JACK and the Beanstalk

retold by Stella Williams Nathan

illustrated by Dora Leder

A GOLDEN BOOK • New York
Western Publishing Company, Inc.
Racine, Wisconsin 53404

Once upon a time there was a boy who lived with his mother in a tiny cottage. They were very poor. One day his mother said to him, "Jack, you must take our cow to market and sell her so we can buy food."

Jack set out at once. On the way, he met an old man.

"That's a fine-looking cow," said the old man. "If you'll give her to me, I'll give you some magic beans."

Jack stared at the red and yellow beans. How exciting! He took the beans, said good-bye to his cow, and hurried back home.

Jack's mother was very angry when she saw what he had done. "Silly boy!" she exclaimed. "Now we shall starve!" She threw the beans out the window.

When Jack awoke the next morning, his bedroom was dark. He ran to the window and saw a tremendously tall beanstalk outside. It seemed to reach up to the sky.

"They *were* magic beans!" Jack shouted. He jumped out the window and quickly climbed the beanstalk.

At the top, he saw a beautiful castle sparkling in the sun. An old woman greeted him as he hopped off the beanstalk. "Don't go near the castle, young man," she said. "A wicked giant lives there. Long ago, he stole your father's fortune and left him a poor man."

"Then I certainly must get it back!" Jack exclaimed, and he strode right to the castle door.

The giant's wife answered his knock. "If you want food, I'll give you some," she said. "But you must hurry. My husband *eats* boys for breakfast!"

She gave Jack a slice of bread as big as a tabletop. But even as he ate, there began a great noise outside. Jack leaped into a skillet to hide, just as the giant entered, bellowing:

"Fe, fi, fo, fum,
I smell the blood of an Englishman.
Be he alive or be he dead,
I'll grind his bones to make my bread."

He bent down and peered under the table. "I smell boy!"

"Nonsense," said his wife. "Eat your breakfast."

Grumbling, the giant sat down to ten roasted oxen and four barrels of milk. Then he shouted, "Wife, bring me my magic hen!"

His wife hurried to obey.

"Lay, hen, lay!" roared the giant, and the hen laid a golden egg.

"Very good," said the giant, with a mighty yawn. Soon he was sound asleep.

At the first snore, Jack popped out of the skillet, snatched up the hen, and ran off. When he had climbed back down the beanstalk, his mother gasped with wonder.

"Jack!" she exclaimed. "It's your father's magic hen!"

The next day, Jack climbed the beanstalk again. "I'll give you a bite to eat," said the giant's wife when she saw him. "But hurry. The giant is in a terrible temper because he has lost his magic hen."

Jack was eating a tart as big as a fishpond, when the
castle began to shake. He leaped into a butter churn, just
as the giant entered, bellowing:

"Fe, fi, fo, fum,
I smell the blood of an Englishman.
Be he alive or be he dead,
I'll grind his bones to make my bread."

"Don't tell me you smell boy again," said his wife. "Sit down and eat your breakfast."

Muttering to himself, the giant gobbled twelve roasted pigs and six dozen eggs. Then he shouted, "Wife, bring me my harp!"

Quickly his wife did as she was told.

"Play, harp, play!" commanded the giant, and the harp
played such beautiful music that it soon lulled the giant
to sleep. At once, Jack jumped out of the butter churn,
seized the harp, and ran away.

When he reached the bottom of the beanstalk, his mother was waiting. "Oh, Jack," she said happily, "you have found your father's golden harp!"

When Jack climbed the beanstalk the next morning, the giant's wife was waiting for him. "I'll give you a snack if you wish," she said, "but you are in great danger. The giant lost his harp yesterday, and he's in a terrible rage."

Jack was eating a cupcake as big as a haystack, when he heard the giant coming. He jumped into a pail and listened to the terrible roar:

"Fe, fi, fo, fum,
I smell the blood of an Englishman.
Be he alive or be he dead,
I'll grind his bones to make my bread."

"Sit down and eat your breakfast," said the giant's wife. "Then you'll feel better."

Mumbling angrily, the giant ate fifteen roasted ducklings and two hundred sausages.

"Wife," he growled, "fetch my gold. That will cheer me."

For a long time, the giant played with his gold pieces. When at last he closed his eyes, Jack jumped out of the pail, snatched the gold, and ran.

But the giant had been only pretending to sleep. With a roar, he leaped to his feet. "I told you I smelled boy!" he bellowed as he raced after Jack.

Poor Jack ran faster than he had ever run in his life.

"Mother, get the ax ready!" he shouted from the top of the beanstalk.

As he climbed down, the beanstalk began to sway. Jack looked up and saw that the giant was coming down, too. It was such a frightening sight that Jack dropped the gold and tumbled all the way to the ground.

Quick as a wink, he jumped up and took the ax from his mother. Smack! SMACK! The beanstalk snapped in two. There was a great crash, and the giant lay before them—dead!

Jack's mother gave him a hug and told him he was indeed a brave boy. "You have brought back your father's hen, his harp, and his gold," she said. "We shall certainly live happily ever after!"

For who *could* be sad, with a hen to lay golden eggs, a harp to play beautiful music, and gold to buy bread and cheese and—sometimes—strawberry tarts?

W9-BNX-388

DATE DUE

MY 28 '10			
JE 25 '13			

Electricity and Basic Electronics

by

Stephen R. Matt
Vocational Director/Assistant Principal
Winder-Barrow High School

Publisher
The Goodheart-Willcox Company, Inc.
Tinley Park, Illinois

Library of Congress Catalog Card Number 97-11853
International Standard Book Number 1-56637-406-5

4 5 6 7 8 9 10 98 02 01

Cover image: Michel Tcherevkoff, Image Bank

Library of Congress Cataloging-in-Publication Data
Matt, Stephen R.
    Electricity and basic electronics / by Stephen R. Matt.
        p. cm.
        Includes index.
        ISBN 1-56637-406-5
        1. Electric engineering. 2. Electronics.
I. Title.
TK146.M376   1998
621.3—dc21   97-11853
                                                            CIP

Introduction

Electricity and Basic Electronics is intended to reflect the growing and expanding interest in electricity and electronics. This first course teaches the fundamentals and is a starting point for a career in this most important area.

This text is clearly written and well-illustrated, making it easy for beginning students to understand. Chapters are organized so that content is presented in the logical order of use. They are laid out in a sequence that facilitates learning. Each new concept builds on the information learned in the previous chapter. Safe work habits are stressed throughout the text.

Using this text, students will find it easy to learn fundamentals and apply them. Important details are clarified with use of extra color. Numerous proven projects are included with construction procedures. These not only help motivate students but also build interest and confidence.

Suggested activities at the end of each chapter range from simple to demanding. These activities may be used to challenge the more advanced students or to diversify the program. An effort has been made to relate all activities and projects to actual applications in home and industry.

Stephen R. Matt

Contents

SAFETY PRECAUTIONS FOR THE
ELECTRICITY-ELECTRONICS SHOP

There is always an element of danger when working with electricity. Observe all safety rules that concern each project and be particularly careful not to contact any live wire or terminal regardless of whether it is connected to either a low voltage or a high voltage. Projects do not specify dangerous voltage levels. However, keep in mind at all times that it is possible to experience a surprising electric shock under certain circumstances. Even a normal healthy person can be injured or seriously hurt by the shock or what happens as a result of it. Do not fool around. The lab is no place for horseplay.

1

Learning and Applying the Fundamentals

LEARNING OBJECTIVES

After studying this chapter, you will be able to:
- Name the three things required in any completed circuit.
- Describe the direction and speed of electron flow in a completed circuit.
- Recognize the cartoon character I.C. as a source of helpful hints.
- Explain what is meant by an open circuit.
- Draw the symbols for a lamp, battery, wire, and a speaker.
- Point out the reasons for using an electrical schematic.

Electricity is truly amazing. To better appreciate its benefits, think for a minute what life would be like without electricity. Can you imagine no lights, no radio or stereo, no television or motion pictures?

Very few things operate or exist without some help from electricity. It helps heat your home in winter and cool it in the summer. The clothes you wear are the products of electric sewing machines and the giant electrically-powered machinery that produced the cloth.

Newspapers, magazines, and books are printed on presses operated by electricity. How about all the electrical devices used in hospitals, laboratories, and research centers? Consider the electrical gear used on a rocket, Fig. 1-1.

USE OF ELECTRICITY

Using electricity is a lot like driving a car. It is not necessary for you to be able to repair everything that goes wrong in order to enjoy using these conveniences. To turn on a light at home, for example, all you have to do is flick a switch. To start a car, you turn the switch with an ignition key.

If the light in your home does not come on, or if the car fails to start, you may have to call in a specialist to make the repair. Normally, however, you do *not* have to be an expert service technician to use and enjoy the benefits of the light or the car.

SAFETY

The more you know about a given subject, the easier it will be to perform your own service work. However, a word of warning is given to do-it-yourselfers. Many people who know a lot about a given subject are injured because they get careless. They have often believed that, "It can only happen to someone else, never to me."

Respect electricity and it will serve you well. Treat it carelessly, and one day you may receive the shock of your life.

Fig. 1-1. Space vehicles carry complex electrical equipment. (NASA)

Fig. 1-2. Alexander Graham Bell's first telephone. (Western Electric Co.)

Since Benjamin Franklin flew his now famous kite and key, and Alexander Graham Bell invented the telephone, Fig. 1-2, many important discoveries have been made in the electrical field.

CAUTION: In attempting to duplicate Franklin's kite flying experiment in a thunderstorm, some people have been killed or seriously injured. As you will see in studying this text, there are safer ways of experimenting with electricity.

Over the years, electrical discoveries have led to many things which have made our work easier and life more comfortable. In order to understand today's remarkable advances, it will be necessary to examine many of the early discoveries. Each one has served as a building block in the house of electrical knowledge that people have constructed so far.

LEARNING OPPORTUNITY

ELECTRICITY AND BASIC ELECTRONICS is designed to provide an explanation of theory and, through the many projects, offer practical application of the principles. It also will serve as a foundation for future studies leading to a career in electricity/electronics or in a related field.

To avoid confusion and make learning easier, each new electrical or electronic term and/or unit will be explained as much as possible when it is introduced. In some cases, the explanation will be quite brief. However, you also will be told which chapter will give complete details on that particular subject area. This method of treating new ideas will help you build a strong understanding of the subject with only the facts that are necessary at the time.

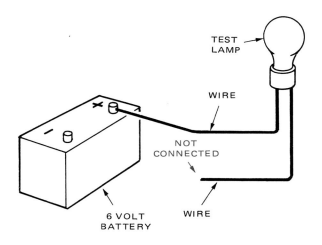

Fig. 1-3. A battery, test lamp and wires are needed to form a simple circuit. However, since a wire is disconnected, this circuit is not completed.

BASIC CONCEPT OF A CIRCUIT

How do you turn on a light? Earlier mention was made of flicking on a switch. What did that action do to result in the light coming on? Understanding this action and reaction will bring you a long way along the path of knowledge about electricity.

First, look at Fig. 1-3. It shows a battery, wires and a test lamp (light bulb and socket). One wire connects the test lamp to the battery. The other wire is connected to the lamp, but not to the battery. Since a wire is disconnected, the test lamp is out. However, when both lamp wires are connected to the battery, Fig. 1-4, the

Fig. 1-4. This circuit has the same parts as in Fig. 1-3. The test lamp is on because the wire is connected to the battery.

lamp will burn brightly. This happens because electricity is flowing through the wires in a "completed circuit."

Any completed circuit requires three things: First, it needs a source of electricity, or energy (in this case, the battery). Second, it needs a load, or something which uses that energy. The load in Figs. 1-3 and 1-4 is the light bulb. Third, it needs a path to get the energy from source to load and back. As you may have guessed, this path is formed by the wires.

There is more to electricity than a simple circuit, but studying circuit makeup is a strong first step toward understanding the subject.

ELECTRONS

As you study these examples of electric circuits in greater detail, you will need to apply physics (matter and energy, and their interaction). Suppose you have a called "electrons" are moving at random (without direction or pattern). These electrons are so small that millions upon millions would fit on the point of a pin.

When the lamp wires are connected, Fig. 1-6, the electrons flow through the wires from the battery to the lamp and back to the battery. How fast do they move? The movement of each little electron takes place at a slow rate of speed. The flow of the individual electrons might be measured in inches per minute.

Notice, also, that when the circuit is completed, the electrons flow through the wires from negative (−) to positive (+). This will be explained in Chapter 3.

The use of a switch was mentioned earlier in this chapter. A switch makes it easy to open or close a circuit, Fig. 1-7. Closing the switch allows the electrons to move or flow. When the switch is opened, none of the electrons can jump across the gap. This is called an "open circuit."

ELECTRONS

Fig. 1-5. Using a very powerful microscope to look inside the wires of Fig. 1-3 shows that the electrons are not flowing.

very powerful microscope and can take a look at what is happening inside the wires, both before and after they are connected to the battery. Note that before connecting the wires, Fig. 1-5, extremely small particles

OPEN
CIRCUIT

SWITCH

CLOSED
CIRCUIT

SWITCH

Fig. 1-7. A switch installed in the simple circuit allows easier opening and closing of the circuit.

ELECTRONS

Fig. 1-6. Using a very powerful microscope to look inside the wires of Fig. 1-4 shows that the electrons are flowing (moving rapidly in one direction).

Fig. 1-8. Vibrating door bell operation. A—Normally, circuit is open at push button switch. B—The instant the push button is depressed, circuit is completed and coil is energized (has magnetism), attracting the bar and striker assembly. C—Bar is drawn against coil, causing striker to ring bell. However, movement of bar causes contacts to break and circuit is opened. Coil is de-engerized (lost its magnetism) and spring pulls bar and striker away from coil. This, in turn, completes circuit at contacts and striker hits the bell again.

10

Basically, a switch provides a simple and convenient way of opening or closing the circuit without having to disconnect and reconnect wires to the battery. A push button can be connected to the circuit to do the same thing at your house or apartment. See A in Fig. 1-8. A person at your door will press the push button, as in B and C, allowing electrons to flow to the door bell. Releasing the push button, as in A in Fig. 1-8, stops the flow of electrons and the sound. As long as the push button is depressed, the circuit repeatedly opens and closes at the contacts (as in B and C), causing the door bell to ring.

Several other methods used to open and close circuits will be explained as you progress in your knowledge of electricity. At the same time, you will learn what is happening electrically, as you go through this book.

BATTERIES

You probably have noticed that the batteries pictured in some of the illustrations are labeled 6 volts. Your flashlight uses two or more 1 1/2 volt cells, like the one shown in Fig. 1-9. These are *not* batteries.

Fig. 1-9. The familiar flashlight battery is not a battery. Proper terminology for the item shown is a "1 1/2 volt cell."

When two or more cells are combined, they form a battery. Another type of battery, Fig. 1-10, is used in cars, golf carts and electric vans.

Although most people refer to cells as "batteries," this is *not* correct. Proper names or terminology are very important in the study of electricity and electronics. Imagine your surprise if you asked somebody for a screwdriver and they gave you a hacksaw. Use the proper name for any particular item or component (part) and save yourself a lot of trouble later.

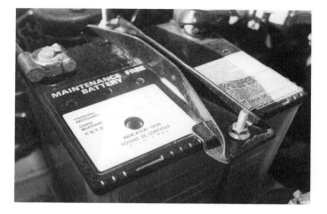

Fig. 1-10. Pictured is a 12 volt battery for automotive use. It is an assembly of six 2 volt cells.

SYMBOLS

Take a closer look at the drawing of the power source, wires and load, Fig. 1-4. Note that the elements of the circuit are drawn in some detail. Now that you are learning more about electricity and electronics, it is necessary to use some other method of showing circuits. Otherwise, drawings will be difficult to make and take a long time to complete.

Therefore, rather than picturing each element, symbols should be used. For example, instead of drawing a cell, use the symbol for a cell, Fig. 1-11.

Fig. 1-11. Symbols are used to identify electrical elements or components in circuit drawings. The symbol for a cell is shown.

Since a battery is a combination of two or more cells, its symbol should be drawn as a group of cell symbols, as shown in Fig. 1-12. Note that the long line in the battery symbol is the positive terminal; the short line is the negative terminal.

Fig. 1-12. The symbol for a battery is a combination of several cell symbols.

When using symbols, a wire is simply drawn as a line. The symbol for "load," on the other hand, will not always be the same. It depends on what element or component you are using for a load. For example, Figs. 1-13 and 1-14 show common loads (speaker, lamp and bell) along with their symbols. There are many others.

Fig. 1-13. A speaker and its symbol are shown.   (Electro Voice)

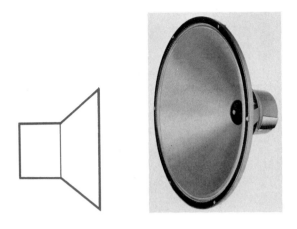

Fig. 1-14. Symbols pictured are: Left. Lamp. Right. Door Bell.

I.C. SAYS:

"Hi! My name is I.C. I will be around from time to time to help you understand new words, phrases and formulas. My body is a printed circuit board with integrated circuits attached. Can you recognize the rest of my parts? You will learn the function of these parts and their symbols in your study of electricity and basic electronics."

Knowing symbols will allow us to redraw some of the circuits we saw earlier in this chapter. Fig. 1-16, would be another way of drawing the circuit shown in Fig. 1-4, using the battery, wires and lamp. If you want

Fig. 1-15. I.C. stands for "integrated circuit." It also is the name of this helpful character made of various parts and symbols.

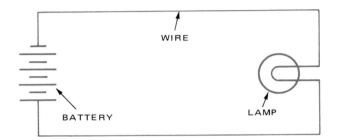

Fig. 1-16. Use of symbols permits us to simplify the pictorial drawing of electrical circuits. Compare this schematic with the drawing in Fig. 1-5.

to add another lamp to the circuit, just put a large dot where the wires connect to one another. Fig. 1-17 shows how this is done.

If two circuits are shown near each other, or if the wires do not connect, leave off the dot, Fig. 1-18. This tells the person reading the drawing that the wires just pass over each other but are not connected.

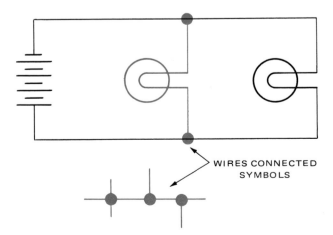

Fig. 1-17. Another lamp has been added to the circuit in Fig. 1-16. Note that a large dot is the symbol for "wires connected."

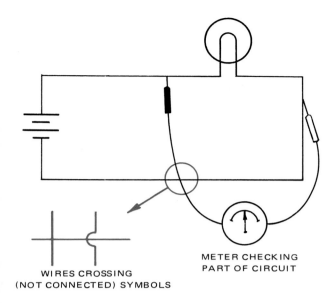

WIRES CROSSING
(NOT CONNECTED) SYMBOLS

METER CHECKING
PART OF CIRCUIT

Fig. 1-18. If the wires of a circuit are near each other, or if the wires cross but do not connect, either one of the two symbols shown may be used.

Drawings using symbols are called "schematics" by most people working in the electrical field. Fig. 1-19 shows what a finished industrial schematic looks like. The television service technician would be lost without a schematic for a TV set brought in for repairs.

Not all television receivers have the same circuits, and even the same brand varies as the models change from year to year. The TV technician usually has several hundered TV schematics. Some companies print

them to sell. Can you imagine the trouble it would be to build the control room shown in Fig. 1-20 *without* a schematic?

PROBES

As you go through this text, you will be shown things you can build. Many of these projects will be illustrated with circuit drawings and photographs to give you a good idea what the finished job looks like.

Some of the projects you will be asked to build require the use of probes to make tests. You can buy a set of probes or make your own, Fig. 1-21. The probes you can make are just nails with wires soldered to them. Then, the whole thing must be cast in plastic to insulate the tips. This is done so you can hold the probes in your hand without fear of electric shock.

Some people use plastic tubing for insulation instead of casting in plastic. Simple ideas like this make projects more economical to build than if you bought the materials from an electronics store. Also, it is more fun to "build your own," and you really can learn how it works. Then, too, if something happens to your project, you will have an easier time fixing it.

ELECTRONS

Earlier, we told you a few facts about electrons. If you used a powerful electron microscope, you would be able to see that everything around you is made up of electrons. These microscopes, however, are much too expensive for a school to buy. Therefore, we will try to

Fig. 1-19. Schematic of an automobile electric clock, illustrating its various circuits and symbols for its electrical components.
(Borg Instruments)

Fig. 1-20. This complex power plant control room is loaded with meters, switches, and buttons which were wired with the help of a schematic. (Georgia Power Co.)

Fig. 1-21. Probe used to perform circuit tests made from nails soldered to wires and cast in plastic. (Project by Rico Righetti)

explain by text and illustration what electrons are and how they act.

One of the simplest atoms is the helium atom, Fig. 1-22. The helium atom has two electrons (negatively charged particles) in orbit around the center of the atom, known as its nucleus. The nucleus is made up of neutrons (particles which have no charge) and protons (particles which have a positive charge). The number of neutrons, protons and electrons varies, depending on which atom you are studying. Some atoms have 50 to 100 electrons in orbit around the nucleus.

Think of the nucleus of an atom as our planet Earth, and the electrons as two satellites orbiting around it,

Fig. 1-23. If a satellite speeds up or slows down, its orbit will change. If you want the satellite to orbit farther from the planet, you must give it more energy, usually by firing a rocket to increase the satellite's speed. To lower its orbit, you would fire rockets that retard (hold back) the forward speed of the satellite.

You can do similar things to electrons to make their orbits change. For example, you can take away some of

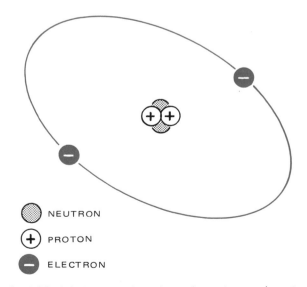

NEUTRON

(+) PROTON

(−) ELECTRON

Fig. 1-22. A helium atom is made up of two electrons (negative charge) and a nucleus composed of neutrons (no charge) and protons (positive charge).

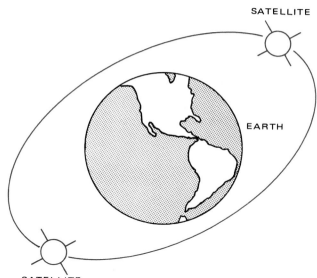

Fig. 1-23. The parts of a helium atom can be compared with the Earth and two satellites orbiting around it. The Earth represents the nucleus and the satellites are the electrons in orbit.

their energy and make them drop to a lower energy level. If you want to shift the electrons to a higher level, you must give them more energy.

As you move away from the simple atoms, such as helium, you get into others that are more complex. Think again in terms of our Earth. You now have a large number of satellites in orbit, but they are not all at the same altitude nor in the same orbit. The more

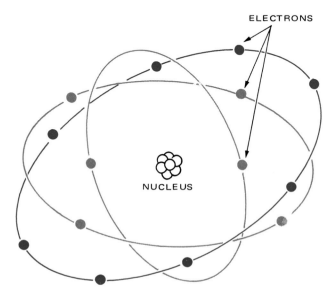

Fig. 1-24. In studying the makeup of more complex atoms, note that electrons orbit around nucleus at different levels.

complex atoms, Fig. 1-24, have many more orbiting electrons at different energy levels.

Earlier you were told that the movement of each separate electron was fairly slow. However, as each electron moves, it sets up a chain reaction from atom to atom. The movement of one electron to the next atom forces a second electron to move. As it moves to another atom, it forces still another electron to move and so on down the line. The movement of all these electrons sets up a wave motion similar to those waves you see at the ocean as they move toward a beach. All of this movement of individual electrons takes place at a high rate of speed.

The movement of the electrons is similar to the example shown in Fig. 1-25. Take a plastic tube 10 miles long and fill it with ball bearings. Once it is filled, force one more bearing into the tube. At the same instant that you force a new one in, another ball bearing must fall out the other end. This is similar to how electrons force a flow from atom to atom at approximately the speed of light (about 186,000 miles per second).

In Chapter 17, you will find that most electronic components depend on electrons to work properly. How we are able to move electrons or shift them around means a great deal to us. For example, electronic components such as diodes and transistors cannot work if we are not able to move those electrons.

Fig. 1-25. Another bearing forced into a full plastic tube will result in one falling out 10 miles away.

PROJECT TESTER AND FUSE SAVER

Do you want to save yourself a lot of trouble after building a project? Put together the project tester shown in Fig. 1-26, then plug it into a wall receptacle. The project tester is just what its name implies. It will serve as an advance guard against project failure when you put the project into operation for the first time.

You can check a new 110 volt project for short circuits (unwanted electron flow) or opens by plugging it into the test receptacle with the switch open. The tester will prevent blown fuses and avoid the possibility of burning up a circuit that has taken hours to build.

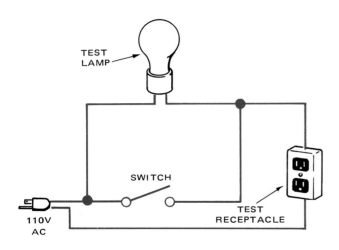

Fig. 1-26. Project tester and fuse saver. First, obtain electrical parts and wire as shown. Then, assemble the unit by making the necessary connections and proceed with the tests as outlined in the text.

Here is how the tester works: first, be sure the tester switch is open. Then, screw in a test lamp of about the same wattage as the project you are building. Next, plug the power lead of your tester into an 11 volt receptacle. Then, plug the lead of your 110 volt project into the test receptacle.

The possible results are:

- With a short, the test lamp will burn brightly.
- Without a short, the test lamp will be dim.
- With an open circuit, the test lamp will not light.

SUMMARY

In this chapter you were introduced to a whole new language. This language includes both terms and symbols. As you study **Electricity and Basic Electronics** do not be afraid to ask questions if you do not understand any of the topics being taught.

The easiest way to learn about anything new is to apply what you are being taught. Don't just read about electricity and electronics, build the projects, make your own drawings, and work on the problems. You will learn best by the practice of doing. The more hands-on activities you do, the more you will learn. Don't just watch someone else build a project, do it yourself.

In this course you will be able to apply what you learn to things that are around you every day. You will be able to apply what you learned in science and math classes. Not only is it fun to learn, but you can also earn a good living with your new knowledge.

KEY WORDS AND TERMS

Battery	Load
Cell	Open circuit
Completed circuit	Probe
Electron	Schematic

TEST YOUR KNOWLEDGE

Do not write in this book. Write your answers on a separate sheet of paper.

1. The three requirements for a complete circuit are _____, _____, and _____.
2. Electron flow usually means flow _____.
   a. from positive to negative
   b. of positive charges
   c. of negative and positive charges
   d. of negative charges
3. Electrons come from the _____ post of a battery and go back to the _____ post.
4. One way to stop the flow of electrons is to _____ the circuit.
5. Electrons travel at _____.
   a. the speed of light
   b. the speed of sound
   c. 100 miles per hour
   d. 1000 feet per second
6. An electrical schematic is _____.
7. Draw the symbols for a cell and for a battery.

ACTIVITIES

1. Explain why there are so many different symbols for an electrical load.
2. Explain why a load is so important to an electrical current.

2 Sources of Electricity

LEARNING OBJECTIVES

After studying this chapter, you will be able to:
- Identify each of the five ways of producing electricity.
- Describe how magnetic fields work to attract or repel each other.
- Explain the concept of magnetic declination.
- Demonstrate at least one use for a continuity tester .
- Draw a simple buzzer circuit.

After reading the first chapter, you probably have several questions about how electricity is produced. This chapter has been designed to provide the answers.

There are many ways and means of making, converting, and generating electricity. Basically, they fall into the following five general methods:
- Chemical energy
- Light
- Pressure
- Heat
- Magnetism

These methods will be explained in some detail in the order given. Specific examples and related projects will be included.

ELECTRICITY FROM CHEMICAL ENERGY

Chemical energy means that electricity is generated through the use of chemicals and their reaction with other materials. The simple cell mentioned earlier is a good example of this means of producing electricity. If you were to cut one of these cells in half, you would see something like Fig. 2-1.

This type of cell is often called a *dry cell*, although the chemicals used (electrolyte material that provides the path for electricity inside a cell) are in the form of a paste. The paste is a mixture of salammoniac, manganese dioxide, and carbon with water. These chemicals react with the zinc can and the carbon rod to produce electricity. When the zinc can is finally eaten away, the cell can no longer produce electricity. It is called a *dead cell*.

Older dry cells would swell up as the zinc can dissolved, and appliances were ruined because electrolyte leaked through the case. Today, most companies making dry cells have solved this problem by building the outer section of the case with different materials.

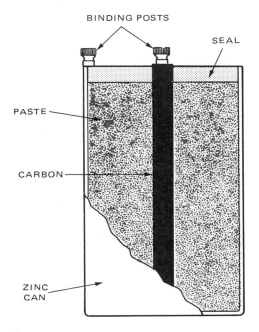

Fig. 2-1. In a dry cell, chemical energy produces electricity. The electrolyte (paste) in the cell reacts with the zinc can and the carbon rod.

BINDING POSTS

SEAL

PASTE

CARBON

ZINC CAN

Fig. 2-2. Emergency lights need to be portable. They are a common application of a dry cell. (Rayovac Corporation)

Dry cells and batteries produce a stream of electrons that flow from negative (–) to positive (+). Remember, this was mentioned in Chapter 1. This flow of electrons in the electrical circuit is called direct current (often abbreviated to dc).

How many things can you think of that get their power from a dc source? Flashlights, emergency lamps or lanterns, Fig. 2-2, portable radios and children's toys use dc as a source of electricity.

CONTINUITY TESTER PROJECT

Figs. 2-3 and 2-4 illustrate a handy item you can make for yourself. It is called a "continuity tester." With it, you can test for broken wires or burned out (open) fuses. Another good use is finding the matching wire ends in a wiring harness (a group of wires routed together).

Fig. 2-3. This schematic for a shop-built continuity tester includes: B_1 — One 1.5 volt dry cell. L_1 — One 1.5 volt test lamp.

To make the continuity tester, connect leads to a 1.5 volt dry cell and a 1.5 volt test lamp, Fig. 2-3. Keep the circuit small. In that way, you can put the dry cell and

Fig. 2-4. The continuity tester can be used to trace the flow of electricity in individual wires in a wiring harness.

lamp in almost anything you want to, such as a hollow plastic tube.

To use the continuity tester, touch the leads to the item under test. If the light comes on, the item has continuity (will conduct electricity). If the light stays off, the item lacks continuity (will not conduct electricity).

You cannot use this continuity tester to check out certain things. The coil in a transformer or a large inductor, for example, offers too much resistance for the low voltage tester. A dc cell of 1.5 volts cannot do the job. Later, you will find why this is so.

If you want to test a wiring harness, Fig. 2-4, hook one lead of the tester to one end of a wire. To find the other end of the wire, touch each of the other wire ends with the other test lead. When the light comes on, you have continuity. Now you have both ends of the same wire. Sometimes, one end of the wiring harness is hard to reach. For this reason, wires are often color coded (each wire has a specific color of insulation).

STORAGE BATTERIES

Cells may contain electrolytes other than the paste type. In Fig. 2-5, for example, you see several cells combined in a storage battery like the one installed in an automobile.

Fig. 2-5. A car's storage battery is made up of six cells filled to a prescribed level with electrolyte.
(ESB Brands, Inc.)

A storage battery uses an acid as its electrolyte. This is an advantage over the dry cell, because the car battery can be recharged over and over again. When an inexpensive dry cell goes dead, it is thrown away and replaced with a new one. The storage battery used in a car, however, is fairly expensive. To save the cost of constantly replacing batteries, they are designed so they can be recharged.

In the case of a car battery, the alternator (generator) does the charging. However, it is possible to drain (discharge) the battery of its charge. If, for example, you leave the headlights on, it may be necessary to use a battery charger, Fig. 2-6, to recharge the battery. In some cases, you will see mechanics or

Fig. 2-6. A portable battery charger serves to keep the storage battery fully charged (high specific gravity).

car owners use two heavy "jumper cables" to start an engine from the battery in a second car. Once the engine in the first car is started, the alternator will begin to recharge the battery.

Fig. 2-7. Cutaway battery reveals relationship of parts. 1—Case. 2—Cover. 3—Positive plates. 4—Negative plates. 5—Separators. 6—Cell. 7—Cell connector. 8—Terminal post. 9—Vent cap.

Consider, however, that car batteries do not last forever. When they get old, it is harder to keep them fully charged. This is especially true if the owner does not take care of the battery, and it is allowed to discharge repeatedly. When this happens, the life of the battery is shortened.

Older batteries or those that have been misused do not hold their charge because chemical action is poor. As the battery is used, the electrolyte begins to react with the metal plates. See 3 and 4 in Fig. 2-7. This causes them to be eaten or dissolved like the zinc can in the dry cell. The major difference, however, is that the metal in a car battery can be made to deposit itself back on its plates. This is done through a chemical action known as charging the battery. This battery charging process is explained in full detail in most chemistry books.

BUZZER PROJECT

Fig. 2-8 illustrates a circuit for a buzzer you can build. This circuit will be seen as part of other circuits which are to follow. In some cases, the buzzer is replaced with a light, or you can use a bell or siren if you wish.

The parts needed to complete this project include a 1.5 volt cell, a 1.5 volt buzzer, a single-pole single-throw switch and sufficient wire to make the connections shown in Fig. 2-8.

Fig. 2-8. This schematic for a buzzer includes: B—One 1.5 volt buzzer. B_1—One 1.5 volt dry cell. S_1—SPST switch.

HYDROMETER TEST

The acid or electrolyte in a battery also can be used to tell you whether or not the battery is fully charged. You may recall seeing a service station attendant checking the battery with a device called a "hydrometer," Fig. 2-9.

First, the hydrometer bulb must be squeezed and released to fill the hydrometer tube with acid from the

Fig. 2-9. A hydrometer is an instrument used to measure specific gravity of electrolyte in each cell to determine state of charge of the battery.

battery. Then, by reading the scale on the float inside, it is possible to tell how much of a charge the battery has available. Many hydrometers are marked to tell you whether the battery is fully charged, half-charged or discharged. This is possible because the acid actually changes in strength. This strength is measured in terms of "specific gravity."

Specific gravity is a comparison of the density of the acid with the density of water. Water has a specific gravity of 1.000. As the battery discharges, the specific gravity of the acid gets closer to the 1.000 mark. In some colder sections of the country, this loss of charge could result in a battery freezing in the winter. Note the table in Fig. 2-10.

FREEZING POINT OF BATTERY ELECTROLYTE

	SPECIFIC GRAVITY	FREEZING POINT
FULLY CHARGED	1.275	−85 DEG. F (−65 C)
	1.250	−62 DEG. F (−52 C)
HALF-CHARGED	1.225	−35 DEG. F (−37 C)
	1.200	−16 DEG. F (−27 C)
	1.175	− 4 DEG. F (−20 C)
DISCHARGED (WATER)	1.150	+ 5 DEG. F (−15 C)
	1.000	+32 DEG. F (0 C)

Fig. 2-10. Chart shows freezing points of battery electrolyte at various specific gravity readings.

ELECTRICITY FROM LIGHT ENERGY

Light energy is another means of producing electricity. In recent years, more and more research has been involved with changing or converting light energy into electricity (photovoltaic).

Light energy becomes especially important in space travel. Figs. 2-11 and 2-12 show solar cells being used in two different satellites. In space, liquid chemicals like the electrolyte used in batteries would be of limited

Fig. 2-11. This spacecraft is the Hubble Space Telescope (HST). It is shown while still in the grasp of the space shuttle Discovery. Solar cells convert light into energy. (NASA)

use. However, the sun is a huge source of power. By using solar cells, it is possible to convert the sun's rays into enough electrical energy to power all the electronic devices in the satellite.

Fig. 2-12. Telestar satellite uses solar cells to convert the sun's rays into electrical energy while orbiting in space. (Western Electric Co.)

PHOTOELECTRIC CELL

Light can be used to produce effects other than storing electricity for later use. For example, a portable light meter or a similar device that senses light inside of a camera is a valuable aid when taking photographs.

In any situation, the film must have just the right amount of exposure to light to produce good photographs. Too much light or too little light will give poor results. By using a light metering device, you are able to know just how much of an adjustment to make to your camera shutter and lens controls for the best possible photographs. Fig. 2-13 will help you to understand why this is so.

Some cameras automatically control the adjustments. Rays of light strike a photoelectric cell (which changes resistance with an increase in the amount of light which hits it). If there is a lot of light, an electrical signal sent to a variable size opening makes the opening smaller. If there is a small amount of light, the signal makes the opening larger.

Other devices use the photoelectric cell to convert light energy into electric energy. For example, have you ever seen a rainstorm occur during the daytime? The next time that happens, watch the streetlights. In some cities, as the sky grows darker, the lights will come on automatically through the use of light sensing devices. The sensor is a photoelectric cell mounted on top of the light assembly.

FIBER OPTICS LAMP PROJECT

You, too, can make a fiber optics lamp. You will need an old can, a light bulb, a single-pole single-throw switch, fiber optics tubing and some wire, Figs. 2-14 and 2-15. To dress up the project, install contact paper on the outside of the can.

The size of the bulb you use will depend on how big and how fancy you wish to get. However, your best bet is to stay down in wattage. This will prevent the bulb

Fig. 2-14. The base of this fiber optics lamps is made from an old can covered with contact paper. (Project by Allan Witherspoon)

LIGHT SENSING PHOTOELECTRIC CELL

MIRROR

LIGHT RAYS

CAMERA

Fig. 2-13. A built-in light meter uses a photoelectric cell to detect the amount of light that will enter the camera.

from overheating the inside of the can. If you decide to paint the outside of the can, use a smaller bulb to avoid burning your design. A base can be cut from wood, so the can does not mar your table. For further protection, glue a felt material on the bottom of the wood base.

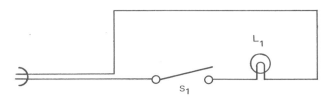

Fig. 2-15. This schematic for the fiber optics lamp includes: L_1—One 110 volt ac lamp. S_1—One SPST switch and one rubber cap with line cord.

ELECTRICITY BY PRESSURE

Pressure is still another method used to generate electricity for many of the things you see and hear around you every day. Piezo is the Greek name for pressure. Therefore, piezoelectricity, or the piezo-electric effect, is the name often mentioned when talking about the effect of electricity from pressure.

A common application of pressure being used to generate electricity is shown in Fig. 2-16. It is a microphone used with a citizens band radio. Another popular use is the tone arm which you place on your favorite record. The telephone, one of the great conveniences of the modern household, also depends on pressure to generate electricity.

All of these devices use crystalline materials, like quartz, in their makeup. When a force is exerted on these materials, they bend or become distorted and electrons are forced to move. Fig. 2-17 illustrates how this is done.

Fig. 2-16. A citizens band radio microphone is a good example of electricity being generated by pressure. (Cobra Electronics Corp.)

Another recent use of quartz is shown in Fig. 2-18. Here it is being used in a wristwatch to aid in keeping accurate time. Fig. 2-19 shows both the mechanical and electric parts of the watch, and its main sections are identified. The quartz crystal is pulsing at 32,768 times per second (Hz) to give off electrical signals. The abbreviation Hz stands for hertz, which will be explained in Chapter 10.

The item in Fig. 2-19 called an "integrated circuit module" is another way of saying the circuits being used are miniaturized (extremely small). Integrated circuits will be described in some detail when you get to Chapter 17. The important thing at this point is to note that quartz is being used to give off an electrical signal, which is what the piezoelectric effect is all about.

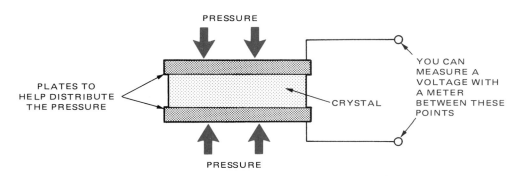

Fig. 2-17. Electricity by pressure can be demonstrated by placing quartz crystal between pressure plates. When pressure is applied, electricity flows.

Fig. 2-18. Another use of quartz crystal is in the "tuning fork" wristwatch. Pressure created by the pulsing of the crystal produces electrical signals. (Bulova Watch Co., Inc.)

ELECTRICITY BY HEAT

Heat also can be used to generate electricity. Many schools have an area called a foundry, set aside for casting hot metals into many different shapes. Other schools have furnaces used for heat treating metals at a specific temperature. Still others have a kiln where ceramic objects are fired. At home, ovens are used to cook our food and to bake cakes and pies. How, then, can we tell the temperatures at which certain things melt and others cook? All this is possible because of thermoelectricity or electricity from heat.

Many of the temperatures needed to handle the tasks mentioned are measured with a device called a thermocouple, Fig. 2-20. A thermocouple consists of two dissimilar metals, such as copper and zinc or constantan and iron joined tightly at one end. To check output voltage, connect the other two ends of the dissimilar metals to a sensitive meter, such as a galvanometer.

A galvanometer is a meter that can sense a very small number of electrons flowing through a circuit. As the electrons flow, the needle on the meter will begin to move. If the flow of electrons increases, the needle will

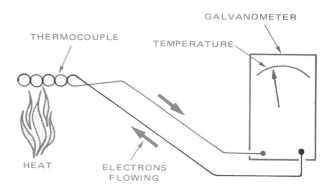

Fig. 2-20. A thermocouple will generate electricity if heat is applied to the connection of two dissimilar metals. If the other two ends of the metals are connected to a meter, the meter needle will indicate the temperature of the thermocouple at the joined end.

Fig. 2-19. "Tuning fork" wristwatch features a quartz power cell. A—Integrated circuit module. B—Electromagnetic coils. C—Tuning fork. D—Power cell nest. (Bulova Watch Co., Inc.)

Fig. 2-21. The principle of the steam turbine powered generator is illustrated. Heat changes water to steam, which forces the fan (turbine wheel) to turn. The turbine output shaft rotates the generator to produce electricity.

move farther across the meter face. To relate this to the thermocouple, consider that when the joined end is heated, the needle of the galvanometer will move, Fig. 2-20. The scale of the meter can then be marked with degrees of temperature.

ELECTRICITY BY MAGNETISM

Using magnetism to generate electricity is the best known and most often used method of all. Yet, for the average person, magnetism probably is the least understood source of electricity.

Everyone knows that electricity is supplied to the community by the power company. The company produces this electricity with a device called a generator. To operate, the generator is turned in a rotary motion, Fig. 2-21. Power companies do this in several ways:

1. By means of waterfalls and water under pressure from giant dams or reservoirs, Figs. 2-22 to 2-25.
2. By means of steam produced by burning coal or oil, Fig. 2-26.
3. By means of steam from nuclear reactors, Figs. 2-27 and 2-28.

We will go into motors and generators in greater detail when we get to Chapter 12. At this time, just bear in mind that the spinning generator will create a magnetic field which is used to give us electricity.

MAGNETISM

All material is either magnetic or nonmagnetic. This characteristic is based on whether or not the material will be attracted to a strong magnet placed near it. Most ferrous metals (those that have iron or steel as part of their makeup) are magnetic. Stainless steel is an exception to this fact because, usually, it is not magnetic.

Fig. 2-22. In a hydroelectric power plant, water under pressure from the high side of the dam is applied to turbine wheels that power electric generators.

Fig. 2-23. The difference in water level on high and low sides of the dam creates the "head" (water pressure) needed to spin the turbines. (Boeing Electronics)

Fig. 2-24. Turbine shaft drives a generator in the hydroelectric power plant. The greater the water pressure on the turbine wheel, the higher the electrical output of the generator.

Fig. 2-25. Electricity generated by magnetism is the method employed by huge generators installed in a power station.

Fig. 2-26. In a steam turbine generator application, coal fires the boiler that generates steam which, in turn, drives the turbine generator that produces electricity.

Fig. 2-27. Nuclear power plants are the modern approach to producing electricity. In this plant, workers are loading fuel cells in the nuclear reactor. (Georgia Power Co.)

Fig. 2-28. Nuclear power complex includes auxiliary building, fuel building and reactor building, at left, which houses a free-standing steel containment and nuclear reactor.
(Consumers Power Co.)

Most nonferrous metals are not magnetic. Nonferrous metals are metals other than iron. Copper, brass and aluminum are examples of these nonmagnetic materials. An easy way to find out whether or not a metal is magnetic is to place a magnet on it. If it is attracted to the magnet, it *is* magnetic.

I.C. SAYS:

"If you look at a magnet attracting a piece of steel, you can see the movement of the steel toward the magnet. However, you cannot see the magnetic field because it is invisible."

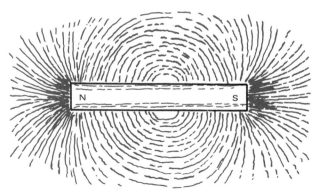

Fig. 2-29. In this magnetic field experiment, first cover a bar magnet with a sheet of paper, plastic or glass. Then sprinkle on the iron filings and tap gently. The iron filings will form the pattern shown between the poles of the magnet.

There *are* some simple ways that make it possible for you to observe a magnetic field. One way is to place a piece of paper, plastic or glass over a bar magnet. Then, obtain some fine steel particles by filing a steel rod or bar. Next, lightly cover the material with filings, sprinkling them right over the magnet, and gently tap it. You will see the filings fall into a pattern of attraction between the north and south poles of the magnet, Fig. 2-29. Do not use particles that are too large or too heavy. If you use a horseshoe magnet, you will see a magnetic field like the one illustrated in Fig. 2-30.

The lines which make up the magnetic field are

Fig. 2-30. Iron filings on a paper, plastic or glass placed over a horseshoe magnet reveals the pattern of lines of force around and between the poles of the magnet.

called lines of flux or lines of force. Figs. 2-31 and 2-32 reveal that the lines of force start from one end of the magnet and are attracted to the other end. The two ends of the magnet are called poles. One is known as the north pole, the other is the south pole. The lines of force are thought to leave the north pole, enter the magnet at the south pole, and complete the path through the magnet to the north pole.

PRINCIPLES OF MAGNETISM

In the 1800s, an Englishman named Michael Faraday first performed the lines of force experiment with iron filings. He also found that when two magnets are used

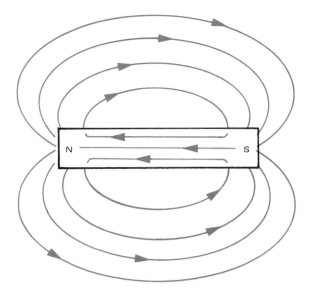

Fig. 2-31. The magnetic lines of force around a bar magnet follow the pattern of iron filings shown in the experiment in Fig. 2-29.

in the experiment, you will get the results shown in Figs. 2-33 and 2-34. From this discovery, he was able to state two basic principles of magnetism:

1. Like poles repel.
2. Unlike poles attract.

Fig. 2-32. The magnetic lines of force around a horseshoe magnet are similar to the pattern of the iron filings in Fig. 2-30.

Whether the two poles are both north or both south, they *will* repel one another, Fig. 2-33. Unlike poles, on the other hand, will always attract each other, Fig. 2-34.

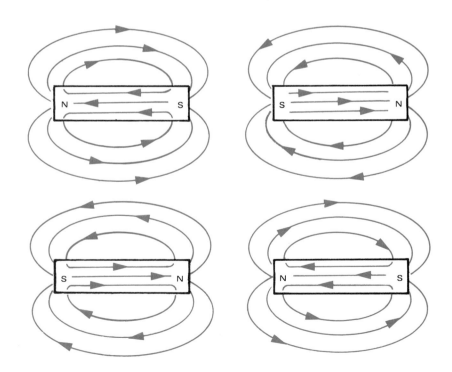

Fig. 2-33. The opposing lines of force of these two bar magnets show that like poles repel each other, whether they are aligned north to north or south to south.

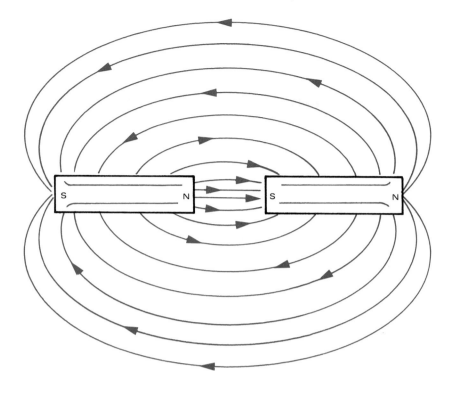

Fig. 2-34. Two bar magnets with unlike poles facing, show lines of force that merge into a pattern of attraction. Note that the lines of force always go from north to south.

I.C. SAYS:

"When you are working with magnets or experimenting with magnetism, the important facts to remember are: like poles repel and unlike poles attract."

MAGNETIC DECLINATION

The north pole of a compass needle is really the north seeking pole, Fig. 2-35. As an experiment, hold a compass level and watch the needle. You will find that the pole of the needle labeled N (north) will align itself in the general direction of the north geographic pole. However, unlike poles attract. Therefore, the compass needle has to be pointing at a south magnetic pole, the earth's "magnetic north" pole.

This north pole/south pole relationship is confusing to most people, so today's accepted terminology is "magnetic north" because it attracts the north seeking pole of the compass needle. Fig. 2-36 will help clarify this point.

From this explanation, it can be seen that the Earth

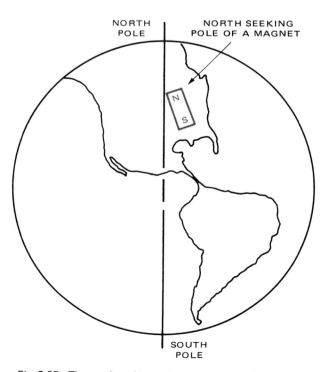

Fig. 2-35. The north seeking pole of a magnet or the pointer of a compass always points in the general direction of the north geographic pole.

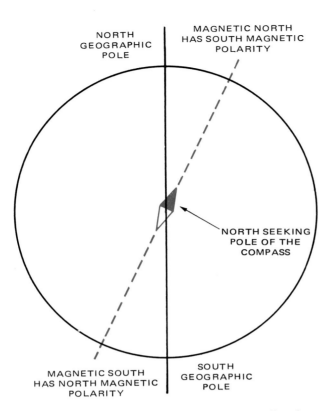

Fig. 2-36. The north seeking pole of the compass needle points at the south magnetic pole, which is termed "magnetic north."

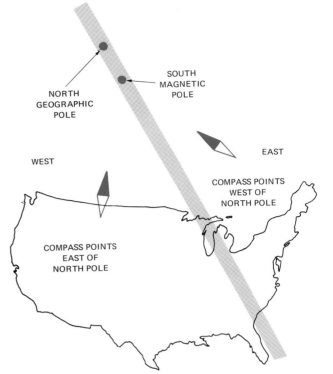

Fig. 2-37. The north geographic pole and "magnetic north" are in similar but separate locations. The compass needle points at both poles only in the narrow band shown in color.

is a giant magnet. The major problem with this theory, is that the two magnetic poles do not line up with the two geographic poles. Depending on where you live on the earth, the magnetic pole may be either east or west of the true north pole. In the United States, people living in the narrow band shown in Fig. 2-37 will have their compasses point toward the geographic and magnetic poles with the same reading. People living to the west of that band will have their compasses point east of the true north pole.

The difference between the geographic and magnetic poles is called "magnetic declination." It is another way of saying that a difference exists between the two poles. Magnetic declination is an important fact that airplane pilots must know. If they fail to make corrections when reading their navigational instruments, it is possible that they will not find the airfield when it is time to land their planes.

BENDING LINES OF FORCE

Earlier in this chapter, we placed paper over a magnet and sprinkled iron filings on it to show magnetic lines of force. Paper is an insulator. An insulator is a material that does not allow electrons to flow through it easily. Bakelite, glass, air, paper and mica are insulators.

Although insulators block the flow of electrons, they do not block the flow of the magnetic lines of force. This is why you are able to see the lines of force formed on the paper. As you saw, you can use plastic, glass or other insulators over the magnet and still perform the experiment with iron filings.

Fig. 2-38 shows how magnetic lines of force can pass right through most nonmagnetic materials. However, there are ways of bending the lines of force so that they can take another path through the magnetic material.

DEMONSTRATION OF MAGNETISM

To demonstrate how electricity is generated through magnetism, perform this experiment using a galvanometer. First, take a coil of wire and attach the two ends to the terminals of the galvanometer, Fig. 2-39. Next, take a bar magnet and quickly insert it into the coil while watching the meter pointer move. Quickly remove the magnet and note that pointer movement is in the opposite direction. The meter pointer moves because the magnetic lines of force cut through the copper coil even though the wire is insulated.

NONMAGNETIC MATERIAL:
PAPER, GLASS, PLASTIC, COPPER OR ALUMINUM

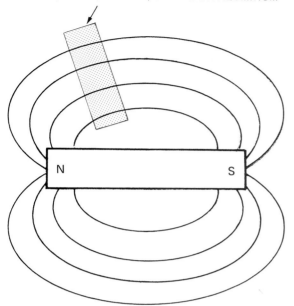

Fig. 2-38. Magnetic lines of force are unaffected by insulators and most nonmagnetic materials.

GALVANOMETER

MAGNET

COIL OF WIRE

Fig. 2-39. Moving a magnet into and out of a coil of wire will cause the needle of a galvanometer to move, first in one direction, then in the opposite direction.

This "cutting" action of the magnetic lines of force generates a small movement of electrons which, in turn, causes the pointer of the meter to move. Different amounts of electrons can be made to move by:

1. Changing the size of the magnet.

Fig. 2-40. Laser beams created by electricity are used to make holograms, which are three dimensional pictures made without a camera. (Western Electric Co.)

2. Using coils with different numbers of copper wire turns.
3. Changing the speed with which the magnet is moved into the coil.

You can see these differences by watching how far the pointer moves on the meter. It is also possible in this experiment to move the pointer by holding the magnet still and moving the coils of copper wire over the magnet. Relative movement between the magnetic field and the conductor causes the pointer to move.

Later, we will see how all these ideas are used to build motors and generators to do specific jobs.

USES OF ELECTRICITY

Five methods are commonly used to generate electricity: chemical energy, light, pressure, heat and magnetism. It also is possible to reverse this procedure and use electricity to create these same five things.

In Fig. 2-40, for example, laser light beams are being used to make holograms. A laser (Light Amplification by Stimulated Emission of Radiation) is a highly concentrated or focused beam of light. The hologram being produced is a three dimensional picture. In Fig. 2-41, for example, you can see the front, side and back views of various chess pieces.

White light, Fig. 2-42, also can be produced through the use of electricity. Special tungsten bulbs are used in this application.

One of the more specialized uses of electricity is

Fig. 2-42. In an application where electricity is used to produce light, tungsten halogen bulbs make white lights for a manufacturing process.   (Guide Div., General Motors Corp.)

Fig. 2-41. These holograms were produced by laser beams. Chess pieces appear in three different perspectives on each hologram plate.

Fig. 2-43. In another factory operation, an electrical discharge machine is shown producing an automobile grille.

Fig. 2-45. Ultrasonic welding of two dissimilar plastics also illustrates electricity being used to produce heat for a manufacturing operation.

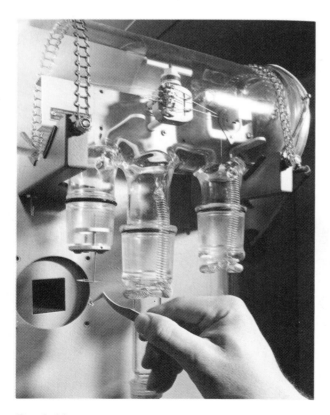

Fig. 2-44. Laboratory thermal analysis equipment is an example of electricity being used to generate heat. (Guide Div., General Motors Corp.)

shown in Fig. 2-43, where an electrical discharge machine is pictured making plastic grilles for automobiles. Two other uses include thermal analysis equipment, Fig. 2-44 and the welding of two different types of plastic through ultrasonics, Fig. 2-45. There are many other examples all around you: telegraph, telephone, buzzers, soldering guns and other devices that are powered by electricity.

SUMMARY

In this chapter you learned about the five methods of generating electricity. You saw examples of how electricity was produced on earth and in outer space. Sources on earth can use huge buildings and pieces of equipment such as the reactors in a nuclear plant. Others use small solar cells like those on a satellite to convert light energy from the sun's rays.

These methods of generating electricity were discovered by scientists who spent long hours working and studying. As their work was perfected, all the comforts of the modern world became a reality. Comforts we take for granted like the lightbulb, automobile, stereo, and computer, would probably not exist today if they hadn't persisted. The buildings in which we live, study, and work, owe part of their existence to the power of electricity.

Can you think of any of the items in your daily life that does not depend in some way on electricity?

KEY WORDS AND TERMS

Continuity tester
Dead cell
Dry cell
Ferrous metals
Laser
Magnetic declination
Magnetic north

Magnetism
Nonferrous metals
Photoelectric cell
Piezoelectric effect
Piezoelectricity
Specific gravity
Thermocouple

TEST YOUR KNOWLEDGE

Do not write in this book. Write your answers on a separate sheet of paper.

1. The basic law of magnetism says that _____ poles repel and _____ poles attract.
2. The north pole of a compass needle is really the north seeking pole. When held level, the compass will always point at _____.
   a. the north geographic pole
   b. magnetic north, which has south magnetic polarity
   c. the south geographic pole
   d. magnetic south, which has north magnetic polarity
3. Name two uses for a thermocouple.
4. One of the materials used to produce electricity by pressure is _____.
5. Which of the following is a type of chemical energy used to produce electricity?
   a. Nuclear power plants
   b. Burning coal to produce heat
   c. The storage battery in a car
   d. Lights in your house
6. A thermocouple is made from _____ dissimilar metals.
7. The magnetic flux lines come out of the _____ pole and go into the _____ pole of a permanent magnet.
8. A _____ is used to measure the specific gravity of the acid used in a storage battery.
9. Name five ways to produce electricity.
10. Why would a battery freeze up in the winter if it is discharged?

ACTIVITIES

1. Find the magnetic declination for your city.
2. Why is a keeper used on a magnet?
3. Where are the poles on a ring magnet?
4. Why does striking a magnet with a sharp blow demagnetize it?
5. Why does a magnet grow weaker with age?

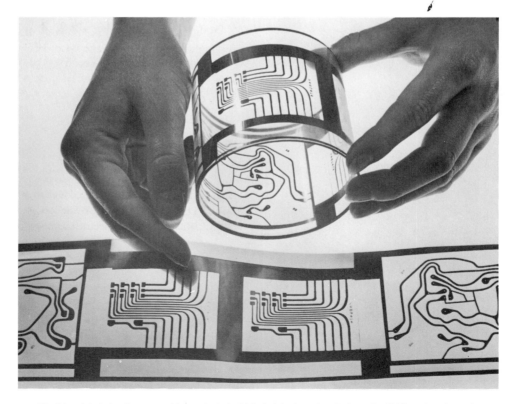

Flexible printed circuits are used to conduct electricity in telephone handsets and switchboard equipment.
(Western Electric Co.)

3

Conductors and Insulators

LEARNING OBJECTIVES

After studying this chapter, you will be able to:
- Identify items which are conductors and insulators.
- Describe the process of stripping the insulation off wire.
- Explain how wire size is measured.
- Draw the symbol for a fuse and tell why it is used to protect a circuit.
- Demonstrate the process of soldering wire and use of a heat sink.

As discussed in Chapter 1, electrons must be provided with a path from the power source to the load. This path usually is in the form of a wire, although it could be any kind of conductor of electricity. *A conductor is any material that easily passes an electric current.*

In some cases, the path for the electrons is provided by printed wiring on specially made *printed circuit boards*, or *PC boards*. See Fig. 3-1. Many radios and television sets have circuits of this type, Fig. 3-2.

Fig. 3-2 Electric circuits in television sets include printed circuit boards. (Heath Co.)

Fig. 3-3 presents a close-up of two typical PC boards. Note that many of the parts are connected with thin strips of copper or silver. This is printed wiring. While it is used extensively in certain applications, many electric circuits still require wire.

WIRE

Wire used in electric circuits can be made from many different materials. Common conductors are shown in the table in Fig. 3-4. When the electrons can flow easily in the material, it is called a good conductor. If it is difficult to pass an electric current through a material, it is known as an *insulator*.

Some good conductors of electricity are copper, silver, and aluminum. Most wire is made from copper because it is a good conductor and can be purchased at a reasonable price. Silver is a better conductor than copper but it is higher in cost and not as readily available.

Fig. 3-1 Printed circuit boards utilized printed wiring to conduct electricity between parts of the circuit.

Fig. 3-3. Close-up of printed circuit boards reveals printed wiring usually made of copper or silver.

There *are* times when silver is used to make wire, such as the printed wire mentioned earlier. However, much more use is made of copper wire, while aluminum wire is used for high voltage lines that carry electricity long distances from the power plant to the users.

SOLID VS STRANDED WIRE

If you examine various pieces of wire, you will see how they differ. One piece may be a solid single wire. Another may be made of many fine strands of wire in the form of a braid, Fig. 3-5. Solid wire does not flex as readily as stranded wire, so it is used in places where, normally, the wire does not move. Stranded wire is used in applications where the wire has to flex.

Wire is used in thousands of different electric circuits. Solid wire, for example, completes the circuit to your lights, washer, dryer and in most circuits routed behind the plaster or dry wall in your home. Stranded wire will be found in lamp cords, toaster cords, and in the heavy-duty cord connected to the iron used to press your clothes. All of these electric cords are moved

CONDUCTOR	APPROXIMATE RESISTANCE*	TYPICAL APPLICATION
SILVER	9.8	ELECTRONIC CIRCUITS
COPPER	10.35	SOLID AND STRANDED WIRE
GOLD	14.6	SPECIALIZED ELECTRICAL INSTRUMENTS
ALUMINUM	17.0	LIGHTWEIGHT WIRE
NICKEL	52.0	RADIO TUBES
STEEL	100	TELEPHONE LINES
CONSTANTAN	295	HEAT MEASURING DEVICES
NICHROME	676	HEATER ELEMENTS
CARBON	2000 +	AUTOMOBILE WIRING

*Resistance is given in ohms per circular mil-foot at 25 deg. on Celsius scale. These terms will be explained as you progress through this and the next two chapters.

Fig. 3-4. Electrical conductors are listed in order of rising resistance. Typical applications are given for each conductor.

Fig. 3-5. Stranded wire with braided covering is used in communications field. A—TV camera extension cable. B—Mobile TV camera coaxial cable. C—Shielded remote control cable. (Belden Corp.)

frequently, and the stranded wire is what makes the moves possible. If solid wire was used, it would break due to the constant flexing.

WIRE COVERING

Wire is made in many different ways. In addition to being either solid or stranded, wire can be coated with varnish, left bare or covered with insulating material, and with a braided covering.

Coated wire usually is referred to as "magnet wire." It can be found in electromagnets, coils for transformers (see Chapter 11) and in the antennas of portable radios. Generally, the varnish coating must be removed when this type of wire is to be soldered.

Fig. 3-6. Data transmission cable contains 66 pairs of color-coded wires, built into a plastic jacket.

However, there is a coated wire available which does not require the protective coating to be stripped off before the wire can be soldered.

INSULATED WIRE

Insulated wire is used for lamp cords, house wiring and telephone cables. *By definition, a cable is an assembly of two or more wires inside a common covering.* Cables used in telephone circuits have color-coded insulation on the individual wires for ease in connecting or tracing wires. See Fig. 3-6.

Since many people are color blind, it is important to remember that certain electrical jobs require working with color-coded wires. Color coding is one reason why some companies insist on giving a color blindness test when they are interviewing people to fill new job openings. It would create a problem if color blind persons were hired as telephone installers or TV camera installers, because some cables have 20 or more color-coded conductors inside.

Fig. 3-7. This 6-conductor TV camera cable includes two coaxial cables with braided covering to shield against interference.

Wire with braided covering, Fig. 3-7, is used extensively in communications work. Applications include lead-in cables that connect antennas to TV sets, leads for electrical instruments and transmission line cables. This type of cable is used because the braided covering reduces interference problems in radio and television reception. It is much more expensive than other wire, but it is used because of its special "shielding" properties. For this reason, wire with braided covering is commonly called "shielded cable."

A coaxial cable, B in Fig. 3-5, utilizes two conductors having the same axis. The outer, braided conductor shields magnetic fields from the inner conductor.

STRIPPING WIRE

When working with insulated wire for electric circuits, it is necessary to remove the insulation before it can be soldered. Stripping usually is done with wire

Fig. 3-8. A wire stripper is a specialty hand tool used to remove insulation from an insulated wire.

strippers, Fig. 3-8, or it can be done with a knife. Use care, however, to insure that the wire is not nicked or strands broken off during the stripping, Fig. 3-9. When this happens, the size of the wire is reduced. This, in turn, reduces the number of electrons that can flow through the wire.

Fig. 3-10 shows what happens when broken strands reduce the size of a wire. In view A, for the sake of comparison, water hoses of two different sizes are shown. Note that as the size of the hose increases, the amount of water passing through also increases. The reverse is also true. When the size of the hose decreases, the amount of water also decreases.

Electron flow through two wires is shown in view B

Fig. 3-9. Sketch shows an insulated wire that has been properly stripped by means of a knife.

in Fig. 3-10. One wire is whole and undamaged. The other is smaller because many strands are broken. *Note that the smaller the wire, the fewer electrons that can pass through.*

Fig. 3-10. The size of the conductor makes a difference in volume of flow, whether the product is water or electricity. A—Large and small hoses. B—Whole and damaged wires.

WIRE SIZE

Fig. 3-11 lists various sizes of wire. Note that the size is given by a number, ranging from 0000 to 40. This numbering system is known as the American Wire Gage (AWG). It is used to give specific information about the various sizes of wire.

Study the chart and you will see that the larger the wire number, the smaller the diameter of the wire. It is important to select the proper size of wire for the job. Otherwise, failure is possible and a fire might result.

I. C. SAYS:

"NEVER USE WATER ON AN ELEC-TRICAL FIRE. Use the correct type of fire extinguisher or common baking soda. Also be sure to disconnect the source of electricity powering the device that caused the fire."

DIMENSIONS AND RESISTANCES OF COPPER WIRE

GAGE NO. AWG OR B & S	DIAMETER OF BARE WIRE IN INCHES	DIAMETER IN MILS	AREA IN CIRCULAR MILS	RESISTANCE FEET PER ONE OHM AT 68 DEG. F
0000	.460	460.0	211600	20400
000	.410	409.6	167800	16180
00	.365	364.8	133100	12830
0	.325	324.9	105500	10180
1	.289	289.3	83690	8070
2	.258	257.6	66370	6400
3	.229	229.4	52640	5075
4	.204	204.3	41740	4025
5	.182	181.9	33100	3192
6	.162	162.0	26250	2531
7	.144	144.3	20820	2007
8	.129	128.5	16510	1592
9	.114	114.4	13090	1262
10	.102	101.9	10380	1001
11	.091	90.74	8234	794
12	.081	80.81	6530	629.6
13	.072	71.96	5178	499.3
14	.064	64.08	4107	396.0
15	.057	57.07	3257	314.0
16	.051	50.82	2583	249.0
17	.045	45.26	2048	197.5
18	.040	40.30	1624	156.5
19	.036	35.89	1288	124.2
20	.032	31.96	1022	98.5
21	.028	28.46	810.1	78.11
22	.025	25.35	642.4	61.95
23	.023	22.57	509.5	49.13
24	.020	20.10	404.0	38.96
25	.018	17.90	320.4	30.90
26	.016	15.94	254.1	24.50
27	.014	14.20	201.5	19.43
28	.013	12.64	159.8	15.41
29	.011	11.26	126.7	12.22
30	.010	10.03	100.5	9.691
31	.009	8.928	79.7	7.685
32	.008	7.950	63.21	6.095
33	.007	7.080	50.13	4.833
34	.006	6.305	39.75	3.833
35	.006	5.615	31.52	3.040
36	.005	5.000	25.00	2.411
37	.004	4.453	19.83	1.912
38	.004	3.965	15.72	1.516
39	.004	3.531	12.47	1.202
40	.003	3.145	9.888	0.9534

Fig. 3-11. Copper wire is charted by gage number, by diameter in inches and in mils and by area in circular mils. Resistance is shown in feet per ohm at 68 deg. F (20 deg. C).

Fig. 3-12. To use an American Standard wire gage, insert bare wire in different slots until it "fits." Then, note gage number.

Other problems that result from the use of under-sized wire are:
1. Toasters do not brown the bread.
2. Electric motors run too slow.

Fig. 3-12 shows how a wire gage is used to determine the size of the wire. The gage is easy to use. First remove the insulation from the wire. Then, hold the gage firmly and place the wire being measured between the slots. Check the size, then use the round hole at the bottom of the slot for easy removal of the wire. The numbers on the outside of the gage are the same numbers found in the table in Fig. 3-11.

INTERCOM PROJECT

You can build a simple intercom for use in your home. Use two permanent magnet speakers about 4 in. in diameter. Get speakers with large magnets. Place the speakers in separate rooms and connect them with two wires, Fig. 3-13.

Take turns either talking or listening. Both parties cannot speak at once. You will not be blasted by the volume from this simple intercom setup, but the results will surprise you. Note, however, that this intercom will not work in a noisy building.

AMPERES/AMPS

Earlier in this chapter, we stressed the importance of wire size as it relates to the number of electrons that can flow through the wire. Since the number of electrons is *so large,* when speaking in electrical terms, the word amperes or amps is used instead. A one amp reading, in fact, is another way of stating that

6,240,000,000,000,000,000 (6.24×10^{18}) electrons are flowing past a given point in one second, Fig. 3-14. The term "amp" is explained in detail in Chapter 5.

Changing the 6,240,000,000,000,000,000 electrons to 6.24×10^{18} is called "scientific notation." (See

Fig. 3-13. This simple intercom project consist of two 4 in. diameter permanent magnet speakers and connecting wires.

reference section.) It is a way people working on electrical circuits can shorten the numbers to make them easier to use. The given value for one amp is a "standard" issued by the National Bureau of Standards.

You probably have seen the term "amps" printed on motors, electric frypans and other appliances around your home. There are two reasons why this is important. First, for safety reasons, each of the various

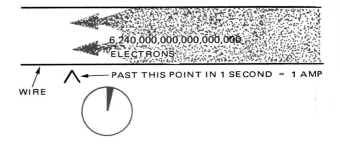

Fig. 3-14. The term amperes, or amps, is used to simplify, and it refers to how many electrons are flowing through a circuit.

appliances must have the proper size lead wire to prevent it from burning up. Second, by keeping a total of the number of amps used by each appliance every hour, the power company can send you the bill for the amount of money owed them for using the electricity.

Remember, the larger the wire, the smaller the AWG number, and the higher the number of amps that the wire will carry without overheating.

RESISTANCE WIRE

If you watch a toaster while it is in operation, you will notice that it gets so hot that the heating element inside turns red. If you look closely after it cools off, you will see that the part that was red is also made from wire. *Actually, this type of wire is made so that it will heat up. It is called "resistance wire."* It is used inside light bulbs, in heating elements for hair dryers and in electric space heaters.

Because resistance wire is designed to heat up, it is not made from copper. Instead, it is made from special

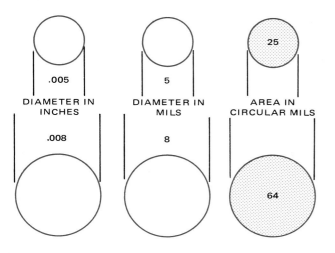

Fig. 3-15. A given size of wire is expressed in inches, mils and circular mils.

metals with names like Nichrome and Constantan. Although most wire is round, resistance wire can also be purchased in a ribbon shape. Ribbon shape resistance wire is what is commonly used in toasters.

CIRCULAR MILS

Round wire is measured in "circular mils." A mil is one thousandth of an inch (.001 in.). A circular mil is the cross-sectional area of a wire that has a diameter of one mil. Note in Fig. 3-15 that as the cross-sectional area (shaded area) gets larger, the number of circular mils is increased by the square of the diameter.

Circular mils are easier to visualize through an example. When you square a number, it means you must multiply the number by itself. Number 5 squared would be 5 x 5, which is equal to 25. Therefore, if you had a wire 5 mils in diameter, Fig. 3-15, the cross-sectional area of the wire would contain 25 circular mils. The second wire shown in Fig. 3-15 has a diameter of 8 mils. Its area then, would be 64 circular mils.

There is a good reason for converting the diameter of wire into circular mils. Working with the cross-sectional area of the wire makes it possible for you to select the right size of wire to safely carry the prescribed number of amps in the circuit.

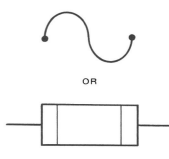

Fig. 3-16. Wiring diagrams and schematics use symbols to identify parts of circuits. Two different fuse symbols are shown.

FUSES

Most electric circuits are equipped with a safety device called a "fuse." It is designed to prevent fires caused by overloading the circuit with too many amps. Fuse symbols most commonly found on schematics are shown in Fig. 3-16.

A fuse is a conductor of electricity containing a thin element made of aluminum and other metals. When too many amps pass through the fuse, the thin element will overheat, then melt. This opens the circuit and stops

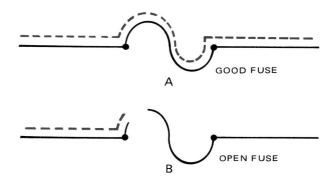

Fig. 3-17. The most popular fuse symbol is used to indicate a good fuse. An open fuse is shown with a break in the symbol. A—Electrons can flow. B—Electrons are stopped.

the electrons from flowing, Fig. 3-17. Fuses range in size from 1/100 amp to heavy-duty units able to carry several hundred amps.

The reason for using a fuse in the circuit is to keep the wires from burning up or having other parts of the circuit damaged. When the element does melt most people say, "The fuse has blown." When it does blow, the bad fuse must be replaced with a new one. It also is very important to find out *why* the fuse blew. Something must be wrong with the circuit, or the circuit is being overloaded.

FUSE TESTER PROJECT

Build the fuse tester shown in Figs. 3-18 and 3-19 by obtaining the following materials and assembling them according to the construction procedure given.

Fig. 3-18. Shop-built fuse tester emits a buzzing sound if the fuse is good. (Project by Allan Witherspoon)

No.	Item
1	1.5 to 3 volt dc alarm buzzer.
1	1 in. x 3 in. x 2 in. chassis box.
1	Penlight battery (cell).
1	1/4 in. x 6 in. x 14 in. plywood.
4	1/2 in. screw eyes.
1	Battery holder.
2	1 ft. lengths of stranded copper wire (uncoated).

CONSTRUCTION PROCEDURE

1. Cut a hole in chassis box and mount buzzer.
2. Install battery and mount chassis box at bottom of plywood.
3. Position screw eyes on plywood in a triangular shape.
4. Connect wires on screw eyes as shown in diagram.
5. Drill a 1/4 in. hole in plywood for hanging fuse tester on the wall.

To use the tester, Fig. 3-18, pick up a fuse and place it between the two wires on the plywood. Move the fuse inward until it makes contact with both wires. The buzzer will sound off if the fuse is good. If it fails to buzz, the fuse is blown.

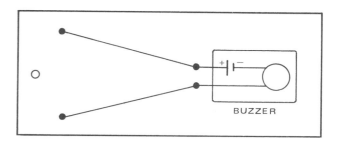

Fig. 3-19. Fuse tester schematic shows the arrangement of parts. See the text for construction details.

BLOWN FUSES

Blown fuses are shown in Fig. 3-20. The blackened section is the result of a short circuit. This condition will result if a large number of amps are surging through the circuit. When this happens, the thin metal strip is heated to a very high temperature and turns into a vapor, which discolors the fuse window.

Fig. 3-20. When fuses of the snap-in or screw-in type blow, the element vaporizes.

The term, "short circuit" is explained in Fig. 3-21. Notice that a short circuit bypasses the load. This allows an extremely high number of amps to flow in the circuit, which is what the fuse is meant to stop.

Fig. 3-21. A short circuit occurs when two bare wires come into contact and bypass the load, allowing a large number of amps to take a shortcut.

SLOW BLOWING FUSES

Some circuits normally have a large number of amps flowing for short periods of time. You probably have seen some lights in your home go dim when certain appliances (such as the refrigerator) first turn on. If you have an electric saw, you may notice the same dimming effect when the saw is turned on, or if the saw slows down while cutting a large piece of wood. At times like this, you do not want the fuse to blow if the overload is only going to last a few seconds. To prevent this, a slow blowing fuse, Fig. 3-22, is made by some manufac-

Fig. 3-22. Slow blowing fuses generally have a dual element to help withstand a brief overload.

turers. Note that the dual element pictured is heavier at one end. Some types of slow blowing fuses are designed to withstand an overload for 12 to 25 seconds without blowing.

Fig. 3-23 illustrates some of the many fuses that are

Fig. 3-23. Fuses are designed for every electrical protection need. (Bussman Div./Cooper Ind.)

manufactured. Fig. 3-24 pictures a fuse holder with a fuse in place to protect the circuit from being overloaded. This unit is designed for easy removal and replacement of the blown fuse.

Fig. 3-24. Fuse holders usually are placed for easy access and designed for quick fuse replacement.

The electric circuits in many older homes are protected with fuses. In most newer homes, however, the circuits are protected with circuit breakers, Fig. 3-25. A circuit breaker has a distinct advantage over a fuse. When an overload occurs, the circuit breaker "trips," and the circuit is opened. *Unlike a fuse, the circuit breaker does not have to be replaced after it trips.* It works like a switch. If an overload trips it, all you have to do is turn it off, then back on and the circuit is completed again.

Fig. 3-25. A circuit breaker will open automatically when a current overload flows through it.

Fig. 3-26. This portable receptacle is fitted with a toggle switch and plug type fuse. (Bussman Div./Cooper Ind.)

SWITCHES

As mentioned in Chapter 1, switches are used to open and close circuits without having to go through the inconvenience of removing and attaching wires. Fig.

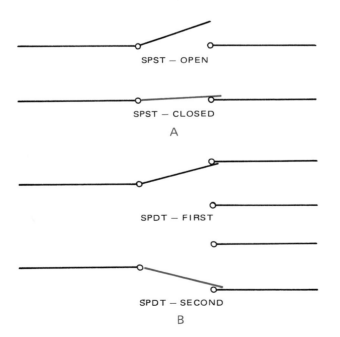

Fig. 3-27. Symbols for single-pole switches. A—Single-pole single-throw switch in open/closed position. B—Single-pole double-throw switch in first/second positions.

3-26 shows one of the common types of switches, along with a plug type fuse. The purpose of the glass top is to help prevent shocks when you change a blown fuse.

The symbols for various switches are shown in Figs. 3-27 and 3-28. The letters SPST stand for single-pole

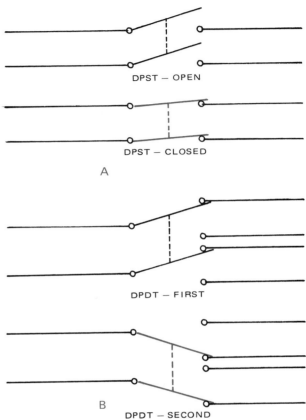

Fig. 3-28. Symbols for double-pole switches. A—Double-pole single-throw switch in open/closed positions. B—Double-pole double-throw switch in first/second positions.

single-throw; SPDT is single-pole double-throw; DPST is double-pole single-throw; DPDT is double-pole double-throw. To make it easier to understand, each switch is shown in both the normal position and in the second position after the switch is thrown.

Switches are wired into circuits so that one or two circuits are completed by closing (throwing) the switch. When the circuit is open, no electrons can flow and the switch is said to be OFF. When the circuit is closed, electrons can flow and the circuit is said to be ON.

The number of switches available ranges in the hundreds. To mention a few, there are: slide switches, rotary switches (Fig. 3-29), plunger switches, push button switches (Fig. 3-30) and roller arm switches.

Fig. 3-29. Rotary switches come in many styles and shapes, including these open frame types.
(Centralab Electronics Div. of Globe-Union Inc.)

Some switches will indicate that a piece of magnetic material is close to it. These are known as "magnet actuated proximity switches."

AUTO BURGLAR ALARM PROJECT

You can put a switch to good use in building an auto burglar alarm. First look at the horn circuit on your car, Fig. 3-31. When you push the horn button or press the horn ring, the horn "blows." When you release the pressure, the blowing stops. You can use the same sound to scare away a car thief. Do this by wiring a switch into the horn circuit as shown in Fig. 3-32.

When the switch is installed and the car is in use, keep the burglar alarm switch in the open position. When you leave your car, close the switch and hide it where only you can find it. As soon as someone starts the engine, the horn will start blowing and frighten the would-be thief away.

When *you* want to start the engine of your car, turn off the alarm switch. Always keep this in mind or the blasting sound of the horn will surprise you, too.

Fig. 3-30. Lighted and unlighted push button switches are used in many applications such as car radios,
telephone, intercoms and elevators in buildings. (Centralab Electronics Div. of Globe-Union Inc.)

Fig. 3-31. This schematic shows a simplified circuit for the horn on a passenger car.

Fig. 3-32. Install a burglar alarm switch into the horn circuit as shown. When the ignition switch is turned on (closed), the alarm will sound off.

INSULATORS

As mentioned earlier, insulation is a material used to cover wire. Wires are insulated to keep them from touching each other or contacting other conductors. If they did touch, it would cause a bright spark called an "arc." Anytime there is an arc, there is danger that a fire will start or a fuse will blow. Therefore, for protection and safety, wire is manufactured with an insulating cover molded on it.

Insulation comes in white, black, red, green, blue, yellow and many other colors, combinations of colors and striped patterns. Insulation also prevents any person touching the wire from getting a shock. Imagine plugging in an uninsulated radio lead and receiving a shock or bad burn. Usually, the plug is molded from an insulating material, which offers a high resistance to the flow of electrons.

The best insulators are rubber, shellac, glass, mica, plastics, and paper. In Fig. 3-33, the plastic ends (connectors) on the wires in the instrument panel module (unit), are insulators. The electrical tape and plastic shields are also forms of insulators. When a large number of wires are taped together, or encased in protective tubing, the assembly is called a *wiring harness*. Figs. 3-34 and 3-35 show a few of the many insulators you will find being used in conjunction with electric circuits.

SOLDERING

Many times, it will be necessary to connect wires or attach them to an electrical part. Usually, this is done by soldering the connection. *Solder is a metal mixture used to connect metal parts or components.* Generally, the mixture is made of tin and lead. For example, a mixture of 60 percent tin and 40 percent lead is known

Fig. 3-33. Car instrument panel circuits are combined in a wiring harness. They are protected from damage by arcing by various types of insulators.
(Packard Electric Div., General Motors Corp.)

Conductors and Insulators

Fig. 3-34. Insulators for electric circuits come in many shapes and forms. Insulators shown are termed "structural ceramics" by professionals in the field.
(Centralab Electronics Div. of Globe-Union Inc.)

as 60/40 solder. This 60/40 mixture is used by most people because it melts at a lower temperature than other types (70/30 or 40/60).

I. C. SAYS:

"Here is a word of warning. Solder will melt at 370 deg. F or higher. At these temperatures, you can get a bad burn. Do not let any of the melted solder touch your skin. Also, do not touch the soldering iron or gun used to melt the solder."

Typical soldering irons are shown in Figs. 3-36 and 3-37. A soldering iron with multiple temperature settings is shown in Fig. 3-36. The proper way to use a soldering iron is shown in Fig. 3-37. By using it this way, you can avoid seriously burning yourself.

Fig. 3-35. See if you can pick out the insulators on top of this power pole.

STEPS IN SOLDERING

To make a satisfactory solder joint, several important steps are necessary. First, strip the insulation or coating from the ends of the wire to be soldered. Next, make a strong mechanical connection to insure good electrical flow after solder has been placed on the

joint. If the joint is not mechanically tight, you will get poor electrical flow because solder is not as good a conductor as copper.

Fig. 3-36. This soldering iron kit provides a built-in heat source. Note heat control knob. (Heath/General Electric)

Then, use a soldering iron Fig. 3-37, to heat the mechanical connection on one side while applying the solder from the other side. Do not put the solder directly on the soldering iron; a poor solder joint may result. By heating one side, the connection will get hot enough to melt the solder on the other side. Use only enough solder to flow over all the surfaces and wires at the connection. Too much solder will result in poor appearance, and solder may drip into places where it is not wanted.

When enough solder has melted on the connection, remove the iron. Do not move the parts being soldered until the solder has cooled. If you accidentally move the parts while the connection is cooling, apply the iron

Fig. 3-37. The correct soldering technique is to heat one side of the connection while applying solder from the other side.

and reheat the joint. This technique will insure a good solder connection. The finished soldering joint should be completely covered by the flowing solder, bright and smooth, with all wires firmly held in place. Study the soldering sequence in Figs. 3-38 through 3-41.

Fig. 3-38. The first step in soldering is to heat the joint.

Fig. 3-39. The second step in soldering is to apply the solder.

Fig. 3-40. The third step in soldering is to remove the iron and allow the solder to cool.

Fig. 3-41. The fourth and final step in soldering is to cut off excess wire.

If the solder is dull looking or if it has lumps or small beads of solder, the job is poorly done. This is known as a "cold solder joint," which is the mark of someone who has not learned the correct way to solder. When you know how, even printed wiring, Fig. 3-42 can be repaired with solder. Small breaks or cracks can be fixed by heating the bad spot and applying a small amount of solder.

Fig. 3-42. Small breaks in a printed wiring circuit can be soldered. The circuit shown is for a car instrument panel. (Packard Electric Div., General Motors Corp.)

TYPES OF SOLDER

Most hardware and building supply stores carry two types of solder, rosin core and acid cord. *Use only rosin core solder when doing electrical work.* Acid core solder is used for sheet metal work. If it is used for electrical work, it will eat through connections and damage parts.

Rosin core solder means that the solder has a small opening in the center, filled with special material called "flux." Flux is a general term for materials used to remove impurities (called "oxides") from the surfaces being joined by the solder. The clean surfaces permit the solder to stick to the connection when it reaches the correct temperature.

HEAT SINKS

Items like transistors, diodes and even some resistors (parts to be described in detail later) can be damaged from the heat created by the soldering iron. Therefore, when soldering near delicate electrical parts, protect them with a heat sink. A heat sink is a better conductor of heat than the electrical part, so it will pick up the heat and stop it from going to the nearby part.

The heat sink shown in Fig. 3-43 is made from an alligator clip and a piece of copper. One end of the

Fig. 3-43. A satisfactory heat sink can be made from an alligator clip and a piece of copper. (Project by Ron Simons)

copper is cut to fit the clip. The other end is broad and flat to give off absorbed heat. This heat sink is easy to solder together and convenient to store for use when needed. When preparing to solder electrical work, place the heat sink between the electrical part to be protected and the joint to be soldered, Fig. 3-44. Needle nose pliers and other metal objects also can be used as heat sinks.

Fig. 3-44. The heat sink is a means of attracting and giving off heat to protect delicate electrical parts from heat damage.

POOR SOLDER JOINTS

Check these common reasons why some solder joints are unsatisfactory:
1. Not heating connection to proper temperature so solder can flow.
2. Applying solder to iron instead of on joint opposite iron.
3. Using too much solder.

The only way to learn to solder is to do it. Learning to solder is like learning to ride a bicycle. In both cases, the only way to learn is by trying.

PROTECTING THE WIRE

Cables and wires have to be protected in some job locations. Often, where there is danger of having the

Fig. 3-45. Wires between switches, receptacles and electrical loads must be installed in protective tubing. A—Flexible steel conduit. B—Thinwall conduit.

insulation worn away, cut or scraped, the wire is protected by placing it in a hollow pipe called "conduit." In some applications, it is protected by flexible steel conduit, or "greenfield." Both types of protection are shown in Fig. 3-45.

Another covering used to protect wire is called "spaghetti," Fig. 3-46. It is a hollow insulating material

Fig. 3-46. "Spaghetti" is a common term used for a hollow insulating material used to cover spliced and soldered wires.

similar to a plastic straw. When splicing two pieces of wire, remove the insulation from both ends. Slide a piece of spaghetti over one of the ends. Then, connect the two pieces of wire and solder them together. Next, slide the spaghetti over the completed connection so that it completely covers the bare ends of both wires. This method of protection will prevent bare wire from coming into contact with other wires or metal parts, causing an arc or giving someone an electric shock.

Another material, called "heat shrink," also can be used to protect wires. It looks much like spaghetti. With heat shrink, however, heat is applied to it after assembly and the material actually gets smaller in size. This shrinking action makes the covering fit more tightly on the wire.

ELECTRICAL CODES

Guidelines for proper routing of wires, and other safe practices, vary from city to city, depending on local electrical codes. The National Electrical Code contains the general rules and regulations that contractors, builders and manufacturers must follow. Local codes supplement (add to) National Code requirements. These codes have been established to protect those people who are not familiar with some of the dangers of electricity. City and state building inspectors visit new buildings under construction to make sure that codes have been followed.

If you are becoming more interested in the electrical field, get yourself a small set of tools, Fig. 3-47, and a heat sink for project work and other supervised activities. With the kit shown, you should be able to do the soldering and handle electrical work involved with small nuts, screws and other fasteners.

Fig. 3-47. A basic set of tools for simple electrical work should include pliers, screwdrivers, nut drivers, soldering iron and a supply of solder. (Heath Co.)

SUPERCONDUCTORS

Scientists continually experiment with new methods of producing and transporting electricity. Some recent developments have come in the field of superconductive materials. Superconductivity is the point at which a conductor loses its resistance to electricity. In past years, the point of superconductivity was thought to be around −452° Kelvin. However, scientists are now discovering that some special materials can be manufactured to have little or no resistance to the flow of electrons at even warmer temperatures. This type of research will result in some exciting new possibilities for the use of electricity.

Superconductivity may finally allow electricity to be stored by methods other than batteries. Just think, electricity could be sent around a loop of superconductive material until it is ready to use. Generating stations could be made smaller because their output could be stored for later use. Generators designed for peak demands would no longer be needed. A reserve supply of electricity could be built up by running a smaller generator overnight.

Another application of superconductors is in the computer industry. With no resistance to electron flow, computer circuits could operate at blinding speed. This could result in supercomputers small enough to fit on a desktop.

A third and important possibility lies in the distribution of electricity. If electric lines have no resistance, electricity can be sent great distances without loss of energy. This means hydroelectric plants located in remote mountain areas could ship electricity to distant urban areas. Also, electricity could be produced in desert areas using photoelectric cells and then carried where needed without energy loss.

SUMMARY

In this chapter, you learned the difference between insulators and conductors. You found that there are many different kinds of materials used as conductors. Copper is, however, the most widely used conductor material. Plastic, ceramic, and rubber are the most widely used insulating materials. Insulators are put to use in tasks where the flow of electrons must not take place easily.

A fuse is installed in a circuit to prevent a surge of electrons from burning up or destroying its components. Using too small a conductor can restrict the flow of electrons. Poor solder joints could also do the same. Resistance wire is a material used to restrict the flow of electrons on purpose. Resistance causes the wire, such as is found in a space heater or toaster, to produce heat that is needed to do the job. The National Electrical Code provides an abundance of information on the proper installation of electrical wiring.

KEY WORDS AND TERMS

American Wire Gage (AWG)
Amp
Ampere
boards
Arc
Circuit breaker
Circular mills
Cold solder joint
Conductor
Conduit
Double-pole double-
    throw (DPDT)
Double-pole single-
    throw (DPST)
Flux
Fuse
Heat sink

Insulator
Magnet wire
Printed circuit (PC)

Resistance wire
Rosin core solder
Shielded cable
Short circuit
Single-pole double-
    throw (SPDT)
Single-pole single-
    throw (SPST)
Solder
Soldering iron
Superconductivity
Switch
Wiring harness

TEST YOUR KNOWLEDGE

Do not write in this book. Write your answers on a separate sheet of paper.

1. The purpose of soldering in electrical circuits is to _____.
2. *True or False?* Rosin-core solder should be used for all electrical work.
3. What two precautions should you observe when soldering?
4. Three good materials for conducting electricity are _____, _____, and _____.
5. Name three commonly used insulator materials.
6. Which size wire is larger, No. 12 or No. 16?
7. Describe how a wire should fit into the slot on the American Wire Gage to determine its size.
8. Name two tools used to remove insulation from wires.
9. How is a circuit breaker reset after it has opened the circuit?
10. What kind of wire is used in heating elements?
11. List three nonmagnetic materials.
12. Acid core solder should not be used for _____.
13. Draw the schematic for a circuit to show how a single-pole, single-throw switch can be used to control a 6 volt lightbulb connected to a storage battery.
14. Draw a circuit for a continuity tester.

ACTIVITIES

1. Why are the ends of stranded wire twisted together and tinned before it is used?
2. List the different mixtures of solder and find the temperature where each will melt.
3. Many companies use a method of soldering which does not use soldering irons or guns. Find out what they call this type of soldering and how it is done.
4. There are many different types of insulation used on wire. Make a list of different kinds and their colors.
5. How is insulation put on wires?
6. How is the rosin flux put into the core of the solder? How do companies make the solder with a hollow center?
7. List the different types of fuses you can find and determine how much current they will carry without blowing.
8. How is stranded wire made?
9. Find out what types of tests are given to see if a person is color blind.
10. What is flux and how is it made?
11. Where does copper come from? Make a map of the different places where it is found.

4 Resistors and Capacitors

LEARNING OBJECTIVES

After studying this chapter, you will be able to:
- Draw the symbols for resistors and capacitors.
- Describe some of the uses for thermistors.
- Contrast the different types of capacitors.
- Demonstrate the proper way to handle and discharge capacitors.
- Compute the value of a resistor by its color code.
- Explain the difference between a farad, microfarad, and picofarad.

In Chapter 3, you studied electrical conductors and insulators. You found that good conductors are made from materials that allow electrons to flow easily. Conductors are used to form a path or circuit for electrons to flow from source to lead and back again.

Insulators, on the other hand, are poor conductors of electricity. They are made from materials that offer strong resistance to the flow of electrons. Because of this non-conducting characteristic, insulators are used to contain the flow of electricity in planned circuits and to prevent severe electrical shock when you touch wires, plugs, or switches.

RESISTORS

Conductors, then, allow electrons to flow and insulators do not. In between these two extremes, we have other materials that conduct electricity but make it difficult for electrons to flow. These are called *resistors*. One familiar type of resistor is a resistance wire. A resistance wire offers so much resistance that it turns bright red and gives off enough heat to make toast, heat rooms, and dry people's hair.

The resistance of a given material to electron flow is based on a comparison with copper. See the table in Fig. 3-4 of Chapter 3. Silver, for example, is listed higher on the table than copper because it has lower resistance and is a better conductor. Aluminum, nichrome, and carbon have higher resistance so they are poorer conductors.

Since carbon resists the flow of electrons much more than copper, carbon is often used in making resistors. The material, size, and makeup of the resistor determines its resistance value, which is measured in ohms.

Resistors can be purchased in hundreds of different values, ranging from about 1 ohm to over 22 million ohms. Fig. 4-1 shows some of the common types of resistors that are used in electrical circuits.

RESISTOR SYMBOLS

The symbols for a resistor (or resistance) are shown in Fig. 4-2. Do not confuse the second symbol in the illustration with the symbol for a fuse. Unlike the fuse symbol, there are no lines in the box in the resistor symbol.

Fig. 4-1. Many resistors are used in this electrical circuit. Note identifying stripes on the body of each resistor.

Fig. 4-2. These two symbols are the most popular resistor symbols used in schematics.

In some schematics, you will see what looks like an upside down horseshoe (Ω) being used instead of the word "ohm." This symbol is the Greek letter "omega." In other circuits, you may find the letter "R" being used. This letter helps locate the place to put the resistor on the circuit board when you assemble the kit. In Fig. 4-3, for example, note R 29.

Later in this text, we will see still other symbols and letters being used in drawings to represent some common electrical components.

Fig. 4-3. Installing resistors on a coded circuit board. (Acme Electric Corp.)

TYPES OF RESISTORS

Resistors are of two types, either fixed or variable. A fixed resistor has one specific value, such as 150 ohms. A variable resistor has a range of values or it can be adjusted to the resistance needed for a specific circuit.

FIXED RESISTORS

Fixed resistors vary in makeup. They may be molded composition, metal film, carbon film or wirewound. Fig. 4-4 shows various types of fixed resistors that are available. The big difference between resistors lies in the heat they create and the heat they can safely get rid of to the air around them. Therefore, the amount of heat in the area where they are being used and the humidity of the area, are two typical problems which a designer must consider when drawing a circuit that uses resistors.

A molded composition resistor is often referred to as a carbon resistor. Break apart a composition resistor

Fig. 4-4. Fixed resistors. A—Wirewound. B—Thin Film. C—Composition.

and you will find that it is made of a carbon material and a "binder" that holds the carbon together. Note also that the wire leads at either end of the resistor do not go all the way through. They stop soon after entering the body of the resistor. The different numerical values of resistors depend on the amounts of carbon and binder used in their construction.

Carbon resistors come in many different sizes. Those most commonly used range from approximately 3/32 in. to about 5/16 in. in diameter. (Wirewound and thin film types will have still different sizes.)

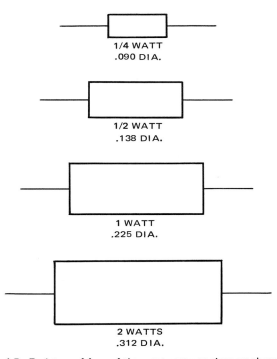

1/4 WATT
.090 DIA.

1/2 WATT
.138 DIA.

1 WATT
.225 DIA.

2 WATTS
.312 DIA.

Fig. 4-5. Resistors of four of the most common sizes are shown by wattage and diameter.

The different sizes of carbon resistors, Fig. 4-5, also tell the amount of heat that a given resistor can transfer or dissipate to the outside air. Carbon resistors are rated at 1/8, 1/4, 1/2, 1 and 2 watts.

The term "watts" will be described in detail in Chapter 5. For the time being, just think of this term as the amount of heat the resistor can stand without being destroyed.

THIN FILM RESISTORS

Thin film resistors are sort of a compromise between carbon resistors and wirewound resistors. The primary differences are in size and cost. Fig. 4-6 shows how thin film resistors are constructed. The substrate shown is an insulating material something like ceramic.

Fig. 4-6. Four steps in the construction of thin film resistors.

WIREWOUND RESISTORS

Wirewound resistors, Fig. 4-7, are built in a different manner. They are constructed by winding a long length of wire around a core. The length of wire, its diameter, and material from which it is made determine the value of the resistor.

After the core is wound, a ceramic insulating coating is applied to the body of the resistor. This coating protects the wires when the resistor is put to use. Each end of the winding is attached to a terminal used to install the resistor in the circuit.

Fig. 4-7. A wirewound resistor is made up of a core wound with a continuous piece of wire and coated with ceramic insulation.

Wirewound resistors are used in circuits where large amounts of heat must be dissipated (given off) to the surrounding air. As a result they usually are made much larger than carbon resistors. Some wirewound resistors are over 1 in. in diameter and 10 in. long. Power ratings range from about 3 watts to over 200 watts; much higher than carbon resistors. For this reason, they are much more expensive than the smaller carbon types.

Fig. 4-8. An adjustable wirewound resistor and its symbol.

ADJUSTABLE WIREWOUND RESISTORS

Some wirewound resistors are adjustable. This type of resistor is not completely covered with the ceramic material that protects the windings. As you can see in Fig. 4-8, these resistors have a small portion of one side exposed. A slider arm is mounted across the exposed portion as a means of adjustment.

To make a resistance adjustment, move the slider arm along the resistor, then clamp it in a given position. By changing the slider arm location, different amounts of resistance can be obtained. This type of resistor is not designed to be adjusted very often. If repeated adjustments were made, the resistor would soon wear out from the action of the slider arm on the exposed copper.

VARIABLE RESISTORS

Variable resistors, Fig. 4-9, are used in applications where it is necessary to make frequent adjustments of resistance values. Some common usages are as follows:

Resistors and Capacitors

Fig. 4-9. Variable resistors fill a variety of electrical needs. (Centralab Electronics Div. of Globe-Union Inc.)

1. When you adjust the volume of your stereo or television set.
2. When you change the speed of your car windshield wipers.
3. When you dim lights in your house.
4. When you change the speed of variable speed drill in your home workshop.

In each case, you are adjusting a variable resistor. Remember, too, that this type of resistor will do many other things for you, depending on how it is used.

POTENTIOMETER

Variable resistors are also known as potentiometers, rheostats and trimmer resistors, Fig. 4-10. These names refer to some of the many uses found for variable resistors. A potentiometer, for example, allows the electrons to have two paths: one through part of the resistance, then to the load; the second path goes only through the resistance, Fig. 4-11. The rheostat allows only one path.

Fig. 4-10. Potentiometers and trimmer resistors are popular forms of variable resistors.

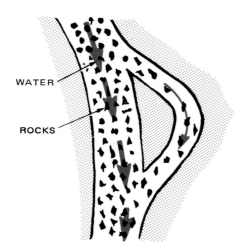

When there is more than one path for electrons, you have what is called a "parallel circuit." This will be explained more fully when you get to Chapter 7. At this point, you should know that if more than one path is present, some of the electrons will travel down each path. The amount depends on the size of the path and how much resistance is in the path, Fig. 4-12.

VARIABLE NEON VOLTMETER PROJECT

Here is a small voltmeter, Fig. 4-13, which you can use to find the exact circuit voltage. After you have built the circuit (inset) and mounted it in a box, you can calibrate the instrument. Connect the test leads to a variable power supply. *Do not* exceed 600 volts. Turn the dial on the potentiometer to the point where the light goes out. Mark this voltage value on the front of

Fig. 4-13. A variable neon voltmeter is pictured. Note the inset schematic showing circuit. NE 2-Bulb. R_1-200K resistor. R_2-300K potentiometer. (Project by Allan Witherspoon)

your voltmeter box. Keep changing the variable power supply and making this test until you have all of the values you want marked on the front of your voltmeter. Be sure to use grommets where the wires come through the metal box.

RHEOSTAT

The rheostat is a device that just adds resistance to the circuit. It serves to put greater restriction in the path of the electrons, Fig. 4-14. The further the electrons must travel through the rheostat's resistance before getting to the load, the more resistance the electrons must overcome. So, the more resistance you

Fig. 4-11. Arrows indicate path of electron movement in two similar circuits. Note there are two paths in circuit with potentiometer and one path in circuit with rheostat.

Fig. 4-12. The principle of splitting the path of electron flow is illustrated by water flowing in the mainstream and in a branch. Rocks show resistance to flow.

Fig. 4-14. A rheostat adds resistance to the circuit. A—Easy flow of electrons. B—More difficult flow of electrons. C—Very difficult flow of electrons.

want in the circuit, the further you have to turn the movable arm of the variable resistor.

TRIMMER RESISTORS

A trimmer resistor, Fig. 4-15, is a variable resistor that is similar to a potentiometer in construction. It is

Fig. 4-15. Trimmer resistors used in fine tuning applications. (Centralab Electronics Div. of Globe-Union Inc.)

used to make very small changes in the resistance of a circuit. Fine tuning of certain circuits in television sets, stereos and other communication devices are typical applications of trimmer resistors.

VALUES

Resistors are included in most circuits as a part of the design. They come in many different shapes and sizes. Generally, to help you identify a given resistor, a number is printed on its body, telling you its value. You will see numbers like 5 ohms or 450 ohms. Values such as 3.8k ohms or 3 meg ohms are a short method of labeling the size of the resistor without having to write out all the zeros.

The letter k stands for kilo, which is the same as *thousand*. A 3.8k resistor, for example, would have a value of 3800 ohms. Meg is another way of writing *million*. Therefore, a 3 meg resistor would have the value of 3,000,000 or 3 million ohms.

Pursuing this method of marking resistors further, what is the value of a 2.7k resistor? This would be 2700 ohms. How about 7.9 meg? This resistor would have a value of 7,900,000 ohms or 7.9 million ohms. The term meg and kilo are very commonly used with resistors and for sizing other electrical components, which you will learn about later.

COLOR CODE

Some resistors are color coded with rings or bands to indicate their size, Fig. 4-16. Most resistors have four bands, while others have five. At this point, an explanation of how to read these bands is in order. First, note in Fig. 4-16, that the bands are closer to one end of the resistor. Therefore, when you read its value,

Fig. 4-16. These resistors are part of a stereo tuner.

always place the resistor so the bands are to your left, Fig. 4-17. The value placed on the resistor depends on the order in which you read the colors.

I.C.SAYS:

"When using a carbon resistor, it may be soldered into the circuit in either direction. We will discover later that many other components can be mounted only one way. If they are installed any other way, they might be destroyed."

Next, we will get down to the business of *reading* the code. Basically, each color represents a number. The colors used for the first three bands are:

COLOR	NUMBER IT REPRESENTS
Black	0
Brown	1
Red	2
Orange	3
Yellow	4
Green	5
Blue	6
Violet	7
Gray	8
White	9

Fig. 4-17. The right way to read the color bands on a resistor is to position the resistor with the bands at your left.

To make a reading, list each of the colors used in the three bands. Then, list their respective numbers as follows.

Red — 2   Green — 5   Orange — 3

Write the first two numbers in order. In this case, the numbers would be 25. The third color tells you the number of zeros to add. Therefore, we would have a resistor with a value of 25 with 3 zeros or 25,000 ohms.

If the color bands are brown, yellow and red, write the code as follows:

Brown — 1   Yellow — 4   Red — 2

This indicates a resistor value of 14 with 2 zeros or 1400 ohms.

If the color bands are red, violet and blue, write the code as follows:

Red — 2   Violet — 7   Blue — 6

This indicates a resistor value of 27 with 6 zeros or 27,000,000 ohms.

The values of these three resistors could be written as follows:

$$25,000 \text{ ohms} = 25 \text{ k ohms}$$
$$1400 \text{ ohms} = 1.4 \text{ k ohms}$$
$$27,000,000 \text{ ohms} = 27 \text{ megohms}$$

The fourth band, if used, will either be gold or silver. This band tells how close the rated value of the resistor is to the actual value. Usually, the resistor is coded to some percentage, (range of values) specified by the manufacturer. This is known as its tolerance.

The reason for having a tolerance on resistors is because of problems in controlling the exact amount of carbon and binder used to make each resistor. When making a "batch," a very small change in amounts called for will result in a group of resistors that are not all the same exact value. Therefore, the manufacturer will give their value within a range or tolerance from one value.

Possible resistor tolerances are:

Gold   Plus or minus 5 percent (± 5%)
Silver   Plus or minus 10 percent (± 10%)
No 4th band   Plus or minus 20 percent (± 20%)

Using our previous examples, assume that the 1400 ohm resistor had a gold fourth band. Its value and tolerance would be:

1400 ohms plus or minus 5 percent (± 5%)
5 percent of 1400 ohms is
1400 ohms x .05 = 70 ohms

Therefore, this resistor would have a value of 1400 ± 70 ohms. This would mean that if you measured the resistor with a meter that showed values in ohms, the value could go as high as 1470 ohms or as low as 1330 ohms and still be within the manufacturer's tolerance. This is possible because:

1400 ohms + 70 ohms = 1470 ohms
1400 ohms − 70 ohms = 1330 ohms

A 25,000 ohm resistor with a silver fourth band would be:

25,000 ohms plus or minus 10 percent (± 10%)
10 percent of 25,000 ohms is
25,000 ohms x .10 = 2500 ohms

Therefore, its range would be:

25,000 ohms ± 2500 ohms or from
27,500 ohms to 22,500 ohms

A 27,000,000 ohm resistor with no fourth band would be:

27,000,000 ohms plus or minus 20 percent (± 20%)
20 percent of 27,000,000 ohms is
27,000,000 ohms x .20 = 5,400,000 ohms

Therefore, its range would be:

27,000,000 ohms ± 5,400,000 ohms or from
32,400,000 ohms to 21,600,000 ohms.

Another way of stating this range would be, "Between 32.4 megohms and 21.6 megohms." This is the manufacturer's tolerance for 27 megohm resistor with no fourth band.

Occasionally, you will find a gold or silver color on the third band of a carbon resistor. When you do, write down the first two numbers based on the color code, then divide by 10 for a gold band or by 100 for a silver band. For example, if you have a resistor with stripes of red, green and gold, you would have:

Red — 2   Green — 5   Gold — Divide by 10

This resistor would have a value of 25 divided by 10, which equals 2.5 ohms.

A resistor with colors of red, green and a silver third band would be:

Red — 2   Green — 5   Silver - Divide by 100

This resistor would have a value of 25 divided by 100 which equals .25 ohms. Resistors of this size will not be found in many circuits.

FIFTH BAND

Earlier, we mentioned the possibility of a resistor having a fifth band. When such a resistor is found, it also will be color coded. The fifth band is used to predict the percentage of failure per thousand hours of use. It is based on tests which the manufacturer has conducted on similar resistors. The coding is:

Brown   —   1.0 percent
Red   —   0.1 percent
Orange   —   0.01 percent
Yellow   —   0.001 percent

For example, if a group of resistors all had a brown fifth band, only one out of each one hundred (1.0 percent) would be likely to fail during one thousand hours of use. Reading a resistor is similar to learning to multiply. The more you do it, the easier it becomes. To sum up the entire resistor code, look at Fig. 4-18.

SHELF LIFE

Resistors tend to heat up when they are used in a circuit. Therefore, when reusing a resistor, make sure it

RESISTOR VALUES

COLOR	1st & 2nd BAND DIGITS	3rd BAND MULTIPLY BY	4th BAND TOLERANCE ± %	5th BAND FAILURE RATE LEVEL %/ THOUSAND HOURS USE
BLACK	0	1	—	
BROWN	1	10	—	1.0
RED	2	100	—	0.1
ORANGE	3	1000	—	0.01
YELLOW	4	10000	—	0.001
GREEN	5	100000	—	
BLUE	6	1000000	—	
VIOLET	7	10000000	—	
GRAY	8	100000000	—	
WHITE	9	1000000000	—	
GOLD	—	0.1	5	
SILVER	—	0.01	10	
NO COLOR	—	—	20	

Fig. 4-18. Table shows resistor color code and tolerances.

is still good. This can be done by using an ohmmeter to measure the resistance. This type of measuring instrument will be described in detail when you get to Chapter 8.

Resistors can be stored for long periods of time without going bad. If they have been on a shelf and never used in a circuit, they can be considered as good as new. Some electrical devices should be used as soon as possible after they have been purchased. Batteries, for example, will age when stored on a shelf.

TOLERANCES

Some popular resistors are made in large quantities to cover the full range for each tolerance. If you want to buy resistors with a 20 percent tolerance, you can cover the range with fewer sizes.

Note in Fig. 4-19 that a 10 ohm resistor with 20 percent tolerance would range from 8 to 12 ohms; a 15 ohm resistor, 12 to 18 ohms; a 22 ohm resistor, 17.6 to 26.4 ohms. Because of the overlap in their ranges, it is not necessary to get resistors with values in between the ranges.

When a 10 percent tolerance is required, the number of resistors needed to fill the range will increase. See

20% TOLERANCE RESISTORS

RESISTOR SIZE IN OHMS	TOLERANCE RANGE
10	8 — 12
15	12 — 18
22	17.6 — 26.4
33	22.4 — 39.6
47	37.6 — 56.4
68	54.4 — 81.6
100	80 — 120
150	120 — 264
330	224 — 396
470	376 — 564
680	544 — 816
1000	800 — 1200

Fig. 4-19. Table specifies resistor sizes in ohms and 20 percent tolerance range.

10% TOLERANCE RESISTORS

SIZE IN OHMS	TOLERANCE
10	9 — 11
12	10.8 — 13.2
15	13.5 — 16.5
18	16.2 — 19.8
22	19.8 — 24.2
27	24.3 — 29.7
33	29.7 — 36.3
39	35.1 — 42.9
47	42.3 — 51.7
56	50.4 — 61.6
68	61.2 — 74.8
82	73.8 — 90.2
100	90 — 110
120	108 — 132

Fig. 4-20. Table covers resistor sizes in ohms and 10 percent tolerance range.

Fig. 4-20. When a 5 percent tolerance is required, Fig. 4-21, the range gets smaller and still more resistors are needed to fill the overlap.

Note also in Fig. 4-19 that all 20 percent tolerance resistors are included in the 10 percent tolerance group. Both of these groups are also included in the 5 percent tolerance group. Bear in mind, too, that manufacturers charge more for resistors they must produce in limited quantities. By keeping all of these tolerances and ranges in mind, it is possible to save the expense of buying all different sizes of resistors.

THERMISTORS

One other type of resistor called a "thermistor" deserves special mention. See Fig. 4-22. Thermistors have come into popular usage in electric circuits of heating and cooling systems. The name, thermistor, was derived from the phrase THERMally sensitive resISTOR.

Most thermistors differ from conventional resistors in how they react to temperature changes. A resistor starts to heat up when electrons begin to flow in the

SIZE IN OHMS	TOLERANCE RANGE
10	9.5 — 10.50
11	10.45 — 11.55
12	11.40 — 12.60
13	12.35 — 13.65
15	14.25 — 15.75
16	15.20 — 16.80
18	11.10 — 18.90
20	19.00 — 21.00
22	20.90 — 23.10
24	22.80 — 25.20
27	25.65 — 28.35
30	28.50 — 31.50
33	31.35 — 34.65
36	34.20 — 37.80
39	37.05 — 40.95
43	40.85 — 45.15
47	44.65 — 49.35
51	48.45 — 53.55
56	53.20 — 58.80
62	58.90 — 65.10
68	64.60 — 71.40
75	71.25 — 78.75
82	77.90 — 86.10
91	86.45 — 95.55
100	95.00 — 105.00
110	104.50 — 115.50

Fig. 4-21. Table shows resistor sizes in ohms and 5 percent tolerance range.

Fig. 4-22. Thermistors are thermally sensitive resistors. Since thermistors can detect slight temperature changes, they often are used as safety switches. (Fenwal Electronics, Inc., Div. of Walter Kidde & Co., Inc.)

circuit. As the temperature rises, resistance increases in an effort to reduce the amount of moving electrons so the resistor can cool off. In contrast, most thermistors will have an opposite reaction. As the temperature rises, resistance decreases. As mentioned, most thermistors react this way; others behave just like resistors.

Actually, there are two different kinds of thermistors, the negative temperature coefficient (NTC) type and the positive temperature coefficient (PTC) type. The NTC type *decreases* in resistance as the temperature rises. The PTC type, like a conventional resistor, *increases* in resistance as the temperature rises.

Since thermistors have this special ability to react to temperature changes, they are used to measure temperatures, protect electric motors from overheating, sense liquid levels, Fig. 4-23, or serve as safety switches in fire or frost alarms.

Fig. 4-23. In another application, thermistors can be used to sense liquid levels.

The frost alarm application is very important to people who are concerned with the danger of frost on fruits and vegetables. A killing frost could destroy hundreds of thousands of dollars worth of food in just one night. Thermistors are used because they are able to detect small differences in temperature.

There are two terminals, Fig. 4-24, on most thermistors, permitting them to be installed into circuits in the same way as resistors. To get a better understanding of the use of resistors and thermistors, read Chapter 5. It is designed to clear up the kinds to be used, their wattage value, the type of circuits where they are found, and the value in ohms for each one.

CAPACITORS

Another key part found in many electric circuits is a "capacitor," Fig. 4-25. The basic job of a capacitor is to

store electrons until they are needed by the circuit in which the capacitor is installed. Although many different symbols for a capacitor are in current use, the symbol shown in Fig. 4-26 is a popular choice.

Fig. 4-24. Thermistors generally have two leads or terminals for use in connecting this type of resistor into the circuit.

CAPACITOR ACTION

To understand how a capacitor works in a circuit, try relating it to a water jug placed in a cooler in an office. First, it must be filled. Next, people take water by the cupful until the jug is empty. Then, it must be refilled.

With the capacitor, the sequence is the same. First, it must be charged with electrons. Next, it must give up the electrons as needed. Then, the capacitor must be recharged so it can give off more electrons when called on to do so.

In Chapter 9, we will go into details of capacitor operation for some circuits. At this point, however, all you need to know is that a capacitor can be charged and discharged.

CAPACITOR CONSTRUCTION

A capacitor consists of two or more plates and an insulator. The plates are made from material that can be charged, such as aluminum foil. In order to hold this

Fig. 4-25. Capacitors store electrons, holding the electrical charge until the circuit needs it.
(Sprague Electric Co.)

charge, an insulator (dielectric) must be placed between the plates, Fig. 4-27. If the plates touch one another, the charge will be lost. These losses, in turn, will appear as heat in the capacitor. The more rapidly we charge and discharge the capacitor, the more heat we will create. If these heat gains are not held to a reasonable level, the capacitor will be destroyed.

Fig. 4-26. This simple sketch depicts the most commonly used symbol for a capacitor.

TYPES OF CAPACITORS

To hold down the heat, capacitors are designed to do specific jobs. Because of this, capacitors are given names like "tantalum electrolytic," shown in Fig. 4-28, "film capacitors" in Fig. 4-29, "ceramic capacitors" in Fig. 4-30, and "mica capacitors" in Fig. 4-31.

Mica capacitors are used in applications where it is necessary to charge and discharge the capacitor billions of times in a second.

Fig. 4-27. The dielectric in a capacitor is the insulator placed between the plates that store the electrical charge.

Fig. 4-28. Tantalum electrolytic capacitors utilize paper soaked with electrolyte as insulator between tantalum plates or sheets.
(Sprague Electric Co.)

63

Fig. 4-29. A film capacitor usually is made up of two conductors separated by a plastic film.

Fig. 4-31. Mica capacitators are made of foil segments with sheets of mica serving as insulators. These capacitors are used in high current transmitting applications. (Sprague Electric Co.)

Fig. 4-30. A ceramic capacitor uses a ceramic material as an insulator between the two conductors. (Centralab Electronics Div. of Globe-Union Inc.)

FLASHER PROJECT

This is a good project you might make for a little brother or sister. Paint a picture of a rabbit or some other animal against a flowered background. Then drill small holes at the center of the flowers for five NE 2 bulbs. Finally, hook up the circuit so the lamps flash. See Fig. 4-32.

When electrons fill (charge) a capacitor, the capacitor discharges, making the lamp flash. Then the capacitor begins to recharge again and the process is repeated. Changing the size of the resistors will change how often the lights flash. Large ohm resistors will increase the time needed to charge the capacitor. Smaller value resistors will decrease the charging time, making the lamps flash more often.

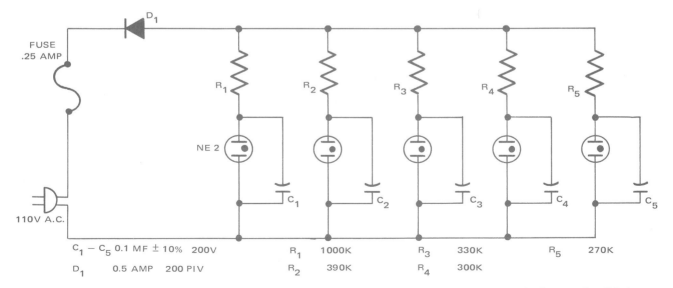

$C_1 - C_5$ 0.1 MF ± 10% 200V	R_1	1000K	R_3	330K	R_5	270K
D_1 0.5 AMP 200 PIV	R_2	390K	R_4	300K		

Fig. 4-32. Front view, back view and the schematic for building the flasher toy described in the text. In the parts list, C is for capacitor, R is for resistor, D is for diode, NE 2 for the bulbs. (Project by Don Winchell)

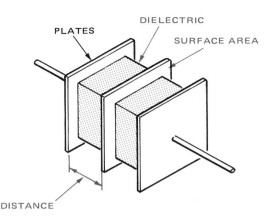

Fig. 4-33. The three factors which determine capacitance are: plate surface area (total of all plates); distance between plates; value of dielectric material (see Fig. 4-35).

FACTORS AFFECTING CAPACITANCE

At this point, you probably are asking yourself "What are the important things I need to know about capacitors?" There are three important factors that determine the capacitance of a capacitor, Fig. 4-33. These are:
1. Surface area of the plates.
2. Distance between the plates.
3. Insulating material used between the plates. This insulating material is usually known as "dielectric."

SURFACE AREA

To get a better understanding of capacitance, look at some examples. First, look at the surface area of the plates, while keeping the distance between the plates

Fig. 4-34. Plate area determines the difference in capacitance of these two aluminum electrolytic capacitors. Note that one at left is marked 100000 mfd; right 56000 mfd.

and dielectric equal for both. The capacitor with the most plate surface area will have the greatest capacitance, Fig. 4-34. This is because the capacitor would have more space to store an electrical charge. *Increase the surface area and you will increase the capacitance.* Remember though, this is only true if everything else is kept equal and the plates are perfectly parallel to each other.

DISTANCE BETWEEN PLATES

The second thing which affects our capacitance is the distance between the plates. Again, we will keep the dielectric and surface areas constant. If the two charged plates are moved apart (double the space between them), the strength of the capacitor's charge will be lowered. In effect, the strength is inversely proportional to the distance between them.

Suppose, for example, the distance between the plates is increased by one thousandth of an inch (.001 in.). Will the capacitance increase or decrease? Since the strength is inversely proportional, capacitance will get weaker. *If the distance between the plates is reduced, capacitance will increase.*

DIELECTRIC

The third affect on capacitance concerns the type of dielectric (insulating material) used in the capacitor. Remember from Chapter 3 that an insulator resists the flow of electrons. See Fig. 4-35 for dielectrics used in capacitors. Approximate values are given.

DIELECTRIC CONSTANTS OF CAPACITOR MATERIALS

MATERIAL	DIELECTRIC CONSTANT
AIR	1.0
ALUMINUM OXIDE	10.0
BEESWAX	3.0
CAMBRIC (VARNISHED)	4.0
CELLULOID	4.0
GLASS (PYREX)	4.2
GLASS (WINDOW)	7.6
MICA (CLEAR INDIA)	7.5
MYLAR	3.0
PAPER (KRAFT)	4.0
PORCELAIN	6.2
QUARTZ	5.0
TANTALUM OXIDE	11.0
VACUUM	1.0

Fig. 4-35. Dielectric materials are listed at left; dielectric constants for figuring capacitance are given at right.

FORMULA

To better understand the three major factors that affect capacitance, examine the following formula:

$$C = 0.2235 \frac{KA}{d} (N\text{-}1)$$

Where

C is the capacitance in picofarads (pF).
K is the dielectric constant.
A is the area of one plate in square inches.
d is the distance between the plates in inches.
N is the number of plates.

Example:

What is the capacitance of four 1 in. square plates separated by quartz which is 0.001 in. thick?

$$C = 0.2235 \frac{KA}{d} (N\text{-}1)$$

$$C = 0.2235 \frac{5 \times 1 \text{ sq. in.}}{0.001 \text{ in}} (4\text{-}1)$$

$$C = 0.2235 \frac{5}{.001} (3)$$

$$C = 0.2235 \times 5000 \ (3)$$

$$C = 3352.5 \text{ pF}$$

If we double the distance between the plates by increasing the thickness of the quartz to 0.002 in. thick, we have:

$$C = 0.2235 \frac{KA}{d} (N\text{-}1)$$

$$C = 0.2235 \frac{5 \times 1 \text{ sq. in.}}{.002} (4\text{-}1)$$

$$C = 0.2235 \frac{5}{.002} (3)$$

$$C = 0.2235 \times 2500 \ (3)$$

$$C = 1676.25 \text{ pF}$$

As you can see, doubling the distance cut the capacitance to one-half of the previous example.

TERMS

Note that the capacitance in the example is given in picofarads. The original discoverer of the capacitor was Pieter van Musschenbrock, but the basic unit of capacitance was named "farad" after Michael Faraday.

A capacitor has a capacitance of one farad when, with one volt applied to its plates, it stores one coulomb of charge on each of its plates. A coulomb is equal to 6.24×10^{18} electrons. You may be familiar with the term "volt," having seen it marked on batteries. We will cover what a volt is and how it works with other units in the next chapter.

The farad is a very large unit and is not used much. Most capacitors are rated picofarads and microfarads. A microfarad is one-millionth of a farad, while a picofarad is one-millionth of a microfarad. The chart which follows will give you an idea of how this works.

1 farad (F)	= 1,000,000 microfarads (μF)
1 microfarad (μF)	= 1,000,000 picofarads (pF)
1 picofarad (pF)	= .000001 microfarad (μF)
1 microfarad (μF)	= .000001 farad (F)
1 picofarad (pF)	= .000 000 000 001 farad (F)

It is common to use the term microfarads down to about 0.0001 μF. The term picofarads is used up to about 1000 pF (.001 μF). Even though a crossover point exists, the idea is to try to use the smallest amount of numbers.

DISCHARGING CAPACITORS

At this point, you probably are saying to yourself that these are pretty small numbers. As small as they may seem, they carry enough electrical charge to kill.

I.C. SAYS:

"CAUTION: Before you pick up any capacitor, make sure it has been discharged."

Use care when working with electrical circuits that include capacitors. Always assume that any capacitor is "charged." Therefore, use some special means of discharging it before attempting to handle it. Fig. 4-38 shows a discharging device that is safe and easy to use, simply by touching a probe to each capacitor terminal.

Some people make the mistake of using a screwdriver or a short section of insulated wire. Two things can result. First, you could ruin the capacitor by discharging it this way. Second, if the capacitor is very large, it is possible to cause an arc. In some cases, such as the capacitors in an electronic flash for a camera, you could even melt the end of the screwdriver.

CAPACITOR DISCHARGER PROJECT

Capacitor discharging devices can be useful when working on radios, television sets and other electrical circuits involving capacitors. However, the right kind of equipment is needed to do the job properly. Fig. 4-36

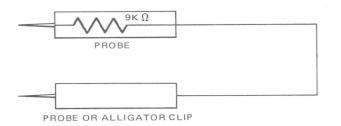

PROBE

PROBE OR ALLIGATOR CLIP

Fig. 4-36. Schematic for a capacitor discharger shows a two probe setup. An alligator clip can be substituted for plain probe.

gives details on how to build a capacitor discharger. Fig. 4-37 reveals a resistor built into the probe and how the boot fits over the alligator clip.

Parts needed to build this capacitor discharger include: two probes or one probe and an alligator clip; one 9K 1 watt resistor (or larger, depending on the capacitor to be discharged); three feet of 14 AWG wire.

Building procedures are as follows:

1. Obtain parts and check resistor ratings.
2. Drill out the inside of one probe to accomodate the resistor or resistors.

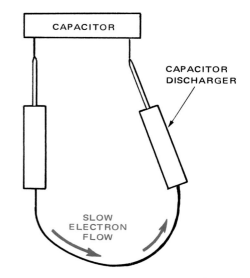

Fig. 4-38. The resistor built into one probe of the capacitor discharger slows the flow of electrons to avoid a damaging sudden discharge of the capacitor.

3. Strip the wire on both ends and make good mechanical joints. Connect the wire to one end of the resistor and connect the other end of the resistor to the metal part of the probe. Connect the other end of the wire to the second probe or alligator clip, if used.
4. Screw the handles on the metal part of the probes. To use the capacitor discharger, attach the alligator clip (or probe) to one terminal of the capacitor and

A

B

Fig. 4-37. Two probe and alligator clip setups are shown for use with capacitor discharger. Note insulating boot on the lower clip.

touch a probe to the other terminal for at least five seconds. See Fig. 4-38. This will give the capacitor time to discharge slowly.

The principle of operation of the discharger is simple. The wire acts as a path for the electrons to flow from one set of capacitor plates to the second set of plates. The resistor slows up the discharging process and stops arcing by avoiding a sudden buildup of heat.

ELECTROLYTIC CAPACITORS

Electrolytic capacitors deserve special attention. They are made in a different way, Fig. 4-39, and provide more capacitance for their size than any other type of capacitors.

Fig. 4-39. In manufacturing an electrolytic capacitor, one aluminized sheet is coated with a layer of oxide. As a result, the capacitor becomes "polarized" (has a positive side and a negative side).

Fig. 4-40. In use, electrolytic capacitors must be installed positive to positive and negative to negative. Ends of capacitors are marked with a + and —. (Fisher Radio)

Instead of having its plates separated by a dielectric, the electrolytic capacitor consists of two aluminum sheets separated by a layer of paper soaked with a liquid chemical called "electrolyte." All three sheets are rolled together, sealed in a container and dc voltage is applied between the two aluminized sheets.

The charge of electricity causes a thin oxide layer to be formed on one of the aluminized sheets. As a result, the capacitor is said to be "polarized." This means that one side of the capacitor is positive; the other side is negative. See Fig. 4-40. The oxide acts as the dielectric. It has a high resistance to the flow of electrons in one direction and very low resistance in the opposite direction.

I.C. SAYS:

"Electrolytic capacitors are marked with a positive (+) end and a negative (—) end. If they are not connected into circuits positive to positive and negative to negative, the oxide film will be ruined. In some cases, the capacitor may explode."

ELECTROLYTICS DEFORM

An electrolytic capacitor will slowly deform (decrease in capacitance) if not used for awhile. If not used, then given a sudden surge of electrons, it may be ruined. This surge can be caused by just installing the electrolytic capacitor in a circuit. When electrolytics are purchased from a store or taken off a shelf after being stored for a long time, they must be charged slowly.

Many capacitors have voltage ratings marked on their outside cover. See Fig. 4-41. The electrolytic capacitor shows in marked WVDC, which stands for "Working

Fig. 4-41. Many capacitors are labeled with a voltage rating in addition to capacitance. This electrolytic capacitor is marked 150 volts. (Sprague Electric Co.)

Voltage Direct Current." To reform an electrolytic, hook up a circuit shown in Fig. 4-42. It is important that the voltage output of the power source is *lower* than the voltage marked on the outside of the capacitor.

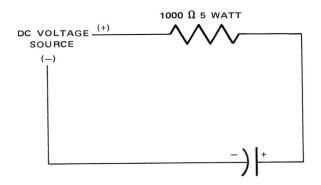

Fig. 4-42. This schematic shows an electrolytic capacitor being reformed (charged) to build up its capacitance. Note that it is installed positive to positive and negative to negative.

HOLDING A CHARGE

Remember that capacitors can hold a charge for many hours and, in some cases, for several days. Before you handle any capacitor, make sure it is discharged.

SUBSTITUTING CAPACITORS

When repairing a circuit or building a new one, install capacitors of the specified voltage rating. If you cannot find a capacitor of the correct voltage rating, substitute one that has a higher voltage rating. If you install one with a lower rating, you are asking for trouble.

SOLDERING CAPACITORS

There are a couple of precautions you should take if you have to replace a capacitor in a circuit.
1. Make sure the new capacitor is soldered in place the same way as the old one when it was installed. If you get too close or too far away from the chassis (the metal box on which electronic components are mounted and wired), it may shift the capacitance. For example, this could result in a hum from a repaired radio.
2. Be sure the new leads are the same length as the old ones. This could affect the resonant frequency (described in Chapter 14).
3. Use a heat sink between the capacitor and the solder

joint, as explained in Chapter 3. Some capacitors have a dielectric that could be melted by the heat from a soldering iron.

SUMMARY

In Chapter 4, you have learned the difference between a fixed and variable resistor. You also learned how to use the color code to determine the value and tolerance of a resistor. Two types of thermistors are available. NTC thermistors decrease in resistance as its temperature rises. PTC thermistors, similar to resistors, increase in resistance as their temperature rises.

Capacitors are devices that are used to hold an electrical charge. They vary in size from large ratings in farads to smaller values in the microfarad or picofarad range. There are three factors that determine capacitance. They are the insulating material, surface area, and the distance between the plates. Since a capacitor can hold a charge for long periods of time, make sure it is discharged before handling.

KEY WORDS AND TERMS

Binder	Picofarad
Capacitor	Polarized
Dielectric	Positive temperature
Electrolyte	coefficient (PTC)
Electrolytic capacitor	Potentiometer
Farad (F)	Resistor
Fixed resistor	Rheostat
Microfarad (μF)	Thermistor
Negative temperature	Trimmer resistor
coefficient (NTC)	Variable resistor
Ohm (Ω)	Working Voltage Direct
	Current (WDVC)

TEST YOUR KNOWLEDGE

Do not write in this book. Write your answers on a separate sheet of paper.
1. What is the basic unit of measure for capacitance?
2. Change .0001 microfarads into picofarads.
3. List two different types of capacitors.
4. You never touch a capacitor without _____.
5. Because an _____ capacitor is made in a special way, you must watch its polarity when you put it into a circuit.
6. How long can a capacitor store (hold) its charge?
7. List the following readings from highest to lowest capacitance.

    3 farads   700 picofarads
    600 microfarads   .03 farads
8. Name two things that affect the amount of capacitance.

9. A potentiometer is another name for a _____.
   a. variable capacitor
   b. polarized capacitor
   c. fixed resistor
   d. variable resistor
10. Copy these colors on a separate paper and place the number alongside each color that corresponds to the color code found in the resistor.

   _____ White   _____ Blue
   _____ Orange   _____ Black
   _____ Gray   _____ Green
   _____ Red   _____ Violet
   _____ Yellow   _____ Brown

ACTIVITIES

1. How do you know which tolerance resistor to use in a circuit?
2. Find out how a company actually makes carbon resistors.
3. Visit a store that sells electrical components and see how many different sizes of resistors they sell. Make a list of the sizes.
4. Make a list of the places in your car or home that use variable resistors.
5. Make up some memory device to help you remember the first letters in the resistor color code.
6. Why is it important to know the failure rate of resistors? Why do dome resistors lack a fifth band to show failure rate?
7. Make your own capacitor using knowledge that you have gained about things used in their construction.
8. See if you can find a capacitor with a rating over one farad. Where are these types of capacitors used?
9. What is the smallest capacitor rating you can find in a book? What is the smallest size capacitor you can find in some circuit?
10. What kind of capacitor holds its charge for the longest period of time? Where is it used?
11. Should capacitors and resistors be soldered into circuits the same way? Should you pay attention to which direction each lead is hooked into a circuit?
12. Find an easy way to store resistors and capacitors when you are laying them out for soldering into a circuit.

To identify a color-coded resistor, turn the varicolored wheels at the top until the color of the wheels matches the color of the bands on the resistor. Then, read the numbers in the windows.

5 Ohm's Law

LEARNING OBJECTIVES

After studying this chapter, you will be able to:

- Calculate the value of voltage, current, and resistance using Ohm's Law.
- Determine the amount and cost of the electricity used in your home by reading your kilowatt hour meter.
- Compute your body resistance by measuring it with an ohmmeter.
- Apply the power formula to determine wattage.
- Explain the difference between a milliamp and microamp.

George Simon Ohm (1787-1854), a German scientist, discovered how amps, resistance, power, and watts are tied together mathematically. Ohm found a simple method for figuring a third value when only two values are known. This method is Ohm's Law.

THREE VARIABLES OF OHM'S LAW

If you take any three numbers, such as 2, 3, and 6, you can arrange them so that if you omit one and replace it with a variable, you can find its value. For example, if you wrote $2 \times 3 = $ A, all you would have to do is multiply to find that A = 6. If you had the equation $2 \times A = 6$, you would rearrange the equation as such: $6 \div 2 = A$. After performing the division, you would get A = 3. Ohm's Law is just as easy to use.

When using Ohm's Law, the variables are *voltage*, *current*, and *resistance*.

Just as you were able to determine that $2 \times 3 = 6$, you can say that voltage in a circuit is equal to current multiplied by resistance. The formula would be:

Voltage = Current × Resistance.

Common practice is to substitute letters for words in a formula. The letter E is used to represent voltage, the letter I is used to represent current, and the letter R is used to represent resistance. The formula would read:

$$E = I \times R.$$

However, it still means that voltage is equal to current times resistance.

ELECTROMOTIVE FORCE

The letter E in the formula stands for voltage. It refers to the pressure that is required to force the electrons through the circuit. Therefore, voltage is often called *electromotive force*. To get a better understanding of this, see Fig. 5-1. The flow of electrons in an electrical circuit is compared with the flow of water from a squirt gun. If no pressure is exerted on the gun, no water will flow. The more pressure exerted on the gun, the greater the amount of water that will flow and the farther it will travel. This same principle applies to the type of pressure that must exist in an electrical circuit.

The pressure or voltage in electrical circuits can come from many different sources. See Figs. 5-2 and

NO WATER

NO PRESSURE

LIGHT FLOW OF WATER

LIGHT PRESSURE

HEAVY FLOW OF WATER

HIGH PRESSURE

Fig. 5-1. Just as increased pressure on a squirt gun forces more water to squirt farther, increased electrical pressure (voltage) forces more electrons to flow.

Fig. 5-2. A "cell" is one possible source of electrical pressure in a low voltage circuit.

5-3. At this point, we are only discussing direct current (dc) sources, such as batteries. There is another whole group of voltage sources that give alternating current (ac). These sources are described in Chapter 10.

Fig. 5-3. A "battery" is the source of electrical pressure in an automobile electrical system.

CURRENT

The letter I in the formula is for "Intensity" of current flow. Earlier, we discussed the millions of electrons that pass a given point in the circuit in one second when current is flowing. Numbers this large are hard to work with, so the current flow rate is shortened to read in amperes (amps). *One amp is equal to 6.24 x 10^{18} electrons flowing past a given point in one second.* This given value for one amp is a "standard" issued by the National Bureau of Standards.

The term "ampere" was named in honor of Andre Marie Ampere (1775-1836). As you continue reading, you will find that many laws and even some circuits have names which honor the people who first discovered them.

RESISTANCE

The letter R stands for resistance to, or the opposition to, the flow of electrons. This resistance is measured in ohms. Earlier, we saw from our table of wire sizes that the resistance went up as the length of wire increased. We also saw that as the wire got larger in diameter, we could get a longer piece of wire and still have the same resistance.

All three elements, E, I and R, can be measured with meters similar to the one shown in Fig. 5-4. These are:

Voltage is measured with a voltmeter.

Current is measured with an ammeter.

Resistance is measured with an ohmmeter.

Fig. 5-4. A multimeter is used to measure voltage, amperage and ohms. (AEMC Instruments)

Many times, meters can be used to help find some missing values. It is also possible to find out the value of E, I or R by using Ohm's Law.

Fig. 5-5. As a visual aid to learning Ohm's Law, try covering the letter for the unknown value. For example, cover I and the formula becomes $I = \dfrac{E}{R}$.

By shifting letters around, it is possible to get different forms of Ohm's Law. A study of Fig. 5-5 should help you follow these changes. Depending on which values you know, you can select a formula for finding the unknown value. The three basic formulas created by Ohm's Law are:

$$E = I \times R \qquad I = \frac{E}{R} \qquad R = \frac{E}{I}$$

CIRCUIT VOLTAGE

The simple circuit shown in Fig. 5-6 offers a problem that you can solve by applying Ohm's Law. In this circuit, the symbol for a battery is used to show the source of voltage. The wires are shown by lines. The symbol for resistance is the load, or bulb. The circular symbol with a large A indicates a test ammeter. The voltage, in this case, is unknown.

Looking at known values, the amount of current flowing in the circuit is 3 amps. The resistance is 2 ohms. To determine the voltage needed to light the bulb, use Ohm's Law as follows:

$E = I \times R$ Most people do not use the x to show multiplication. Instead, they would simply write out the formula as:

$E = I R$ Then, by substituting known values for the letters

$E = 3 \text{ amps} \times 2 \text{ ohms}$

$E = 6 \text{ volts}$

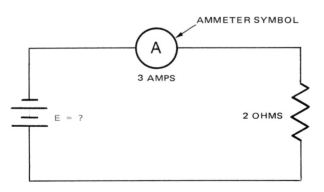

Fig. 5-6. This simple electrical circuit poses a problem that can be solved by applying Ohm's Law, $E = I \times R$.

Therefore, put a 6 volt battery in the circuit. If you mistakenly use a 3 volt battery, Fig. 5-7, the bulb will not light properly. A 3 volt battery does not produce enough pressure (voltage) to push the right number of electrons through the resistance of the bulb.

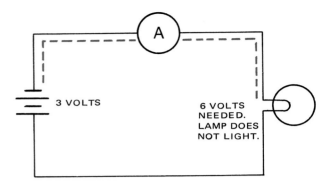

Fig. 5-7. The voltage is too low in this circuit to force electrons through the resistance of the lamp.

If you had selected a 12 volt battery, Fig. 5-8, it would produce *too* much pressure. Battery voltage would push so many electrons through the bulb that the filament would get hot and burn out. Replacing the bulb would not solve the problem. No matter how many new 6 volt bulbs you put in, each new one would burn out. You must reduce the voltage of the battery or add resistance to the circuit to reduce the current flow.

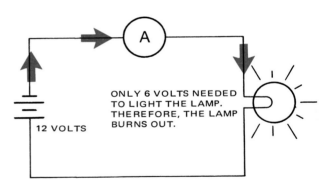

Fig. 5-8. If the voltage is too high for the low resistance of the lamp, you must reduce the voltage or add a resistor to the circuit.

VOLTMETER PROJECT

You can make a voltmeter, Fig. 5-9, for use in checking whether an electrical circuit is 110 volts or 220 volts. Obtain the following materials and assemble them according to the construction procedure given:

No.	Item
1	R_1 — 220K resistor.
1	R_2 — 470K resistor.
1	R_3 — 180K resistor.
2	NE 2 neon bulbs.
2	Probes.
2 oz.	Casting plastic.

Fig. 5-9. You can test circuit voltage with this voltmeter. If one lamp lights, the circuit is 110 volts. If both lamps light, the circuit is 220 volts. (Project by Scott Murwin)

CONSTRUCTION PROCEDURE

Build the project by following the schematic shown in Fig. 5-10. After the circuit has been assembled, it is encased in plastic.

1. Wire the circuit shown in Fig. 5-10.
2. Connect 12 to 15 in. of wire to the circuit.
3. Make a mold about 1/2 in. larger than the size of your finished circuit. Make the mold from a manila folder and tape the edges. Use paste wax to coat the inside of the mold.
4. Punch two small openings in the mold for the lead wires.
5. Pass the lead wires through the holes. Tape around the holes to hold the circuit centered in the mold and to prevent leakage.
6. Mix the casting plastic and pour it over the circuit.
7. After the plastic cures, remove it from the mold, file, sand, and buff it.
8. Attach insulated probes to the lead wires.

To use the voltmeter, touch the two probes to the circuit being tested. If one light comes on, there is 110 volts. If both lights come on, there is 220 volts.

CIRCUIT AMPERAGE

How much current could flow through a 36 ohm resistor in a car radio powered by a 12 volt battery? Using one formula, you would first list what is known:

$$I = \frac{E}{R}$$

$$I = \frac{12 \text{ volts}}{36 \text{ ohms}}$$

$$I = \frac{1}{3} \text{ amp or .33 amp}$$

The completed formula tells you that about 1/3 of an amp of current would flow through the resistor.

Study Fig. 5-11. What size resistor would you pick to keep the current to 3 amps or less? Listing the things you know, you would have:

$$R = \frac{E}{I}$$

$$R = \frac{12 \text{ volts}}{3 \text{ amps}}$$

$$R = 4 \text{ ohms}$$

This means that a resistor of at least 4 ohms should be used.

If you picked a 6 ohm resistor, the current would be kept below 3 amps:

$$I = \frac{E}{R}$$

$$I = \frac{12 \text{ volts}}{6 \text{ ohms}}$$

$$I = 2 \text{ amps}$$

This is lower than the high limit you set, but it is acceptable.

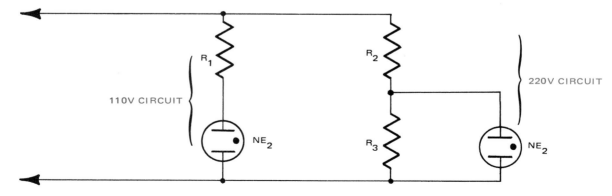

Fig. 5-10. This schematic for the voltmeter gives the wiring arrangement and basic connections. Probes are shown at the left.

If you picked a resistor of 2 ohms, you would be in trouble:

$$I = \frac{E}{R}$$

$$I = \frac{12 \text{ volts}}{2 \text{ ohms}}$$

$$I = 6 \text{ amps}$$

This setup would result in a blown fuse (if circuit is fused) or an overheated resistor (if circuit is not fused). These examples show the importance of choosing the right resistor in terms of its resistance value.

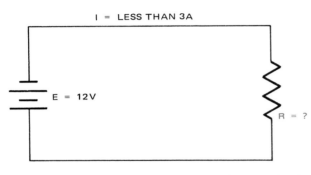

Fig. 5-11. A circuit having an unknown resistance value is shown. Ohm's formula $R = \frac{E}{I}$ will help supply the answer.

WATTAGE

To find the right resistor for a given circuit, you have to pick a resistor of the correct wattage. Earlier, we found that wattage of a resistor tells how much heat it will dissipate. As long as the resistor can transfer heat into the air around it, the resistor will not overheat; if it cannot, the resistor will be ruined.

A formula for "power" has been worked out which uses many of the same terms as Ohm's Law. By putting down known values, the formula will permit you to figure out the correct wattage resistor to use. The formula is:

$$P = E I$$

The unit of electrical power is the watt, named after James Watt (1736-1819). Here, again, the term is named after an important person in the early history of electricity.

A watt is the amount of work done in one second by one volt moving a charge of one coulomb. A coulomb equals 6.24×10^{18} electrons per second. This means we can replace the coulomb with amperes and get the formula $P = E I$. Per second, of course, means "in one second."

Fig. 5-12. What amount of power (wattage) is used in this circuit? Power formula $P = IE$ will help solve this problem.

KILOWATT HOURS

Fig. 5-12 shows a simple circuit. To find the number of watts being used, work out the formula: $P = E I$. You know that $3 \times 2 = 6$ and that $2 \times 3 = 6$. It does not

APPROXIMATE COST OF OPERATION OF APPLIANCES

APPLIANCE	AVERAGE WATTAGE	EST. COST PER MO. AT $0.08 PER KWH
TOOTH BRUSH	1.1	.006
CLOCK	2	.12
HAIR DRYER	381	.1
SEWING MACHINE	75	.08
SHAVER	15	.08
TOASTER	1146	.26
VACUUM CLEANER	630	.30
RADIO	71	.58
WASHING MACHINE	512	.68
COFFEE MAKER	894	.70
TELEVISION, B & W	45	.66
TELEVISION, COLOR	145	2.12
DISHWASHER	1201	2.42
REFRIGERATOR/ FREEZER MANUAL DEFROST	—	4.66
CLOTHES DRYER	4856	6.61
RANGE W/OVEN	12,200	7.84
REFRIGERATOR/ FREEZER AUTO. DEFROST	—	11.96
WATER HEATER	4474	29.82
CENTRAL A/C	1670/TON	70.00

Fig. 5-13. Wattages and cost of operation are given for many popular appliances. Note that higher cost is in direct proportion to higher wattages. (Edison Electric Institute)

JULY 1 READING	71190
JUNE 1 READING	59244
	11946 KILOWATT HOURS

Fig. 5-14. Read kilowatt hour meters from right to left. In this diagram, black hands indicate June reading; green hands point to July reading. The difference between these readings is the number of kilowatt hours of electricity used.

matter which number comes first in multiplying numbers. Therefore, an easy way to remember the formula for power is to think of PIE (P = IE). In our problem, the circuit has an electromotive force (voltage) of 120 volts and a current of 3 amps. Therefore, substituting values for letters, we would have:

P = I E
P = 3 amps x 120 volts
P = 360 watts

You might ask if 360 watts is a lot of power or a small amount. For a helpful comparison of typical wattage ratings, consider some of the appliances you have around your home. Also, see Fig. 5-13. The cost of operation shown in this table is based on the number of kilowatt hours (KWH) used. The power company charges about eight cents for one kilowatt hour. A kilowatt hour is equivalent to one thousand watts of electricity being used in one hour.

To keep a record of how much electrical power you use every month, the power company installs a meter at your home, Fig. 5-14 shows how they keep a record of your power use by means of this meter. By recording meter readings at regular intervals, the company is able to bill you for the exact amount of electricity used.

The power formula (P = E I) is just as flexible as the basic formula (E = I R) established by Ohm's Law. By shifting letters around, as in Fig. 5-15, you can come up with different forms of the power formula for use in finding unknown values in electrical circuits.

MILLI AND MICRO AMPS

In previous examples of electrical circuits, the word "amps" was established as the basic unit for the amount of current flowing through a load. The term "amps" is used when referring to circuits carrying relatively large

VARIATIONS IN OHM'S LAW AND THE POWER FORMULA

E	I	R	P
I R	$\dfrac{E}{R}$	$\dfrac{E}{I}$	I E
$\dfrac{P}{I}$	$\dfrac{P}{E}$	$\dfrac{P}{I^2}$	$I^2 R$
$\sqrt{PR}$	$\sqrt{\dfrac{P}{R}}$	$\dfrac{E^2}{P}$	$\dfrac{E^2}{R}$

Fig. 5-15. All of Ohm's formulas and all power formulas are arranged in chart form. Read down from headings, E, I, R and P to get formula desired.

amounts of current, such as power plants, Fig. 5-16, high tension (voltage) lines, house wiring and in many household appliances.

In many circuits, however, you will find that current flow is less than one amp. In fact, the current may be so low that you will have numbers such as .001 amp. Rather than say "one thousandth or one millionth of an amp," the names "milli" and "micro" are used.

A milliamp (mA) is .001 or one thousandth of an amp. A microamp is .000001 or one millionth of an amp. Very often, you will find the word "micro" replaced with what looks like a smaller letter u (μ), the symbol mu. You saw this symbol in the last chapter when we worked with capacitors.

Consider the circuit illustrated in Fig. 5-17. The voltage is 120 volts and the resistance is 120,000 ohms. What is the current? Laying out the formula, you would have:

$$I = \dfrac{E}{R} \qquad I = \dfrac{120 \text{ volts}}{120,000 \text{ ohms}} \qquad I = .001 \text{ amp}$$

Fig. 5-16. This highly instrumented control room for a large power plant serves as the brain center for the generation of electricity. (Consumers Power Co.)

The current in this case would be equal to 1 milliamp or 1 mA.

If the resistance in the previous example had been 120 Meg ohms, we would have:

$$I = \frac{120 \text{ volts}}{120,000,000 \text{ ohms}}$$

$$I = .000001 \text{ amp}$$

The current in this case would be equal to 1 microamp or 1 μA.

As mentioned, the term "milli" and "micro" are used when referring to circuits carrying less than one amp of current. These terms also find use with reference to low voltage circuits in radios, television sets and many other communications systems, Fig. 5-18. In this case, the proper terms are "millivolts" and "microvolts."

Fig. 5-17. This student is wiring an electrical circuit from a schematic. See the accompanying text for a problem in how to find an unknown current value by applying Ohm's Law.

Fig. 5-18. These students are testing a completed circuit. (Hickok Teaching Systems, Inc.)

78

BODY RESISTANCE

Have you ever considered what happens to the human body when it is involved with electricity? Fig. 5-19 shows an electrician doing a typical job of circuit testing. If she were to make a mistake, would she be killed (electrocuted)? The quick reply is "Maybe."

To be able to answer this question properly, several things must be known. First, every person's body is a

Fig. 5-19. Technician is performing a test on some telephone wiring she has just finished installing. (Southern Bell)

giant resistor. To measure your body resistance from hand to hand, hold the ohmmeter probes as shown in Fig. 5-20, and compare the reading to others. You will find that everyone has a different amount of body resistance, and most will fall in a range from 10K to 150K ohms. The reason you differ is because of different weights, heights, size of bones and many other body chemistry factors. In other words, no two people are exactly alike.

If you measure your body resistance on a hot summer day, then measure it again on a cool day, you will get different readings. This is caused by the fact that when you perspire, your body resistance changes. You can prove this by wetting your fingers and measuring your body resistance again. Note that this reading is lower.

Fig. 5-20. You can measure body resistance by means of an ohmmeter. Note that when you increase pressure on the probes, the resistance reading drops.

PRESSURE VS RESISTANCE

Measure your body resistance by holding each probe loosely between your thumb and forefinger. Take a second reading while squeezing down as hard as you can. Is there any difference in the two readings? The reason for the different results is because "squeezing" places a larger amount of surface area of skin in contact with the probes. The larger the area in contact, the less the resistance.

What does all this have to do with the danger of being shocked or even killed while working with electricity? These examples show that every person has a different body resistance. No two people will be affected the same way by coming into contact with electricity. One person might be shocked while another may receive serious injury from the same source. The result also will depend on weather conditions and whether or not the victim was perspiring. (Remember, when you perspire, your body resistance goes down.)

CAUTION: Avoid touching anything electrical in a damp basement or an area with water on the floor. See Fig. 5-21. At home, never touch anything electrical soon after coming out of a tub or shower.

Professional electrical technicians are taught the safe way to work on equipment when they must be below ground or in tunnels. See Fig. 5-22.

DON'T TOUCH UNGROUNDED APPLI-
ANCES WHILE STANDING IN WATER.

Fig. 5-21. Standing or walking in water on the floor will reduce body resistance, making the careless person more susceptible to severe electrical shock. (Consumers Power Co.)

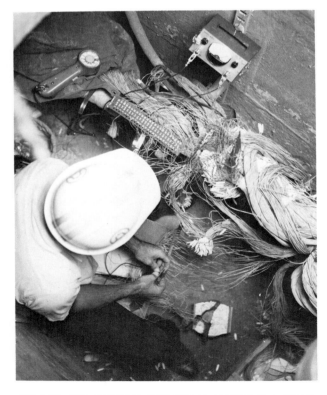

Fig. 5-22. This telephone technician is working in a tunnel, safely testing the wiring with an ohmmeter. (Southern Bell)

CURRENT PATH

Fig. 5-23 shows the path of electricity going through the heart. When this happens the heart seizes and stops beating. Some people think they can release their grip on a wire when they discover that it is carrying current. Electricity travels at the speed of light (186,000 miles

HOT ELECTRICAL WIRE

Fig. 5-23. Picking up a hot electrical wire can cause electrocution because of the direct path of current through the heart.

per second), and no human can react that fast. When you touch a current carrying wire, it is too late to change your mind.

When you touch a "hot" wire, the muscles in your hand and arm contract as shown in Fig. 5-24. This

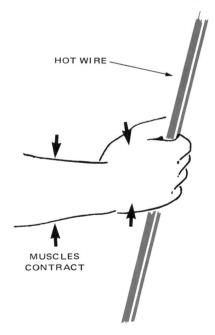

HOT WIRE

MUSCLES
CONTRACT

Fig. 5-24. Holding a hot electrical wire will cause muscles to contract, making it impossible to let go of the wire.

Fig. 5-25. Body resistance is reduced when the grip tightens on a hot wire. When this happens, current goes up and severe electrical shock may result.

means that instead of letting go of the wire, you are forced to grip it even harder. When this happens, the surface area in contact increases and your body resistance goes down. If the current has a path through your heart, you run the risk of serious injury. If there is no path through the heart, your chances of survival are greatly increased. Therefore, keep one hand behind your back or in your pocket (if possible) when working on a current-carrying wire.

Obviously, your best chance of survival would be to turn off the current by removing a fuse or opening a circuit breaker. This eliminates the source of power when working on a circuit.

If the conditions are right, it takes less than one amp to kill you!!

Body resistance has an important effect on your chances of survival when working with electricity. This is easy to understand when you know Ohm's Law.

Imagine that you are working on a 120 volt circuit in your home. Since E = IR, you know that I x R must be equal to 120 volts. Therefore:

$$I = \frac{E}{R}$$

$$I = \frac{120 \text{ volts}}{\text{body resistance}}$$

Body resistance is estimated at 50,000 ohms

$$I = \frac{120 \text{ volts}}{50,000 \text{ ohms}}$$

$$I = .0024 \text{ amp or } 2.4 \text{ mA}$$

As the body resistance falls, the current goes up. See Fig. 5-25.

SOLDERING IRON/ETCHING TOOL PROJECT

Here is a device you can build and use for soldering or etching metal, Fig. 5-26. The carbon tip is used for soldering or it can be replaced with a copper tip for etching (writing on) metal.

Obtain the following materials and assemble them according to construction procedures given in Fig. 5-27.

No.	Item
3	Battery clips 4 in. or 50 amps, lead-plated steel.
1	Handle, 1 1/4 in. dia., 5 in. long wood dowel.
1	15 ft. lamp cord, No. 18 twin lead copper wire.
1	15 ft. ground wire, No. 10 insulated copper wire.
3	Machine screws, 1/2 in. No. 8-32 RH, brass.
1	Tip extender, 3/4 in. dia., 1 1/2 in. long, brass or thinwall conduit.
1	Bushing, 1/2 in. dia., 3/4 in. long, brass or copper.
1	Tip, 3/8 in. dia., 1 1/2 in. long, carbon.
1	Tip, 3/8 in. dia., 1 1/2 in. copper.

Fig. 5-26. A shop-built soldering iron/etching tool is easy to build and fun to use. (Project by Ken Koenig)

This project is designed to be used with a car battery, Fig. 5-28. To solder with this tool, hold the tip a short distance from the metal workpiece once the arc is started. *It will draw a large amount of current. Therefore, do not solder for long periods of time unless the battery is recharged.* It cannot be used on painted metal. Also avoid metal coated with grease or oil.

When using this tool for soldering, bring the carbon tip into contact with the bare metal. This completes the circuit and creates an arc. The arc is very bright and

Fig. 5-27. Construction details are shown for the soldering iron/etching tool pictured in Fig. 5-26.

could harm your eyes. Therefore, wear some type of welding goggles.

If you use the carbon tip for soldering the car body, you do not have to connect the second lead. This is because the car is grounded to the other battery terminal. When you use the tool in other ways, you must connect a heavy wire from the metal being soldered back to the battery. See Fig. 5-28.

If you use a copper tip instead of a carbon tip, the copper will etch the metal. Use the tool this way to mark your property with your name and social security number. Be sure that the wire is large enough to handle the current.

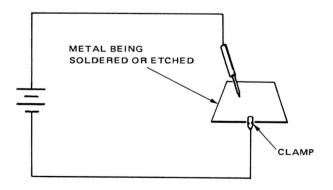

Fig. 5-28. This schematic shows the electrical hookup for the soldering iron/etching tool. If the soldering iron is connected to the car's battery and work is done on that car, the second electrical lead is unnecessary.

SUMMARY

You found that the Electromotive Force in a circuit is its voltage. It was found by first measuring the current (labeled I) and the resistance (labeled R). Next, multiplying the current times the resistance will yield the voltage ($E = I \times R$). If the voltage in a circuit remains fixed, as the current increases, the resistance will decrease. You can measure the voltage, current, and resistance by using a meter.

Wattage is a measure of the amount of power for a circuit. Power (labeled P) is found by multiplying the voltage (labeled E) by the current (labeled I). The formula is written:

$$P = E \times I.$$

The amount of electrical power used in your home is measured in kilowatt-hours. The number of kilowatt-hours are measured with a meter that the power company attaches to your house. The difference in the reading from month to month is multiplied by the cost of power in your location. The larger the number of kilowatt-hours used each month, the higher your electric bill.

It is important that you *not* become a part of the circuit in *all* electrical work. If the path of the current goes through your heart you could be killed instantly. It takes less than one amp for that to happen. Make it a practice not to become part of the circuit when you take measurements, touch wires, or make electrical connections. Don't get into the habit of touching exposed metal on probes and wires when checking low voltage circuits. You might forget and make that mistake on higher voltage circuits.

KEY WORDS AND TERMS

Coulomb   Ohm's Law
Current   Power
Electromotive force   Voltage
Hot wire   Watt
Kilowatt hour (KWH)

TEST YOUR KNOWLEDGE

Do not write in this book. Write your answers on a separate sheet of paper.

1. Using the correct letters, write three different equations using Ohm's Law.
2. The unit of measure for resistance is the _____.
3. Explain what is meant by "hot" in an electrical circuit.
4. If we increase the voltage in an electrical circuit containing a lightbulb, what might happen? Why?
5. An electrical circuit has a voltage of 10 volts and the current flowing through it is 2 amperes. What is the resistance of the circuit?
6. Voltage means about the same thing as electrical _____.
7. List two devices that can produce a voltage.
8. The term "milliamp" means _____ of an amp.
9. A circuit has a current of 2.150 amperes flowing in it. How many milliamperes does that equal?
10. Give another name for voltage.
11. *True or False?* It takes less than 1 amp to kill you if it travels through your heart.
12. What is the unit of measure for electron flow in a circuit?
13. The unit of measure for electrical power is the _____.
14. Write the basic formula for calculating electrical power.
15. The unit used to measure the quantity of electricity used in your home is the _____.

ACTIVITIES

1. How did George Ohm discover the law named in his honor?
2. If you wanted to protect a circuit that carried 6 amps, what size fuse should you use?
3. If you wanted to install a fuse in a circuit carrying 1 amp, what size fuse should you use?
4. How much current can flow in a 1/2 watt resistor before it would burn up?
5. Take a reading of the meter that measures the amount of electricity you use in your home. Take another reading two weeks later. Find out from the power company what they charge for electricity and use this information to figure out what it cost you for those two weeks.
6. Take readings each morning and evening for two weeks on home's meter. When do the peak readings take place?
7. Many of your home appliances are rated in watts. How much current flows in each of these appliances? Make a list of the appliances starting with the one that uses the most current and ending with the one that uses the least current.
8. Measure your body resistance on a cool day and again on a hot day. Is there a difference? Why? Do the same thing while lightly squeezing the probes and again by squeezing the probes as hard as you can. Is there a difference? Why?
9. Knowing the speed of electricity, how many times will it travel around the world in one minute? In 30 seconds? In 5 seconds? How long would it take for it to travel from the east coast to the west coast of the United States?
10. Show the number of ways electricity can go through your heart while working with electrical tools or appliances.

6 Series Circuits

LEARNING OBJECTIVES

After studying this chapter, you will be able to:
- Construct a series circuit using various components.
- Measure the current flow and voltage drop in a series circuit with meters.
- Calculate the total resistance, voltage, and current in a circuit.
- Use a continuity tester to find the two ends of a wire in a cable.
- Determine the polarity of batteries and connect them in series in a flashlight.

You will find two different types of circuits on most electrical prints. These are known as *series circuits* and *parallel circuits*, Fig. 6-1. In this chapter, we will be dealing with series circuits. In the next, we will cover parallel circuits.

There are times when electrical circuits have both series and parallel branches (paths for current to flow) on the same schematic. Note in Fig. 6-1 that there is only one branch in the series circuit, while the parallel circuit has a number of branches.

ELECTRON PATH

Many times, it is necessary to make up a circuit that has its components hooked in series. Fig. 6-2, for example, illustrates a circuit with four lamps connected in series. Electrons flowing in this circuit have only one path to follow. Starting at the source of voltage, the electrons will travel through each lamp and finally return to the source. Therefore, when current is flowing in a series circuit, the same number of electrons will pass through each component.

Basically, then, every part of a series circuit carries the same amount of current flow (amperage). You can prove this by wiring a four-lamp circuit with an ammeter placed in the line behind each resistance (lamp). Close the switch and read the number of amps showing on each meter, Fig. 6-3. Each will read the same. However, if you open the switch or remove one of the wires, Fig. 6-4, all meter needles will drop to zero. This final test proves that the electrons have stopped moving.

NOTE: An ammeter is always connected in series with the components of any electrical circuit. When hooking up an ammeter to an existing circuit, some part of the circuit must be disconnected to permit installation of the tester. Usually, it is placed between a disconnected wire and its terminal.

Fig. 6-1. Electrical symbols for the power source, resistors, and wires form simple series and parallel circuits.

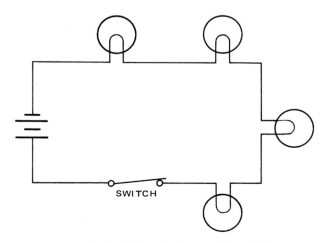
Fig. 6-2. Path of electron flow in a completed circuit.

SWITCH

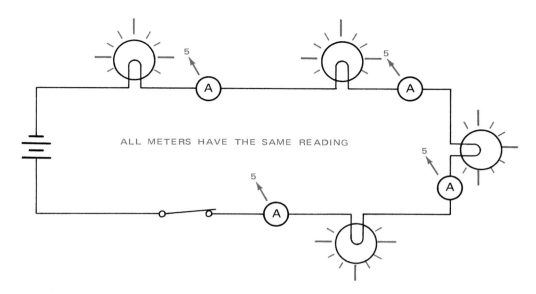

Fig. 6-3. Ammeters placed behind resistances in a completed series circuit will read the same amperage.

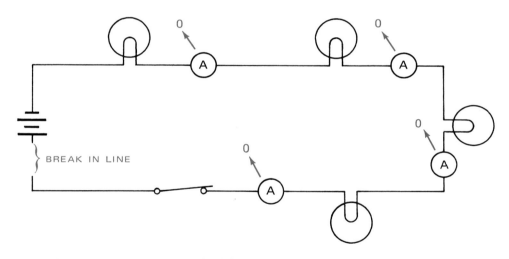

Fig. 6-4. With same circuit shown in Fig. 6-3, a break in the line will cause ammeters to read zero.

A voltmeter, on the other hand, is always connected in parallel to or across the circuit. There is no need to disconnect wires or uncouple electrical parts.

DEAD MAN'S SWITCH PROJECT

A dead man's switch, Figs. 6-5 and 6-6, is a useful project for anyone who owns and/or operates a lathe, drill press or other chuck type machine. Too often, the chuck key is left in the chuck. Then, when the machine is started, the chuck key is thrown out with great force. If the key strikes someone, he or she could be badly injured. A simple way to avoid this problem is to use a

dead man's switch inserted in the power line to the machine. The switch will keep the machine from starting to operate while the chuck key is in the chuck.

To build the project, obtain the following materials and assemble them according to Fig. 6-6.

No.	Item
1	Microswitch.
1	Surface mounting outlet box and plain cover.
1	Wood block.
2	Wire nuts.
1	110 volt three wire extension cord.
1	Junction box grounding clip w/wire.
2	1/2 in. connectors.

Fig. 6-5. Dead man's switch. Note that chuck key is inserted in opening to complete the circuit. (Project by John Kleihege)

With the dead man's switch connected to the machine power cord and a 110 volt receptacle, the machine will not operate unless the chuck key is dropped in the hole in the cover of the outlet box, Fig. 6-5. In this position, the key will close the microswitch and allow current to pass to the on-off switch on the machine.

Fig. 6-6. Dead man's switch construction. Switch protects operator from being hit by chuck key left in machine.

AMPS IN A SERIES CIRCUIT

In working with the circuit shown in Fig. 6-3, we proved that every part of a series circuit carries the same amount of current flow. Further proof of this can be had by examining three different test circuits, each having a total resistance of 45 ohms.

First, look at a series circuit with a 90 volt power source, one 45 ohm resistor and a test ammeter, Fig. 6-7. When this simple circuit is completed, the meter will read 2 amps.

Fig. 6-7. Simple series circuit with one resistor. Electrical values are given.

A second test circuit shown in Fig. 6-8 has a 90 volt power source in series with three 15 ohm resistors and an ammeter. When the last wire is connected, the meter will read 2 amps.

Finally, a third test circuit, using a 90 volt power source has three different resistors (10, 15 and 20 ohms) and an ammeter, Fig. 6-9. Again, 2 amps of current are flowing in the circuit. These three circuits are only used as examples. Do not actually hook them up because the high current will burn up the resistors.

TOTAL RESISTANCE

Each test circuit, Figs. 6-7, 6-8 and 6-9, carries the same number of amps. We proved this by reading the ammeter in each circuit.

In Chapter 5, however, we found that it is possible to figure how many amps are flowing in a given circuit by applying Ohm's Law. We can put this law to use while working with the test circuits just covered. In Fig. 6-7, for example, apply Ohm's Law as follows:

$$I = \frac{E}{R}$$

$$I = \frac{90 \text{ volts}}{45 \text{ ohms}}$$

$$I = 2 \text{ amps}$$

Fig. 6-8. Three resistors of equal value in a series circuit have same total resistance as single resistor in Fig. 6-7.

In order to apply this formula to the other two test circuits, you need to know the total resistance of the circuit. To find the total resistance, simply add the values of the individual resistances:

$$R_{Total} = R_1 + R_2 + R_3 \ldots$$

The ellipsis (...) means that something has been omitted. In this case, it means that you keep adding resistance values until you have accounted for all individual resistors and/or resistances.

In the circuit shown in Fig. 6-8, you have three resistors of equal value. Compute total resistance and how much amperage is flowing as follows:

$$R_T = R_1 + R_2 + R_3$$

$$R_T = 15 + 15 + 15 = 45 \text{ ohms}$$

$$I = \frac{E}{R}$$

$$I = \frac{90 \text{ volts}}{45 \text{ ohms}}$$

$$I = 2 \text{ amps}$$

Fig. 6-9. Three resistors of unequal values in a series circuit also have same total resistance as single resistor in Fig. 6-7.

In Fig. 6-9, you have resistors of three different values wired into the series circuit. Compute total resistance and amperage as follows:

$$R_T = R_1 + R_2 + R_3$$

$$R_T = 10 + 15 + 20$$

$$R_T = 45 \text{ ohms}$$

$$I = \frac{E}{R}$$

$$I = \frac{90 \text{ volts}}{45 \text{ ohms}}$$

$$I = 2 \text{ amps}$$

These three test circuits having different individual resistance setups show that total resistance governs how much current is flowing in a series circuit.

Now try a sample problem. What would the total resistance be in the series circuit shown in Fig. 6-10? There are five components in the circuit: a lamp with 15 ohms resistance; a fixed resistor with 45 ohms resistance; a variable resistor set at 100 ohms resistance; a switch, fuse and wire.

NOTE: Although the switch, fuse and wire do have some resistance, it usually is overlooked in circuit calculations because the amounts are so small. Most circuits, for example, will use wire in the range of 12 to 22 AWG (American Wire Gage). Turn to Chapter 3, Fig. 3-11. According to this table of resistances, you would need 629 feet of No. 12 wire, or 61 feet of No. 22 wire, to get one ohm of resistance. Few circuits, other than house wiring, have enough wire to affect total resistance to a great degree. Most circuits which you will be wiring on a bench in the school shop will involve just a small amount of wire.

In the series circuit in Fig. 6-10, then, compute total resistance and amperage as follows:

$$R_T = 15 + 45 + 100 \text{ ohms}$$

$$R_T = 160 \text{ ohms}$$

$$I = \frac{E}{R}$$

$$I = \frac{80 \text{ volts}}{160 \text{ ohms}}$$

$$I = 0.5 \text{ amps or } 500 \text{ mA}$$

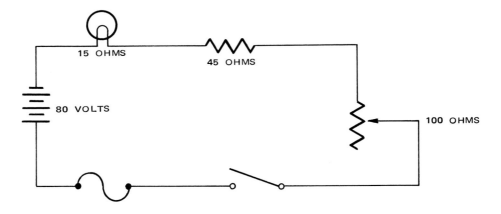

Fig. 6-10. Finding the total resistance of a series circuit is simply a matter of adding individual resistances.

Remember, in a series circuit, you must use the total resistance to find the amperage. To find the amperage in Fig. 6-11, first total the resistances:

$$R_T = R_1 + R_2 + R_3$$

$$R_T = 200 + 1000 + 1200 \text{ ohms}$$

$$R_T = 2400 \text{ ohms}$$

To compute the amperage use Ohm's Law:

$$I = \frac{E}{R}$$

$$I = \frac{24 \text{ volts}}{2400 \text{ ohms}}$$

$$I = .01 \text{ amp or } 10 \text{ mA}$$

We can prove it by reading the milliammeter, which is also in the circuit.

Note that the source of voltage in Fig. 6-11 is a generator. You will find that a generator is used in some circuits instead of (or in conjunction with) a battery. The generator will produce voltage and save the effort of having to change batteries every time they lose their charge.

POLARITY

There are a lot of electrical items that cannot be plugged into a wall outlet for a source of voltage. These items include flashlights, children's toys and portable tape recorders, all of which operate off dry cells. Most use more than one cell because of the need for higher voltage.

Fig. 6-11. Series circuit with a generator as the power source.

When you prepare to put cells in these devices, note that there are markings on each cell, and on the device, to show you the right way to make the installation. Each cell has a positive (+) pole and a negative (−) pole. To get proper voltage needed to operate a given electrical device, it is necessary to face these poles in the proper direction. This is what is known as "correct polarity." If you face the cells in the wrong direction, you will have "incorrect polarity."

Fig. 6-12 illustrates why polarity is important. Note that when all cells face in the same direction, their individual voltages *add* (1 1/2 + 1 1/2 + 1 1/2 + 1 1/2 = 6). If one cell faces the opposite way, it will reduce total voltage (1 1/2 + 1 1/2 − 1 1/2 + 1 1/2 = 3).

Polarity, then, is the proper identification of positive and negative terminals of a battery, cell or component in an electrical circuit. The polarity of electrical devices will affect: the direction in which a meter needle moves; how bright a flashlight will light; which direction a motor will turn; whether or not some devices will operate.

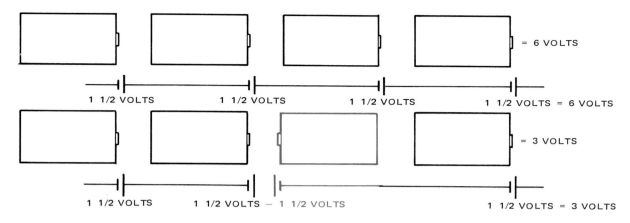

Fig. 6-12. Polarity of cells connected in series. Top. Correct polarity. Bottom. Incorrect polarity, with resulting loss of voltage.

All of which goes to prove that the sum of voltages in a series circuit depends on their polarity. If the polarity is correct, the voltages will add. If not, circuit

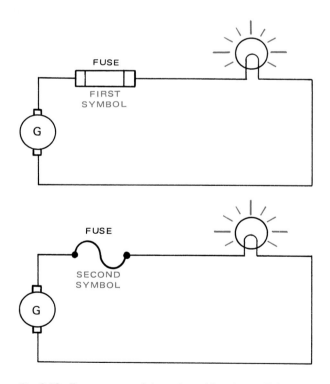

Fig. 6-13. Fuse connected in series with a lamp. Either fuse symbol is acceptable.

voltage will be reduced. One exception is a resistor installed in a series circuit. Resistors do not have polarity problems because they do not have positive and negative poles.

CONTINUITY LIGHT

There are times when you must install wire or components in a circuit so that they are in series with one another. In Fig. 6-13, the fuse (both symbols are shown) is in series with the lamp. After the circuit has been in operation for awhile, something could happen that would create an overload and blow the fuse.

If the lamp in this circuit does not light because of a blown fuse, there are several ways of checking it. The simplest way would be to see if the element is burned through (appears to be broken or completely missing).

Another way of checking for a blown fuse is to use a continuity light, Fig. 6-14. When the element is broken the light will not come on. If the element is good

Fig. 6-14. Continuity light will come on if alligator clips touch each other or if they are placed in contact with both ends of a good fuse.

(solid), the continuity light will come on. This tells you that the circuit is continuous, which is why we call the tester a "continuity light."

A continuity light also can be used to check wires to find out whether or not a "break" in a wire exists. If there is a break in the copper under the insulation, you cannot see it. A continuity light will help pinpoint the location of the break.

In another application, a continuity light will reveal both ends of a given wire from among a group of wires bundled together, Fig. 6-15. When we get to the chapter on meters, you will be shown how to make a continuity check with an ohmmeter.

LIGHT COMES ON WHEN PROBES MATCH CORRECT WIRE ENDS

CABLE WITH WIRES INSIDE

Fig. 6-15. A continuity light can be used to find two ends of the same wire in a cable or wiring harness.

MULTIPLE OUTLET EXTENSION CORD PROJECT

How many times have you found yourself in need of another electrical outlet? After you hook up an extension cord, you run into the problem of trying to run two power tools. Fig. 6-16 shows details of a little device which will solve that problem. This extension cord outlet box has four receptacles that can be turned on and off with a switch. It also has indicator lamps to tell you whether or not the power is on. If you should overload either side, it is protected by a fuse.

The mutliple outlet extension cord is shown in Fig. 6-16. One view pictures the completed outlet box; another shows details of its internal construction; the schematic illustrates circuit hookups.

To build the project, obtain the following materials:

No.	Item
1	Outlet box.
2	NE 2 lamps with dropping resistors.
2	Fuse assemblies (w/3 to 4 amp fuses).
2	DPST switches.
2	110 volt duplex receptacle w/ground.
1	Male plug (cap) w/ground.
1	18/3 extension cord.
1	Grommet or cord strain relief.

CONSTRUCTION PROCEDURE

Check all parts and decide on size of box. You can either build one or buy it from a local electrical supply store. Proceed as follows:

1. Lay out location of fuses, lamp, resistors, switches and receptacles. Allow enough room, so it will be easy to wire and build.
2. Cut holes in cover for various parts.
3. Mount receptacles in cover and wire them. Use black covered wire to attach to brass electrical fitting on receptacle; attach white wire to silver fitting. Use green wire for grounds.
4. Mount resistors (100,000 ohms or more) and indicator lights, splicing them into line. Keep all connections well insulated, especially if you use a metal box.
5. Mount fuses and switches, then wire them in position.
6. When wiring is completed, close either switch. The indicator lamp should come on. If not, a fuse may be blown.
7. Wire an extension cord of desired length to box as shown in Fig. 6-16. Use a wireman's knot inside box, so wire cannot be pulled out during use.
8. Mount the male plug on the other end of the extension cord. Be sure to use a grounded 110V receptacle to give you the protection you need when using portable power tools.

PUTTING THE PROJECT TO WORK

Plug the extension cord into the 110V receptacle and unwind as much of the cord as you need to bring the multiple outlet box to the job.

You may wish to make a stand on wheels for the multiple outlet box, so you can roll the outlet box and stand to each job. In addition, you can drill a 1/2 in. hole at each corner of the stand and install short wooden dowels. Then, wrap the cord around the dowels.

VOLTAGE

In order to study voltages, look back at some of the circuits made up earlier in this chapter. Take the one shown in Fig. 6-7, having a 90 volt power source and a 45 ohm resistor. First, measure the voltage at the source, using a voltmeter as shown in Fig. 6-17. It will read 90 volts. Next, connect the meter across the resistor as indicated in this illustration. It, too, will read 90 volts. Remember, we mentioned that the wiring in these test circuits has almost no resistance.

However, if we add another resistor to the circuit, Fig. 6-18, we start to see some changes. Note the three voltmeters connected across the circuit at various points. All indicate voltage, and the one across the

Fig. 6-17. A voltmeter is always connected in parallel with an electrical circuit.

Fig. 6-16. Multiple outlet extension cord. Top. Completed project. Center. Internal view of outlet box. Bottom. Schematic for use in assembling this project. (Project by Mike O'Berski)

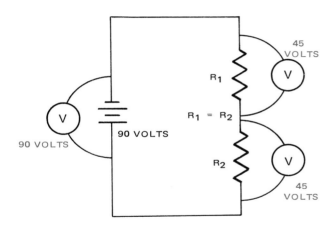

Fig. 6-18. Voltmeter readings taken across two resistors in a series circuit.

power source reads 90 volts. The two voltmeters connected across the resistors are equal, and the sum of their voltages (45 + 45 = 90) is equal to the reading on the voltmeter connected across the power source.

VOLTAGE DROP

Voltage drop is voltage measured across each resistor. The circuit shown in Fig. 6-18 has a 90 volt power source and three 15 ohm resistors. Make voltmeter tests at the points shown in Fig. 6-19. Note that the voltmeter across the power source reads 90 volts, while

the voltmeters across the resistors read 30 volts each. If you add these voltages, you will find that they again total voltage of the power source. No matter how many resistors are placed in a series circut, the total applied voltage (amount put out by the power source) will be divided among them.

Therefore, we have established that voltage across each resistor is called voltage drop; also that the sum of all voltage drops will be equal to the applied voltage. This discovery was named in honor of the discoverer. It is one of "Kirchhoff's Laws," and it states simply that "Total voltage drop in a series circuit will be equal to the applied voltage."

With this in mind, consider voltage drops in the circuit shown in Fig. 6-20, having four 10 ohm resistors and a generator that produces 40 volts. What would you expect each voltmeter to read? Voltmeters 1 through 4 would read 10 volts each, while voltmeter number 5 would read 40 volts. Each resistor, however, may or may not drop voltage the same amount. The amount of voltage drop depends on the value of each resistor.

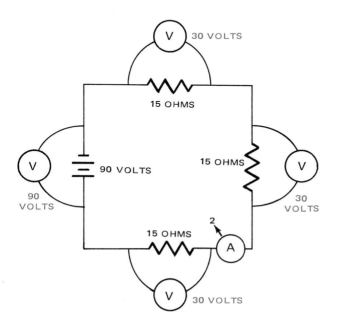

Fig. 6-19. Voltmeter readings taken across three resistors of like values in a series circuit.

Fig. 6-20. Voltmeter lead connections are shown for measuring voltage drops across each of four resistors of like values, and across all four resistors at once.

OHM'S LAW IN SERIES CIRCUITS

The amount of voltage drop across a given resistor can be determined by either of two methods. We can use a voltmeter to measure its value or we can use Ohm's Law. We worked with a voltmeter in getting voltage drop values in the last four circuits. Now we will use Ohm's Law to figure voltage drops across three different resistors in the series circuit shown in Fig. 6-21, then follow up with voltmeter readings.

First, compute the total resistance using symbols and abbreviations learned in Chapter 1.

$$R_T = R_1 + R_2 + R_3$$

$$R_T = 10\Omega + 15\Omega + 20\Omega$$

$$R_T = 45\Omega$$

Next, divide the source voltage by the total resistance:

$$I = \frac{E}{R_T}$$

$$I = \frac{90V}{45\Omega}$$

$$I = 2A$$

Fig. 6-21. Voltmeter readings taken across each of three resistors of unequal values.

Then, multiply each resistance by the amps running through the circuit in Fig. 6-21. This will give you the voltage drop across each resistor.

The voltage drop across R_1 would be:

$$E_1 = IR_1$$

$$E_1 = 2A \times 10\Omega$$

$$E_1 = 20V$$

You can see that using the E in this formula could be confusing. So instead of using the E, do as many people do: use a V for the voltage drop across each resistor.

$$V_{R_1} = 20V$$

Figuring out the rest of the circuit, you would have:

$$V_{R_2} = IR_2$$

$$V_{R_2} = 2A \times 15\Omega$$

$$V_{R_2} = 30V$$

$$V_{R_3} = IR_3$$

$$V_{R_3} = 2A \times 20\Omega$$

$$V_{R_3} = 40V$$

TOTAL VOLTAGE DROP

Total voltage drop in a series circuit should be equal to voltage at the source. To find total voltage drop in the circuit shown in Fig. 6-21, use the following formula:

$$E_T = V_{R_1} + V_{R_2} + V_{R_3}$$

Next, substitute the individual voltage drop values you worked out in solving the last problem:

$$E_T = V_{R_1} + V_{R_2} + V_{R_3}$$

$$E_T = 20V + 30V + 40V$$

$$E_T = 90V$$

You can see that 90 volts does equal our source voltage.

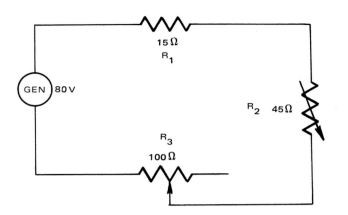

Fig. 6-22. Calculating unknown voltage drops. First determine total resistance, then amperage. Using Ohm's Law, figure individual voltage drop across resistors and come up with total voltage drop for the circuit.

Try another example, using Fig. 6-22. First find the total resistance:

$$R_T = R_1 + R_2 + R_3$$

$$R_T = 15\Omega + 45\Omega + 100\Omega$$

$$R_T = 160\Omega$$

Next, find the amperage:

$$I = \frac{E}{R}$$

$$I = \frac{80V}{160\Omega}$$

$$I = 0.5A \text{ or } 500 \text{ mA}$$

Then, find the voltage drop across each resistor.

$$V_{R_1} = I \times R_1$$

$$V_{R_1} = 0.5A \times 15\Omega$$

$$V_{R_1} = 7.5V$$

$$V_{R_2} = I \times R_2$$

$$V_{R_2} = 0.5A \times 45\Omega$$

$$V_{R_2} = 22.5V$$

R_2 is the symbol for variable resistor.

$$V_{R_3} = I \times R_3$$

$$V_{R_3} = 0.5A \times 100\Omega$$

$$V_{R_3} = 50V$$

Finally, add up the individual voltage drops to see if their sum equals the applied voltage:

$$E_T = V_{R_1} + V_{R_2} + V_{R_3}$$

$$E_T = 7.5V + 22.5V + 50V$$

$$E_T = 80V$$

FOOT SWITCH PROJECT

How many times have you wanted to turn on electrical power, but both hands were full? You could have handled this problem if you had a foot switch, Fig. 6-23, attached to an electrical outlet. By merely pushing down on the switch with your foot, you could have controlled the flow of power to some electrical device.

To build this project, you will need the following items:

No.	Item
1	Foot switch.
1	Double outlet receptacle.
1	Male plug.
2	Black lead wires.
1	White lead wire.

CONSTRUCTION PROCEDURE

Study Fig. 6-23 and proceed as follows:
1. Install white wire and one black wire in male plug.
2. Connect other end of white wire to double outlet receptacle.
3. Connect other end of black wire to foot switch.
4. Use other black wire to connect foot switch to double outlet receptacle.

There are many good uses for a foot switch, including photo enlarging. Operator uses left hand to feed light sensitive paper to an easel under enlarger lens. Foot switch is pressed down to turn on enlarger light. Operator times exposure, releases foot switch and uses right hand to remove exposed paper from easel and drop it in developer.

Fig. 6-23. A foot switch connected in series with an electrical device frees both hands. Top. Foot switch and twin receptacle. Bottom. Schematic for use in constructing this project.
(Project by Dave Wightman)

SUMMARY

Electrons flowing in a series circuit have only one path in which they can flow. Therefore, every part of a series circuit has the same amount of current flowing through it. When you measure the current, an ammeter is always connected in series with the components. A voltmeter is connected across (in parallel with) the circuit. If you know the voltage and total resistance of the circuit, you can calculate the current using Ohm's Law ($I = E/R$). The sum of voltage that drops across all the components in a series circuit, will be equal to the applied voltage.

The total resistance (R_T) of a series circuit can be found by adding up the values of each resistance ($R_T = R_1 + R_2 + R_3$).

Polarity refers to the proper identification of the positive (+) and negative (–) poles of the device. A battery will have its poles marked to help you connect them in the circuit in the correct manner.

KEY WORDS AND TERMS

Ammeter
Kirchhoff's laws
Series circuit

Total resistance
Total voltage drop
Voltmeter

TEST YOUR KNOWLEDGE

Do not write in this book. Write your answers on a separate sheet of paper.
1. There is only one _____ in a series circuit, while a parallel circuit has several.
2. Every part of a series circuit carries the same amount of _____.
3. An ammeter is always connected _____ components of an electrical circuit.
4. A voltmeter is always connected _____ components of an electrical circuit.
5. What is polarity?
6. What does R_T stand for?
7. Draw the symbol for ohms.
8. Give the Ohm's Law formula for finding the amount of current flow or amperage in an electrical circuit.
9. If you had three resistors connected in series, each with a value of 30 ohms, how much total resistance would you have?
10. How much current will flow in a circuit having a 24 volt power supply, a 200 ohm resistor, and a 2200 ohm resistor in series?
11. To find the voltage drop across a resistor, we can use a voltmeter to measure its value, or we can use _____.

ACTIVITIES

1. Why will several lights in your house go out if you open a circuit breaker?
2. If a continuity light will not light up when checking a coil, what is indicated?
3. Visit a new house under construction. What type and size of wire is being used? Where is the ground wire, and what color is it?
4. List some places or things where you will find three or more sources of resistance connected in series.
5. Explain why a continuity light should never be used on a circuit while it is connected to its source of power.
6. List Kirchhoff's laws and tell what they mean.
7. Make a list of the people who have electrical laws named after them. Show the dates when these people lived. Notice in which years most of their discoveries were made.
8. Where did omega, the name of the symbol used for resistance, first come from? How old is the term?
9. Which electrical devices in your home have the greatest resistance? If they are listed in watts, explain why your answer is correct.

7 Parallel Circuits

LEARNING OBJECTIVES

After studying this chapter, you will be able to:
- Construct a parallel circuit using various components.
- Measure the current flow and voltage drop in a parallel circuit with meters.
- Calculate the total resistance, voltage, and current in a parallel circuit .
- Design and connect a circuit on a breadboard.
- State a simple rule for the total resistance if all the resistors in the parallel circuit have the same value.

After learning how series circuits work, your next assignment is the study of "parallel circuits," Fig. 7-1. As you work your way through this chapter, you will see why all circuits cannot be wired in series. Parallel circuits have broad application, including radios, television sets, and the wiring in your home.

CURRENT IN A PARALLEL CIRCUIT

A parallel circuit is one which has two or more paths (branches) through which electrons flow. For example, electron flow in a parallel circuit may be related to water flowing down a riverbed, Fig. 7-2. First, note the full flow down the main branch of the river. Then, when the water reaches the two islands, the river splits and takes three paths. Since each path is the same size, the same amount of water will flow in each.

The same thing is true of electrical circuits. In Fig. 7-3, note that the electrons have only one path to follow when they leave the generator (or battery). Then, when three equal paths are provided, the electrons split up evenly in taking those paths.

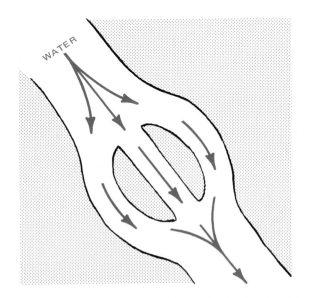
Fig. 7-2. Water flowing downriver will divide evenly when branching into three equal parts.

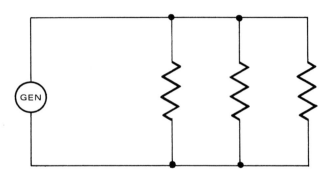
Fig. 7-1. A parallel circuit provides two or more paths for the flow of electricity.

Fig. 7-3. Electron flow in a parallel circuit also divides evenly when three equal electrical paths are provided.

96

RESISTANCE IN A PARALLEL CIRCUIT

Again relating water flow to electron flow, note that the river shown in Fig. 7-4 also flows down three different paths. However, since these paths are unequal in size, the water will not divide equally. Most of the water will flow through the largest path, which is the

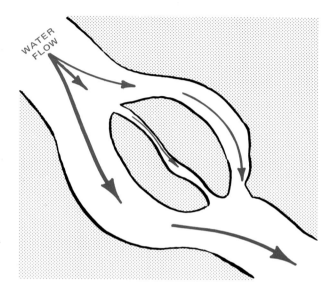

Fig. 7-4. Water flowing downriver will divide unevenly when branching into several unequal paths.

one that offers the least resistance. Lesser amounts of water will flow through the smaller paths, or those offering the most resistance.

The same thing is true of electron flow in an

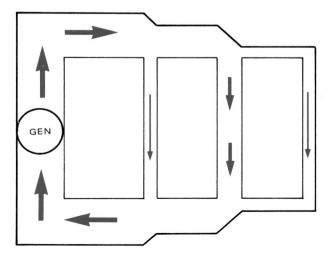

Fig. 7-5. Electron flow in a parallel circuit also divides unevenly when the electrical paths are unequal.

electrical circuit of the parallel type. If the circuit has three unequal paths, the total number of electrons flowing will divide unequally.

Basically, then, the branch of a parallel circuit that offers the smallest amount of resistance will provide the easiest path for electron flow, Fig. 7-5. Ohm's Law can be used to determine the number of electrons flowing, but first, it is necessary to find the total resistance of the circuit.

Total resistance in a parallel circuit can be computed in various ways. One convenient method is by means of the "conductance" formula. Conductance is the reciprocal (opposite) of resistance. It is the current carrying ability of any wire or electrical component. Resistance, on the other hand, is the ability to oppose the flow of current.

Use this conductance formula, then invert the answer to find total resistance:

$$\frac{1}{R_T} = \frac{1}{R_1} + \frac{1}{R_2} + \frac{1}{R_3} \cdots$$

In the portion of a parallel circuit shown in Fig. 7-6, the two resistors connected in parallel have values of 20 ohms each. Substitute these values for factors (numbers or symbols in mathematics) in the formula as follows:

Fig. 7-6. Parallel paths of equal resistance permit the same amount of current to flow in each electrical path. Total resistance in this circuit is 10 ohms (see text).

$$\frac{1}{R_T} = \frac{1}{R_1} + \frac{1}{R_2}$$

$$\frac{1}{R_T} = \frac{1}{20} + \frac{1}{20}$$

$$\frac{1}{R_T} = \frac{2}{20} = \frac{1}{10}$$

Invert both sides of the equation (equal factors):

$$\frac{R_T}{1} = \frac{10}{1} = 10 \text{ ohms}$$

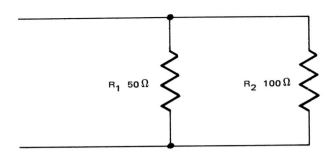

Fig. 7-7. Parallel paths of unequal resistance vary the amount of current flowing in each electrical path. Total resistance of this circuit is 33.3 ohms (see text).

Try another total resistance example. In Fig. 7-7, R_1 is rated at 50 ohms, R_2 is 100 ohms. Again use the formula:

$$\frac{1}{R_T} = \frac{1}{R_1} + \frac{1}{R_2}$$

$$\frac{1}{R_T} = \frac{1}{50} + \frac{1}{100}$$

$$\frac{1}{R_T} = \frac{2}{100} + \frac{1}{100} = \frac{3}{100}$$

Invert both sides of the equation:

$$R_T = \frac{100}{3} = 33.3\,\Omega$$

I.C. SAYS:

"For a quick check to see if your work is okay, look at your answer. The R Total (R_T) must be smaller than either of the resistors used in the circuit."

If your R Total comes out larger than either of the resistors, the answer is wrong. Recheck your work. Study Fig. 7-8 to see why this is so.

COMBINING PATHS
FOR EQUIVALENT SIZE

Fig. 7-8. Two electrical paths combined are equivalent to one path of larger size.

TOTAL RESISTANCE

By using the conductance formula for finding the total resistance in a parallel circuit, you are trying to show an "equivalent circuit," Fig. 7-8. An equivalent circuit is one that takes out all resistors and replaces them with just one resistor. In this way, you can find the amount of current that the power supply is being asked to deliver. It will tell you what effect the load has had on the power supply. Remember, you do not want to overload the circuit or blow a fuse.

Anytime you have resistors in parallel you are making a larger path for the electrons to flow. Anytime you combine two or more paths into one path for electron flow, that path will get larger. *Therefore, when you find the R Total in a parallel circuit, it must offer less resistance to the flow of electrons; and it must be smaller than any one of the resistors in the parallel circuit.*

Fig. 7-9 shows a circuit with three resistors. Compute R_T as follows:

$$\frac{1}{R_T} = \frac{1}{R_1} + \frac{1}{R_2} + \frac{1}{R_3}$$

$$\frac{1}{R_T} = \frac{1}{500} + \frac{1}{500} + \frac{1}{1000}$$

$$\frac{1}{R_T} = \frac{2}{1000} + \frac{2}{1000} + \frac{1}{1000} = \frac{5}{1000}$$

$$\frac{1}{R_T} = \frac{1}{200}$$

Invert both sides of the equation:

$$R_T = 200\,\Omega$$

Note, again, that R Total is smaller than any of the resistors in the circuit.

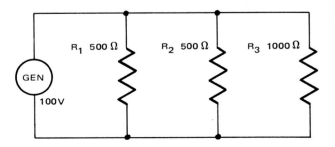

Fig. 7-9. This parallel circuit with three resistors has a total resistance of 200 ohms (see text).

CURRENT

Now that you have found R Total, the next thing to do is find the amount of current flowing in the circuit. Again, we can use Ohm's Law and the values from Fig. 7-9:

$$I = \frac{E}{R}$$

$$I = \frac{100V}{200\,\Omega}$$

$$I = .5A$$

Because R Total was used, the value .5A is the amount of current flowing in the total circuit.

To find the amount of current flowing in each resistor, again use Ohm's Law. In R_1 (and R_2), the amount of current flow would be:

$$I = \frac{E}{R}$$

$$I = \frac{100V}{500\,\Omega}$$

$$I = .2A$$

In R_3 the current equals:

$$I = \frac{E}{R}$$

$$I = \frac{100V}{1000\,\Omega}$$

$$I = .1A$$

Adding these three current values gives .5 amp (.2 + .2 + .1), which is equal to the total current flowing in the circuit.

ERRORS IN CURRENT VALUES

Fig. 7-10 shows the same circuit as Fig. 7-9, with five ammeters installed in the lines. Ammeters 1 and 5 both show .5 amp. Each reading indicates total current flow in the circuit. Ammeters 2 and 3 read .2 amp, and ammeter 4 reads .1 amp. These values represent current flow through each resistor in the circuit. Again, adding these three current values gives .5 amp, which is the total current flowing in the circuit.

These examples serve to illustrate that total current flow in a parallel circuit is equal to the sum of the currents flowing through the branches of the circuit.

Fig. 7-10. This parallel circuit with ammeters in the lines show effect resistors of different values have on current flow.

Therefore, in a circuit using three resistors, the formula would be:

$$I_{Total} = I_1 + I_2 + I_3$$

I_1, I_2 and I_3 represent the amount of current flowing through each resistor.

I.C. SAYS:

"If you actually hook up this circuit, you may get different results. This difference is because of the tolerance of various resistors. Your results may vary from plus or minus 5 percent if the resistors have a gold fourth band; plus or minus 10 percent if they have a silver fourth band; plus or minus 20 percent if they have no fourth band."

BREADBOARDING

Fig. 7-11 shows a student who has set up a parallel circuit based on an activity in an electricity workbook. The student has wired the circuit, using parts from a kit. When working with circuits, kits are an easy way to get started. However, before you solder any circuit together, it would be wise to "breadboard" it first.

Breadboarding, Fig. 7-12, is a way of laying out the circuit to see if it works. The various components of a given project are mounted on a perforated board and connected temporarily for test purposes. By bread-

Fig. 7-11. Student traces a circuit on an electrical project built from a kit in the school shop. (Hickok Teaching Systems, Inc.)

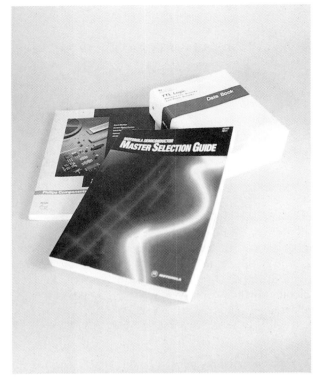

Fig. 7-13. Replacement parts catalogs usually include a cross-reference section for use when substituting replacement parts for original equipment.

Fig. 7-12. "Breadboarding" a circuit is a means of testing circuit operation before soldering parts and connections. (Interplex Electronics, Inc.)

HEP Semiconductor Replacement Cross-References

DEVICE	HEP	DEVICE	HEP	DEVICE	HEP	DEVICE	HEP	DEVICE	HEP	DEVICE	HEP
399C	R0092	429-0958-41	R0050	576-0003-011	728	617-67	730	690V043H63	254	690V109H44	R0050
399D	R0092	429-0958-42	53	576-0003-012 (NPN)	56	617-68	729	690V047H56	253	690V109H46	53
404-2 (Syl)	729	429-0958-43	Z0408	576-0003-012 (PNP)	717	617-69	238	690V047H57	253	690V109H72	R2502
404A	R0160	429-0986-12	56	576-0003-017	57	617-70	632	690V047H60	632	690V110H30	55
404B	R0162	429-0989-68	R0050	576-0003-018	56	617-71	243	690V047H61	134	690V110H31	54
34C	R0162	430 (Zen)	730	576-0003-019	57	617-87	243	690V049H81	56	690V110H32	50
	R0162	431-26551A	C6056P	576-0003-020	56	617-117	245	690V052H23	250	690V110H33	50
	R0137	429-1 (Syl)	243	576-0003-021	56	617-156	134	690V052H24	254	690V110H34	243
				576-0003-022	736	617-161	733	690V052H50	134	690V110H36	243
				-0003-023	709	617-162	R0054	690V056H31	639	690V110H55	242
					3	617-163	R0054	690V056H32	639	690V116H20	53
						(RCA)	245	690V056H33	633	693G	55
							246	690V056H34	632	699 (GE)	736
								690V057H24	254	700-04	801
								...7H25	637	702-810	R9001
								703-1	254		

Fig. 7-14. Cross-reference listings in parts catalogs give original equipment numbers alongside of replacement parts numbers.

boarding first, you can be sure that:
1. Wiring of components has been done properly.
2. Components of correct value have been used.
3. Circuit will work.

In this manner, you can prove to yourself that the circuit works before you solder it together. "After soldering" is the wrong time to find out the circuit does not work. To remove solder from connections and check out components takes a lot longer than if it were done on a breadboard first.

You will find that some circuits in magazines and books do not work very well. Some do not work at all, or you may have to substitute one manufacturer's components for another's. When this happens, use a substitution manual or look up the cross-reference list in a replacement parts catalog, Figs. 7-13 and 7-14.

Occasionally, a circuit fitted with substitute parts will work poorly or not at all. This occurs because some electrical parts have important and critical (vital) values. If substituted for, circuit design may be changed. It is better to find out about circuit problems on a breadboard first.

USES FOR PARALLEL CIRCUITS

Next, let us see how parallel circuits can be of value to you. Suppose you have a radio and want to attach two speakers to it. You look through a pile of speakers and find some marked 4 ohms, 8 ohms and 16 ohms. However, the back of the radio is marked 4 ohms, meaning it calls for one 4 ohm speaker.

Since you wish to install more than one speaker, you do have a problem. One answer to selecting the right speakers for the project is to make up a parallel circuit, using two speakers marked 8 ohms each, Fig. 7-15. Working out total resistance for this parallel circuit, you will find that two 8 ohm speakers connected in parallel equal 4 ohms of total resistance.

$$\frac{1}{R_T} = \frac{1}{R_1} + \frac{1}{R_2}$$

$$\frac{1}{R_T} = \frac{1}{8} + \frac{1}{8}$$

$$\frac{1}{R_T} = \frac{2}{8} = \frac{1}{4}$$

Invert both sides of the equation:

$$R_T = 4\,\Omega$$

Fig. 7-15. In this circuit, two speakers are connected in parallel, each having 8 ohms resistance to match radio's requirement for 4 ohms total resistance (see text).

The problem is solved. The total resistance of the two speakers now matches the 4 ohms marked on the back of the radio.

ELECTRIC PUZZLE PROJECT

Here is a puzzle that you can build with four switches, a lamp and two dry cells. The whole idea is to wire the project so that the lamp will come on if a mistake is made while working the puzzle.

Each switch, in turn, represents a child, a chicken, corn and a fox. The trick is to operate the four switches so that the child can get all three possessions safely across the river. On the shore is a rowboat which is used to carry the child and only one possession at a time. The "catch" is: the fox will eat the chicken or the chicken will eat the corn if left together on one side of the river.

If you wire the switches as shown in Fig. 7-16, there is a way for the child to get all three possessions safely across the river. Try your skill to see if you can figure out how to do it. Remember, the child can move only one possession per trip across the river.

When working the puzzle, imagine that the switches span the river. S_1 in Fig. 7-16 and 7-17 is for controlling the child's crossings. S_2 is for the chicken. S_3 is for the corn. S_4 is for the fox.

Fig. 7-16. Electric puzzle. Right. Finished project. Below. Drawing shows switches, lamp and wiring hookups. (Project by Dick Butcke)

The answer follows the construction procedure.

No.	Item
2	1.5V dry cells (B_1).
1	3V dc lamp (L_1).
3	SPDT knife switches $(S_1, S_3$ and $S_4)$.
1	DPDT knife switch (S_2).

Lead wire, wooden box, baseboard, lamp socket and holder for cells.

CONSTRUCTION PROCEDURE

Assemble the materials for this project as follows:
1. Lay out the location of the switches and lamp on the baseboard.
2. Drill all necessary holes in baseboard.
3. Wire and install all switches and the lamp according to the diagram in Fig. 7-16.
4. Assemble the wooden box and install the switchboard on it, as pictured in Fig. 7-16.

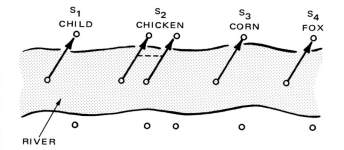

Fig. 7-17. When working the electric puzzle shown in Fig. 7-16, think of the switches as the child, chicken, corn and fox moving back and forth across the river.

Here is the correct switching sequence, Fig. 7-17, that will get the child and possessions to the opposite side of the river:

1st Trip	Child (S_1) and chicken (S_2).
Return Trip	Child (S_1) alone.
2nd Trip	Child (S_1) and corn (S_3).
Return Trip	Child (S_1) and chicken (S_2).
3rd Trip	Child (S_1) and fox (S_4).
Return Trip	Child (S_1) alone.
4th Trip	Child (S_1) and chicken (S_2).

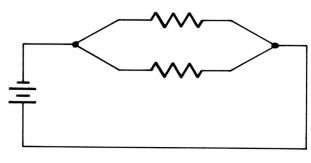

Fig. 7-18. Parallel circuits can be drawn in many different ways. Drawings shown are typical arrangements of power source and resistors.

SCHEMATIC DRAWINGS

You will find parallel circuits drawn in many different ways. So far in this chapter, we have shown simple rectangular circuits with resistors placed parallel to each other in add-on fashion. Fig. 7-18 shows two other ways of drawing parallel circuits.

Note in Fig. 7-19 that the two resistors are connected to separate branches of the circuit, putting them in parallel electrically, but not in parallel position on the drawing. When resistors are *connected in parallel*, it is not necessary to *draw them parallel* to each other.

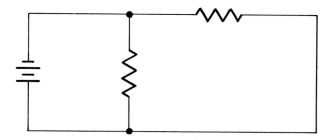

Fig. 7-19. In this parallel circuit, one resistor is shown on a cross wire. The second resistor is placed at right angles rather than parallel to the first resistor.

PARALLEL POWER SOURCES

Power sources also can be connected in parallel. In Fig. 7-20, note that three batteries are connected in parallel across the load. This arrangement is set up when one power source simply cannot supply enough current for an extended time.

In Fig. 7-21, three batteries are connected in parallel to the load (a lamp). This is done for a reason. There are times when a load will draw so much current that it will shorten the life of the power source. When this happens, it is necessary to install several power sources (batteries, in this case) in parallel. This enables them to

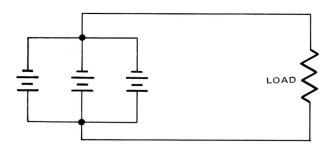

Fig. 7-20. Multiple power sources connected in parallel share the electrical load and last longer.

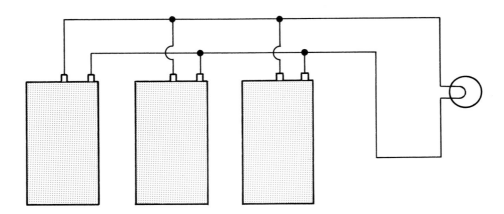

Fig. 7-21. This circuit drawing is another way of showing three power supplies connected to the circuit in parallel.

share the current draw from the load and extend the life of the total power supply. In later chapters, you will see that most people will replace batteries with a power source which converts the ac into dc. Only batteries or power sources that have the same voltage should be connected in parallel.

EQUAL RESISTORS IN PARALLEL

In Fig. 7-22, you see two resistors connected in parallel, each having a value of 100 ohms. When a parallel circuit has two resistors of the same value, another formula can be used to find total resistance. R_T will be equal to R divided by the number of resistors.

In Fig. 7-22, for example, R equals 100 ohms and N is the number of resistors:

$$R_T = \frac{R}{N}$$

$$R_T = \frac{100}{2}$$

$$R_T = 50\,\Omega$$

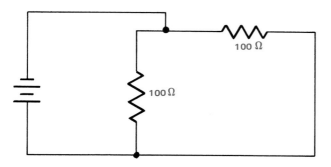

Fig. 7-22. Two 100 ohm resistors connected in parallel offer 50 ohms total resistance (see formula in text).

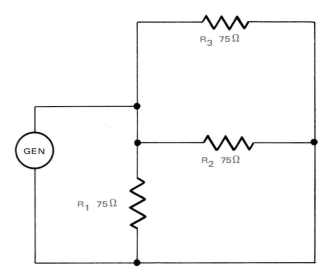

Fig. 7-23. Three 75 ohm resistors in parallel offer 25 ohms total resistance (see text).

In Fig. 7-23, three resistors are connected in parallel. Use the same formula to find total resistance:

$$R_T = \frac{R}{N}$$

$$R_T = \frac{75}{3}$$

$$R_T = 25\,\Omega$$

This means that if you want to substitute one resistor for the three in this parallel circuit, replace them with one 25 ohm resistor.

Fig. 7-24 shows a typical power amplifier chassis with all components in place. A complex electrical

Fig. 7-24. This power amplifier is made up of many parallel circuits. (Fisher Radio)

device such as this has many parallel circuits. It also has series circuits, which were described in the last chapter, and series parallel circuits, which will be explained in Chapter 9.

VOLTAGE

Voltage in a parallel circuit can be found by using a voltmeter and some common sense about hooking up the leads. Using the meter means reading it directly as you did before. However, the voltmeter leads must be connected across the circuit. Look at Fig. 7-25. Note that by connecting a voltmeter across each resistor and the source, all leads are connected to the same two lines. Therefore, all meters are reading the same *source voltage.*

Consider another resistance experiment. If you installed a voltmeter across the line as in Fig. 7-26, you would get a reading of zero. There is no reading because voltage drop across a short piece of wire is very small. It is so small, in fact, that you would need a highly sensitive meter to record the drop.

Take the No. 14 wire in Fig. 7-26, for example. It is carrying 2 amps of current. Going back to the table in Fig. 3-11 on page 39, you will find that No. 14 wire has 1 ohm resistance for 396 feet of wire. Therefore, one foot of wire between the clips of the voltmeter has a resistance of .00252 ohm.

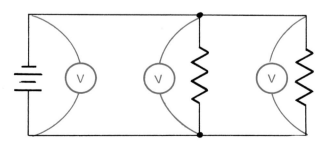

Fig. 7-25. When measuring voltage in this parallel circuit, connect voltmeter across power source or load.

Fig. 7-26. There is no voltage drop when measuring across a wire, because its resistance is so small.

$$R = \frac{1 \text{ ft.}}{396 \text{ ft./ohm}}$$

$$R = .00252 \text{ ohm}$$

Using Ohm's Law to find the voltage drop:

$$E = IR$$

$$E = 2A \times .00252\Omega$$

$$E = .00504V$$

You can see that a very sensitive voltmeter would be needed to make this voltage measurement. Since there is practically no voltage drop, we can forget it when using meters. See Fig. 7-26. *Therefore, the voltage in a parallel circuit is the same across each resistor.*

SUMMARY

In this chapter, you have learned that:

- Total current flow in a parallel circuit is equal to the sum of the currents flowing in the branches.

$$I_{Total} = I_1 + I_2 + I_3$$

- Voltage is the same across each path of a parallel circuit.
- Total resistance in a parallel circuit is the reciprocal (opposite) of conductance. Use this conductance formula, then invert the answer:

$$\frac{1}{R_{Total}} = \frac{1}{R_1} + \frac{1}{R_2} + \frac{1}{R_3}$$

- When resistors connected in a parallel circuit have the same value, the total resistance is equal to the value of one resistor divided by the number of resistors. The formula would be $R_T = \frac{R}{N}$.

KEY WORDS AND TERMS

Branch	Equivalent circuit
Breadboard	Parallel circuit
Conductance	

TEST YOUR KNOWLEDGE

Do not write in this book. Write your answers on a separate sheet of paper.

1. What is the total resistance in a circuit having four 200 ohm resistors connected in parallel? Use either formula to solve this problem.
2. Show the formula you used to get the answer to No. 1.
3. How many branches are there in a parallel circuit?
4. What is a quick check to see if the answer to a parallel circuit problem is right?
   a. The answer must be smaller in value than any of the resistors in the circuit.
   b. The answer must be larger in value than any of the resistors in the circuit.
5. In a parallel circuit, how much of the current will flow in the path of least resistance?
   a. A small amount
   b. Most
   c. All
6. Three resistors are connected in parallel. If they are all of equal value, how would you find the equivalent (one resistor) circuit?
7. When you measure the current in a circuit, you may get different results than if you solved the problem using the formula. Why?
8. *True or False?* "Breadboarding" is a method of wiring up a circuit to check its operation before soldering.
9. Before soldering a circuit together, it would be wise to check its operation. Why?
10. The voltage in a parallel circuit is _____ across all branches.
11. *Yes or No?* When two resistors are connected in parallel, they must be placed parallel to each other on the circuit drawing.

ACTIVITIES

1. Why do speakers have different ratings?
2. Why does a voltmeter read zero when it is connected across a piece of wire?
3. Why do you get a voltage drop across a piece of resistance wire and not across copper wire or aluminum wire?
4. What are some of the ways companies use to remove solder when they must repair circuits that have been soldered?
5. Why do some circuits found in books and magazines fail to work?
6. Make a list of some of the places where you can find resistors connected in parallel.
7. Why can a bird land on electric wires between telephone poles without getting shocked or killed?

Series Parallel Circuits

LEARNING OBJECTIVES

After studying this chapter, you will be able to:
- Construct a series parallel circuit using various components.
- Measure the current flow and voltage drop in a series parallel circuit with meters.
- Calculate the total resistance, voltage, and current in a series parallel circuit.
- Design, connect, and explain a wheatstone bridge circuit on a breadboard.
- Explain how an automobile can use a one wire system to operate its electrical components.
- Show how to hook up and calculate series, parallel, and series parallel circuits with capacitors.

When series circuits and parallel circuits are combined, the resulting single circuit is commonly called a *series parallel circuit* or *network*. Most series parallel circuits are very complex. However, if you follow some simple guidelines, you will be able to reduce any series parallel circuit to its simplest form to determine current and voltages.

Part A in Fig. 8-1 illustrates a simple series parallel circuit having three 60 ohm resistors. The first step in figuring values in this type of circuit is to determine which resistors are in series with the power supply and which resistors are in parallel. Note that R_1 is in series, while R_2 and R_3 are in parallel.

Use the following formula (from Chapter 7) for finding the equivalent resistance (R_{EQ}) of the two resistors of equal value in the parallel element of the circuit shown at A in Fig. 8-1:

$$R_{EQ} = \frac{R}{N}$$

$$R_{EQ} = \frac{60}{2}$$

$$R_{EQ} = 30\Omega$$

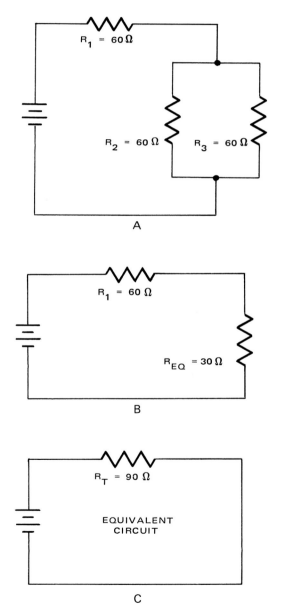

Fig. 8-1. Series parallel circuit has three resistors. A—R_1 is in series, R_2 and R_3 are in parallel. B—Equivalent resistance is 30 ohms. C—Total resistance is 90 ohms.

Next, use the following formula for finding total equivalent resistance in the newly formed series circuit. See Part B.

$$R_T = R_1 + R_{EQ}$$
$$R_T = 60 + 30$$

$$R_T = 90\Omega$$

This gives you an equivalent circuit, Part C, having total resistance of 90 ohms.

LOCATION OF RESISTANCES

You might think that if you placed the series element of a series parallel circuit *ahead of* the parallel element, it would make a difference when figuring total resistance. This would be true for figuring the amount of current flow in various parts of the circuit, but not for total resistance.

For example, Part A in Fig. 8-2 shows a circuit with the series element ahead of the parallel element. Now if you go through the same steps in figuring total resistance that you did in Fig. 8-1, you *will* get the same answer (90 ohms): In Part B, the equivalent resistance (R_{EQ}) of R_1 and R_2 is 30 ohms. When this is added to the 60 ohms of R_3, Part C, you would again have an equivalent circuit with a total resistance of 90 ohms.

CIRCUIT LAYOUT

To make circuits a little easier to read, most people who draw them follow certain basic rules of construction. First, they try to lay out the circuit so that the top part is positive and the bottom part is negative. See Fig. 8-3. A second general rule is to lay out the circuit so that the input is on the left and the output is on the right, Fig. 8-4. This means that the power supply would be drawn on the left and the load (such as lamps), on the right.

Knowing about these two circuit drawing practices will save you a lot of time when you look at schematics. In the past, these "rules of construction" were not observed. Today, it is easy to see how a simple idea like this can be very valuable in troubleshooting electrical circuits.

ORDER FOR SOLVING
TOTAL RESISTANCE

You might think that all series parallel circuits are solved for total resistance by first looking for a parallel circuit. This is not true, although the previous examples make it appear that way. The schematic at Part A in Fig. 8-5, for example, has resistors of 10 ohms, 20 ohms, and 30 ohms. The first step in solving this circuit is to take the two resistors in series (R_2 and R_3) and find their equivalent:

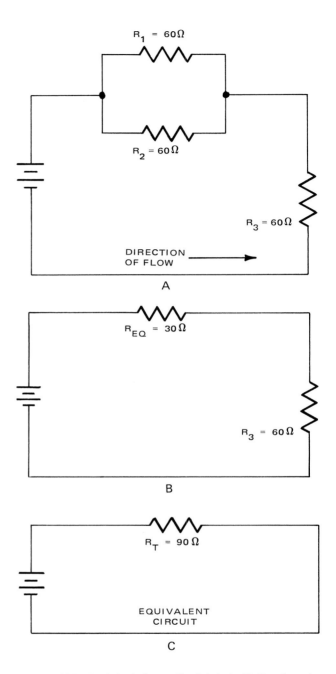

Fig. 8-2. This circuit is similar to Fig. 8-1, but with the elements reversed. A—Series element R_3 is ahead of parallel element R_1 and R_2. B—Equivalent resistance is 30 ohms. C—Total resistance is 90 ohms.

$$R_{EQ} = R_2 + R_3$$
$$R_{EQ} = 10 + 20$$
$$R_{EQ} = 30\Omega$$

This gives us the equivalent of two 30 ohm resistances in parallel, shown at Part B in Fig. 8-5.

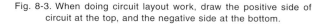

Fig. 8-3. When doing circuit layout work, draw the positive side of circuit at the top, and the negative side at the bottom.

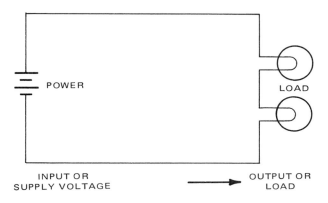

Fig. 8-4. Good circuit layout practice calls for power supply to be drawn at left and load at right

In order to solve this equivalent circuit for total resistance, use the formula for parallel branches of equal value:

$$R_T = \frac{R}{N}$$

$$R_T = \frac{30}{2}$$

$$R_T = 15\Omega$$

Part C in Fig. 8-5, shows the equivalent circuit (for the series parallel circuit at Part A) with a total resistance of 15 ohms.

TV ANTENNA COUPLER PROJECT

Three resistors can be wired in a special TV antenna coupler circuit so that you can hook up two television sets to one antenna. To build this project, carefully follow the construction procedure while studying the diagram in Fig. 8-6.

Few parts are needed:

No.	Item
3	910 ohm resistors.
	300 ohm TV feed line.

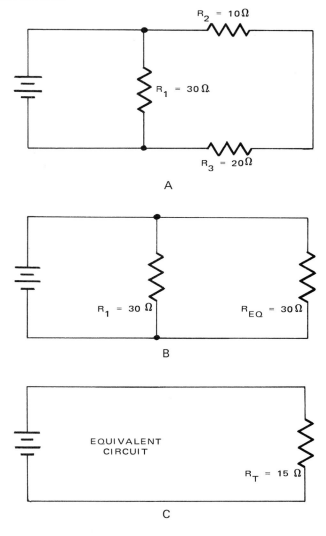

Fig. 8-5. Series parallel circuit has resistors of unequal value. A—First solve the series element, R_2 and R_3. B—Equivalent resistance is 30 ohms. C—Total resistance is 15 ohms.

CONSTRUCTION PROCEDURE

When soldering the connections, keep the resistor leads short and run standard TV feed line right up to the soldered joints. Pay close attention to the circuit diagram in Fig. 8-6.

1. Solder R_1 leads to the antenna leads, along with one feed line from each TV set antenna terminal.
2. Solder one lead of R_2 to one lead of R_1. Solder the other lead of R_2 to a TV feed line running between antenna terminals on TV set No. 1 and TV set No. 2.
3. Solder one lead of R_3 to other lead of R_1. Solder other lead of R_3 to TV feed line running between antenna terminals on TV set No. 1 and TV set No. 2.

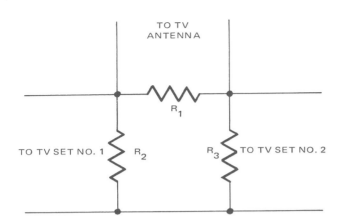

Fig. 8-6. Schematic shows how to hook up two television sets to one antenna. Resistors are 910 ohms each.

With this coupler, your need for a second TV antenna is eliminated. It also serves to isolate and cut down on inter-action between the two operating TV sets.

POWER SUPPLIES IN SERIES

At this point, we should look at what will happen if our power supplies are hooked up in series. See Part A in Fig. 8-7. Later, we will see how power supplies are used to provide different parts of our circuits. This can be done by means of two batteries or by using a *voltage divider* (to be covered later in this chapter).

The series parallel circuit shown in Part A in Fig. 8-7 can be solved for total voltage and total resistance in just a few simple steps. First, note that the power supplies *are* in series. This means that we can add the voltages of the two batteries and come up with the equivalent power supply shown in Part B:

$$E_{EQ} = E_1 + E_2$$
$$E_{EQ} = 12 + 12 = 24V$$

Next, take the two resistors in series and figure their equivalent resistance as shown at Part C:

$$R_{EQ} = R_1 + R_2$$
$$R_{EQ} = 12 + 12 = 24\Omega$$

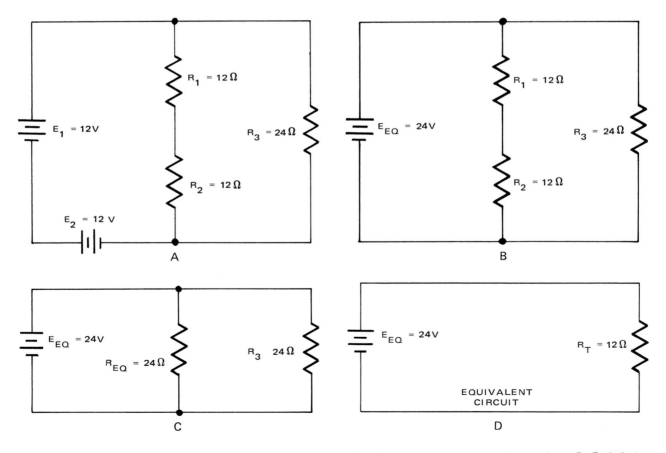

Fig. 8-7. Solve this circuit for total power supply and total resistance. A—Circuit has two power supplies and three resistors. B—Equivalent power supply is 24 volts. C—Equivalent resistance is 24 ohms. D—Total resistance is 12 ohms.

Then, solve for equivalent resistance of two resistors of equal value in parallel. This, in turn, will give us the total resistance of the equivalent circuit shown in Part D in Fig. 8-7:

$$R_T = \frac{R}{N} \qquad R_T = \frac{24}{2} \qquad R_T = 12\Omega$$

The answers to the questions concerning electrical values presented at Part A in Fig. 8-7 are: total voltage = 24V; total resistance = 12Ω.

CURRENT FLOW

You probably are asking yourself, "Why go through all this work?" The answer is: "We must use these methods to determine the total current flowing in any series parallel circuit."

Circuit analysis is just another way of saying that you must break down the full circuit network to determine the amount of current in each part. The same thing is true for finding the voltage drop across each part of the circuit.

Circuit analysis also reveals open circuits and short circuits. An open circuit occurs when the path for current is broken. This can occur accidentally or through the use of a switch. A short circuit is one which has practically no resistance. Therefore, the current will cause the fuse to blow or the circuit breaker to open.

Looking at Part A in Fig. 8-8, our circuit analysis starts with the power supply:

E = 24V

Next, we need to figure an equivalent resistance for the two resistors in series:

$$R_{EQ} = R_1 + R_2$$

$$R_{EQ} = 12 + 12 = 24\Omega$$

Then, use the formula for finding total resistance of parallel branches of equal value:

$$R_T = \frac{R}{N}$$

$$R_T = \frac{24}{2} = 12\Omega$$

We now have an equivalent circuit with a power supply of 24 volts and a total resistance of 12 ohms. See Part B. Using these values in a formula based on Ohm's Law, you can solve the circuit for total current (amperage) as shown at Part C:

$$I = \frac{E}{R} \qquad I = \frac{24}{12} = 2A$$

Total current, then, is 2 amps. This *does not* mean that 2 amps will be flowing in each branch of our circuit. It *does* mean that the generator must be able to supply

A

B

C

Fig. 8-8. Analyze this circuit for current output and amount of current through each element. A—Power supply is 24 volts. B—Total resistance is 12 ohms. C—Current output is 2 amps, with 1 amp flowing through each element of circuit.

2 amps to the circuit. With this information, you can go back and find the current in each branch:

$$I = \frac{E}{R_{EQ}} \quad \text{or} \quad I = \frac{E}{R_3}$$

$$I = \frac{24}{24} = 1A$$

CAPACITORS IN PARALLEL

We introduced you to capacitors in Chapter 4. At that time, we covered various types of capacitors and how they are built. You also saw one symbol for a capacitor. Now, you will see how they work in electrical circuits.

Part A in Fig. 8-9 shows two capacitors in parallel, having ratings of 30 microfarads (μF) and 40 microfarads. To get total capacitance, use the following formula for capacitors in parallel:

$$C_T = C_1 + C_2 + C_3 + \dots$$

In our example, this would result in the equivalent circuit shown at Part B in Fig. 8-9:

$$C_T = C_1 + C_2$$

$$C_T = 30 \ \mu F + 40 \ \mu F$$

$$C_T = 70 \ \mu F$$

Total capacitance of this equivalent circuit is 70 microfarads.

The formula for finding total capacitance of capacitors in parallel is much different than the formula for finding total resistance of resistors in parallel. It *is* very similar to the formula you used for resistors in series.

The reason why capacitors in parallel differ from resistors in parallel can be seen in Fig. 8-10. Remember, one of the things which increases capacitance is a larger plate area. When we have two capacitors in parallel, we have a greater number of plates and more electrons on the plates. Therefore, total capacitance (C_T) really means more plate area.

CAPACITOR SYMBOLS

A popular capacitor symbol is shown at Part A in Fig. 8-11. You can see that this is an easier symbol to draw than the one in Fig. 4-26. For this reason, you will find the simpler one used on many schematics.

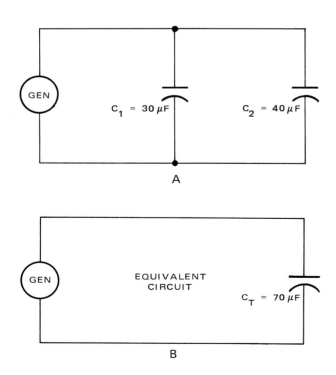

Fig. 8-9. Find total capacitance of this circuit. A—Two capacitors of unequal value in parallel. B—Total capacitance is 70 μF.

Fig. 8-10. When capacitors are placed in parallel, capacitance in circuit increases because plate area is larger.

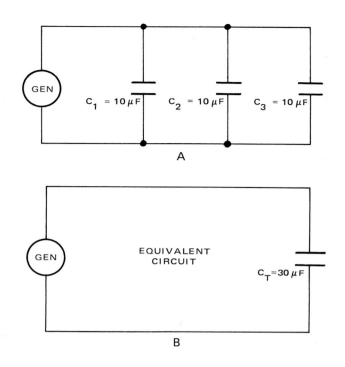

Fig. 8-11. Solve this circuit for total capacitance. A—Three 10 µF capacitors in parallel. B—Total capacitance is 30 µF.

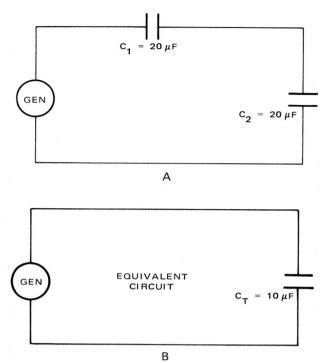

Fig. 8-12. Analyze this series circuit for total capacitance. A—Two 20 µF capacitors in series. B—Total capacitance is 10 µF.

To find the total capacitance in the circuit presented at Part A, Fig. 8-11, use this formula:

$$C_T = C_1 + C_2 + C_3$$

$$C_T = 10 + 10 + 10 = 30 \text{ µF}$$

Therefore, the equivalent circuit shown at Part B in Fig. 8-11, would have a total capacitance of 30 microfarads.

CAPACITORS IN SERIES

If we have a circuit with capacitors hooked up in series, how would you find the equivalent circuit? As you might expect, we would use a formula similar to the one for finding the total resistance of resistors in parallel:

$$\frac{1}{C_T} = \frac{1}{C_1} + \frac{1}{C_2} = \frac{1}{C_3} + \dots$$

The circuit shown at Part A in Fig. 8-12 has two capacitors in series, each having a rating of 20 microfarads. To find the total capacitance in this series circuit:

$$\frac{1}{C_T} = \frac{1}{C_1} + \frac{1}{C_2}$$

$$\frac{1}{C_T} = \frac{1}{20} + \frac{1}{20}$$

$$\frac{1}{C_T} = \frac{2}{20} + \frac{1}{10}$$

Invert both sides of the equation:

$$C_T = 10 \text{ µF}$$

Therefore, total capacitance of this equivalent circuit, Part B, Fig. 8-12, is 10 microfarads.

DISTANCE BETWEEN PLATES

You may wonder why capacitors placed in series will offer less capacitance than a single capacitor. The reason is quite simple. In Fig. 8-13, you can see that the distance between the outer plates of C_1 and C_2 will increase when placed in series. This, in turn, will lower the capacitance of the circuit.

In Chapter 4, we established that an increase in the distance between the plates of capacitors will lower the capacitance. One way manufacturers do this is by putting a thicker dielectric between the plates. Another way is by making the plates adjustable. In later chapters, we will be working with an adjustable unit known as a "variable capacitor." By adjustment, you can either increase or decrease the distance between plates, and thereby lower or raise the capacitance of the capacitor.

SERIES PARALLEL CAPACITORS

If you have a circuit with capacitors in a series parallel network, you can solve it for total capacitance by the same

Fig. 8-13. When capacitors are placed in series, capacitance in circuit decreases because distance between plates increases.

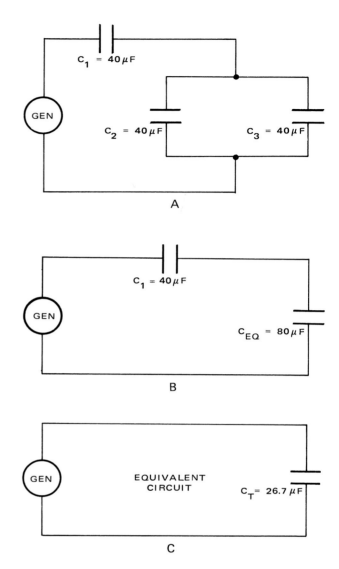

Fig. 8-14. Find total capacitance of this circuit. A—Three capacitors of equal value. B—Equivalent capacitance of capacitors in parallel is 80 μF. C—Total capacitance is 26.7 μF.

methods used to handle series and parallel circuit problems. Looking at Part A in Fig. 8-14, you have a circuit with three capacitors, each with a rating of 40 microfarads. To solve this circuit for total capacitance, first work on the parallel element.

Use this formula for capacitors in parallel:

$$C_T = C_2 + C_3$$

$$C_T = 40 \ \mu F + 40 \ \mu F$$

$$C_T = 80 \ \mu F$$

The equivalent capacitance of the two capacitors in parallel is 80 microfarads, as shown at Part B in Fig. 8-14.

Then, use this formula for capacitors in series:

$$\frac{1}{C_T} = \frac{1}{C_1} + \frac{1}{C_{EQ}}$$

$$\frac{1}{C_T} = \frac{1}{40} + \frac{1}{80}$$

$$\frac{1}{C_T} = \frac{2}{80} + \frac{1}{80} = \frac{3}{80}$$

Invert both sides of the equation:

$$C_T = 26.7 \ \mu F$$

Total capacitance of this equivalent circuit is 26.7 microfarads, as shown at Part C in Fig. 8-14.

As you can see, total capacitance is smaller than the capacitance of any capacitor in the circuit. If you solve for total capacitance and the answer is larger than the value of the individual capacitors, you have made a mistake and must refigure to find your error. Again, this is just like resistors in series parallel problems which you solved earlier.

CAPACITOR/RESISTOR COMBINATIONS

You know how to find equivalent circuits for both capacitor networks and resistor networks. The next question would seem to be: "What happens when capacitors and resistors are combined in the same circuit?" Circuits of this type cannot be solved by means of the simple formulas we have used so far. You must cover additional material before you can solve this type of network. When we get to Chapter 13, you will be shown how to do it.

ELECTRIC COMBINATION LOCK PROJECT

A toggle switch can be used in a number of ways. Basically, it is designed to open or close an electrical circuit by a flip of the little switch lever. However, by wiring five toggle switches in series, you can make an electric combination lock.

Make up the circuit by assembling the following parts as pictured in Fig. 8-15:

No.	Item
5	Toggle switches.
1	Right angle plate.
	Insulated primary ignition wiring.

CONSTRUCTION PROCEDURE

The trick to setting up the circuit is to mix up the switch connections; do not have all switch levers "on" in the same position. One good automotive application for this electric combination lock is to wire it into a dash-mounted ignition switch circuit to foil car thieves. Proceed as follows:

1. Wire the switches together, using your own code for "off/on" position of the switch levers. See Fig. 8-15.
2. Disconnect the negative cable from the car battery.
3. Disconnect the primary wire from the battery terminal of the ignition switch.

4. Run a wire from the disconnected ignition switch wire to the open terminal on the No. 1 toggle switch.
5. Run a wire from the battery terminal of the ignition switch to the open terminal on No. 5 toggle switch.
6. All switches have to be "closed" to activate the circuit.

Only the person knowing the right combination of lever positions can complete the circuit to the ignition switch.

You also can use a toggle switch setup like this to create an interesting game. Install a 6V battery and a lamp or buzzer in the circuit, Fig. 8-16. Then, see who can flip the switches the least number of times to light the lamp or sound the buzzer. Do not solder the connections, because you will want to change the combination and restart the game.

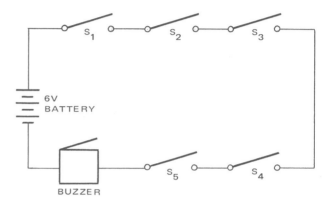

Fig. 8-16. The electric combination lock can be used in this buzzer game. Again, the right combination of switch lever positions will complete the circuit and sound the buzzer.

Fig. 8-15. Pictured is an electric combination lock made by wiring five toggle switches and assembling them on a right angle plate. Schematic shows the hookup for an automobile ignition switch. (Project by William Miller)

GROUNDS

We have mentioned the term "ground" in previous chapters. *A ground is an electrical connection between a circuit and the earth or a metallic object that takes the place of the earth.*

Fig. 8-17 shows two types of ground symbols that normally appear on drawings. At times, these symbols are used interchangeably. There *is* a difference, but all you need to know at this point is that a ground is a path for current.

Fig. 8-18 is a schematic of a signaling system that can be used to turn a light on and off. Trace the ground circuit from the power supply through a wire to the load (a lamp). Note, too, that two ground symbols are used, indicating that the ground circuit is to act as a second wire in the system. When the switch is closed, Fig. 8-18, the circuit is completed and the lamp lights.

Radios and television sets also use this arrangement. In these applications, the chassis serves as the ground circuit.

ONE WIRE SYSTEM

Automobiles use a *one wire electrical system.* This means that the frame of the vehicle serves as a path for ground, rather than having a return wire to the power supply. The one wire system is easier to trace and simpler to service. Fig. 8-19 illustrates a series circuit of this type. Fig. 8-20 shows a parallel circuit.

All U.S. car manufacturers ground the negative post of the battery. Some manufacturers of imported cars use the positive ground principle. Regardless of which system is used, all automotive electrical circuits are completed, either directly or indirectly, by using the car frame as the second wire or path.

Fig. 8-21 gives some of the electrical circuits you can find on a car. The ground paths for the headlights and taillights are shown. The ground path for the alternator is through its housing to the engine, then to the engine ground strap attached to the frame or to the negative post of the battery.

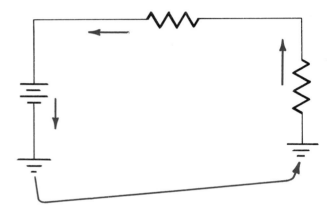
Fig. 8-19. A simple one wire series circuit. Note path from ground connection-to-ground connection.

GROUND   CHASSIS GROUND

Fig. 8-17. Two ground symbols used on circuit drawings.

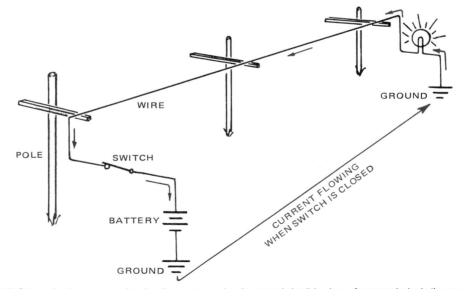

WIRE

POLE

SWITCH

GROUND

BATTERY

GROUND

CURRENT FLOWING WHEN SWITCH IS CLOSED

Fig. 8-18. Schematic shows a one wire signaling system, using the ground circuit in place of a second wire in the system.

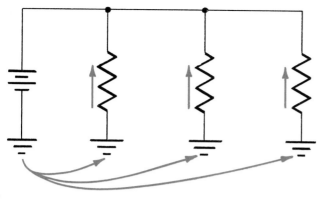

Fig. 8-20. A simple one wire parallel circuit. Note multiple paths to ground in this application.

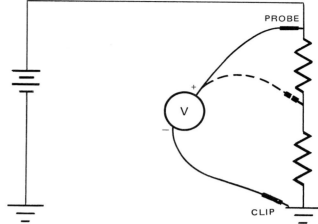

Fig. 8-22. One wire system speeds voltmeter checks for continuity and voltage drop.

There are some real advantages in using the one wire system. It simplifies test procedures. Note in Fig. 8-22 that you can make voltage checks by clamping the negative lead of your voltmeter to a good ground point. Then, use one hand to move the second probe to various points in the circuit to take voltage readings.

The one wire system has other drawing and testing advantages. For example, Fig. 8-23 shows two different ways of drawing the same simple series circuit. By removing the wire from the right side of this circuit and replacing it with ground symbols, you will have the one wire system shown at Part A in Fig. 8-24. Note that polarity is marked at either end of each resistor. This is helpful when making voltage drop tests.

POLARITY

When the polarity of a resistor is indicated on a drawing, it is done only with respect to the polarity of the power supply. See Fig. 8-24. Part A shows that resistor R_1 has a positive side and a negative side. The side of R_1 nearer the positive post of the battery is marked plus (+), and the side farther away is marked minus (−).

Resistor R_2 is marked in just the opposite way, because the negative post of the battery is closer to it. Therefore,

Fig. 8-21. Automobiles use frame for grounding the various electrical circuits.

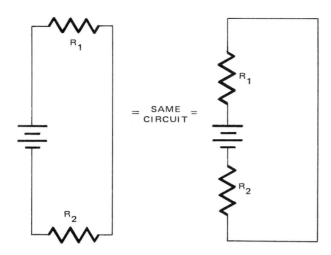

Fig. 8-23. A simple series circuit is shown with resistors placed at different points. Resistance values remain the same.

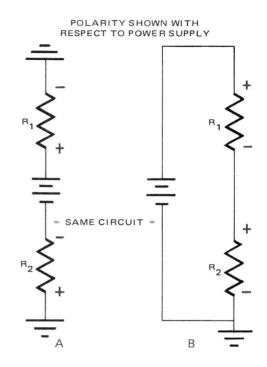

Fig. 8-24. This series circuit has polarity indicated at ends of resistors. A—One wire system grounded at two points. B—Complete circuit with return wire and ground connection.

the polarity of this resistor is also marked with respect to the polarity of the power supply.

If you reconnect this circuit without the grounds, you will see the polarities shown at Part B in Fig. 8-24. Again, the two ends of each resistor are labeled with respect to the power supply. Although the lower end of R_1 is marked minus (–), and the upper end of R_2 is marked plus (+), there is no difference between these points.

To illustrate how this form of polarity works, look at the simple series circuit in Fig. 8-25. If you measure the voltage between point A and point B, you will get 15 volts. Likewise, the voltage between B and C will be 15 volts. The voltage across both resistors from A to C will read 30 volts (voltage of the power supply).

A resistor always causes a drop in voltage if there is current through it. In Fig. 8-25, you dropped 15 volts

across R_2 and its polarity is minus (–) on the bottom and plus (+) on the top. Although the bottom of R_1 is marked minus (–) with respect to the top, it still has a voltage of 15 volts across it.

REFERENCE POINT

In order to have a better understanding of voltage drop, we could pick some reference point and call it zero.

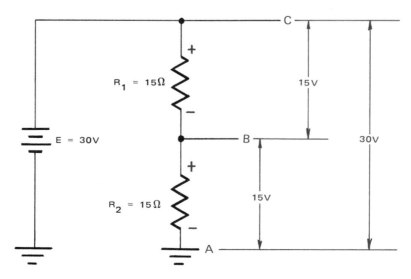

Fig. 8-25. Values are given for voltage drop tests taken across each resistor in turn, then across both resistors. Also note polarity of the resistors.

Everything above zero would be positive, while everything below zero would be negative.

This reference point can be compared with 0 deg. on a Celsius thermometer. See Fig. 8-26. Again, any reading above zero is positive; below zero is negative. You could get a reading of 20 deg. above the reference point (20 deg. C) or 20 deg. below the reference point (–20 deg. C). In this application, the reference point is where water freezes. With voltages, you also can establish a reference point.

In Fig. 8-27, you have a power supply with a 30 volt potential. By grounding the circuit at the reference point, you can make voltage measurements in relation to that point. *In this situation, the ground is said to be a reference point from which voltage measurements are made.*

If you measure between point B and point A, you will get a reading of –10 volts. If you measure from B to C, you will get a reading of +10 volts. Finally, measuring from B to D, you will get a reading of +20 volts.

Note that from point A to point D, the potential difference is still 30 volts (which matches our power supply). Since you are using the ground as a reference point, you will get both negative and positive voltages from the same power supply. This is the whole idea behind a *voltage divider.*

VOLTAGE DIVIDER

If you want to have different voltages for different parts of a circuit, you can construct a voltage divider. In effect, a voltage divider is nothing more than a series parallel circuit.

You cannot design a good voltage divider without first looking at the load resistance. Note in Fig. 8-27 that if you make a voltage divider with three 15 ohm resistors, you would get 10 volts drop across each one. However, as soon as you add another resistor (load), Fig. 8-28, there

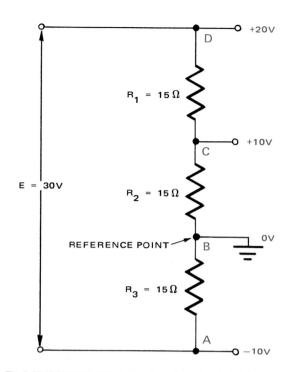

Fig. 8-27. Voltage values are given for voltage drop tests taken across resistors from A to B (–10V), B to C (+10V) and B to D (+20V). Note that the circuit is grounded at reference point B.

Fig. 8-28. Three 15 ohm resistors and one 15 ohm load resistor serve as a voltage divider that routes different voltages to different parts of the circuit.

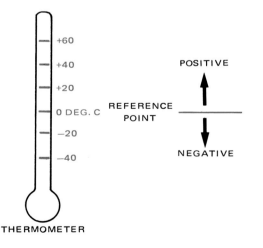

Fig. 8-26. On a Celsius thermometer scale, the zero mark is considered the reference point. All readings above zero are positive, all readings below zero are negative.

is a further change. The load resistor serves to drop the total resistance of the lower part of the voltage divider. Use this formula for finding the equivalent resistance of resistors of equal value in a parallel circuit:

$$R_{EQ} = \frac{R}{N}$$

$$R_{EQ} = \frac{15}{2} = 7.5\Omega$$

The equivalent resistance of these two 15 ohm resistors in the lower part of the voltage divider is 7.5 ohms. As a result of this resistance change, what will happen to the current in the circuit?

Remember that as resistance goes down, current goes up. Therefore, with the addition of the load resistor, the circuit will now carry higher amperage. It is important, then, when constructing a voltage divider circuit, to watch both resistance values and current values. Review Fig. 8-28 to make sure you understand how a voltage divider works.

WHEATSTONE BRIDGE

Of special use in series parallel circuits is a device known as a *wheatstone bridge*. It is used to find the value of an unknown resistor in a circuit. Much more accurate than an ohmmeter, a wheatstone bridge will give values within very close tolerances.

Fig. 8-29 shows a simple series parallel circuit with four resistors. Find the current flowing in I_1 and I_2:

$$I_1 = \frac{E}{R_{EQ}}$$

$$I_1 = \frac{132V}{12\Omega + 32\Omega}$$

$$I_1 = \frac{132V}{44\Omega}$$

$$I_1 = 3A$$

$$I_2 = \frac{E}{R_{EQ}}$$

$$I_2 = \frac{132V}{9\Omega + 27\Omega}$$

$$I_2 = \frac{132V}{36\Omega}$$

$$I_2 = 3.66A$$

Now that you have determined the current value in each branch, Fig. 8-30, find the voltage drop across each resistor.

$$V_{R_1} = I \times R_1$$

$$V_{R_1} = 3A \times 12\Omega$$

$$V_{R_1} = 36V$$

$$V_{R_2} = I \times R_2$$

$$V_{R_2} = 3A \times 32\Omega$$

$$V_{R_2} = 96V$$

$$V_{R_3} = I \times R_3$$

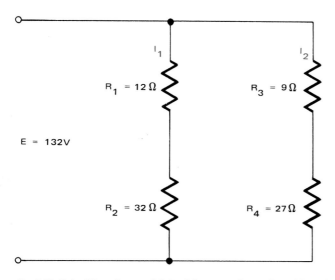

Fig. 8-29. Solve this series parallel circuit for current flow at I_1 and I_2. Use the formula $I = \frac{E}{R_{EQ}}$.

Fig. 8-30. With the amount of current established, next determine voltage drop across each resistor by using the formula $V_R = I \times R$.

$$V_{R_3} = 3.66A \times 9\Omega$$

$$V_{R_3} = 32.94V$$

For our purposes, round off 32.94V to 33V.

$$V_{R_4} = I \times R_4$$

$$V_{R_4} = 3.66A \times 27\Omega$$

$$V_{R_4} = 98.82V$$

Call this 99 volts.

VOLTAGE DROP — WHEATSTONE BRIDGE

If you put the individual current values and voltage drops in the circuit shown in Fig. 8-30, what would you get for a voltage reading? You should expect the voltmeter to read 3 volts. Note that there is a 3 volt difference in potential between the 12 ohm resistor and the 9 ohm resistor. This same 3 volt potential exists across the two lower resistors.

The principle behind a wheatstone bridge is to get the voltmeter to read zero. A zero reading would mean there is no difference in potential between the elements of this resistor bridge. If you could redraw the circuit, and make one resistor an unknown value, you would have the setup shown in Fig. 8-31. With a little shifting around of Ohm's Law formulas, you would find that the following ratio exists:

$$\frac{R_1}{R_2} = \frac{R_3}{R_x}$$

If you substitute known values into this formula, you will get:

$$\frac{R_1}{R_2} = \frac{R_3}{R_x}$$

$$\frac{12\Omega}{32\Omega} = \frac{9\Omega}{x}$$

$$12x = 288$$

$$x = 24\Omega$$

This formula shows that if our unknown resistor had a value of 24 ohms, this circuit would be balanced. In both cases, the voltages on each side would be balanced.

In actual practice, three resistors are assembled in one unit, along with an adjustable resistor and a galvanometer. With the sensitive galvanometer, you can get a much more accurate balance in resistor matching process. Fig. 8-32 shows a typical circuit for a finished wheatstone bridge.

CLIMB THE LADDER GAME PROJECT

Here is a game you can make, using an electrical power supply, two pieces of copper tubing, and strips cut from old cans. See Fig. 8-33. Wire the metal strips so that it is difficult, yet possible, to move the copper plugs from hole to hole without breaking the circuit to the bulb.

Fig. 8-31. Wheatstone bridge concept: Voltmeter should read zero when voltages are balanced on each side of circuit. Value of resistor R$_x$ should be 24 ohms.

Fig. 8-32. Typical wheatstone bridge setup: Variable resistor R$_2$ can be adjusted to obtain desired balance of voltages in circuit. This, in turn, pinpoints value of resistor R$_x$.

No.	Item
1	1/3 in. plywood base, 4 in. x 10 in.
2	1/4 in. plywood sides, 2 in. x 10 in.
20	Brads.
2	Cans cut into 20 1/4 in. x 1 1/4 in. strips.
2	Lengths of copper tubing, 1/2 in. x 3 in.
1	Flashlight bulb.
1	6 ft. length of 18 gage wire.
1	6V battery.

A

CONSTRUCTION PROCEDURE

Build the game as follows:

1. Drill ten 1/2 in. holes in plywood base. See Part A in Fig. 8-33.
2. Drill one 1/4 in. hole for bulb.
3. Nail 20 metal strips to underside of base, alongside holes as at Part B.
4. Squeeze one end of each piece of copper tubing to keep it from falling through hole. See Part A.
5. Bend up strips as shown at Part B.
6. Make a small hole in tail end of each strip for wires.
7. Cut wire to lengths shown at Part C and insert wires in holes in strips.
8. Hook up battery and bulb.
9. Test all connections for continuity, then solder.
10. Nail plywood sides to base.
11. Finish to suit.

You can use a step-down transformer, 110V ac to 6V ac, as a power supply for this project. If you make it so that it can be removed, you will be able to use it for other projects. A dropping resistor can be wired in for a 3 volt bulb, if used.

To play the climb the ladder game, allow the player to move only one hole at a time up to the bulb. By using the right combination of moves, the player should be able to reach the bulb without turning the light off.

SUMMARY

By using several simple formulas, you can reduce any series parallel circuit to its simplest form to determine current and voltages.

For easier reading, circuit drawings should be laid out with the top of the schematic being positive and the bottom being negative. The power source should be on the left side and the output or load on the right. Circuits can also be drawn with the power source at the top but the load should still be on the right-hand side.

When solving series parallel problems, the equivalent resistance of the circuit should be found first. That information can then be used to calculate the total current for the circuit.

B

L_1 POWER SUPPLY

WIRING TO SUIT PUZZLE

C

Fig. 8-33. Climb the ladder game. A—Copper plugs must be moved from hole to hole without breaking the circuit to the bulb. B—Underside of game board reveals metal strips and wiring. C—Drawing shows one possible series of hookups for wiring game board. (Project by Randy Schafer)

Capacitors wired in parallel increase the capacitance of a circuit. The formula $C_T = C_1 + C_2 + C_3$ is similar to the formula for adding resistors in series. The formula for capacitors in series is similar to that used for resistors in parallel.

A one-wire system is used to connect the electrical components on an automobile. The metal body of the car is used to complete the electrical connection in place of a return wire. This is why cars, which are subject to rusting, may lose some of their circuits as they age. The rust prevents completed circuits or causes added resistance that can dim lights or cause other problems.

KEY WORDS AND TERMS

Ground	Total capacitance
Network	Variable capacitor
One wire electrical system	Voltage divider
Rules of construction	Wheatstone bridge
Series parallel circuit	

TEST YOUR KNOWLEDGE

Do not write in this book. Write your answers on a separate sheet of paper.

1. A _____ is another name for a circuit having series and parallel branches.
2. *True or False?* The current in a series parallel circuit is the same in all parts of the circuit.
3. Explain one of the methods used in drawing circuit layouts to make the circuits easier to read.
4. What is an equivalent circuit for a series parallel circuit?
5. If two 3 volt power supplies are connected in series, the net result will be either _____ or _____.

6. If two capacitors of 4 microfarads are connected in series, what is the total capacitance? Show your work.
7. The larger the plate area on a capacitor, the _____ capacitance.
8. Draw at least two symbols for a capacitor.
9. If two capacitors of 4 microfarads are connected in parallel, what is the total capacitance? Show your work.
10. An increase in the distance between plates in a capacitor will result in _____.
11. What is a short circuit?
12. What is an open circuit?
13. What is a ground?
14. What is a wheatstone bridge used for?

ACTIVITIES

1. Why do you see some cars with a black strap hanging down to the ground? Cars are not produced with these straps. Why not?
2. Modern electric drills are made with a 3 prong plug, one of which is a ground. Why do some people cut off the ground prong? Is that really the safe thing to do?
3. Is there a difference between a negative or positive ground found on different cars? Which system is better?
4. What will happen if you are not careful when using jumper cables on cars with weak batteries? Will European and U.S. cars be "jumped" in the same way?
5. Metrics are used in most electrical measurements. Why did it take so long for other trades to convert to the metric system?
6. Why are there so many ways of drawing the same symbols?
7. Some people claim that they check for voltage by using their fingers. What could happen to those people?
8. Make a list of some of the places where grounds are used.

How many types of meters can you find in this control room? (Georgia Power Co.)

9

Meters

LEARNING OBJECTIVES

After studying this chapter, you will be able to:
- Interpret the value of a meter reading based on the position of the range switches.
- Connect meter probes in the circuit in correct and safe fashion so as to get the reading desired.
- Explain the purpose of the mirror on the meter face.
- Judge which portion of the meter to use for the most accurate reading.
- Describe the purpose and use of the *Left-Hand Rule*.

In this chapter, we will study two types of meters. First, we will discuss pointer type meters (also called analog meters), Fig. 9-1, then, we will discuss digital readout meters, Fig. 9-2. *These meters are sensitive instruments used to measure and indicate electrical values.*

POINTER TYPE METERS

A pointer type meter has a calibrated dial (face with marked values) and a needle that "points" to the value of the electrical unit under test. The meter shown in Fig. 9-3 will measure current and voltage.

Pointer type meters are used in many fields. Auto technicians use them to make tests and measurements on automobile electrical systems. Most cars are powered by a 12V battery and an electronic device called an *alternator*. All circuits are dc, so meters are necessary to help pinpoint the source of electrical problems. Without meters,

Fig. 9-2. Compact digital multimeter displays an exact reading of the test result.

Fig. 9-1. Cross section of a typical pointer type meter. (AC Spark Plug, Div., General Motors Corp.)

Fig. 9-3. This pointer type meter used by auto technicians will measure current (amps) and voltage.

technicians would lose valuable time when troubleshooting or making adjustments on customers' cars.

Pointer type meters are also used by electricians in industrial plants, by television repair technicians, and by anyone who fixes house wiring, dishwashers, ranges, clothes dryers, furnaces, and air conditioning units. Even when products are manufactured, meters are used to make sure the products pass inspection before they are sold.

DIGITAL READOUT METERS

Digital readout meters "spell out" the specific value of the electrical unit under test, Fig. 9-2. This type of meter has some special uses, such as computerized automobile engine analyzers, exhaust emission testers, and digital readouts on the instrument panels of cars, Fig. 9-4.

One advantage digital readout meters have over pointer type meters is that they are accurate within 0.1 percent. Most people cannot read a pointer type meter with anywhere near that degree of accuracy. Both meters, however, hook up with circuits much the same way.

SEGMENTED DISPLAYS

One type of digital readout has groups of seven small segments that form a number on the meter face according to which segments light, Fig. 9-5. In this way, all numbers from

Fig. 9-5. Portable digital multimeter has seven segments per digit. Illuminated segments form numbers. (Weston Instruments, Inc.)

zero through nine can be shown by lighting up the proper segments. For example, numbers two and six would light up as shown in Fig. 9-6. Number eight lights up the entire seven segments. Can you figure out the rest of the numbers?

AMMETER

In earlier chapters, we studied series circuits and parallel circuits. We also introduced you to the use of some meters. Now, the first meter we will study further is the ammeter.

Fig. 9-4. Digital readout on the instrument panel of a car. (Buick)

Fig. 9-6. Lighted segments on digital readout meter face form numbers 2 and 6.

Note in Fig. 9-7, that the ammeter is always connected in series with the power source and the load in order to measure load current. You also must pay attention to polarity (positive and negative terminals) when using an ammeter in a dc circuit (see CURRENT READINGS and VOLTAGE READINGS later in this chapter).

With an ammeter connected in series, it is possible to measure the amount of current flowing in the circuit. You know that automotive circuits are dc, because they are powered by a battery. Our next step in studying pointer type meters is to find out why they work in dc circuits.

HOW AMMETERS WORK

Most dc meters are constructed so that current flows through in one direction only. This is why they are called *dc* or *direct current* meters.

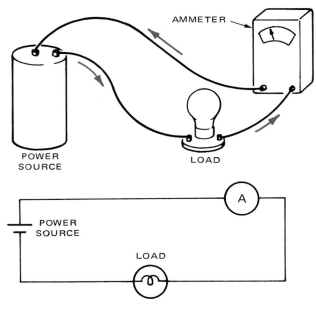

Fig. 9-7. An ammeter is always connected in series with the power source and load.

When direct current flows in a wire, it only goes in one direction. We also know that when current flows, a magnetic field is created. You can prove this by setting up a metal filings experiment similar to the one performed earlier. In preparing for this experiment, however, we will put a current-carrying wire through a piece of paper. As a result, the magnetic field will look like the one you see in Fig. 9-8. Typically, it will be made up of circles around the wire. The only problem with this magnetic field is that it is too weak to do much good. Therefore, we must find a way to make the field stronger. One of the easiest ways to do this is to wrap the wire into the shape of a coil.

To make the coil, wind the wire around an insulating material called a coil form, Fig. 9-9. Remember, insulation cannot stop the magnetic lines of force; they will cut right through it. This coil will make the magnetic field stronger, and form a field with a north pole and south pole.

If you took an ordinary magnet and placed it in the field, you would notice that the two poles always line up in a certain way. Then, if you pass a direct current through the wire in one direction, the north pole will be established at one particular end of the magnet. However, reverse the direction of current and the north pole will shift to the other end.

LEFT-HAND RULE

There is a way that you can tell in advance which end of the coil will have the north pole. If you point the fingers of your left hand in the direction the current flows, your thumb will point to the north pole. See Fig. 9-10. As a result, this has come to be known as the Left-Hand Rule. "Wrap a coil" and see for yourself.

Fig. 9-8. Metal filings show the magnetic field around a wire.

Fig. 9-9. Wire wrapped on a coil form provides the means for making a magnetic field experiment.

Fig. 9-10. The left-hand rule for coil polarity determines which end of the coil is the north pole.

Fig. 9-11. Major parts of a galvonometer. Note the coil and permanent horseshoe magnet.

GALVANOMETER

When we have a magnetic field, we will find attraction and repulsion. You learned this when working with magnets. Fig. 9-11 shows a *galvanometer,* which will detect and indicate small amounts of current. The place where the needle pivots for its swing back and forth is known as a jeweled movement. This movement is made a special way to help reduce friction in the meter. By doing this, the pointer on the meter will move very easily. The more friction in the movement, the less accuracy you get in your meter readings. Therefore, you must keep friction down to the smallest amount possible.

The galvanometer contains a permanent magnet with a north pole and a south pole. Note also, in Fig. 9-11, that there is a coil of wire between the poles. As current passes through the meter a magnetic field is created in the coil. This magnetic field will be affected by the north and south poles of the magnet. As soon as there is magnetic attraction or repulsion, the pointer on the meter will begin to move. The greater the flow of current through the coil, the more the pointer will swing. Fig. 9-12 will show you why this happens.

RANGE SELECTOR SWITCH

When making metered tests, it is possible to pass too much current through the meter. A surge of high current will drive the pointer right off the end of the scale and damage the meter movement. To prevent this from happening, many meters have a *range selector switch.* See Fig. 9-13. When working with unknown meter readings, you should start by adjusting the range selector switch to

Fig. 9-12. Meter movement occurs when the north pole of the horseshoe magnet repels the north pole of the coil.

127

Fig. 9-13. Meters with more than one scale of values generally have a range selector switch. Note the many positions on this digital readout meter switch. (AEMC Instruments)

Fig. 9-15. "Pegging the meter" occurs when the range selector switch is set too low and the pointer swings hard against right end of scale.

I.C. SAYS:

"Remember, when reading unknown currents or voltages, always start with the range selector switch in the highest position. This can prevent damage to your meter."

its highest value, Fig. 9-14. Then, reduce the switch setting until the meter is able to read the current.

This same operating technique is used for all electrical meters with multiple ranges. It will help prevent the problem known as *pegging the meter,* which refers to a test that buries the pointer of the meter off the end of the scale, Fig. 9-15. This mistreatment could ruin a meter or bend the pointer.

Some meters have a peg (small pin) at the end of the scale. When the pointer hits it, the meter is "pegged." The usual cause of pegging is failure to check the setting of the range selector switch.

HOW A RANGE SELECTOR WORKS

To get a better understanding of how a range selector works, see Fig. 9-16. Note that when you turn the range selector switch, you add another resistor to the circuit. This resistor is commonly called a *shunt.* It provides a parallel path for the current to flow and automatically positions the pointer in a different range of values.

Take a closer look at a shunt resistor in Fig. 9-17. Consider that the moving coil on a meter has a resistance of about 50 ohms, depending on the type of meter used. Since the coil can be rated at 50 ohms, a shunt can be placed in parallel to it. If the shunt is a resistor which has a value less than 50 ohms, and it is connected in parallel to the moving coil, more current will flow through the shunt than goes through the coil.

START TESTING WITH RANGE SELECTOR SWITCH AT HIGHEST VOLTAGE OR AMPERAGE

Fig. 9-14. The range selector switch on this multimeter provides several ranges for testing amperage, voltage, and resistance. Always read unknown values on highest range first.

By using this knowledge, it is possible to put a shunt in parallel to the coil that will allow us to select the range of current we wish to measure. To make it easier for the user, the

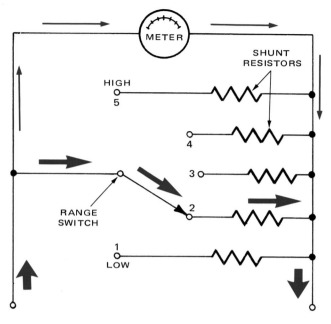

Fig. 9-16. A range selector switch operates on the principle of adding resistors when the switch is turned from range to range.

Fig. 9-17. A shunt resistor in a range selector switch provides a parallel path for current flow in a different range of values.

manufacturers mark the range on the front of the meter. In effect, when you turn the range selector switch, you are adding or subtracting a resistance in parallel with the meter movement. This also keeps the coil of the meter from being burned up by high current passing through it.

D'ARSONVAL MOVEMENT

The meter we have been looking at has a moving coil movement inside a horseshoe magnet, Fig. 9-18. This is known as a *D'Arsonval movement*. A D'Arsonval meter has the type of movement found in ammeters, voltmeters, ohmmeters, and wattmeters. A D'Arsonval meter has a jeweled movement to cut down the amount of friction and to ensure the accuracy of its readings.

While a D'Arsonval meter is reliably accurate, one problem is that the movement is very sensitive. If you drop the meter and the movement receives a shock, it is possible that the jeweled movement or the whole meter will be permanently damaged. In either case, the meter is ruined.

DAMPING SPRING

When using a meter to measure electrical current, it is possible that the sudden surge of current will swing the pointer right off the scale. To prevent this, a damping (shock absorbing) spring is attached to the pointer of the meter. See Fig. 9-18.

When current passes through the meter, the *damping spring* prevents the pointer from going full scale so fast that it will ruin the meter. Then, when current is removed from the meter, the damping spring keeps the pointer from dropping too quickly.

Fig. 9-18. A D'Arsonval meter movement features a moving coil inside a horseshoe magnet. The damping spring keeps the pointer from reacting too quickly to surges of current flow.

Damping action, then, is helpful in most electrical test procedures. However, it does create a problem if the flow of electrons lasts for only a few milliseconds. In this situation, a meter equipped with a damping spring will not react quickly enough to give accurate readings.

USING AMMETERS AND MULTIMETERS

Now that you have seen how meters are constructed, we will study their use. In order to take current readings with an ammeter or multimeter, you need to know: how to "hook up" to the electrical circuit; how to set the switches and connect the probes (if the meter is so equipped); and how to read the meter.

To hook up an ammeter to take current readings:

1. Open the circuit at some convenient point. The only way we can get readings is by making sure that current is flowing through our ammeter.
2. Connect the negative test lead of the meter (usually black) to the disconnected part of the circuit on the negative side of the power source. See Fig. 9-19. Connect the positive test lead (usually red) to the disconnected part of the positive side of the power source.
3. Read the meter.

I.C. WARNS:

"Remember that current will be flowing when this circuit is under test. Make sure that you do not touch any of the metal on the probes or you, too, will be in the circuit. Shock may result."

To hook up a multimeter to take current readings:

1. Open the circuit.
2. Set the function switch to the + dc position, as shown in Fig. 9-20.

3. Plug the two probes into their proper jacks: black to the negative terminal on the meter; red to the positive terminal on the meter.
4. Set the range selector switch to the correct position for the circuit under test. If you are working with unknown currents, place the switch in the highest position, Fig. 9-20. This will prevent you from "pegging the meter."
5. Touch the probes to the disconnected parts of the circuit, Fig. 9-21.
6. Read the meter. If necessary, lower the position of the range selector switch until you are able to get a reading.

READING THE METER SCALES

Reading the current value scales on a multimeter calls for special instructions. If you use a multimeter to measure the number of milliamperes flowing in a given circuit, the pointer will move along the direct current (dc) scales shown in Fig. 9-22. To make it easier to read these current scales, we will look at that part of the meter face in Fig. 9-23.

Our multimeter has four possible ranges of current readings.

1. 500mA. Set the range selector switch to 500mA. Take a reading on the scale ending with 50, then multiply this meter reading by 10. In the example shown in Fig. 9-24, the actual current value would be $23 \times 10 = 230mA$.
2. 100mA. Set the range selector switch to 100mA. Take a reading on the scale ending with 10, then multiply this meter reading by 10. In the example shown at

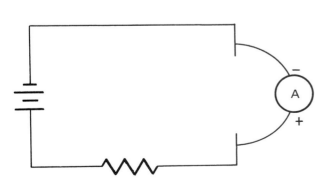

Fig. 9-19. Schematic shows hookup of ammeter in series with circuit: open circuit; connect meter test leads; read meter.

Fig. 9-20. To read current on a multimeter; connect probes to proper jacks; set function switch; set range selector switch; connect meter leads into circuit; read correct scale on meter.

Fig. 9-21. Schematic shows correct hookup of multimeter test leads for measuring current flow (in amps or milliamps).

SCALES USED TO READ
DIRECT CURRENT FLOW

Fig. 9-22. Arrows point to scales used to read direct current test
results in amps or milliamps.

FOR 100 mA, 10 mA
and 1 mA READINGS

FOR 500 mA
READINGS

Fig. 9-23. Read dc milliamps on scale that corresponds with range
selector switch setting.

4. 1mA. Set the range selector switch to 1mA. Take a
reading on the scale ending with 10, then multiply
this meter reading by .10. In the example shown at
Part C in Fig. 9-25, the actual current value would be
$4.6 \times .10 = .46$mA.

METER READING TIPS

In addition to reading the correct scale on a meter, there
are some other reading tips worth noting. In Fig. 9-26, for
example, a small mirror is located behind the pointer of the
meter. *To read this meter accurately, you must position
yourself so that the pointer and its reflection in the mirror
line up.* If you are able to see the reflection, you are not in

Part A in Fig. 9-25, the actual current value would be
$4.6 \times 10 = 46$mA.

3. 10mA. Set the range selector switch to 10mA. Take a
direct reading on the scale ending with 10. In the
example shown at Part B in Fig. 9-25, the current
value is 4.6mA.

230 mA

Fig. 9-24. Controls are set for 500 mA range as indicated on the scale ending with 50. Reading is 23 x 10 = 230 mA.

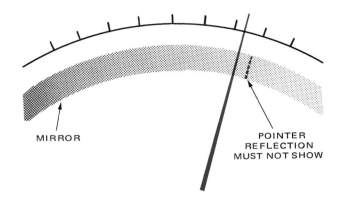

Fig. 9-26. Pointer on the meter must be sighted in a direct line and at right angles to the meter face.

the right position to take an accurate reading. When this happens, move your head in either direction until you cannot see the meter's reflection. Then, take the reading.

If the meter does not have a mirror behind the pointer, look straight down at the pointer and meter face for best readings.

When reading multimeters, the most accurate readings can be obtained when the pointer is near the center of the scale. Fig. 9-27 shows the range where most meters have

their best accuracy. Try to avoid reading the meter at either end of the scale. The reason why can be found by studying the meter face in Fig. 9-28. Note that the high numbers at the left end of the top scale are very close together. This is the upper range of the ohms scale. If you tried to take a reading in this area, you could make a mistake of several hundred ohms and not even know it.

MICROAMPERES

There are times when you will have to read currents in the microampere range (μA). Again, you can use the multimeter to get readings of these small values. Note in Fig. 9-29, however, that the position of one of our probes has been changed. The black test lead stays in the negative jack on the meter; the red test lead must be plugged into the 50 μA jack.

Continue making the settings by placing the range selector switch in the 50 μA position; leave the function

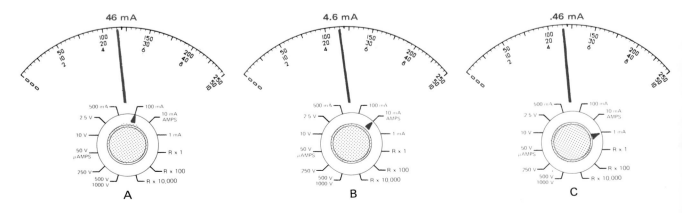

Fig. 9-25. The range selector switch settings for the scale ending with 10 are: A–199nA. B–10mA. C–1mA. The individual readings are: A–46mA. B–4.6mA. C–.46mA.

Fig. 9-27. Portion of meter face in color indicates area in which the most accurate readings may be obtained.

switch in the + dc position. Then, open the circuit and contact the disconnected parts with the probes while observing the correct polarity (positive probe to the positive side of the power source; negative probe to the negative side).

Take a reading on the meter scale ending with 50. This will be a direct reading in microamperes, as shown in Fig. 9-29. The reading on this test circuit is 34 μA.

AMPERES

It also is possible to use the multimeter for measuring current values up to 10 amps. To do this: connect the black test lead to the − 10 amp jack; connect the red test lead to the + 10 amp jack, Fig. 9-30. Move the range selector switch to AMPS, which also is the 10 mA position. Leave the function switch in the + dc position. Open the circuit and contact the disconnected parts with the probes while observing the correct polarity. Take a direct reading on the meter scale ending with 10. The reading on the test circuit shown in Fig. 9-30 is 6A.

NUMBERS ARE VERY CLOSE TOGETHER

Fig. 9-28. Circled area shows why you should try to avoid taking readings at the extreme ends of a meter scale.

Fig. 9-29. Range selector switch setting for a maximum of 50 microamps. Direct reading on the scale ending with 50 is 34 μA.

Fig. 9-30. Range selector switch setting for a maximum of 10 amps. Reading on scale ending with 10 is 6A.

I.C. SAYS:

"Be sure to turn off circuit power before you remove your meter leads. You do not want your body to become a resistor in parallel with your meter."

MULTIMETER APPLICATIONS

The *multimeter* has many uses or applications. You will find that a number of special dc ammeters are available for making specific tests. The ammeter shown in Fig. 9-31, for example, is used by auto technicians in taking battery cell tests. In this chapter, the multimeter has been used to measure current in amperes, milliamperes, and microamperes. It also can be used to measure voltage (volts) and resistance (ohms).

LIE DETECTOR PROJECT

How would you like to build a "poor man's" lie detector? One particular design is shown in Fig. 9-32. After you have created your own design, mount the parts in compact

Fig. 9-31. Special ammeters are available with either high or low range scales or with multiple scales. (Sun Electric Corp.)

fashion, keeping the connecting wires as short as possible. Procure the following materials:

No.	Item
1	15 volt battery (B_1).
1	Milliammeter (M_1).
1	12K resistor (R_1).
1	1.5K resistor (R_2).
1	SK3005 transistor (Q_1).
1	SPST switch (S_1).
2	Copper plates, about 4 sq. in. each.
1	Box of your design and wiring.
1	Battery holder.

CONSTRUCTION PROCEDURE

Assemble the materials as follows:
1. Mount the resistors and transistor in the box.
2. Attach the switch and milliammeter to the cover. Use epoxy to attach the copper plates.
3. Wire the lie detector circuit as shown in the schematic in Fig. 9-32.
4. After all other connections are made, install the battery between the switch and transistor.
5. Install the cover on the box.
6. Turn off the switch and zero the meter with the mechanical adjustment screw.

Turn on the switch and use a jumper wire to complete the circuit across the copper plates. You should get a reading of at least 0.8mA. If not, check the condition of

A

B

Fig. 9-32. Build this lie detector in your school shop. A–Completed project. B–Schematic shows hookup and arrangement of parts. B_1–Battery. Q_1–Transistor. $R_{1,2}$–Resistors. S_1–Switch. (Project by Mike O'Berski)

the dry cell. In effect, you now have a simple ohmmeter to check body resistance.

Once the project passes this test, have someone put a hand on the copper plates. Turn on the switch and ask a question. If the person tells a lie, moisture on the palm will reduce resistance and the meter needle will deflect to the right. When this happens, you will know that this person is telling a lie.

VOLTAGE READINGS

A voltmeter or multimeter is used to measure voltage values in an electrical circuit. When measuring voltage of unknown value, take the same approach you took when measuring current with an ammeter. Set the range selector switch to the highest position to avoid "pegging the meter."

When using a multimeter with controls similar to those shown in Fig. 9-33, start testing by setting the range selector switch at 500V. Set the function switch in the + dc position. Remember, too, that meters used in taking dc measurements are affected by polarity. Connect the meter in parallel to (across) the circuit, Fig. 9-34. Touch the positive probe of the meter to a connection on the positive side of the power source; touch the negative probe to a connection on the negative side.

VOLTMETER RANGES

Most voltmeters have one or two ranges or scales. Multimeters have many ranges. Fig. 9-35 shows a multimeter being used to measure the voltage drop across a resistor. Fig. 9-36 provides a closeup of the controls and simplified meter scales used to show voltage values.

Fig. 9-33. Always start testing for unknown voltage values by placing range selector switch in its highest position.

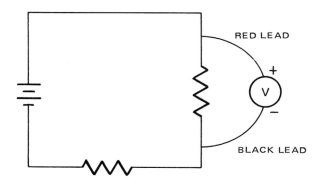

Fig. 9-34. Schematic shows a typical voltmeter hookup across the circuit. Always connect test leads so that voltmeter is in parallel to circuit.

Fig. 9-35. Proper hookup is shown for connecting a multimeter into a dc circuit to measure voltage drop across a resistor.

Our multimeter has five possible ranges of voltage readings.

Fig. 9-36. Scale used for multimeter reading shown in Fig. 9-35.
Actual voltage value is 25 x 10 = 250V.

1. 500V. Set the range selector switch to 500V. Take a reading on the scale ending with 50, then multiply the meter reading by 10. In the example shown in Fig. 9-36, the actual voltage would be 25 × 10 = 250V.
2. 250V. Set the range selector switch to 250V. Take a direct reading on the scale ending with 250.
3. 50V. Set the range selector switch to 50V. Take a direct reading on the scale ending with 50.
4. 10V. Set the range selector switch to 10V. Take a direct reading on the scale ending with 10.
5. 2.5V. Set the range selector switch to 2.5V. Take a reading on the scale ending with 250, then multiply the meter reading by .01, or move the decimal two places to the left.

Example: Set the selector switch in 2.5V position.

Reading on 250V scale is 235.0

235.0 × .01 = 2.350 or

2.35 Volts

I.C. WARNS:

"Do not touch any meter leads or any part of an electrical circuit unless you are absolutely sure the power is off. It only takes about 0.1 amp to kill you. To get that amperage through your arm, across your heart and out your other arm takes about 30 volts. Before you touch anything electrical, make sure that the power supply is turned off. Otherwise, you run the risk of electrocution."

ALTERNATING CURRENT READINGS

The multimeter you have been using has two sets of scales marked dc and ac. The dc scale, of course, stands for direct current electricity. This is the scale you have referred to in all your amperage and voltage tests. The ac scale stands for alternating current electricity.

In Chapter 10, we will fully discuss alternating current (ac). For now, a couple of explanatory notes are in order. Possibly you noticed that the function switch on the multimeter has an ac position. To take both current and voltage readings in ac circuits, the function switch should be moved to the ac position. Later, you will learn that polarity is not important when hooking up your meter to an ac circuit.

VOLTAGE-POLARITY CHECK PROJECT

There will be times when you want to check whether a circuit has ac or dc voltage and a meter is not handy. With the voltage-polarity checker shown in Fig. 9-37, you can check for ac, dc, and polarity (if circuit is dc). You can check circuits in the range of 110 to 480 volts. Higher voltages will cause *arcing* in the neon lamp.

Procure the following parts:

No.	Item
1	NE 51 neon lamp.
1	220K, 1 watt resistor.
2	Probes.
3	1′ lengths, AWG 18 insulated wire.

Attach a probe to each of two lengths of wire. Connect the other end of one wire to the resistor; connect the end of the other wire to the neon lamp. Connect a third length of wire to the resistor and lamp.

TEST PROCEDURE

To check voltage, touch the probes across the circuit to be tested. The lamp will light when voltage is present. If both electrodes in the lamp glow, you have an ac power source. If only one electrode glows, the voltage is dc. When only one lamp electrode lights, it will be on the side of the lamp connected to the probe touching a negative point in the system. Therefore, you also have a polarity check on dc circuits.

OHM READINGS

As you have seen, a multimeter can be used to measure amps and volts. It also can be used to measure ohms

Fig. 9-37. Voltage-polarity checker project. Top. Arrangement of parts. Bottom. Test of dc circuit will light lamp electrode touching negative point in circuit.

(resistance) in an electrical circuit. For this reason, a multimeter usually is called a VOM (volt-ohm-milliammeter).

Note that the range selector switch on the multimeter shown in Fig. 9-38 has positions marked R × 1, R × 100, and R × 10,000. These settings tell you that the resistance (R) value on the top scale of the VOM must be multiplied by either 1, 100, or 10,000, depending upon the position of the range selector switch.

ZERO THE METER

When a multimeter is going to be used for measuring resistance, the first thing to do is *zero the meter*, Fig. 9-38. To zero the pointer on the ohms scale, simply take the red probe (in the positive jack) and touch it to the black probe (in the negative jack). Note that when the probes touch, the pointer will swing to the right, toward the zero on the top scale of the meter.

If the pointer does not stop exactly on zero, you will have to adjust the "zero ohms pot" (potentiometer) until the pointer does align with the zero mark. See Fig. 9-38. The zero ohms adjustment must be made each time you move the range selector switch to a new resistance position. This will ensure an accurate resistance test reading every time. If you do not zero the ohmmeter, your reading will be off the same amount that your meter is out of adjustment.

READING THE METER

With the pointer set to zero ohms, you can proceed with your resistance test. You have a single top scale to

read on the multimeter and the range selector switch has three positions: R × 1, R × 100, and R × 10,000.

Consider these settings and readings:

1. If the range selector switch is in the R × 1 position and the pointer on the meter is in the position shown in Fig. 9-39, what is the resistance value in ohms? Note that the pointer is between 5 and 10 ohms. If you count the major marks between 5 and 10, you will find that the actual meter reading is 8 ohms. Since the selector switch is set on R × 1, then the ohms value is 8 × 1 = 8.

2. If the range selector switch is in the R × 100 position, then the ohms value is 8 × 100 = 800.

3. If the range selector switch is in the R × 10,000 position, then the ohms value is 8 × 10,000 = 80,000.

Take a group of resistors and make your own resistance measurements. The only way you can be sure that you are using the meter correctly is by practicing.

Fig. 9-38. To zero your ohmmeter, touch one probe with the other and adjust the zero ohms control until the pointer aligns with zero.

Fig. 9-39. Resistance measurement is being made with range selector switch in the R x 1 position. Reading is 8 x 1 = 8Ω.

OHMMETER SAFETY PRECAUTIONS

A word of caution is in order at this point. *Whenever you work with an ohmmeter, the power must be off in the circuit under test.* All *ohmmeters* have dry cells inside that act as the power source. Ohmmeters and multimeters need these dry cells to serve as the voltage supply needed to force current through the resistor being tested.

If you accidentally connect an ohmmeter to a live circuit, you probably will damage the meter. If you happen to leave the range selector switch in the ohms position and attempt to test voltage, the meter may explode. In effect, you are using the voltage from the circuit's power source to charge the dry cells in the VOM at a very high rate. This huge rush of electrons could cause the meter to blow apart.

Most multimeters have a built-in overload device. If you take a *voltage reading* with the selector switch in the *ohms position,* it will "pop" the reset button. If so, remove the probe from circuit contact, set the range switch to the desired voltage range, and push the reset button. The meter is ready to go again.

In any case, always disconnect the power source from the circuit before connecting an ohmmeter or multimeter. Also, when you are through using a multimeter, put the range selector switch in the highest voltage position, or in the OFF position if the meter has one. This precaution will take the dry cells out of the circuit, and they will last longer.

LIFE OF POWER SOURCE

As the dry cells inside the ohmmeter or multimeter begin to age, the "zero ohms pot" must be adjusted more and more. Finally, it will get to the point where the meter cannot be zeroed. When this happens, replace the dry cells inside the meter. If you do not, all your readings will be wrong.

Remember, not all VOMs look alike. Get familiar with different "makes." Although they look different, they still make the same kinds of measurements, Fig. 9-40. Note that this multimeter has a range selector switch, zero adjustment, and a function switch.

COIL RESISTANCE OF METERS

The various meters we have discussed have coils as part of their construction. Since coils also have some resistance, you want to be sure that coil resistance does not affect your meter readings. Meter movements with

Fig. 9-40. This volt-ohm milliamp (VOM) meter has one range selector and one function switch.

the lowest full-scale current ratings are called "sensitive," because the pointer will move with small amounts of current flowing through the meter.

When a voltmeter is rated for sensitivity, it is said to have so many "ohms-per-volt." This rating applies to both the resistance in the meter movements as well as to the resistors in the range selector switch. Voltmeters having the highest ohms-per-volt rating will have the least effect on the measurements you make. The most common types of voltmeters have ratings of 20,000 to 30,000 ohms-per-volt.

Some old meters may not have their resistance rating marked on them. In this case, set up the test circuit shown in Fig. 9-41, and use the following method of finding the coil resistance of the meter.

First, adjust R_1 until the meter reads full-scale deflection, Fig. 9-42. The 1.5V dry cell acts as a power supply. Note that you have a parallel circuit: a portion of the current will flow through the resistor; the rest will flow through the meter. The resistance value for R_1 will start somewhere between 400 and 600 ohms.

After you have obtained full-scale deflection on the meter, close switch S_2, Fig. 9-43. Adjust the R_2 potentiometer (50,000 ohms) until the meter reads half-scale. Now you have an equal split through R_2 and the meter. Close switch S_1 and fine tune the adjustment on R_2 again. Since the current has split evenly between R_2 and the meter, their resistances should be the same. Measure the resistance of R_2 and you also have the resistance of the meter.

Fig. 9-41. Basic circuit used to determine unknown resistance of meter coil.

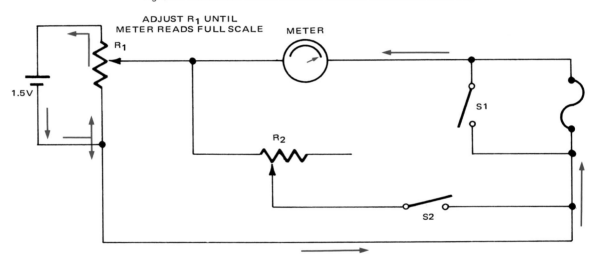

Fig. 9-42. First basic step to find unknown meter resistance is to adjust R_1 to get full scale reading on meter.

Fig. 9-43. Second step is to adjust R_2 until the meter reads half-scale. Resistance value of meter, then, is the same as resistance value of R_2.

Generally, meters are used to measure voltage, current, and resistance. Combination meters are also available. The one shown in Fig. 9-44 measures voltage on one side and temperature on the other side.

VACUUM TUBE VOLTMETER

The last type of meter to be covered in this chapter is known as a *VTVM*. The letters stand for *Vacuum Tube Voltmeter,* Fig. 9-45. A VTVM must be plugged into a 110 volt ac outlet. Before it will work properly, it must warm up for awhile because it has a vacuum tube inside. We will not discuss tubes of this type in this book. However, you know that such a meter exists.

The VTVM has a high input resistance on all ranges. Usually, however, it is read in the megaohm region. That means that the VTVM will not affect circuit readings as much as the VOM did. The meter movement in a VTVM is the moving coil, permanent magnet type. Ranges and scales are different on a VTVM and a VOM. One difference is that the VTVM has a center-zero scale.

VTVMs also use a series of different types of probes, Fig. 9-46. Other differences are beyond the scope of this text. When you get ready to use a VTVM, check with your instructor for assistance.

Fig. 9-44. Volts-temperature tester. Note four ranges on the range selector switch and multiple scales on meter face. (Sun Electric Corp.)

Fig. 9-46. Typical probe assembly furnished with, or as an accessory for, a vacuum tube voltmeter. (Heath Co.)

Fig. 9-45. This vacuum tube voltmeter (VTVM) has broad application. Note seven voltage and resistance ranges on the range selector switch. (Heath Co.)

SUMMARY

You must pay close attention to the polarity when a dc meter is hooked up in a circuit. If not, you could permanently damage the meter. An ammeter must be connected in series with the circuit being tested. Voltmeters must be connected in parallel with the circuit you are checking.

Always start checking the values of an unknown circuit with the range switch set above the expected value. The range switch can be reduced until the reading appears somewhere in the middle of the scale of a pointer type meter. This is the most accurate portion of the meter. Avoid the numbers on either end of the scale, they are less accurate. A digital meter must also be set to the proper range to avoid damage to its movement.

A word of caution when using an ohmmeter: be sure the power is off in the circuit being tested. The meter could blow apart while testing a live circuit, causing damage to the meter or to yourself.

KEY WORDS AND TERMS

Analog meter	Ohmmeter
Damping spring	Ohms-per-volt
D'Arsonval movement	Pegging the meter
Digital meter	Range selector switch
Direct current (dc)	Shunt
Galvanometer	Vacuum tube voltmeter
Left-Hand Rule	(VTVM)
Multimeter	Zero the meter

TEST YOUR KNOWLEDGE

Do not write in this book. Write your answers on a separate sheet of paper.

1. Draw a simple circuit showing where a voltmeter should be placed to measure the voltage.
2. Damping a moving coil meter is necessary because _____.
3. Draw a circuit with a dry cell connected to a lamp. Show where an ammeter should be connected to get the proper reading.
4. Name at least three different types of measurements that can be made and the meters used to make them.
5. Give one of the big advantages of a digital readout meter.
6. State the Left-Hand Rule.
7. A _____ is a meter used to take measurements of very small electrical currents.
8. When working with unknown voltages, it is best to start taking measurements with the range selector switch set at _____.
9. Describe what is meant by "pegging the meter."
10. A _____ is connected to a meter so that it can be used to measure current values higher than that which the meter originally was manufactured to measure.
11. The _____ probe should be plugged into the positive terminal and the _____ probe should be plugged into the negative terminal.
12. Why should you *never* touch the metal tips of probes?
13. A microampere is _____ of an ampere.
14. Before you disconnect meter test leads from a circuit, you should _____ to prevent electrical shock.
15. *True or False?* It takes less than 1 amp of electrical current to kill you.

ACTIVITIES

1. Why are there so many different types of meters?
2. Compare the cost of digital readout meters with pointer type meters. How much have they changed in the last five years? Why?
3. How many different types of lighted segments can be found on digital readout type meters? Why do they differ?
4. How is damping done on meters without moving coils?
5. List the costs of different brands of meters which read the same current values. Why do the costs vary?
6. Make a list of voltage readings. Start with the highest voltage you are able to discover anywhere, then go down to the smallest value of voltage you can find.
7. In some situations, electricians working in industry do not turn off the electricity before making measurements. Why not?
8. Does the utility company turn off the electrical power when you have a power line down because of a storm?
9. Telephone company technicians can tell within a couple of miles where a broken wire is located. How can they do this without leaving their office?
10. Why does the telephone in your home have such small wire?
11. Some meters made by the same company must have their dry cells replaced more often than others. Why?
12. The dry cells in some modern meters will not run down if you accidentally leave the meter set in the ohms range for a long time. Why not?
13. How does a digital wristwatch get its power to operate?
14. Ask a number of electricians, "Which is the best meter?" Why do they disagree?

Top: Advances in the electricity and electronics field have allowed great improvements in telephone design. This phone has an LCD 12-digit readout that confirms operating modes and displays such functions as the number called, the duration of the call, and the time. Bottom: This portable radio contains a calorie pedometer with an LCD display that gives information regarding the user's stride, pace, and distance traveled.

10 AC Voltage

LEARNING OBJECTIVES

After studying this chapter, you will be able to:
- Describe how alternating current is produced.
- Demonstrate how to view a sine wave on an oscilloscope.
- Determine the frequency, period, and amplitude of a sine wave.
- Calculate and explain what is meant by the RMS value of a sine wave.
- Determine your personal audio range using the proper electrical equipment.

When you studied Ohm's Law in Chapter 5, you learned about electrical current that flowed in only one direction. The electrons left the negative post of the battery, flowed through the circuit, and returned to the positive post of the battery. This is called *direct current* (dc) electricity.

In this chapter, we are going to deal with *alternating current* (ac) electricity. Basically, *alternating current is any current that reverses its direction of power at regular intervals.*

Fig. 10-1. Technician working on a television set uses a sine wave on an osilloscope to aid in making troubleshooting tests. (Hewlett-Packard)

In Fig. 10-1, for example, a technician is looking at a *sine wave* on his oscilloscope screen. A *sine wave is a wave form of a single frequency alternating current.* The scope is an instrument that can pick up traces of charged particles moving at a high rate of speed, even though the particles may reverse themselves in an up and down motion.

HOW AC IS PRODUCED

Imagine that you have a pair of magnets like the ones shown in Fig. 10-2. The dotted lines indicate that there is a magnetic field between the poles of the two magnets. (See Chapter 2.) If you pass a piece of wire quickly through the field so that the wire cuts through the lines of force, Fig. 10-3, a current would be "induced" in the wire. At this point, we'll say that induced means "created in the wire." The induction principle will be explained later in the text.

Fig. 10-2. Lines of forces between north pole and south pole of magnets show extent of magnetic field.

WIRE MOVING DOWN THROUGH
THE FIELD WILL "INDUCE"
A CURRENT IN IT

Fig. 10-3. A wire passing through a magnetic field will cut the lines of force and induce electric current in the wire.

In order to understand the example shown in Fig. 10-3, there are three important points to remember:

1. A voltage is induced in the wire only when the wire cuts across lines of force.
2. The faster the wire cuts the lines of force, the higher the voltage induced in the wire.
3. If we reverse the motion of the wire, we reverse the polarity of the induced voltage.

Keeping these points in mind, look at the coil of wire lying in a magnetic field in Fig. 10-4. If you cut

Fig. 10-4. A coil of wire is placed inside the magnetic field. If the coil is cut at the dotted line, cut ends will show what happens when coil rotates.

across the coil at the dotted line, you will have the end view shown in Fig. 10-5. The cut ends of the wire are labeled A and B, so that you can see what happens to each side of the coil as it begins to move, then rotates (spins) inside the magnetic field.

Fig. 10-5. This end view of coil inside magnetic field shows cut ends of coil marked A and B. See Fig. 10-4.

To help you understand how the coil rotates, take a wagon or bicycle and turn it upside down so it cannot move. Mark two spots A and B, Fig. 10-6, and slap the wheel so that it starts to spin. Trace A and B for one complete revolution (turn), and note that they both end up at their original starting point.

The important thing, however, is that both A and B can be traced through one revolution of the wheel. Likewise when the coil of wire cuts through the lines of force of the magnetic field in Fig. 10-7, you can trace A and B throughout the complete revolution. In electrical terms, however, one revolution of the coil is called a "cycle."

Fig. 10-6. A rotating bicycle wheel illustrates path followed by marks A and B. Marks A and B in Fig. 10-5 follow a similar path.

TRACING POINTS ON THE SINE WAVE

To experiment with the coil and magnet, consider the sine wave shown in Fig. 10-7. Then, start rotating the coil around its axis. At Point 1, the coil of wire is moving parallel to the lines of force in the magnetic field. It is *not* cutting the lines of force. Therefore, no voltage is induced in the coil.

At Point 2, the coil is moving at right angles to the lines of force, and a maximum amount of voltage is induced in the coil. This is the highest point our sine wave will reach.

Again, at Point 3, no voltage is induced. Note that the end of the coil marked A is starting to cut the lines of force in the opposite direction from when it moved past Point 1. This causes the voltage induced in the coil to reverse its polarity. It now starts to generate voltage in the negative direction.

At Point 4, the voltage induced in the coil as it rotates through the magnetic field will reach its lowest point (negative voltage). Here again, the coil is cutting the maximum number of lines of force, but in the opposite direction.

Finally, at Point 5, we have returned to our starting point. No lines of force are being cut, and we are back to the zero point on our reference line.

SINE WAVE FACTORS

The curved line in Fig. 10-7 is known as a "sine wave." When we talk about a sine wave, you will need to know its frequency, period and amplitude.

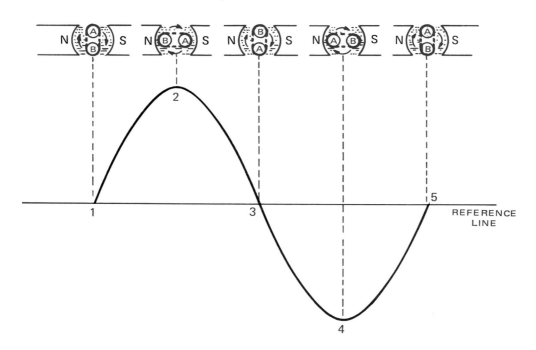

Fig. 10-7. One sine wave (curved line) is generated through one rotation of the coil inside the magnetic field. Coil cuts through maximum number of lines of force in positions 2 and 4.

I.C. SAYS:

"Here are some definitions. Frequency means the number of cycles completed per second. Period is the length of time required to complete one cycle. Amplitude refers to the value of the sine wave."

FREQUENCY

The definition for the electrical term frequency is "number of cycles per second." If the coil pictured in Fig. 10-7 rotated at a speed of five revolutions per second, it would produce five complete sine waves in each second. See Fig. 10-8. *The frequency of this sine wave is five cycles per second, or five Hertz (5 Hz).*

If we rotated the coil faster, the number of cycles would increase and the frequency would be higher. The term "60 cycles per second" is used with reference to house current. This means that your home electrical supply is being generated at a frequency of 60 Hz (Hertz means cycles per second). Some parts of Canada and Australia, and some countries in Europe, generate their electricity at a frequency of 50 Hz.

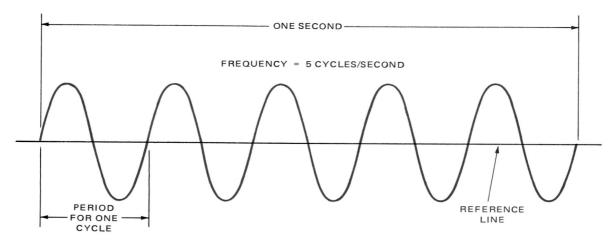

Fig. 10-8. Five sine waves in one second equals a frequency of five cycles per second and a period of one/fifth second.

PERIOD

In Fig. 10-8, the period of the sine wave will be 1/5 of a second. *A period is the time we need to complete one cycle.* Since we generated five complete cycles in one second, the time it takes for one cycle can be found by dividing one by the number of cycles per second (frequency):

$$\text{Period} = \frac{1}{\text{frequency}}$$

$$\text{Period} = \frac{1}{5 \text{ cycles/second}}$$

$$\text{Period} = \frac{1}{5} \text{ second for each cycle}$$

You can see that as frequency increases, the period of time it takes for each cycle gets shorter. For example, if you have 60 cycles per second alternating current in your home, the period will be:

$$\text{Period} = \frac{1}{\text{frequency}}$$

$$\text{Period} = \frac{1}{60 \text{ cycles/second}}$$

$$\text{Period} = \frac{1}{60} \text{ second per cycle}$$

AMPLITUDE

Note that each cycle shown in Fig. 10-8 has a high point and a low point. The highest point is known as the peak value for the sine wave. See Fig. 10-9. *If you*

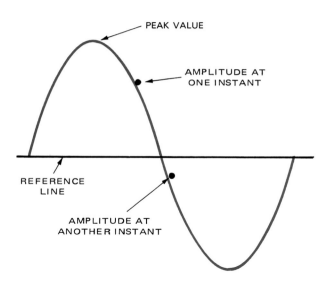

Fig. 10-9. The amplitude of a sine wave is its height above or below reference line at any given time.

wanted to know the height of the wave, you would ask for its amplitude.

However, we are talking about a sine wave that is changing in both directions. At one point in the cycle (peak value), the wave will reach its maximum amplitude in the positive direction. At another point, it will reach its maximum amplitude in a negative direction. This value is taken from a reference line as shown in Fig. 10-10. Therefore, we always have two peaks on a sine wave: a negative peak and a positive peak. The voltage difference between the negative peak and positive peak is commonly called the "peak-to-peak voltage" of a sine wave.

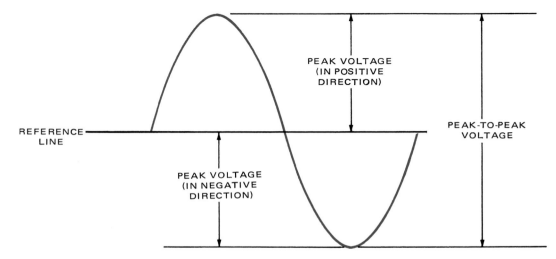

Fig. 10-10. Peak voltage (peak value) is maximum amplitude above or below reference line.
Peak-to-peak voltage is sum of the two peak voltages.

PEAK VOLTAGE

Peak and peak-to-peak voltage and current are very important in our study of electronic devices such as diodes, rectifiers and transistors. These devices can be overloaded very easily. If we do not know the value of peak voltage, a diode could be burned up in just a fraction of a second; just about as fast as a fuse rated at 1/100 amp.

In Fig. 10-11, you have an ac voltage with a peak amplitude of 100 volts. Note that the voltage only reaches 100 volts twice during each cycle. Also note that zero volts occurs twice during each cycle.

The symbol most commonly used to indicate an ac power supply is given in Fig. 10-12.

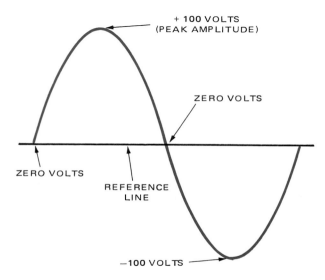

Fig. 10-11. In this specific example of a sine wave, peak amplitude is 100 volts, both above and below the reference line.

Fig. 10-12. This symbol for the ac power supply is used when drawing schematics.

DEMAGNETIZER PROJECT

Do you want to build a simple project that will demagnetize screwdrivers, drill bits or other metal parts? It can be done easily with a simple coil of wire.

You can salvage one of these coils by disassembling an old motor or you can build one yourself, Fig. 10-13.

To make the demagnetizer, wrap about 2000 turns of No. 28 magnet wire on a 4 in. form. Then, splice and solder the ends of the wire to the two wires of a 110V ac lamp cord. Wrap the entire coil with plastic electrical tape. Then, plug the lamp cord into a 110V receptacle and put the demagnetizer into operation.

To demagnetize an object, simply pass it through the coil. The magnetic field produced by the coil will mix up the pattern of electrons in the metal object, causing it to become demagnetized.

Fig. 10-13. Simple coil "demagnetizer" is wired for 110V ac. Metal parts are demagnetized as they pass through coil. (Project by William Miller)

HEAT FACTOR

In Chapter 5, you read that a certain amount of heat is developed in a resistor when the circuit is completed. For comparison, Fig. 10-14 shows similar ac and dc circuits. One has a 100 volt peak ac power supply hooked up to a 50 ohm resistor. The other circuit has a 100 volt dc power supply hooked up to an identical 50 ohm resistor. Which voltage would you expect to produce more heat? *Remember, ac voltage reaches 100 volts only twice in each cycle, while dc voltage stays at a steady 100 volts.* The answer is: dc voltage will produce more heat in the resistor, Fig. 10-15. (Both a + increase and a − increase cause heating.)

RMS VALUE

After many experiments, scientists have come up with a practical way of comparing the heating values of ac and dc voltages. They found that if you multiplied

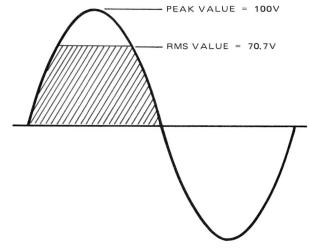

Fig. 10-16. The RMS value of an ac sine wave is, in effect, 70.7 percent of its peak value.

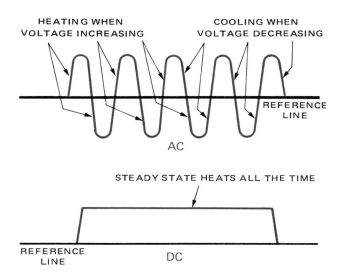

Fig. 10-14. In a test of heat values, identical resistors in similar ac and dc circuits are compared.

Fig. 10-15. More heat is created by dc voltage. Note that ac voltage heats on rise of sine wave only.

the amplitude (peak value) of an ac sine wave by the number .707, you would get an RMS value (effective value) for the ac wave. See Fig. 10-16.

The formula is: RMS = peak voltage x .707

Looking back at Fig. 10-14, we can relate the RMS formula to that ac circuit:

RMS = 100V x .707
RMS = 70.7V

The RMS value of 70.7 volts means that the 100 volt peak ac voltage will have as much heating value as a dc voltage of 70.7 volts. RMS value is so important that whenever people in electrical and electronic work speak of an ac voltage or current, they usually are talking about the RMS value.

A good example of RMS value is the 110 volt power supply found in your home. This is actually the RMS value for the voltage. Peak voltage would be higher. Remember, too, that sine waves can apply to both voltage and current. The formula will work just as well for either of these electrical values.

The letters RMS stand for Root Mean Square. This is just another way of using mathematics to solve problems. You do not have to be concerned with how this factor .707 came about. At this point, we are interested only in knowing how to use the results.

SQUARE WAVE

A "square wave" is another type of wave that is in common use in electricity and electronics. See Fig. 10-17. A square wave is easy to produce by making up a circuit that consists of a battery, switch and resistor.

Consider the circuit shown in Fig. 10-18. When the switch is open, the voltage across the resistor is zero. When the switch is closed at Point A in Fig. 10-19, the voltage across the resistor jumps up to battery voltage. It stays at that voltage until the switch is opened again at Point B. This will happen every time you open and close the switch.

If the switch is closed and opened once every second, we have a square wave with a frequency of one

Fig. 10-17. A technician picks out a portion of a square wave for examination using an oscilloscope. (Hewlett-Packard)

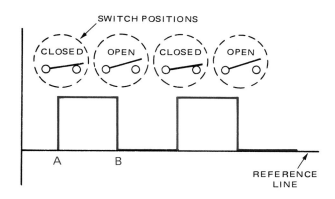

Fig. 10-19. A square wave can be produced by turning the switch on and off at regular intervals.

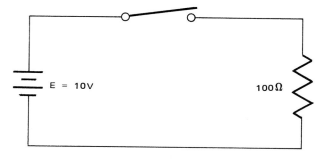

Fig. 10-18. This simple circuit will produce a square wave.

Hertz (Hz). "Hertz" is another way of saying cycles per second (cps) for both square waves and sine waves.

The peak amplitude of the wave shown in Fig. 10-20 is 10 volts. The period of this wave is one second. Note that even though the reference line is at the "bottom" of the wave form, we still have a square wave whose peak-to-peak amplitude is 10 volts.

As you can see, sine waves and square waves have three things in common: frequency, amplitude and period. These waves are an important area of study in electricity and electronics because they are the two most common types of alternating current.

APPLICATION OF SINE WAVES

You have studied the makeup of sine waves. Now we will look at a practical application. First, take a sine wave with a frequency of 400 Hz and a RMS voltage of five volts. Hook up a loud speaker, as shown in Fig. 10-21, and you will hear a sound. The sound is called a "tone." If you increase the voltage of the wave, the tone will get louder. If you increase the frequency of the wave, the tone will get higher in pitch.

Most people can hear sounds as low as 20 Hz and as high as 20,000 Hz. As they get older, their hearing

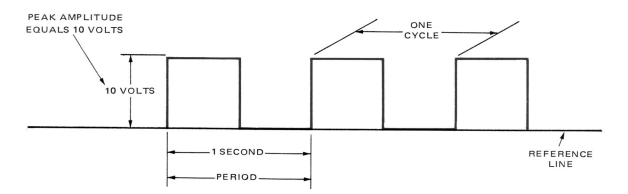

Fig. 10-20. By opening and closing the switch once every second, we can produce a square wave with a frequency of one Hertz.

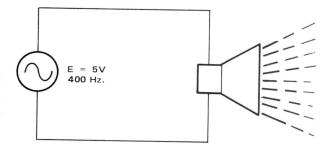

Fig. 10-21. We can produce sound by means of sine waves by putting a loud speaker in the circuit.

range gets smaller. They may only be able to hear sounds between 100 Hz and 15,000 Hz. Usually, frequencies between 20 Hz and 20,000 Hz are called "audio frequency or AF waves."

SIGNAL GENERATORS

Most ac waves you will deal with in electronics can be produced by a machine called a "signal generator." See Fig. 10-22. These machines are used to produce ac

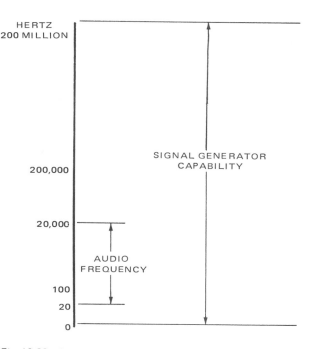

Fig. 10-23. A signal generator can produce sounds far beyond audio frequency (range of human hearing).

Fig. 10-22. Signal generators produce ac voltages having a broad range of frequencies. (Interplex Electronics, Inc.)

voltages having a frequency as low as 20 Hz or as high as 200 million Hz, Fig. 10-23.

Signal generators have many control knobs, three of which are found on all makes, Fig. 10-24. The frequency selector knob lets the operator choose the frequency. The amplitude control adjusts the amplitude of the wave produced. The function selector permits the operator to choose either a sine wave or a square wave.

There are many different types of signal generators made. It is impossible to describe every type. Because of this, you may have noticed several switches on your generator that we have not mentioned. If you are unsure about operating any of the controls, ask your instructor for an explanation.

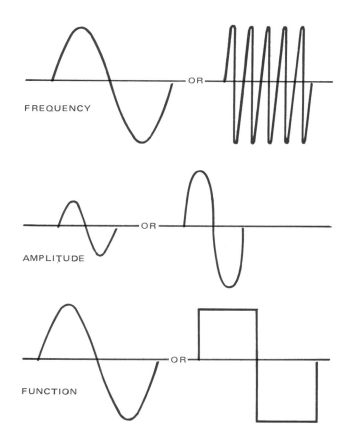

Fig. 10-24. Symbols are given for controls of signal generators.

Fig. 10-26. This AM/FM radio dial covers an AM band from 540 kHz to 1700 kHz. (Panasonic)

Why do signal generators produce frequencies higher than 20,000 Hz if we cannot hear them? In Fig. 10-25, you see the frequency range for radio, television, telephone, and astronomy equipment. Radio stations are able to send both voice and music through the air by means of waves that your radio can pick up and change into frequencies that we can hear. See Fig. 10-26.

FREQUENCY RANGE

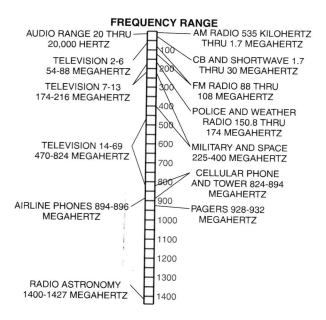

Fig. 10-25. Telephone, television, and astronomy equipment transmit and receive in a wide range of frequencies well above that of human hearing. (1 kHz = 1000 Hz, 1 Megahertz = 1,000,000 Hz)

Waves at these high frequencies are called radio frequency waves or RF waves. Radios probably will be covered in your next course, but the most important point to remember is that waves are around us everywhere and are a very important part of electronics.

PHASE RELATIONSHIP

Phase relationship is the last topic in our study of waves. In Fig. 10-27, we have two waves drawn on the same time scale. The black sine wave represents voltage, while the blue wave represents current. Note that each wave reaches its maximum amplitude at the same time, and both reach their zero level at the same time. When this happens, we say that voltage and current are "in phase."

Actually, an in-phase situation occurs when the circuit contains resistance only. In actual practice, most circuits contain resistors, capacitors, inductors and other components. To give you the basics you need to establish a foundation for working with other, more complex circuits, we *must* start at this level. Once you know the basics, it is easier to understand why other combinations of components have particular circuit applications.

In the next chapter, we will introduce you to "inductors." Then, we will combine resistors, capacitors and inductors in various circuits. At that point, you will see that voltage and current may be out-of-phase, Fig.

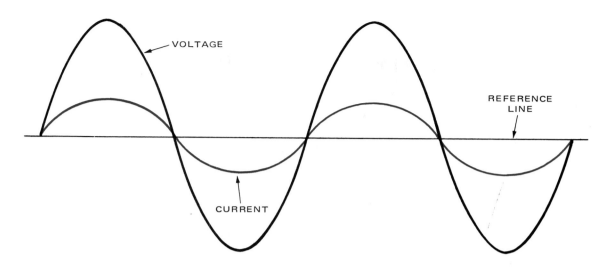

Fig. 10-27. Two sine waves are shown "in phase." Note that they peak at the same time, also reach zero level (reference line) at the same time.

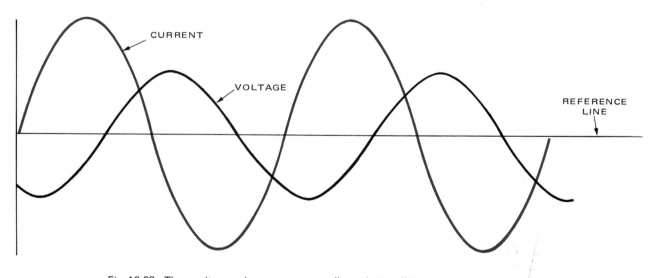

Fig. 10-28. These voltage and current waves are "out-of-phase." Note how the peaks vary, and the waves do not meet at the reference line.

10-28. Then, you will understand how all of these components work together toward accomplishing a desired result.

"FAKEQUAD" PROJECT

You can build a conversion unit that connects to your stereo set to help produce simulated quadrophonic sound. Since the sound *is* faked, this project is called "Fakequad."

Study Fig. 10-29, then procure the following items and assemble them as directed in the construction procedure:

No.	Item
2	20 Ω , 20W resistors.
2	Terminal strips, 2 posts.
2	Terminal strips, 4 posts.
1	Breadboard, 6 in. x 10 in.
1	Plastic box, 6 in. x 10 in. x 2 5/8 in.

A

B

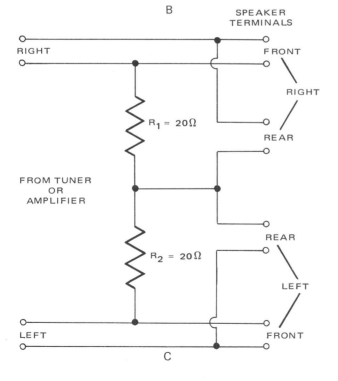

SPEAKER
TERMINALS

C

Fig. 10-29. "Fakequad" is a project designed to fake quadraphonic
sound by bringing sound from two tracks through four speakers.
(Project by Ron Simons)

CONSTRUCTION PROCEDURE

Set up and assemble the project materials as follows:
1. Locate and drill holes for terminal posts and mounting screws.
2. Install small wooden blocks on bottom of breadboard to serve as spacers for bottom clearance in plastic box.
3. Install resistors on bottom of breadboard, feeding lead wires through to top of board.
4. Assemble and mount terminal pins on top of breadboard. See B in Fig. 10-29.
5. Using the schematic shown at C, wire terminal pins on breadboard to terminal strips on top of box.
6. Interconnect proper pins to top terminal posts, as shown at B.
7. Use an ohmmeter to check for shorts or opens in wiring. Repair as required.
8. Solder all connections.
9. Install cover on box and label terminal screws as shown at A.
10. Bring in leads from stereo tuner or amplifier to right and left terminals of "Fakequad" unit.
11. Hook up four speakers to right front, right rear, left front, and left rear terminals.
12. Position speakers around room.

SUMMARY

An alternating current (ac) is one that reverses its direction at regular intervals. A generator produces ac when it is rotated by falling water, steam, heat from coal, oil, or nuclear plants. Another way to produce an alternating current is by passing coils of wire through a magnetic field. The current in the wire is produced by induction.

The frequency of the ac produced in the United States is 60 Hertz (Hz) while in some other countries it is 50 Hz. You can determine the peak value, frequency, and other important values by examining a sine wave on an oscilloscope. To determine the dc heat equivalent value for an ac wave, you can use the formula: RMS = peak value × .707. RMS stands for Root Mean Square.

Square waves can also have a specified frequency and amplitude. Digital music, commonly heard on CDs, benefits from using square waves to produce the crisp, clear sounds heard today.

KEY WORDS AND TERMS

Alternating current (ac)	Peak-to-peak voltage
Amplitude	Period
Cycle	Root mean square (RMS)

Frequency
Hertz (Hz)
In phase
Peak voltage

Signal generator
Sine wave
Square wave

TEST YOUR KNOWLEDGE

Do not write in this book. Write your answers on a separate sheet of paper.
1. Draw a sine wave.
2. What is the voltage of the three wire service that is brought into your home?
3. Frequency is _____.
4. Period is _____.
5. What is the frequency of the current in your home?
6. If you had 100 volts peak, would it give you more or less heat than 100 volts RMS? Show your work.
7. What is the audio range for most people?
8. Say that the resistance of a heating element on an electric range is 20 ohms. How much current does the element use if it is connected to a voltage source of 240 volts? Show your work.
9. Is the voltage in your home measured in RMS or peak voltage?
10. *True or False?* A signal generator is used to produce sine waves and square waves.
11. Change the following:
    1600 kHz equals _____ Hz.
    200 million Hz equals _____ kHz.
    20,000 Hz equals _____ kHz.

ACTIVITIES

1. Why does the power company transport its electricity in ac instead of dc?
2. Recently, a few companies have switched to dc as a means of transporting power for long distances. Where are these companies? Why are they doing it?
3. Make a list of some of the different frequencies used by radio stations in your city.
4. Make a list of the different frequencies used by television stations around your area of the country. Why are these different than radio stations?
5. The National Electric Code governs most electrical construction. What is it? Why do building inspectors follow it?
6. Besides the sine wave, what are some of the other types of waves found in electrical work?
7. What happens to your hearing as you get older? Why does that affect the range of frequencies that you can hear?
8. Why can a dog hear higher frequencies than humans?
9. Microwave ovens are used to cook food in just a few minutes instead of the long periods of time previously needed. How do they work? Would these ovens hurt you if they were turned on without the door being in place?
10. Where are most of the major power companies located in your area of the country?
11. Why are so many people unwilling to have nuclear power plants located near their homes?
12. Where is the biggest generating plant in your area located? How much electricity does it generate in a single day? How long would a city of 30,000 people be able to operate on that much energy?
13. How much electricity does your family use in a single year?
14. Make a list of five countries which consume the most electricity.

11 Electromagnetic Induction

LEARNING OBJECTIVES

After studying this chapter, you will be able to:
- Demonstrate how to induce a voltage using a coil, magnet, and a galvanometer.
- Show how to create an electromagnet using insulated wire, a dc power supply, and an iron rod.
- Explain four things which affect the amount of inductance in a coil.
- Draw the symbols for a fixed and adjustable inductor.
- Calculate the power and current on the secondary of a transformer.

As you learned in Chapter 2, a current passing through a wire will set up a magnetic field around the wire. In Chapter 10, you found that the reverse effect is also true: that a magnetic field will induce current to flow in a wire. In this chapter, we will discuss *electromagnetic induction*. This is a means of generating electromotive force or voltage (EMF) in a conductor by creating a change in the magnetic field. This, in turn, causes electrons to flow in the conductor. See Figs. 11-1 and 11-2.

HOW VOLTAGE IS INDUCED

To prove to yourself that electromagnetic induction works, perform the following experiment:

Obtain a dc galvanometer, a hollow coil of wire, a bar magnet that is small enough to pass through the coil, and some hookup wire. Assemble the equipment as shown in Fig. 11-1. Thrust the magnet into the coil, then quickly remove it, while watching for movement of the galvanometer pointer.

If you observe carefully, you will detect a slight pointer movement, both when you put the magnet into the coil and when you remove it. This means that current is flowing in the wire *only* when the magnetic field is changing. If you fail to get pointer movement, you probably did not move the magnet quickly enough.

Remember that any magnet has a magnetic field coming from its north pole. Also bear in mind that the lines of force in this field will go right through any insulating material, such as the coating on the wire in the coil. Further proof of this is found in working with a simple electromagnet, Fig. 11-2.

If we pass direct current through the coil of the electromagnet, the iron rod within the coil will attract iron filings. This will happen even though we are using insulated wire. Keep this fact in mind because much of what you learn about the applications of electricity is affected by this source of electricity called "electromagnetic induction."

GALVANOMETER

Fig. 11-1. In this experiment, sudden movement of a magnet inside a coil of wire will change the magnetic field and induce voltage in the coil.

Fig. 11-2. In a demonstration of magnetism by induction, iron filings will be attracted to the iron core of an electromagnet when direct current flows through the wire coil.

INDUCED EMF

In Fig. 11-1, the current flows in the wire coil because the changing magnetic field has induced (caused) electromotive force (EMF) or voltage in the coil. This voltage is often called "induced EMF."

Consider, too, that instead of thrusting the magnet into the coil, we could have held the magnet in a fixed spot and moved the coil over it. EMF still would have been induced in the wire. This type of induction will be explained in more detail in Chapter 12.

INDUCTANCE

In Chapter 10 and again earlier in this chapter, you found that a changing magnetic field will induce EMF in a coil of wire. In Fig. 10-7, the magnetic field is, in effect, changing because the coil is rotating in the field. This, you recall, caused major changes at 90 deg. and 270 deg. where the coil cut through the maximum number of lines of force. At 0 deg. and 180 deg., the coil cut through the minimum number of lines of force.

MAGNETIC COUPLING

Now look at the hollow coil of wire shown in Fig. 11-3. If electrical current is passing through the wire, a magnetic field will be created around the coil. In a dc circuit, the magnetic field will expand and remain there.

EXPANDS AND REMAINS

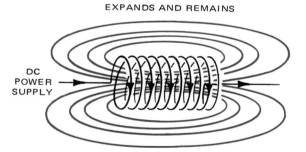

Fig. 11-3. Passing a direct current through a hollow coil of wire will create a magnetic field that will expand, then remain around the wire coil.

However, if current flow in the coil changes, as in the ac circuit shown in Fig. 11-4, a *changing* magnetic field is set up. The magnetic field in an ac circuit will expand and collapse. Note in Fig. 11-5 that the changing field set up by each turn of the coil passes through other turns of the coil. This is known as "magnetic coupling."

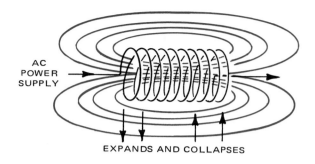

Fig. 11-4. Passing an alternating current through a hollow coil of wire will create a changing magnetic field that will expand and collapse.

FIELD FROM ONE PORTION OF WIRE COIL CUTS THROUGH OTHER SECTION

Fig. 11-5. The changing magnetic field created by alternating current in each turn of the coil will cut through the other coils, resulting in "magnetic coupling."

Actually, the changing magnetic field in one turn of the coil will set up an EMF in the other turns of the coil. If the turns are closer together, the lines of force will cut through all the turns of the coil. The further you stretch out the coil, the fewer the number of lines of force that can cut through the wires of the coil.

You might ask, "How does this EMF affect current in a coil of wire?" The answer is: "*Voltage induced tends to oppose or resist the current in the wire, and any part of a circuit that has this property is called an inductor.*"

The two students working on a circuit in Fig. 11-6 are using an oscilloscope. If we used a scope, we could close the switch for the circuit and see that the "wave" on the scope screen does not immediately climb to its peak. Instead, there is a small delay in its rise from the time reference line. Fig. 11-7 shows that the pattern would look like a slanted line on a scope, since the voltage induced tends to oppose the current. This is why the induced voltage is called a "counter EMF."

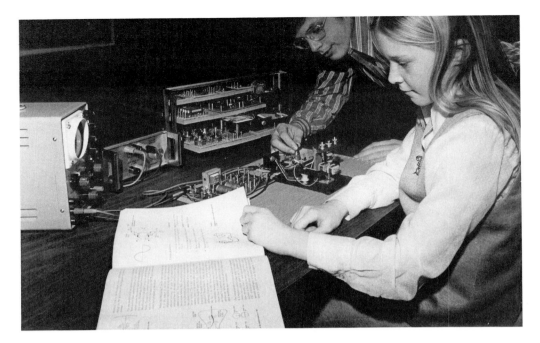

Fig. 11-6. Use diagrams and a parts list to aid in assembling a project. The oscilloscope at left serves to verify whether or not the electrical circuit is satisfactory. (Hickok Teaching Systems, Inc.)

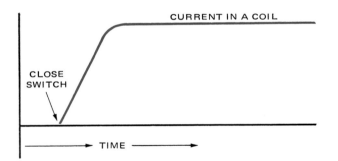

Fig. 11-7. An oscilloscope pattern of a circuit having induced voltage will show a slanted line because counter EMF tends to oppose changing current flow.

I.C. SAYS:

"Any part of a circuit that opposes a change in current is called an "inductor.""

INDUCTOR SYMBOLS AND USES

The most common form of an inductor is a coil of wire. As might be expected, the more turns of wire you have, the higher the inductance of the coil.

There are several symbols for inductors. The basic symbol, along with related symbols, is shown in Fig. 11-8. Note that they are drawn like a coil of wire, which is just what an inductor is supposed to be.

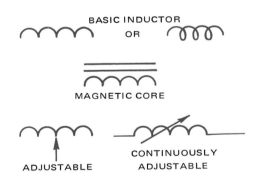

Fig. 11-8. Various symbols may be drawn to indicate the use of inductors in electrical circuits.

Occasionally, you will hear an inductor being called a "choke." A radio frequency (RF) choke would be one which is used where high frequency waves are found. Fig. 11-9 shows one such RF choke in a capacitive discharge ignition (CDI) system for an automobile.

We will not go into CDI circuitry. However, the purpose of the system is to increase the life of spark

Fig. 11-9. Inductors are called "chokes" (circled component) in high frequency wave applications, such as this capacitive discharge ignition system.   (Delta Products, Inc.)

plugs and reduce the number of engine tune-ups needed. The chokes can have either air or an adjustable ferrite (soft iron) core, Fig. 11-10.

HENRY

Just as we needed a unit of resistance for resistors, we also need a unit of inductance for inductors. The

Fig. 11-10. This inductor, or high frequency choke, has an adjustable ferrite core. Many of these variable inductors are used in radios and television sets.

unit for inductance is the "henry." By definition, if one volt of EMF is induced when the current is changing at the rate of one ampere per second, the coil has an inductance of one henry (H).

INDUCTOR IN A DC CIRCUIT

Consider the circuit shown in Fig. 11-11. When the switch is open, the current through the coil is zero. Then, when the switch is *closed*, the current tries to start flowing through the inductor. Since the current is now changing (increasing in value), the inductor will oppose this change. When the current finally reaches its maximum, there is no further change (increase) in current, so the inductor will no longer oppose the current.

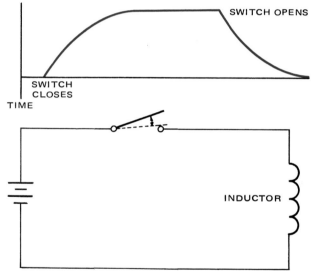

Fig. 11-11. An inductor opposes changes in current flow, particularly when a switch is closed or opened. Note the effect of "switching" on the wave pattern.

From these examples, you can see that an inductor only has an effect on a dc circuit when the current starts to flow. The same thing is true when we *open* the switch. The inductor will oppose the change in current when the voltage falls to zero.

Based on changing magnetic fields, you can see that an inductor will have little or no effect on a dc circuit, but it will have a large effect when used in an ac circuit.

WHAT AFFECTS INDUCTANCE

There are several things that affect the amount of inductance in a coil, Fig. 11-12:

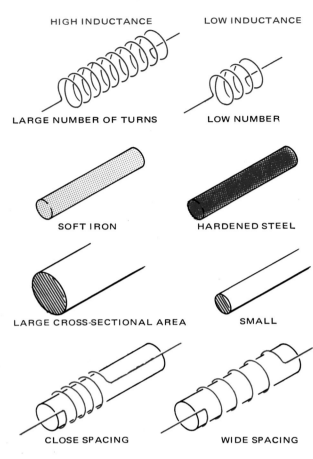

HIGH INDUCTANCE LOW INDUCTANCE

LARGE NUMBER OF TURNS LOW NUMBER

SOFT IRON HARDENED STEEL

LARGE CROSS-SECTIONAL AREA SMALL

CLOSE SPACING WIDE SPACING

Fig. 11-12. The amount of inductance in a coil of wire is affected by the physical makeup of the coil.

1. Number of turns of wire in coil.
2. Type of core.
3. Cross-sectional area of core.
4. Length of coil compared to number of turns of wire

NUMBER OF TURNS

The more turns of wire on a coil, the more lines of flux there will be to act on other turns. If you had only one turn of wire in the coil, the amount of inductance could be forgotten. However, if you multiply that inductance by the number of turns, it will have a large effect on the circuit.

CORE

If you use a core material such as soft iron, you will get more inductance than if you use hardened steel. The flux lines of the magnetic field created in the core actually add to the flux lines from the coil. Together, these two create a greater counter EMF. It should be noted, however, that magnetic cores have a greater inductance than those with air cores or insulating cores.

CROSS-SECTIONAL AREA

If the core of the inductor has a large cross-sectional area, it will create more flux lines than a small core. Lengthening the core is not practical, because then you must space out the wire in the coil and lose the value of using a core.

SPACING

Spacing the turns of wire in the coil does affect the amount of inductance in the circuit. If you space out the turns, the lines of flux from each turn cannot cut through one another.

MAGNETIZER/DEMAGNETIZER PROJECT

Here is a project that will allow you to magnetize or demagnetize small tools. There are times when a magnetized screwdriver can be a big help in tight quarters. There are other times when a magnetized tool will hinder an assembling operation.

See the two views of the magnetizer/demagnetizer pictured at A and B in Fig. 11-13. Then, study the schematic shown at C. Procure the necessary parts and assemble the project according to the construction procedure that follows.

No.	Item
1	Handmade inductor.
1	20 μF, 200V electrolytic capacitor.
1	400 mA (or higher), 300V silicon diode.
1	200 Ω, 5 W wirewound resistor.
1	Momentary contact push button switch.
1	DPDT toggle switch.
1	110V ac lamp cord.
1	6 in. x 3 in. x 2 in. plastic box and cover.

CONSTRUCTION PROCEDURE

Build the inductor first, then install it in the cover of the box. See A and B in Fig. 11-13. Complete the project as shown at B and C.

1. Saw off both ends of ten 20 penny nails, leaving them approximately 2 1/4 in. long.
2. Spray each nail with a thin coating of lacquer.
3. When dry, wrap nails with adhesive tape to form the core of the inductor.
4. Cut two circles of cardboard and put one at each end of the core, leaving about 1 in. of space between the cardboard circles.
5. Wrap layers of No. 36 magnet wire around the core, totaling about 4500 turns.
6. Before cutting the wire, scrape enamel to bare a

Electromagnetic Induction

To use the magnetizer/demagnetizer, plug the unit into a 110V ac outlet. Place the toggle switch in the magnetizer position. While depressing the push button, pass the small tool across the core a few times to magnetize the tool. To demagnetize a tool, put the toggle switch in the demagnetize position. While depressing the push button, pass the tool across the core several times.

INDUCTORS IN SERIES

As mentioned earlier, inductance values are given in henrys (H). Lesser values are measured in millihenrys (one thousandth of a henry) or microhenrys (one millionth of a henry). Their abbreviations are: mH for millihenry; μH for microhenry.

Fig. 11-13. Magnetizer/Demagnetizer. A—Top view of completed project. B—Parts attached to underside of cover. C—Schematic includes: L_1—Inductor. C_1—Capacitor. D_1—Silicon diode. R_1—Wirewound resistor. S_1—Push button switch. S_2—DPDT toggle switch. (Project by Robert Wong)

spot for attaching an ohmmeter lead. Bare starting end of coil wire and connect the other ohmmeter lead to it. Resistance should be between 425 and 450 ohms. If resistance is lower, add turns of wire to coil and recheck resistance value.

7. Cut a hole in the cover just large enough for one end of the core to protrude about 1/4 in. through the cover.

8. Tape the finished coil, leaving both wire ends outside the tape. Scrape enamel from wire ends and solder two hookup wires to them. Tape soldered joints to coil.

9. Epoxy the core to the cover so that it cannot move. Allow 24 hours drying time.

10. Install and wire other parts to underside of cover. See B and C in Fig. 11-13. Observe correct polarity when connecting silicon diode (D_1) and electrolytic capacitor (C_1).

When an inductor is shown in a circuit drawing, it is labeled with a capital L. Inductors will be found in series, parallel and series parallel circuits. In Fig. 11-14, three inductors (L_1, L_2, L_3) are used in series with an ac power supply.

When analyzing a series circuit for total inductance, we use the following formula:

$$L_{Total} = L_1 + L_2 + L_3 \ldots$$

In the circuit shown in Fig. 11-14:

$$L_T = L_1 + L_2 + L_3$$

$$L_T = 2 \text{ mH} + 3 \text{ mH} + 4 \text{ mH}$$

$$L_T = 9 \text{ mH}$$

Fig. 11-14. Inductors of three different millihenry values are used in this ac-powered series circuit. Find total inductance.

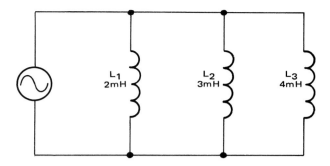

Fig. 11-15. In a setup similar to Fig. 11-14, three inductors are wired in parallel with the ac power supply. Find total inductance.

INDUCTORS IN PARALLEL

If the same three inductors were found in a parallel circuit, Fig. 11-15, we would use this formula:

$$\frac{1}{L_{Total}} = \frac{1}{L_1} + \frac{1}{L_2} + \frac{1}{L_3} + \ldots$$

Solving for total inductance, we would find:

$$\frac{1}{L_T} = \frac{1}{L_1} + \frac{1}{L_2} + \frac{1}{L_3}$$

$$\frac{1}{L_T} = \frac{1}{2 \text{ mH}} + \frac{1}{3 \text{ mH}} + \frac{1}{4 \text{ mH}}$$

$$\frac{1}{L_T} = \frac{6}{12 \text{ mH}} + \frac{4}{12 \text{ mH}} + \frac{3}{12 \text{ mH}}$$

$$\frac{1}{L_T} = \frac{13}{12 \text{ mH}}$$

Invert both sides of the equation:

$$\frac{L_T}{1} = \frac{12}{13} \text{ mH or } 923 \, \mu \text{ H}$$

The same concept used to solve total resistance in series parallel circuits can be used to analyze inductor values. Consider the circuit shown in Fig. 11-16. You recall that an inductor has no effect on a dc circuit, except when the switch is closing or opening. Therefore, we can analyze this circuit as if the inductor is shorted out.

Note in the equivalent circuit shown in Fig. 11-16 that only E (voltage) and R (resistance) are given. Based on these values, you can solve this circuit for I (amperage) by using Ohm's Law:

Fig. 11-16. Since an inductor has no effect on the constant current flow of a dc power supply, it can be left out when solving circuit problems.

$$I = \frac{E}{R}$$

$$I = \frac{10V}{20 \, \Omega}$$

$$I = .5A \text{ or } 500 \text{ mA}$$

INDUCTOR/RESISTOR COMBINATIONS

You have been shown how to find total inductance in various types of electrical circuits. Ordinarily, the next step would involve the analysis of a circuit that contains both inductors and resistors. However, just as we found in working with capacitors and resistors in Chapter 9, more information is required before you can analyze these more complicated circuits.

When we get to Chapter 13, you will be shown how to solve circuits having inductor/resistor combinations.

MUTUAL INDUCTANCE

One use of inductance can be demonstrated by placing two coils of wire close to each other, Fig. 11-17. Connect a changing current to coil No. 1 and a changing magnetic field will be produced around it. Some of the lines of force of the magnetic field around coil No. 1 will cut through the windings of coil No. 2. These changing lines of force will induce voltage in the windings of coil No. 2. This induced voltage, in turn, will cause a current to flow in coil No. 2. This is quite a trick, since we caused a current to flow in the second coil without a wire joining the two coils.

When two coils of wire are close enough to be linked by a magnetic field, they are said to have "mutual inductance." This is the basic principle of transformer operation. You can use different kinds of metal in the cores of the coils and see what effect they have on the inductance. Another thing you can do is place pieces of

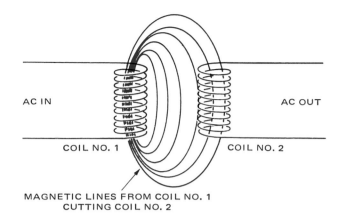

Fig. 11-17. In this demonstration of mutual inductance, ac flow in coil No. 1 will induce voltage across coil No. 2.

metal next to each coil as in Fig. 11-18. The lamp will give you visual proof of the test results.

The amount of mutual inductance in this experiment will depend upon three things:
1. Inductance of coil No. 1.
2. Inductance of coil No. 2.
3. Number of lines of force set up by coil No. 1 that cut across coil No. 2.

Fig. 11-18. Testing how different core materials affect inductance in an ac circuit.

FORMULA FOR MUTUAL INDUCTANCE

The formula for mutual inductance is:

$$M = K\sqrt{L_1 L_2}$$

M = Mutual inductance.

K = Coefficient of coupling (percent of coupling).

L_1 = Inductance of coil No. 1.

L_2 = Inductance of coil No. 2.

Suppose we have two coils placed near each other: one with an inductance of 12.5 henrys; the other with an inductance of 2 henrys. Alternating current is passed through coil No. 1, creating lines of force. When this occurs, it is found that 50 percent of these lines of force cut across coil No. 2. The problem is to find the mutual inductance between the two coils.

First, we know that L_1 = 12.5 H and L_2 = 2 H. We also know that K = .5 (50 percent). Then, substituting these values for factors in the mutual induction formula, we have:

$$M = K\sqrt{L_1 L_2}$$

$$M = .5\sqrt{12.5 \times 2} = .5\sqrt{25}$$

$$M = .5 \times 5$$

$$M = 2.5 \text{ H}$$

Fig. 11-19. The basic idea for transformer design is a pair of wire coils wound around the same core.

TRANSFORMERS

The main use of mutual inductance is in transformer operation. A transformer usually consists of a pair of coils wound around the same iron core or shell, Fig. 11-19. The coils are wound on the same core to insure that the magnetic coupling between the two coils is as high as possible.

Fig. 11-20 shows a basic type of transformer. This type is known as a "laminated core transformer." The

Fig. 11-20. Cutaway view shows the makeup of a laminated core transformer. (Acme Electric Corp.)

core is made from thin strips of metal that look like the letter E. See Fig. 11-21. These pieces are stacked in a special way to produce a closed core assembly, Fig. 11-22. Another design of laminated core transformer uses strips in the shape of the letter U. These strips are stacked in "shell core transformers," Fig. 11-23.

Fig. 11-21. E-strip core material for building transformers is fed into a heat treating furnace. (Acme Electric Corp.)

Fig. 11-22. This laminated core transformer is called a "closed core" type.

Fig. 11-23. When the laminations are U-shaped, the assembled transformer is called a "shell core" type.

WHY THE CORE IS LAMINATED

If a solid core were used in a transformer, or if the thin strips of metal in a laminated core were stacked one on top of the other, a lot of heat will result. Heat means a loss of energy, so this heat buildup must be avoided.

Heat is created in the transformer when alternating currents (Eddy currents) are forced to flow in the core because of induced voltage. See Fig. 11-24. The larger the voltage created by the fields, the greater the heat generated in the transformer. The greater the heat, the greater the energy loss. In the trade, this loss is known as "Eddy-current loss."

One way transformer manufacturers cut down on transformer heat is by coating each metal E or U strip

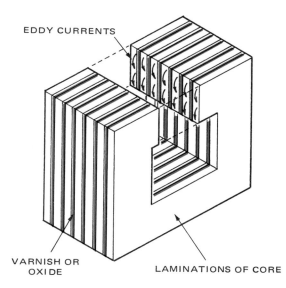

Fig. 11-24. Alternating current flow in the transformer core will break down into tiny loops or Eddy currents.

with varnish or oxide. In effect, then, each piece in the stacked core is separated by an insulator (similar to capacitor construction). This arrangement keeps large voltages from developing in the core, thereby holding down the alternating current flow that builds heat.

The copper for transformers also must be separated by an insulating material, just like insulation on coils of wire. The copper is wound into coils, Fig. 11-25. The

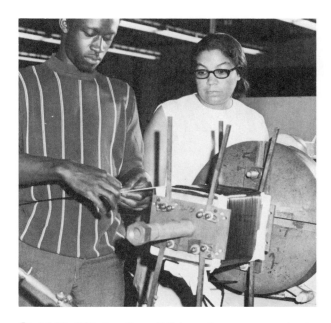

Fig. 11-25. "Winding the coils" is an important step in the early stages of the transformer manufacturing process. (Acme Electric Corp.)

coils are put together with the laminated cores, Fig. 11-26, then they are bolted together and made ready for sale. A view of the finished transformer in Fig. 11-27 will give you an idea of how it all fits together.

A second basic transformer is the ferrite-core type. See Fig. 11-28. It consists of a single, powdered iron bar wound with at least two coils. Ferrite-core transformers are used extensively as power transformers in high frequency applications.

PRIMARY AND SECONDARY

Basically, a transformer's job is to transfer electrical energy from one circuit to another by means of electromagnetic induction. The transformer winding connected to the energy source is called the "primary." The winding from which you receive the energy is called the "secondary."

Fig. 11-28. The ferrite core transformer is another popular design. Basically, the coils are wound around a soft iron core. See Fig. 11-18.

Fig. 11-26. Coils and laminated cores are put together in the start of final assembly of the transformers.

STEP-UP TRANSFORMERS

Transformers are widely used in electronics because they can step-up or step-down voltages. The transformer shown in Fig. 11-29 has 100 turns of wire in the primary winding and 600 turns in the secondary winding. If we connect 110V ac to the primary, we will get 660V ac from the secondary. This is an example of a "step-up" transformer.

The relationship between voltage and the number of turns can be expressed by the following equation:

$$\frac{N \text{ primary}}{N \text{ secondary}} = \frac{E \text{ primary}}{E \text{ secondary}}$$

N equals number of turns

E equals voltage

Using the previous example, here is how we get our result:

Fig. 11-27. Laminated core transformers are bolted together and come off the final assembly line for packing and shipment. (Acme Electric Corp.)

$$\frac{N_P}{N_S} = \frac{E_P}{E_S}$$

$$\frac{100}{600} = \frac{110V}{E_S}$$

$$100\,E_S = 66,000V$$

$$E_S = 660V$$

By putting 110 volts in the primary, we are able to get 660 volts out at the secondary. You can see by this increase why they call this a "step-up" transformer.

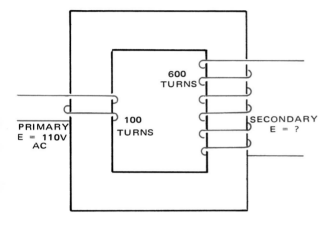

Fig. 11-29. In this simplified version of a step-up transformer, output voltage (E) would be **660** volts. See equation in text.

STEP-DOWN TRANSFORMERS

Next, we will look at a "step-down" transformer, Fig. 11-30. If we apply 1000 volts to a primary winding of 50 turns and the secondary winding has 10 turns, what output would we get?

Use the same formula:

$$\frac{N_P}{N_S} = \frac{E_P}{E_S}$$

$$\frac{50}{10} = \frac{1000}{E_S}$$

$$50\,E_S = 10,000$$

$$E_S = 200 \text{ volts}$$

Fig. 11-30. This step-down transformer carries a nameplate that gives input and output voltage, wattage and cycles per second. Note, too, that the leads are marked primary and secondary. (Acme Electric Corp.)

VOLTAGE-CURRENT RELATIONSHIPS

Transformers are used in electrical circuits because they are very efficient. Almost all the power applied to the primary winding is transferred to the secondary winding, Fig. 11-31. You may recall from Chapter 5, that power is equal to the voltage times current ($P = EI$). We can take this formula and use it in transformer circuit analysis. If we say that transformers are 100 percent efficient and have no losses we would have:

$$\text{Power}_{Primary} = \text{Power}_{Secondary}$$

This equation is equal to:

$$E_P I_P = E_S I_S$$

POWER

Look at the transformer drawing in Fig. 11-31. If the power on the primary winding is 600 watts and the voltage of the secondary is 150 volts, what is the current in the secondary?

Use the following formula:

$$\text{Power}_{In} = \text{Power}_{Out}$$

$$\text{Power}_{Primary} = E_S I_S$$

$$600W = 150V\ I_S$$

$$I_S = \frac{600}{150} = 4A$$

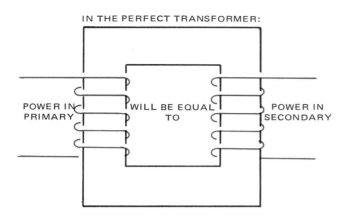

Fig. 11-31. Since transformers are very efficient, you can assume that power (E × I) applied to the primary equals power (E × I) produced by the secondary.

HIGH VOLTAGE TRANSFORMERS

In Fig. 11-32, you can see the coils of a high voltage transformer being wound. The wires sticking out on top of the windings are called taps. They are used to switch the transformer to different voltage levels. Changing to a different tap will change the ratio of primary to secondary windings. This transformer has a different shape than the others we have discussed. Their shape can be described as cylindrical or can-shaped. Again, the coil must be separated by insulation. This prevents the coils from touching one another and shorting out.

High voltage transformers have ratings of over 500,000 volt amperes of electricity (kVA). This type of transformer would not be used in school power supplies or around your home. High voltage transformers are found in industry where they have the need for large amounts of power. Fig. 11-33 shows a finished high voltage transformer.

Fig. 11-33. This high voltage transformer is mounted in its case, ready for stepping up voltages. (Acme Electric Corp.)

High voltage transformers are also found in substations, Fig. 11-34. The transformers on power poles are used to step the voltage down to 240 and 120 volts for use in businesses and homes, Fig 11-35.

SUMMARY

Voltage can be induced in a coil of wire by passing a magnet through the coil. Voltage can also be obtained by holding the magnet stationary and moving the coil past it. In either case, a voltage is produced even if the wire is insulated. In

Fig. 11-32. High voltage transformers look different, but follow the same design principle of coil windings separated by insulation and installed on a metal core.

Fig. 11-34. The transformers in this substation supply the power needs of a community.

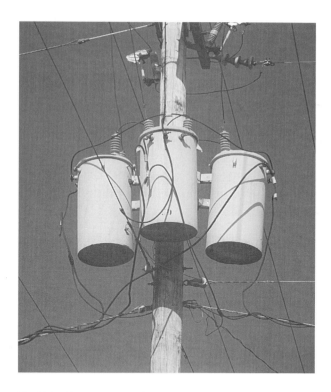

Fig. 11-35. Three power transformers are mounted on a pole. The transformer windings are placed inside a protective container filled with cooling oil.

fact, the wire must be insulated or a short circuit would prevent the process from working properly.

An inductor is a device that resists the change in current in any circuit. You will find inductors used in circuits that protect computers from the effects of voltage spikes caused by nearby lightning.

When two coils of wire are close enough to be linked by a magnetic field, they are said to have mutual inductance. This concept is what enables us to design transformers to step up and step down the voltage. Through mutual inductance, changing the ratio of windings in the primary and secondary produces a voltage change at the secondary.

KEY WORDS AND TERMS

Choke
Counter EMF
Eddy currents
Henry (H)
Induced EMF
Induction
Inductor
Laminated core transformer
Magnetic coupling
Microhenry (μH)

Millihenry (mH)
Mutual inductance
Primary windings
Secondary windings
Shell core transformer
Step-down transformer
Step-up transformer
Total inductance
Transformer

TEST YOUR KNOWLEDGE

1. Name the two windings found on a transformer.
2. Is ac or dc produced in the secondary winding of a transformer?
3. A transformer connected to a 120 volt ac source has 400 turns on the primary winding. If we want to obtain 6 volts from the second winding, how many turns of wire do we need for the secondary? Show your work.
4. *True or False?* Lines of flux cannot cut through insulating material.
5. The part of a circuit that opposes a change in current is called _____.
6. Draw the symbol for an inductor and a capacitor.
7. The unit of inductance is the _____.
8. An inductor will have no effect on _____ circuit.
9. Name three things which affect the inductance of a coil.
10. If we had three inductors connected in series, each having a value of 4 mH, what would the total inductance be? Show your work.
11. Laminations on the core of a transformer help cut down on the _____ loss.
12. The two types of transformers that get their name from how they affect the voltage are _____ and _____.

ACTIVITIES

1. Visit a plant that makes transformers or inductors. How do they wind the coils? Why do these components cost more than resistors?
2. Make a list of the places you find transformers around your house.
3. Some neighborhoods have a device that looks like a large black can attached to its telephone poles. These are transformers. What voltages do they produce?
4. Why do industrial plants operate so much of their equipment at 460 volts instead of the voltage of the appliances in your home?
5. On what voltage do the large electromagnets found in junkyards operate?
6. Why do power companies clear an area under all the high tension transmission lines?
7. How is it possible to run power lines underground without fear of electrocuting people walking over them?
8. The coil on a car is another type of inductor. What would it look like if you cut it into two pieces?
9. Can you make a radio without an inductor?
10. What kind of wire is needed to make an inductor or transformer? What would happen if the wire was not coated with insulation?
11. How do they encapsulate a transformer?
12. If the core of a transformer came apart, what would it sound like? What would happen to the transformer?

12 Motors

LEARNING OBJECTIVES

After studying this chapter, you will be able to:

- Describe the difference between a motor and an alternator.
- Draw the symbols for a motor and an alternator.
- Explain how a motor converts electrical energy into mechanical energy.
- Contrast the different types of motors.
- Calculate the number of poles required for a given RPM of a synchronous motor.

In the 1830s, Michael Faraday made a discovery that has made work easier for all of us. While experimenting with magnets, he found that moving a wire through a magnetic field would produce an electric current. We have seen how this was done in earlier chapters.

The magnet-and-wire experiment is important because it led to the discovery of the operating principles of electric motors and generators. In this chapter, we will study those principles, along with motor and generator types and applications.

MOTORS AND GENERATORS

A motor is a rotating machine that converts electrical energy into mechanical energy. Motors turn our washing machines, dryers, fans, furnace blowers, and much of the machinery found in industry, Fig. 12-1. Today, electric motors provide power for producing most of the mechanical energy used in the U.S.

A generator, on the other hand, is a rotating machine that converts mechanical energy into electrical energy.

Fig. 12-1. Electric motors (circled) are used extensively in industry. (Packard Electric Div., General Motors Corp.)

This mechanical energy could be supplied by a waterfall, nuclear power or in other ways described in Chapter 1.

In the 18th century, a scientist by the name of Oersted discovered that there was a relationship between magnetism and electricity. Oersted noticed that when he connected a wire to the poles of a battery and held the wire *over* a compass needle, the needle moved in one direction. If he held the wire *under* the compass needle, the needle moved in the opposite direction. This was an early discovery of the magnetic lines of force.

SYMBOLS

You recall that if a coil formed by many turns of wire is moved up and down over a magnet, the current created will move the needle on a galvanometer. This is called "induced current." Electric motors and generators work on principles based on the laws of magnetism and induced current.

Fig. 12-2 gives the popular symbols used to represent motors and generators in electrical drawings.

Fig. 12-3. Cutaway view shows major internal parts of a heavy-duty electric motor.

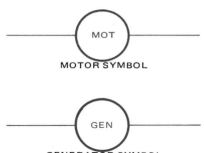

Fig. 12-2. These symbols are commonly used to designate motors and generators in electrical diagrams.

PARTS AND MAKEUP

Both motors and generators are made up of magnets, an armature (moving coils) and a commutator, Fig. 12-3. *A commutator is a device used to reverse electrical connections.* It is required because the armature coils inside motors and generators are in motion, Fig. 12-4. (Shortly, we will see how this works.)

Brushes or terminals are used with the commutator as a means of getting current out of a generator or into a motor armature. When studying motors, you will find a motor that does not need brushes. The most common motor of this type is known as a "squirrel-cage"

Fig. 12-4. The armature/commutator assembly forms the rotor of a dc motor or generator.

induction motor. Since there are so many different types of electric motors, we will explain some of the methods used to classify them.

CLASSIFYING MOTORS AND GENERATORS

There are several ways of classifying motors and generators. First, we can analyze whether they are single phase or polyphase:

NOTE: Single phase ac power is available from home outlets. Three phase ac power is common in industry. Polyphase means more than one phase. Phasing is covered in Chapters 10 and 13.

Single Phase	Polyphase

A. Split phase
  1. Resistance-start
  2. Split-capacitor
  3. Capacitor-start
  4. Repulsion-start
B. Commutator
  1. Series
  2. Repulsion
	A. Squirrel Cage
	B. Wound Rotor

Another way of classifying motors is by ac or dc:

Alternating current	Direct Current

A. Induction
  1. Phase Wound
  2. Squirrel Cage
    a. Split Phase
    b. Shaded Pole
B. Synchronous
	A. Series
	B. Shunt
	C. Compound

You might ask why we must "classify" motors. Since there are hundreds of different kinds of electric motors, you *must* pick the one way of classifying motors which best suits your needs. Relating this to another situation may help you to understand motor classification a little better. Most people, for example, know that automobiles are classified several ways. Some of the ways include:
1. Manufacturer
2. Model
3. Color
4. Engine size
5. Weight

You can see that some of these choices overlap. If you want a car with a specific horsepower rating, you might find that this engine is available only in certain models. Normally, a small four cylinder engine would not be installed in a car weighing over 4500 lb. Likewise, you would not expect a light-duty electric motor to perform satisfactorily in a heavy-duty application.

SELECTION

To find the right motor for your needs, first look at what it will be required to do. Another way is to decide whether you need an ac or dc motor. You also might want to look at torque (twisting force), and possibly

even speed and load given on the motor identification plate. Then, your next step would be to start narrowing down the available types of motors to one which meets your specific needs.

Although we cannot cover all of the different kinds of motors, we will give you the basic principles of operation for most electric motors.

HOW THEY WORK

Start your study of principles of operation by seeing what makes a motor turn. *Both a dc motor and a dc generator work in a similar manner. The basic difference is that a motor is made to turn by putting current into it. A generator, on the other hand, will produce a current when some outside force causes it to turn.* See Fig. 12-5.

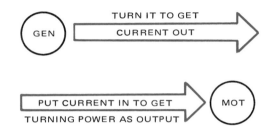

Fig. 12-5. A generator must be turned mechanically to produce current. Current must be applied to a motor to make it turn.

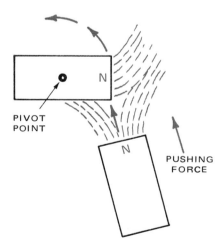

Fig. 12-6. Like poles of two magnets repel each other. If one magnet is pivoted at the center, the pushing force created will cause it to turn.

TURNING MAGNETS

There are two ways you can make a magnet turn. As an experiment, lay down the first magnet so that it is free to move, Fig. 12-6. Then, bring the north pole of the second magnet close to the north pole of the first magnet. Since like poles repel, the first magnet will turn away from the second. The same repelling action (repulsion) holds true if two south poles are used in the experiment.

Another way of making a magnet turn is by setting up as before, but instead of using *like* poles bring the north pole of the second magnet close to the south pole of the first magnet. Since *unlike* poles attract, the first magnet will be attracted to and turn toward the second magnet. See Fig. 12-7.

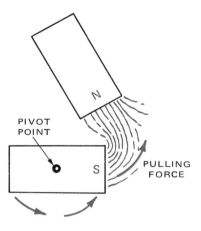

Fig. 12-7. Unlike poles of two magnets attract each other. If one magnet is pivoted at the center, the pulling force created will cause it to turn.

In a further experiment, substitute a coil for the first magnet and a pair of magnets for the second, as shown in Fig. 12-8. To set it up, wrap a coil of wire around a pivoting metal bar and pass a current through the coil. This will create a magnetic field around the coil.

Then, bring the coil and its magnetic field between the opposite poles of the pair of magnets, Fig. 12-8, and the coil will begin to turn. This turning action is the result of attraction or repulsion, depending on the polarity of the parts.

Therefore, the laws of attraction and repulsion (which you learned earlier) are the basis of electric motor operation.

DC MOTORS

To relate our attraction/repulsion experiment directly to electric motor operation, we will start with a simple dc motor, Fig. 12-9. We can pass current through one brush, to the coil and back out the second brush.

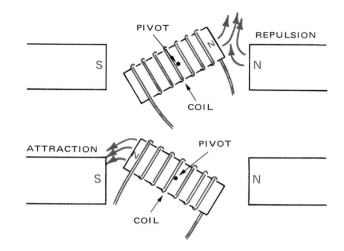

Fig. 12-8. To strengthen the magnetic field and improve the turning action of the pivoting magnet, coils of wire are wrapped around the metal bar to form an electromagnet.

When this happens, the magnetic field of the coil opposes the magnetic field of our magnet. The repelling action of like poles makes the armature start to turn, Fig. 12-10. As the armature turns, its north pole is attracted to the south pole of the magnet. Just as the two unlike poles are about to line up, the polarity of the armature is changed by the commutator, Fig. 12-11. Again, the two like poles will repel each other, and the armature will continue to spin. Therefore, we get this motion from our motor by means of current flow through the set of brushes to the commutator.

COILS

Instead of making a motor with just one coil, most motors have several sets in the armature, Fig. 12-12.

Fig. 12-9. A simple dc electric motor can be formed by connecting the leads of the coil (armature) to the commutator. Fixed brushes carry dc electricity to and from the commutator.

Fig. 12-10. Note that like poles repel each other, causing the armature to start to turn. Once the armature completes a quarter turn, the unlike poles will attract each other and the armature will continue to turn.

Fig. 12-11. After one-half turn of the armature, its poles are reversed by the commutator and the repelling/attracting process is repeated. Note how the split commutator changes the polarity of the armature.

More coils are necessary because we want to get a large magnetic field in the motor housing. If we used just one coil, we would have a very weak motor and it would not provide smooth operation.

Fig. 12-12. Typical way in which the first coil is wrapped on an armature core.

BRUSHES AND COMMUTATOR

Brushes are one of the big problems with electric motors of this type. Usually, they are made of a carbon material. Because of this, the brushes tend to wear out and must be replaced. Many of the small motors used on sewing machines, power drills and other home appliances are equipped with these brushes. See the power tool in Fig. 12-13.

I.C. WARNS:

"If you replace brushes in an electric motor, be sure to unplug the power cord before you start to work. Brushes carry the current which makes motors spin. Avoid electrical shock."

Fig. 12-13. Some power tools use an ac electric motor with armature and commutator. Plug removal permits access to spring-loaded brushes.

Brushes usually are easy to remove. Many can be taken out by using a screwdriver to loosen the brush holder, Fig. 12-14. Most brushes are spring loaded to keep them in contact with the commutator. Be careful on disassembly. Do not lose the springs when you remove the brushes.

If the brushes are not making proper contact with the commutator, the motor will have a weak starting torque. Bad contact can be caused by worn brushes, weak brush spring or brushes sticking in their holders. A dirty commutator also can cause poor electrical contact.

The commutator is made from copper. It should be cleaned with a very fine sandpaper rather than emery cloth, or you may have "shorting" problems later. When you start to clean the commutator, it probably will have a dull, blackened look. As the copper segments clean up, they will regain the shiny copper look.

Fig. 12-14. Sectional view shows makeup of an electric drill. Note brush type motor at rear.

BEARINGS

One of the major causes of electric motor failure is bearing wear. Since motors must spin freely, it is important that the bearings have proper lubrication. Pay close attention to the manufacturer's instructions for lubrication. Some bearings need just two or three drops of oil. If you use too much oil, it will attract dirt and dust that will gum up the bearings. Other pre-lubricated bearings do not need any oil at all. These bearings usually have the right amount and kind of lubricant sealed inside.

Fig. 12-15. An industrial voltmeter can be used to make voltage tests at various points in the electric motor circuit.

VOLTAGE CHECKS

A number of different troubles can cause a motor to fail to start. First use a voltmeter to see if there is voltage at the motor terminals. Fig. 12-15 shows a voltmeter which many industrial electricians carry with them. Note that it reads both ac and dc voltage. Neon lights inside the meter will light up to tell you the voltage level.

Many times, motors have been removed from the mounting to be checked in a repair shop, only to find nothing is wrong with them. Because of their size, Fig. 12-16, some motors have to be lifted by means of a crane. Therefore, if a check with the motor in place

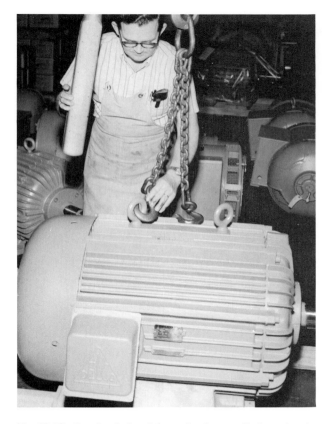

Fig. 12-16. Certain industrial applications call for electric motors so large that a crane must be used to move them. Applications include machine tools, pumps, pulp and paper machines and conveyors. (Delco Products Div., General Motors Corp.)

proves that there is no voltage at the terminals, a lot of time and work will be saved. No voltage would mean that a part other than the motor is at fault. There are some other voltage checks which can be made, Fig. 12-17, without first taking the motor off the machine.

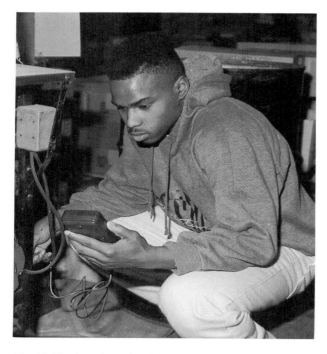

Fig. 12-17. A service technician uses a voltmeter to check a motor that is still in place.

BLOWN FUSE INDICATOR PROJECT

Have you ever spent a lot of time troubleshooting a circuit, only to find a "blown" fuse? To avoid this problem, make up the simple circuit shown in Fig. 12-18. It can be added across the fuse in the original circuit to warn you when the fuse blows. When it does, the lamp will light.

Parts needed for the project include:

No.	Item
1	NE-2 neon lamp.
1	Resistor (value depends on circuit voltage). Connecting wire.

In order to assemble this project, you must know the voltage across the fuse. This information will allow you to select the right size resistor to use. The formula is:

$$\text{Resistance of } R_1 = \frac{\text{voltage}}{.0025}$$

For example, if the fuse is across 110 volts:

$$R_1 = \frac{110V}{.0025}$$

$$R_1 = 44,000\,\Omega$$

Fig. 12-18. Schematic shows how to connect a "blown fuse indicator" across the fuse in the original circuit. R_1 is a resistor. M_1 is a neon lamp.

Based on this computation, then, the 110 volt circuit will require a 44,000 ohm resistor.

Since an NE-2 neon lamp requires between 60 and 65 volts to ionize, this blown fuse indicator is only good for sources greater than 65 volts.

INDUCTION MOTORS

The second major type of electric motor we will cover is the induction motor found on many types of machinery. It does not use a commutator or brushes. Instead, it is constructed with a rotor that spins inside a stator.

One way to get a better grasp of the construction of induction motors is to think of the stator as stationary and the rotor as rotating. The stator consists of a winding or windings on a laminated steel core. The rotor is made of laminated steel, and it has copper bars that fit into slots on the steel core. Two end shields are fitted with bearings to support the rotor shaft.

If you have ever seen a squirrel cage, or treadmill for small animals, you will know why this rotor is called "squirrel cage." See Fig. 12-19.

OPERATION

A magnetic field is created in the stator of an induction motor by passing current through its windings. The lines of force of this magnetic field revolve around the stator windings, inducing a current in the copper bars of the rotor. The rotor, in turn, becomes an electromagnet, and its magnetic field is attracted to the magnetic field of the stator.

Looking at Fig. 12-20, the north pole created in the stator winding will attract the south pole of the rotor winding at point 1. As the magnetic field revolves around the stator windings, it exerts a magnetic pull on the rotor, causing it to turn to point 2, then point 3 and

Fig. 12-19. A squirrel cage rotor serves as the core for an induction motor. Coils of wire are wrapped on the core to form the moving part of the motor.

so on. Finally, it will get to point 21 and start all over again.

Since the rotor can turn in its bearings, it starts to rotate just behind the magnetic field of the stator, Fig. 12-21. These magnetic fields follow one another around the squirrel cage, with the rotor always behind the magnetic field of the stator. If the rotor did manage to

Fig. 12-20. In an induction motor, the magnetic field around the stator windings creates a north pole which, in turn, attracts the south pole of the rotor windings, causing the rotor to turn.

SOUTH POLE BEING DRAGGED ALONG

Fig. 12-21. The magnetic field revolving around the stator windings moves just ahead of the rotating rotor.

"catch up" with the rotating field of the stator, the conductors in the rotor would be standing still with respect to the rotating field. If this condition occurred, no voltage would be induced in the squirrel cage which, in turn, would not have current in it nor magnetic poles set up. There would be no attraction between the rotor and the rotating field in the stator. The rotor would stand still.

For proper operation of an induction motor, the rotor must revolve just a bit slower than the rotating field in the stator can cut through the rotor conductors. This difference is called "slip." Without slip, the rotor will not turn. If the load on the rotor is increased, such as making it turn a heavy weight, we would get greater slip and the motor would run a little bit slower. However, for most purposes, the squirrel cage induction motor is considered to be a constant speed device.

SYNCHRONOUS MOTORS

A third type of motor we will look at is known as the "synchronous motor." In your study of induction motors, you have found that as you pass a current through the stator, you set up a magnetic field. The rotor, in turn, is pulled along by this magnetic field with a small amount of slip. The synchronous motor operates in a similar manner. See Fig. 12-22.

The synchronous motor gets its name from a term used to describe the natural speed of the rotating magnetic field of the stator. In the U.S., the natural speed is tied to the frequency of applied ac power. Here, this frequency is regulated by the power companies at 60 Hz.

In the case of the synchronous motor, the rotating magnetic field is designed to lock onto the rotor. By locking the rotating magnetic field to the rotor, they will operate at the same speed. Because of this locking idea, synchronous motors can be found in various timing devices such as electric clocks. Since power companies regulate the frequency at 60 Hz, these clocks keep very accurate time.

ROTOR TO
TURN CLOCKWISE

Fig. 12-22. Arrows show how a synchronous motor works. The rotating magnetic field locks onto the rotor and turns it at a natural speed.

POLES AND RPM

Other uses can be made of synchronous motors by building them to operate at any one of a number of constant speeds. However, each motor will run at the one speed for which it was built to operate. To get a synchronous motor to operate at another speed, the manufacturer must produce one with a different number of poles.

The formula for figuring the speed of a synchronous motor is:

$$rpm = \frac{frequency \times 120}{P}$$

P = Number of poles in motor

Since the frequency of applied ac power in the U.S. is 60 Hz, all we have to do to change the rpm of a synchronous motor is change the number of poles. For example, if you have a motor with two poles, what is its speed?

$$rpm = \frac{frequency \times 120}{P}$$

$$rpm = \frac{60 \times 120}{2}$$

$$rpm = 3600$$

This means that a two pole synchronous motor will run at a constant speed of 3600 rpm. Synchronous motors do not have variable speeds. If you want a motor that will run at 1200 rpm, how many poles would have to be built into the motor?

$$rpm = \frac{frequency \times 120}{P}$$

$$P = \frac{frequency \times 120}{rpm}$$

$$P = \frac{60 \times 120}{1200} = \frac{7200}{1200}$$

$$P = 6 \text{ poles}$$

Therefore, to get 1200 rpm from a synchronous motor, six poles would have to be built into it. Synchronous motors always have an even number of poles, ranging from two up to 90 poles. A 90 pole motor of this type would run at 80 rpm.

GENERATORS

A dc generator is almost the same as a dc motor. Again, the main difference is that the shaft of the generator must be turned by some means of mechanical power. When the armature starts to turn, magnetic fields are cut inside the generator and current begins to flow. By putting brushes on the commutator, we can then pick off this flow of current.

The commutator is not one continuous ring, Fig. 12-23. Instead, it is made of two separate pieces. To make sure they do not touch each other, a piece of insulating material such as mica is placed between them. If they do touch, it would, in effect, give us a short circuit. All the work done by the generator would be wasted. Instead of getting current out, it would circulate inside the coils of the generator and overheat.

Fig. 12-23. The commutator in this simple generator consists of two metal pieces. Brushes make contact with commutator to pick off flow of current generated in the armature.

DC GENERATOR OUTPUT

The output from a dc generator is not pure dc. It does not give us the same wave we would get out of a battery, Fig. 12-24. Instead, it is a pulsing dc, Fig. 12-25. From Fig. 12-26, you can see that if we could use a four piece commutator, we would get two overlapping sets of pulsing dc. If you look at the peaks

in Fig. 12-27, you can see that we are getting closer to the straight line you think of as being dc.

By using capacitors, Fig. 12-28, we can filter the dc to take out the ripple. The rotating part of the

Fig. 12-24. This dc waveform is typical of battery output. The wave shows a steady voltage above the reference line.

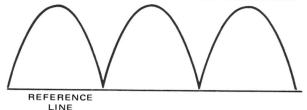

Fig. 12-25. A dc generator produces a pulsing waveform with all waves above the reference line.

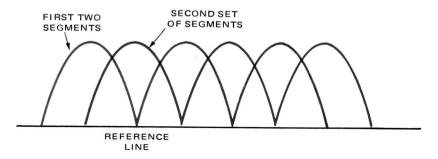

Fig. 12-26. A four-piece commutator will produce overlapping sets of pulsing dc. This is called a "ripple pulse."

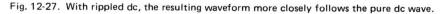

Fig. 12-27. With rippled dc, the resulting waveform more closely follows the pure dc wave.

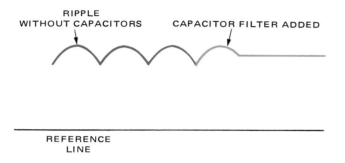

Fig. 12-28. Capacitors can be added to a dc generator circuit to smooth the ripples from rippled dc.

generator is known as the rotor; the stationary part is the stator. The armature usually is part of the rotor, while the field coils are part of the stator.

EDDY CURRENTS

We dicussed eddy currents in transformers in Chapter 11. Eddy currents are also found in generators. When the generator armature cuts through the magnetic field, current is induced in the armature windings and it also circulates within the metal. See Fig. 12-29. The armature is made of several parts and is laminated. The armature windings are wound in the slots of the core. This construction is designed to keep eddy currents as small as possible in the metal core of the armature.

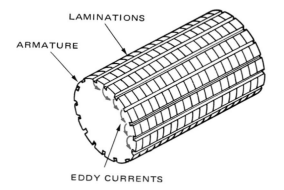

Fig. 12-29. The metal core of a generator armature is laminated to reduce the flow of eddy currents.

AC GENERATOR/ALTERNATOR

The ac generator is called an alternator, especially when it is used in an automotive charging system. See Fig. 12-30. The ac generator uses slip rings, Fig. 12-31, in place of the commutator found on dc generators. The slip rings, or the commutator, are designed to let

Fig. 12-30. Cutaway view reveals the internal makeup of an automotive ac generator (alternator). (Chrysler Corp.)

Fig. 12-31. This simple ac generator has two slip rings and two brushes. Note that each end of the coil wire end leads to a separate slip ring.

the coil turn without twisting or breaking any wires. The ends of the coil are soldered to pick off points. As the coil turns, the slip rings, or commutator, slide past the fixed brushes. This lets us obtain electrical output from the wires attached to the brushes.

THREE-PHASE ALTERNATORS

Many motors and generators use a "three-phase system," Fig. 12-32. Three phase means that the sine wave starts at every 120 deg. instead of the normal 360 deg. In this manner, we can plug the valleys left in a normal sine wave to give us less of a stop-start effect from the dips in the sine waves.

Three-phase alternators are commonly used in automobiles to charge the battery and operate electrical devices. To do this, a rectifier or diode assembly is used,

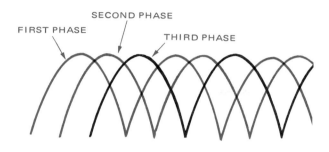

Fig. 12-32. The three-phase system used in generators starts a new sine wave every 120 deg., instead of every 360 deg., to level off dips in the sign waves.

Fig. 12-30. The three-phase system used in generators starts a new sine wave every 120°, instead of every 360°, to level off dips in sine waves. Fig. 12-32.

We will mention rectifiers again when we cover filter circuits. They will be explained in detail in the final few chapters.

For now, just think of a rectifier, or diode, as a one-way street. It limits electrical flow to one direction only. In an automotive alternator, the diodes change the ac to dc.

The alternator is driven by mechanical energy produced by the automobile engine. It will generate current through all three phases of its windings. Because of this, the alternator is able to charge the battery at low engine speed while the dc generator cannot.

SUMMARY

A motor is a rotating machine that converts electrical energy into mechanical energy. An alternator converts mechanical energy into electrical energy. The main parts of a motor include brushes, commutator, armature, and bearings to support the shaft. The laws of attraction and repulsion are the basis for the operation of electric motors.

You can pick the needed speed for a synchronous motor by selecting the number of poles in that motor. Dividing 7200 by the RPM needed for a synchronous motor would give the number of poles required.

A generator does not produce steady state dc like that produced by a battery. The peaks that are produced by the generator can be reduced to a ripple in two ways. First, by increasing the number of pieces in the commutator, produces overlapping sets pulses. Second, adding a capacitor to the circuit also filters the ripple.

KEY WORDS AND TERMS

Alternator
Armature
Brush

Slip
Slip rings
Squirrel cage

Commutator
Generator
Induction motor
Motor
Rotor

Stator
Synchronous motor
Three-phase system
Torque

TEST YOUR KNOWLEDGE

Do not write in this book. Write your answers on a separate sheet of paper.

1. A commutator is a device used to _____.
2. Brushes in a motor are used to _____.
3. *True or False?* Because of their large size, induction motors must have specially made brushes to maintain good contact.
4. Find the rpm of a motor which has four poles and is operated on 60 Hz. Show your work.
5. Why do motors have a varied number of poles?
6. Why should you turn off the power *before* you work on the brushes of a motor?
7. Name one of the major causes of motor failure.
8. The alternator on an automobile is a _____ electrical system which is used to _____ the battery on a car.
9. The rotating part of a generator is called the _____ and the stationary part is called the _____.
10. Eddy currents in a generator are reduced by using _____.
11. *True or False?* The big advantage of a dc generator over an ac generator is that its windings produce pure dc which does not have to be filtered.

ACTIVITIES

1. Get an old motor and take it apart. Label the various parts.
2. Why are brushes for motors made from carbon (the same material used for resistors)?
3. Make a list of places in your home where you use motors. Be careful. Motors may be hidden in places you might not think about.
4. Research to find the specific sizes of the largest and smallest motors being made. Where are they being used?
5. Generators on cars have been replaced by alternators. What is the big advantage of an alternator?
6. Many motors have sealed bearings. How are they made? What makes them so different from regular bearings?
7. Many electrical devices are laminated. What holds them together? List some of the assemblies that are laminated.
8. The alternator on an automobile engine uses a three-phase system. Get the electrical diagram of such a system and see if you can figure out how it works. Where else do you find three-phase electrical systems?

13 Reactance and Impedance

LEARNING OBJECTIVES

After studying this chapter, you will be able to:
- Calculate the value for reactance and impedance in a circuit.
- Describe the principle of vector addition.
- Explain the concept of transformer loading and its effect on the secondary.
- Draw graphs to illustrate the differences between leading and lagging voltage and current in inductive and capacitive circuits.
- Calculate the time required to charge a capacitor in a circuit using the RC time constant formula.
- Use the correct formula to find the voltage drops in inductive and capacitive circuits.

In this chapter, we will look at the behavior of inductors in an ac circuit. In order to find out whether or not inductors have an effect on an ac current, set up a circuit as shown in Fig. 13-1. You will need a 12 volt battery, a switch, test lamp, inductor, and connecting wiring.

When you have the circuit assembled, close the switch and watch the test lamp. Note that, after a slight pause, the lamp lights to full brilliance. This is not too surprising. From your studies in Chapter 11, you know that an inductor will oppose a change in current. Once that current reaches its maximum

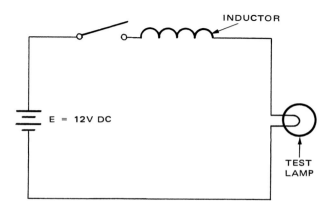

Fig. 13-1. An inductor will oppose a change in direct current flow. When the switch is closed, the lamp will be dimly lit until current flow in the circuit reaches its maximum value.

Fig. 13-2. An inductor placed in an alternating current circuit will offer inductive reactance (opposition) to current flow. Adding the inductor will dim the lamp.

(determined by the resistance of the bulb), the inductor will no longer affect the current. Therefore, the bulb will glow with full brightness.

Now, replace the 12 volt battery with a 12 volt ac source, Fig. 13-2. Since the RMS value of the ac wave is 12 volts, you would expect the bulb to glow as brightly as before. However, when you close the switch, note that the light is less bright. So it seems that an inductor does offer some resistance to the alternating current.

INDUCTIVE REACTANCE

The opposition offered by inductors to any change in current is called inductive reactance. This is an important part of our study of electronics.

The amount of reactance that an inductor presents to ac depends upon two factors:
- Inductance of the inductor.
- Frequency of the varying current or voltage applied to the inductor.

The symbol for inductive reactance is X_L. Its value can be found by working out the following formula:

$$X_L = 2\pi fL$$

Where f is the frequency of the applied voltage, L is the inductance of the coil in henrys, and π is the constant 3.14.

Example:

If an ac voltage with a frequency of 318 Hz and an amplitude of 200 volts is applied to an inductor whose inductance is .5 H, find the inductive reactance of the circuit, Fig. 13-3.

$$X_L = 2\pi fL$$

$$X_L = 2 \times 3.14 \times 318 \text{ Hz} \times .5 \text{ H}$$

$$X_L = 999\,\Omega$$

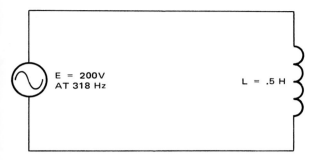

Fig. 13-3. The inductive reactance (X_L) of this ac circuit is 999 ohms, found by using the formula $X_L = 2\pi fL$.

INDUCTIVE REACTANCE = OHMS

The value of X_L is measured in ohms. This is done because reactance affects ac the same way that resistance affects dc. In fact, if we refer back to our example, we can compute the amount of current that is flowing in the circuit.

Use Ohm's Law, replacing the R (resistance) with X_L (inductive reactance). To make our numbers a little easier to handle, round off the X_L value to 1000 ohms. One ohm does not make that much difference. It can exist in the tolerance of a resistor.

$$I = \frac{E}{X_L}$$

$$I = \frac{200V}{1000\,\Omega} = .2A$$

Since this circuit contains only an inductor, you can see that the reactance of the inductor behaves just like resistance.

PHASE BETWEEN VOLTAGE AND CURRENT

If you look at one cycle of alternating current on a sine wave, Fig. 13-4, you will see that we have divided the cycle into 360 electrical degrees. This is the same number of degrees that the generator had to turn to produce the cycle of ac.

I.C. SAYS:

"Remember that one full turn or revolution contains 360 degrees."

When studying the sine wave in Fig. 13-4, note that the current flow is changing at the fastest rate at 0 deg., 180 deg. and 360 deg. Also note that at exactly 90 deg., current flow stops increasing and changes direction.

In Chapter 11, we established that an inductor produces a counter electromotive force that depends upon how fast the current is changing. With this in mind, where would you expect counter EMF to be highest? If you said, 0 deg., 180 deg. or 360 deg., you are right. At these particular times in each cycle, the current is changing at its fastest rate and the voltage across the inductor will be at a maximum.

Based on the sine wave shown in Fig. 13-4, where would you expect the voltage to be at a minimum? The answer is: at 90 deg. and 270 deg. At these points, the current stops changing for a moment and the counter EMF of the coil has dropped to zero.

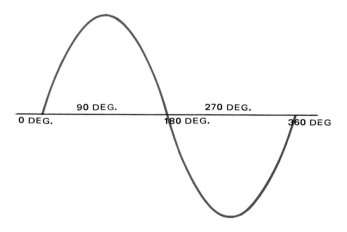

Fig. 13-4. One cycle of alternating current in the form of a sine wave can be divided into 360 electrical degrees.

GRAPHING CURRENT AND VOLTAGE

If you make one graph showing both current flow and EMF produced across the coil, Fig. 13-5, you can see that the current and voltage are both sine waves. While current and voltage waves usually have different amplitudes, at this time we are more concerned with the difference between the phase of the waves.

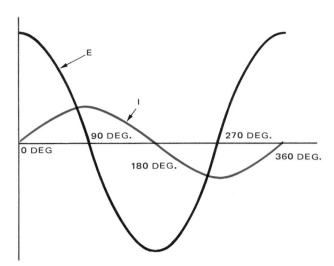

Fig. 13-5. This graph compares out-of-phase sine waves of voltage and current in an inductive circuit.

Fig. 13-6. A series "RL circuit" contains both an inductor and a resistor. Note voltage drop readings across these components.

Note that the zero points of the two waves differ by 90 deg. Therefore, we can say that the voltage across the inductor is 90 deg. out of phase with the current through it.

In Fig. 13-5, the voltage wave crosses the reference line (axis) at 90 deg., while the current wave crosses the line at 180 deg. Since current is 90 deg. "later" than voltage, we say that current "lags" voltage by 90 deg. In this circuit, when the voltage across the inductor is at a maximum, current through the inductor drops to zero. *The current lags the voltage in all inductors.*

AC BEHAVIOR OF SERIES RL CIRCUITS

The next step in the study of inductive reactance is to see what happens when we connect an inductor and a resistor in series. This type of circuit is called an "RL circuit" (R for resistance, L for inductance). If you recall your study of series circuits in Chapter 6, you know that when two elements are in series, they have the same amount of current passing through them.

Hook up a series RL circuit as shown in Fig. 13-6. Pick an inductor with a value of around 100 millihenries and a 47 ohm, 2 watt resistor. Using a voltmeter, measure the voltage across the inductor and the voltage across the resistor. You should get a reading of about 7.5 volts across the inductor and a reading of about 9.4 volts across the resistor.

How can this happen? If these two voltage drops are in series, they should add up to the applied voltage, which is 12 volts. You can see that 7.5 volts + 9.4 volts does not add up to 12 volts.

To answer this question, consider that an inductor has a maximum voltage across it when the current through it drops to zero. A resistor, on the other hand, has zero volts across it when the current drops to zero. In order to add quantities that behave like this, we must use "vectors."

VECTORS

Vectors usually are shown as arrows, Fig. 13-7. The length of the arrow represents the magnitude or size of the vector, while the arrowhead shows the direction of the vector. Vectors can be used to show the value of many different things, such as force, movement, voltage and current.

For example, suppose you walked straight north for three miles, then turned right and walked straight east for four miles, Fig. 13-8. If we let vector A represent your northward travel and vector B represent your eastward travel, you can get a good picture of what has occurred.

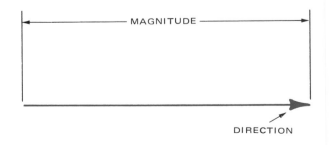

Fig. 13-7. A vector generally is drawn as an arrow. A vector represents direction and magnitude of a given value.

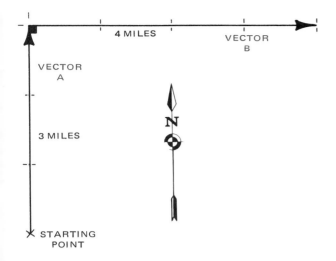

Fig. 13-8. To illustrate the use of vectors, the route of a seven mile walk is charted with vectors A and B.

Note that the little square drawn at the right turn shows that the angle between vector A and vector B is 90 deg. The two most important points you have to think about are:
1. How far have I walked?
2. How far am I from my starting point?

To answer No. 1 is very simple. You have walked a total of seven miles. No. 2 is really quite easy, too. Just join the tail of vector A to the head of vector B, as shown in Fig. 13-9. The figure formed is called a "right triangle," because it has a right angle (90 deg.) in it.

Right triangles have a special relation between their sides. If you take the two shorter sides of the triangle, square them and add these totals, you will get the

length of the longest side squared.

In Fig. 13-9, vector C can be found by using the following formula:

$$(\text{Length of C})^2 = (\text{Length of A})^2 + (\text{Length of B})^2$$

$$C^2 = 3^2 + 4^2$$

$$C^2 = 9 + 16$$

$$C^2 = 25$$

$$C = \sqrt{25}$$

$$C = 5 \text{ mi.}$$

Vector C then, gives us the trip distance from start to finish. Note that even though you walked a total of seven miles, you ended up only five miles from your starting point. From this example, we will see how "adding vectors" can help solve the problem of putting an inductor and a resistor in the same series circuit.

RL VOLTAGES

Take another look at the series RL circuit shown in Fig. 13-6. You should recall the following points:
1. The 7.5 volts across the inductor "leads" the current through the inductor by 90 deg.
2. The 9.4 volts across the resistor is in phase with the current through the resistor.
3. The same current flows through both the inductor and the resistor.

If you keep these three points in mind, you can see that the voltage across the inductor is 90 deg. out of phase with the voltage across the resistor. Fig. 13-10 shows these voltages drawn as vectors. If you want to "add" these voltages, you have to use the same formula we worked out in the last example:

$$C^2 = E_L{}^2 + E_R{}^2$$

$$C^2 = 7.5^2 + 9.4^2$$

$$C^2 = 56.25 + 88.36$$

$$C^2 = 144.61$$

$$C = \sqrt{144.61}$$

$$C = 12.0V$$

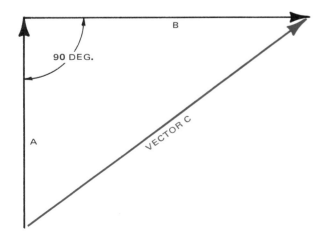

Fig. 13-9. Using vectors A and B from Fig. 13-8, vector C is drawn to complete the right triangle. The formula for solving the length of vector C is $C^2 = A^2 + B^2$.

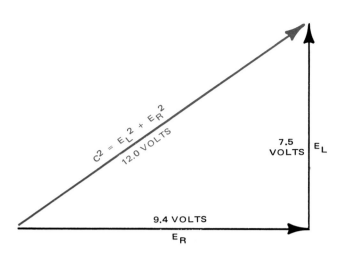

Fig. 13-10. Substituting voltage values for vectors E_R and E_L, use formula shown to solve for total voltage drop in circuit.

From this, you can see that if we add the two voltages like vectors, we get an answer that equals the applied voltage of 12 volts.

IMPEDANCE

By figuring the combination of reactance and resistance as we did in the last example (12.0V), we have "found the impedance" of the circuit. *Impedance, then, is the total opposition that an electrical circuit offers to the flow of varying current at a given frequency.*

You can find the impedance of an RL circuit by adding X_L and R like vectors:

$$\text{Impedance}^2 = X_L{}^2 + R^2$$

Impedance usually is given the symbol Z in formulas and in various forms of circuit analysis. For example, in the series RL circuit shown in Fig. 13-11: the inductor

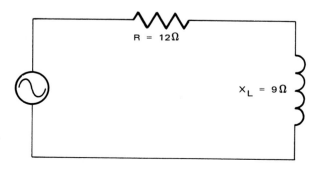

Fig. 13-11. The resistor (R) and the inductor (L) in this series RL circuit offer opposition (impedance) to the flow of alternating current.

has an inductance of 9 ohms; the resistor has a resistance of 12 ohms. Find the total impedance of the circuit:

$$Z^2 = X_L{}^2 + R^2$$

$$Z^2 = 9^2 + 12^2$$

$$Z^2 = 81 + 144 = 225$$

$$Z = \sqrt{225}$$

$$Z = 15\Omega$$

The current will "see" an opposition of 15 ohms to the ac flowing through the circuit.

PHASE ANGLE

Usually a "phase angle" is included with the impedance value. If we draw the two kinds of opposition, Fig. 13-12, we will see that the inductive reactance and the resistance are 90 deg. apart. The angle "A" between the impedance and the resistance is known as the "phase angle." Angle "A" describes the angle (how much out of phase) between the applied voltage and the resulting current.

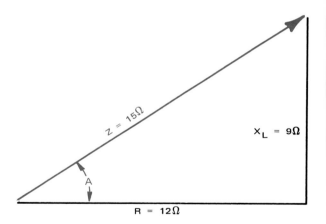

Fig. 13-12. Total impedance (Z) of the circuit shown in Fig. 13-11 is 15 ohms, found by forming vectors X_L and R, and using the formula $Z^2 = X_L{}^2 + R^2$. "A" is the phase angle.

In this text, however, we will not concern ourselves with the phase angle. Rather, we will deal only with the size or magnitude of the impedance. For example, find the magnitude of the current in Fig. 13-13. An ac voltage of 45 volts is applied to the circuit. Total impedance is 15 ohms.

$$I = \frac{E}{Z}$$

$$I = \frac{45}{15}$$

$$I = 3A$$

The current has a magnitude of three amperes.

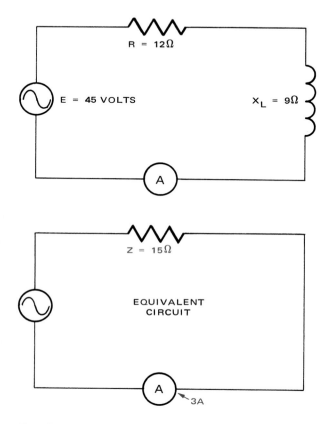

Fig. 13-13. Current flow in this series RL ac circuit is 3 amps, found by figuring impedance (Z) first, then using Ohm's Law $I = \frac{E}{Z}$.

TRANSFORMER LOADING

You recall that we studied transformer operation in some detail in Chapter 11. We found that transformers transfer electrical energy from one circuit to another by electromagnetic induction. When a transformer has no load on the secondary, it will act in a different way than when the secondary is loaded. This is a problem of "phasing." Since we have covered phasing in this chapter, now would be a good time to further explain transformer operation.

UNLOADED TRANSFORMER

When the transformer is not loaded, it is said to have an "open secondary." This means that the primary of the transformer acts just about the same as an inductor. That is: the primary current lags the applied voltage by 90 deg., Fig. 13-14. At the same time, the current will be ahead of the "back EMF" by 90 deg. Back EMF is caused by the magnetic field created when current is flowing in the primary. You can see that the applied voltage and the back EMF have the opposite polarity. Most transformers are built so that the back EMF will be high in the primary when the secondary is open. This is done in an effort to keep the primary current as low as possible when there is no secondary current.

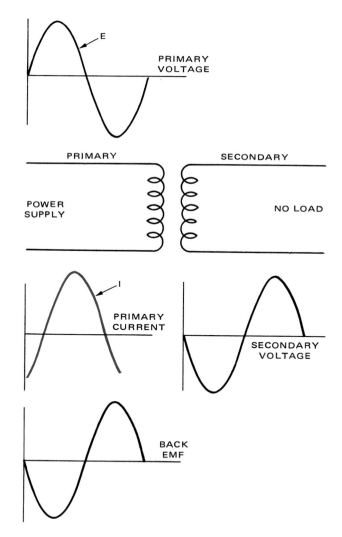

Fig. 13-14. In analyzing the operation of a transformer with no load on the secondary, the primary current lags the applied voltage by 90 deg.

Even though no current flows in the secondary, the expanding and collapsing magnetic field in the primary still cuts through the turns of the secondary winding. This action results in a voltage being induced in the secondary. This induced voltage, however, will be 90 deg. behind the current in the primary. Therefore, the secondary voltage will be a total of 180 deg. out of phase with the primary voltage.

It *is* possible to wind the primary and secondary coils of transformers so that the induced secondary voltage is "in phase" or "out of phase" with the primary. In Fig. 13-15, dots are used to show you whether the terminals are in phase or out of phase.

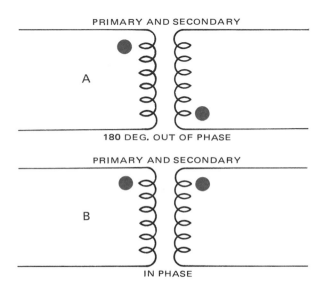

Fig. 13-15. Dots indicate position of terminals on a transformer. A—Primary and secondary windings are out of phase. B—Secondary is wound to bring windings in phase.

LOADED TRANSFORMER

When the transformer's secondary is loaded, we want to get *current* from its windings. As is true in any inductive circuit, the current in the secondary lags the *voltage* in the secondary by 90 deg. See Fig. 13-16. Because of the phase relationship that exists with transformer windings, you can see in Fig. 13-17 that the secondary current is 180 deg. out of phase with the primary current. Therefore, the flux lines of the secondary oppose those of the primary. This will reduce the strength of the primary magnetic field. As a result, there is less back EMF in the primary. With less back EMF, primary current increases, Fig. 13-18. When more current flows in the secondary, more current will flow in the primary.

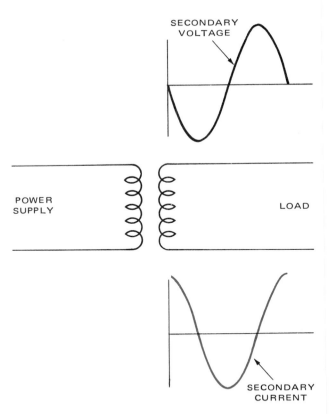

Fig. 13-16. When a transformer's secondary is under load, the current in secondary winding lags secondary voltage by 90 deg.

Fig. 13-17. When a transformer's secondary is under load, the secondary current is 180 deg. out of phase with primary current.

From this explanation, you can see that when we load the secondary there is an automatic increase in primary current. If we overload the secondary, or if it

Fig. 13-18. Since secondary current in a transformer is out of phase with primary current, the primary magnetic field and back voltage are weakened and more current will flow.

becomes shorted, the current in the primary will increase greatly. Therefore, the secondary winding must be fused to protect the primary winding. If not, it is possible that the transformer will burn out.

Transformers are rated in terms of primary voltage, secondary voltage and secondary current. The transformer symbolized in Fig. 13-19 has a secondary voltage of 12.6 volts, and a secondary current of 1.2 amps. Therefore, do not go over 1.2 amps when you load the transformer.

Fig. 13-19. Transformers are rated and labeled for primary voltage (110V), secondary voltage (12.6V) and secondary current (1.2A).

REPULSION COIL PROJECT

You can demonstrate transformer action by building a repulsion coil. Fig. 13-20 shows the coil and plans for its construction.

Procure the following parts and assemble them according to the construction procedure that follows.

Fig. 13-20. The repulsion coil is built basically from wood, wire and welding rods. See the bill of materials and construction procedure. (Project by Derry Jossefides)

No.	Item
1	Plastic or fiber tubing, 3 1/2 in. long with a 3/4 to 1 in. inside diameter.
2	Plastic or fiber ends for tubing, 3 in. in diameter.
20	Welding rods, cut to 4 3/4 in. lengths.
1	115 volt, 15 amp toggle switch.
1	8 amp fuse.
1	Fuse holder.
1	Male plug and lamp cord.
2	Hookup wires, 4 ft. long.
1	2 1/2 lb. No. 22 magnet wire.
1	6 volt light bulb.
1	18-22 gage magnet wire, 30 ft. long.
1	Aluminum tubing, 1 1/2 in. in diameter.
	Wood for base.

CONSTRUCTION PROCEDURE

Start by making the coil, core and base, then assemble the project.

1. Cut plastic or fiber ends and glue them to tubing to make a coil form 3 in. in diameter and 3 1/2 in. long.
2. Wind 2 1/2 lb. of No. 22 magnet wire on coil form. Wrap wire in layers. Do not let coils pile up.
3. Cut welding rods (coat hangers, 16-18 gage steel wire or a large bolt) to 4 3/4 in. lengths.
4. Tape rods together or use epoxy at both ends to hold individual rods together and form the core of the repulsion coil.
5. Make base to fit your needs. See Fig. 13-20.
6. Mount coil on base with wood screws.
7. Attach white wire, black wire, switch and fuse holder to the coil. See Fig. 13-21.
8. Attach lamp cord to fuse holder.
9. Wrap 30 ft. of 18-22 gage magnet wire around a 2 in. pipe. Tape wire together and remove from pipe.
10. Solder light bulb to coil.

Fig. 13-21. Plans for building the repulsion coil project. A—Layout of coil assembly for this transformer action demonstrator. B—Schematic of parts.

When the project is completed, plug the lamp cord into a 110 volt electrical outlet. Drop the ring of aluminum tubing over the core (welding rods) and flip the switch. The ring will shoot up in the air in a surprising demonstration of transformer action.

To further demonstrate the project, lower the coil of 18-22 gage magnet wire over the core and watch the bulb light up.

CAPACITIVE REACTANCE AND IMPEDANCE

We have studied two of the three main components (parts) in electrical and electronic circuits. These are the resistor and inductor. The third main component we want to cover in depth is the capacitor.

HOW A CAPACITOR WORKS

You recall that we studied capacitor construction and typical applications in Chapter 4. *We found that a capacitor is a device that stores electrons until they are needed by the circuit in which the capacitor is installed.*

One type of capacitor is made of two metal plates separated by a layer of air. If you connect this capacitor in a dc circuit, the battery will force electrons onto one of the plates. The excess of electrons on that plate will cause electrons on the other plate to be repelled and flow towards the positive pole of the battery.

As more and more electrons pile onto one plate and repel electrons from the other plate, an electric field is set up between the two plates. Finally, the voltage across the capacitor will be equal to battery voltage and current flow through the battery will stop.

If we take the capacitor out of the circuit, all the energy gained from the battery will remain stored in the electric field of the capacitor. At this point, the capacitor is "charged," because the battery has moved electric charges from one plate to another.

If larger plates are used, there is room for more electrons on each plate. If the plates are brought closer together, the electrons will have a greater repelling effect upon electrons in the opposite plate, and more charge will be built up. The better the dielectric material insulates, the closer the manufacturer can bring the plates together and get more capacitance. *When making tests, the standard unit of capacitance is called a farad.*

BEHAVIOR OF CAPACITORS IN A DC CIRCUIT

In Chapter 4, we also found that if a capacitor is placed in a dc circuit, no current will flow once the capacitor has charged up. You can verify this fact by setting up the circuit shown in Fig. 13-22 and making certain voltmeter and ammeter tests. This test circuit

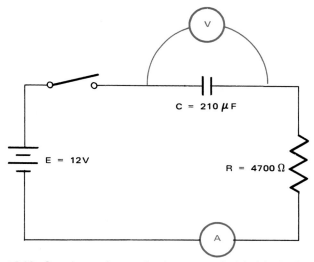

13-22. Capacitor action can be demonstrated with this circuit. Voltmeter/ammeter tests show that once the capacitor is fully charged, no dc will flow.

has a 12 volt dc battery connected in series with a 210 microfarad capacitor, a 4700 ohm resistor and an ammeter. Connect a voltmeter across the capacitor.

To make the tests: Set the voltmeter range selector to the 50 volt scale. Set the ammeter range to read about 10 milliamps. Close the switch and observe the voltage across the capacitor. Voltage builds up slowly, taking about five seconds to reach battery voltage in the circuit. Then, take a look at the ammeter. Once the capacitor has charged up to 12 volts, the ammeter will show no dc flowing in the circuit. A poor quality voltmeter connected across the capacitor could permit a current as high as one milliamp.

I.C. SAYS:

"One of the most important points to remember is that a capacitor blocks the flow of direct current."

TIME CONSTANTS

In the last test setup, you may have wondered what determined how long it took for the capacitor to become fully charged. Actually, the time required for a capacitor to become fully charged depends on two factors:

1. Resistance (R) in the circuit.
2. Capacitance (C) of the capacitor.

If you multiply the resistance (ohms) by the capacitance (farads), you will get a number called the "RC time constant" of that circuit. It takes five of these RC constants for the capacitor to charge up to the voltage of the battery in the circuit:

One RC time constant = R x C
Five RC time constants = Full charge of capacitor

Example:

Connect a 5000 microfarad capacitor and a 2000 ohm resistor in series with a 150 volt battery, as shown in Fig. 13-23. How long will it take the capacitor to charge up to circuit voltage?

$$5000 \ \mu F \ = \ \frac{5000}{1,000,000} \ F$$

$$RC \ = \ 2000 \ x \ \frac{5000}{1,000,000}$$

$$RC \ = \ \frac{10,000,000}{1,000,000}$$

$$RC \ = \ 10 \ seconds$$

Fig. 13-23. Test circuit presents an "RC time constant" problem. How long will it take for the capacitor to charge up to battery voltage?

If the RC time constant is 10 seconds, then it will take the capacitor 5 x 10 = 50 seconds, Fig. 13-24, to charge up to 150 volts. It takes five RC times constants to do all that charging. The amount of time, of course, will vary according to R and C values.

CAPACITORS AND AC

In our last example, you found that it took a while for the voltage to build up across the capacitor.

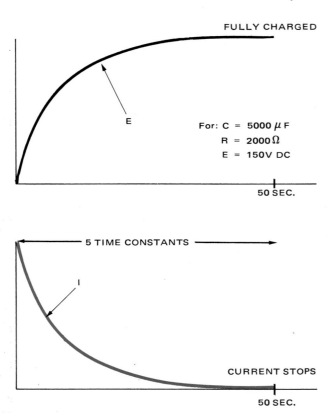

FULLY CHARGED

E

For: C = 5000 μF
R = 2000 Ω
E = 150V DC

50 SEC.

5 TIME CONSTANTS

I

CURRENT STOPS

50 SEC.

Fig. 13-24. The RC time constant for the circuit in Fig. 13-23 is 10 seconds, or a total of 50 seconds to charge the capacitor.

Although the current started to flow in the circuit immediately after the switch was closed, it took almost a full minute for the capacitor to become fully charged and for the current to die down to zero.

Fig. 13-25 shows a graph of both the voltage across the capacitor and the current in the test circuit. From

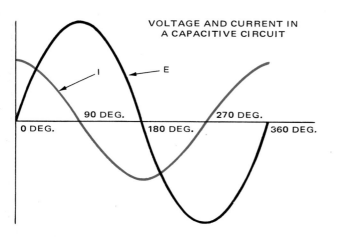

VOLTAGE AND CURRENT IN
A CAPACITIVE CIRCUIT

I   E

0 DEG.   90 DEG.   180 DEG.   270 DEG.   360 DEG.

Fig. 13-25. Graph compares 90 deg. out-of-phase sine waves of voltage and current in a capacitive circuit.

these sine waves of current (I) and voltage (E), you can see that the current "leads" the voltage. *If you connect a capacitor in an alternating current circuit, the current will lead the voltage by 90 deg.*

NOTE: If you recall from our earlier study of inductors, you will remember that just the opposite condition existed. *With an inductor installed in the circuit, the voltage leads the current.*

CAPACITIVE REACTANCE

Capacitors also show reactance when connected in an alternating current circuit. *The opposition offered by capacitors to a change in voltage is termed "capacitive reactance."*

To demonstrate this type of opposition to ac, connect a 12 volt bulb to a 12 volt, 60 Hz ac source, Fig. 13-26, and check the brightness of the bulb. Then, add a nonpolarized 50 microfarad capacitor in series with the lamp and note that the bulb is less bright. This is caused by capacitive reactance, which bears the symbol X_c.

The formula for figuring capacitive reactance is:

$$X_c = \frac{1}{2 \pi fC}$$

E = 12V

C = 50 μF

E = 12V

Fig. 13-26. The lamp burns brightly because there is no capacitor in the circuit. Bottom. A capacitor in an ac circuit will reduce the brilliance of the lamp.

Where

f   is the frequency of the applied ac voltage.
C   is the capacitance in farads.
π is the constant 3.14.

If the capacitance is given in microfarads, the following formula will make your calculations easier:

$$X_c = \frac{1,000,000}{2 \pi fC}$$

VECTOR ADDITION

As with inductors, a capacitor's reactance can be added to the resistance in an ac circuit by using vector addition. Fig. 13-27, for example, shows a series circuit that has a 100 volt, 60 Hz ac power supply, a 220 microfarad capacitor and a 5 ohm resistor.

First, find capacitive reactance (X_c):

$$X_c = \frac{1,000,000}{2 \pi fC}$$

$$X_c = \frac{1,000,000}{2 \times 3.14 \times 60 \times 220}$$

$$X_c = 12 \,\Omega$$

Next, find impedance (Z):

$$Z^2 = X_c^2 + R^2$$

$$Z^2 = 12^2 + 5^2$$

$$Z^2 = 144 + 25$$

$$Z^2 = 169$$

$$Z = \sqrt{169}$$

$$Z = 13 \,\Omega$$

Finally, find the current (I):

$$I = \frac{E}{Z}$$

$$I = \frac{100}{13}$$

$$I = 7.7 A$$

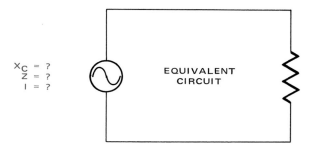

$X_c = ?$
$Z = ?$
$I = ?$

Fig. 13-27. Find the various unknowns in this capacitive circuit. The unknowns include capacitive reactance (X_c), impedance (Z) and current flow (I).

VOLTAGE DROPS

By using vector addition, we found that the impedance of the circuit shown in Fig. 13-27 is 13 ohms. Then, using Ohm's Law and substituting our value of impedance for resistance ($I = \frac{E}{Z}$ instead of $I = \frac{E}{R}$), we found that the current in the circuit is 7.7 amps.

Since this is a series ac circuit, the same 7.7 amps must flow through both the capacitor and the resistor. Therefore, the voltage drops across the capacitor and resistor are:

$$V_c = IX_c$$

$$V_c = 7.7 \times 12$$

$$V_c = 92.4V$$

$$V_R = IR$$

$$V_R = 7.7 \times 5$$

$$V_R = 38.5V$$

Note that if we try to add voltage across the capacitor and the resistor like ordinary numbers, we do not get 120 volts for an answer. This is because the voltages are vectors and must be added like vectors.

Try adding these two voltages like vectors and see if you get the correct answer:

$$V^2 = V_C{}^2 + V_R{}^2$$

$$V^2 = (92.4)^2 + (38.5)^2$$

$$V^2 = 8537.8 + 1482.3$$

$$V^2 = 10,020.1$$

$$V = \sqrt{10,020.1}$$

$$V = 100.1V$$

Note that this answer is the same as the applied voltage of 100 volts.

SUMMARY

The opposition that is offered by inductors to any change in current in a circuit is called inductive reactance. The symbol for inductive reactance is X_L and is measured in ohms. In an inductive circuit, the voltage leads the current.

The opposition that is offered by capacitors to any change in current in a circuit is called capacitive reactance. The symbol for capacitive reactance is X_C and is measured in ohms. In a capacitive circuit, the current leads the voltage.

Impedance is the total opposition that components in a circuit offer to a varying current at a given frequency. The symbol for impedance is Z and is expressed in ohms. Z is found using vector addition.

Transformers are used to convert the electrical energy of a circuit by electromagnetic induction. You can wind the coils of a transformer so the primary and secondary are either in or out of phase with each other.

KEY WORDS AND TERMS

Capacitive reactance	Phase single
Impedance	RC time constant
Inductive reactance	Right triangle
Lag	RL circuit
Lead	Vector
Open secondary	

TEST YOUR KNOWLEDGE

Do not write in this book. Write your answers on a separate sheet of paper.

1. The opposition to ac by an inductor is called _____.
2. The symbol for an inductor is _____.
3. How many electrical degrees are there in one complete revolution?
4. What is meant by impedance?
5. Draw a vector diagram and tell how vectors can be used in ac circuits.
6. What does a capacitor do to current in a dc circuit?
7. Find the RC time constant for a 30,000 ohm resistor and a 200 microfarad capacitor connected in series. Show your work.
8. In what terms is the value for inductive reactance usually given?
9. The voltage on a sine wave would be at its maximum at _____ degrees and _____ degrees.
10. At what number of degrees would you expect to find the counter EMF to be the highest on a sine wave?
11. In order to add voltages in inductive and capacitive reactance circuits, we must use _____.
12. Impedance in a circuit is usually labeled _____ in a vector diagram.
13. Dots are used on schematics with transformers to show _____.
14. It takes about _____ time constants to charge a capacitor up to the voltage of a dc circuit power supply.
15. *True or False?* The RC time constant of all capacitors is approximately equal.
16. Write the formula for the impedance of a circuit with inductive reactance.

ACTIVITIES

1. The electronic calculator has made the analysis of circuits with impedance a lot easier. How is a calculator able to show you the square of a number or square root of a number, multiply, divide, and do all of the other functions so easily?
2. See if you can locate a nomograph for inductive reactance and capacitive reactance circuits. Show how they work.
3. What is a saturable core reactor? How does it work?
4. How do you determine the value of a resistor which can be safely used to discharge a capacitor? What stops the resistor from overheating if you exceed its wattage rating when discharging capacitors?
5. How does an electric shaver make use of a transformer? What is done to its windings in terms of phasing? What stops it from overheating when it is not loaded?
6. Perform some experiments which prove what a capacitor does to the current in a dc circuit.
7. Take three different sizes of capacitors and charge them. Measure the amount of time necessary for the capacitors to lose their charge. Use three different sizes of resistors to discharge them and measure the time needed. What do the results tell you?

14 LCR Circuits

LEARNING OBJECTIVES

After studying this chapter, you will be able to:
- Apply a memory aid to inductive and capacitive circuits.
- Determine the voltage and current of an LCR circuit.
- Calculate the impedance of an LCR circuit.
- Describe what is meant by a resonant circuit.
- Explain the concept of tuning a radio.

In this chapter, we will look at LCR circuits. These are circuits that contain inductance (L), capacitance (C), and resistance (R). We will study their behavior and look at some of the useful things we can do with LCR circuits.

SIMPLE LCR CIRCUITS

Fig. 14-1 shows an LCR circuit connected to a 50 volt ac power supply with a frequency of 100 Hz. LCR values in the circuit include: inductor = .159 henry; capacitor = 21.2 microfarads; resistor = 7 ohms. Since this is an ac circuit, we will have to find the reactance of both the capacitor and the inductor in order to calculate the impedance of the circuit.

To solve the circuit for inductive reactance:

$X_L = 2\pi fL$

$X_L = 2 \times 3.14 \times 100 \times .159$

$X_L = 100\Omega$

When solving for capacitive reactance, the formula must be changed because the value of the capacitor is given in microfarads:

$X_C = \dfrac{1,000,000}{2\pi fC}$

$X_C = \dfrac{1,000,000}{2 \times 3.14 \times 100 \times 21.2}$

$X_C = \dfrac{1,000,000}{13,314}$

$X_C = 75\Omega$

FINDING IMPEDANCE

To find the total impedance of the circuit shown in Fig. 14-1, we have to add the reactances and the resistance like vectors. Note in Fig. 14-2 that the vectors for X_L and X_C are drawn in opposite directions. You can see the reason for this if you recall our earlier study of capacitors and inductors.

Fig. 14-1. A typical LCR circuit contains an inductor (L), a capacitor (C), and a resistor (R). Formulas for finding inductive reactance and capacitive reactance are given in the text.

Fig. 14-2. Vectors drawn for inductive reactance (K_L) and capacitive reactance (X_C), extend away from each other because they represent opposing actions.

In Chapter 13, we found that in an inductor, the voltage leads the current by 90 deg. (a right angle). In a capacitor, the current leads the voltage by 90 deg. See Fig. 14-3. These two events really are opposing actions, which is the reason why the vectors for X_L and X_C are drawn in opposite directions.

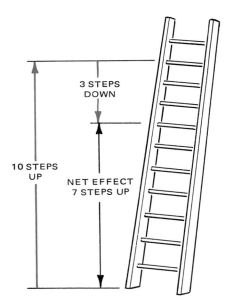

Fig. 14-3. "ELI the ICE man" will serve as a memory aid in your study of inductive (L) and capacitive (C) circuits.

SOLVING X_L AND X_C

Look at the two vectors representing X_L and X_C in Fig. 14-2. The best way to add them is to imagine that each vector represents a displacement. That is, imagine yourself at the bottom of a high ladder. If you climb ten steps straight up, then three steps straight down, you would end up seven steps above your starting point. See Fig. 14-4. As you can see, you just subtract one number from the other to get the result.

Fig. 14-4. When adding positive and negative vectors, think of climbing up (positive) and down (negative) the steps or rungs of a long ladder.

ADDING VECTORS

To relate the "ladder" method of adding vectors to our example, Fig. 14-5, first add the two vectors for X_L and X_C. This will give us a vector 25 units long that points in the same direction as X_L (because X_L is

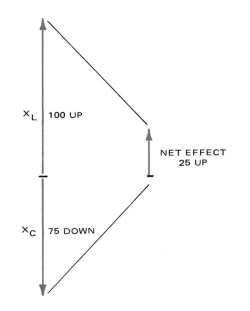

Fig. 14-5. When adding the vectors for inductive reactance (X_L) and capacitive reactance (X_C), make use of the "ladder" method shown in Fig. 14-4.

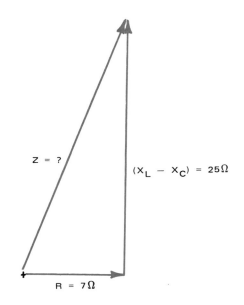

Fig. 14-6. To find total impedance of a circuit, draw the vector diagram shown and use the formula given in the text. Total impedance is 26 ohms.

longer than X_C). We now have two vectors left, Fig. 14-6. The vector with a length of 25 units represents the net reactance of the circuit. The vector with a length of seven units represents the resistive part of the circuit.

Next, place the tail of one vector at the head of the other (do not change the direction of the vector when you move it). This is the same type of vector problem that you solved for total impedance in Chapter 13.

$$Z^2 = 7^2 + 25^2$$

$$Z^2 = 49 + 625$$

$$Z^2 = 674$$

$$Z = \sqrt{674}$$

$$Z = 25.96 \ \Omega \text{ (round off to 26)}$$

FINDING CURRENT

You have found the total impedance of the circuit, Fig. 14-7. Knowing the impedance (26 ohms) and the applied voltage (50 volts), you can use the following formula to find the current flowing through the circuit:

Fig. 14-7. To find the current flowing in this LCR circuit, divide the applied voltage by the total impedance. The current is 1.92 amps.

$$I = \frac{E}{Z}$$

$$I = \frac{50}{26}$$

$$I = 1.92A$$

FINDING VOLTAGE

Once you know the current in the circuit, you can use the following formula to find the voltage across each part of the circuit:

$$V_L = I \times X_L$$

$$V_L = 1.92 \times 100$$

$$V_L = 192V$$

$$V_C = I \times X_C$$

$$V_C = 1.92 \times 75$$

$$V_C = 144V$$

$$V_R = I \times R$$

$$V_R = 1.92 \times 7$$

$$V_R = 13.4V$$

Note that circuits containing reactance often produce voltages that are higher than the applied voltage. Remember that the voltage across the inductor and the voltage across the capacitor are opposite to each other (180 deg. out of phase).

Fig. 14-8 shows the voltages across the components. If you try to add all the voltages like ordinary numbers, you will get an answer that is much higher than 50. Remember, these voltages must be added like vectors.

LCR SAMPLE CIRCUITS

Try solving another LCR circuit to make sure you understand how to do this type of problem. Fig. 14-9 shows a series LCR circuit with a 150 volt, 200 Hz ac power supply. It also has a .219 henry inductor, a 10.6 microfarad capacitor and a 20 ohm resistor. Find the voltages across each of the components in the circuit on a step-by-step basis.

Fig. 14-8. Voltages across LCR components total more than the applied voltage. Individual voltages must be added like vectors to match the applied voltage.

Find reactance of inductor:

$$X_L = 2 \pi fL$$

$$X_L = 2 \times 3.14 \times 200 \times .219$$

$$X_L = 275\Omega$$

Figure reactance of capacitor, based on formula for use when C is given in microfarads:

$$X_C = \frac{1,000,000}{2 \pi fC}$$

$$X_C = \frac{1,000,000}{2 \times 3.14 \times 200 \times 10.6}$$

$$X_C = \frac{1,000,000}{13,314}$$

$$X_C = 75.1\Omega \quad \text{(Round off at 75)}$$

Find net reactance offered by inductor and capacitor:

$$\text{Net reactance} = X_L - X_C$$

$$\text{Net reactance} = 275 - 75$$

$$\text{Net reactance} = 200\Omega$$

Fig. 14-9. This sample LCR circuit must be solved for reactance, impedance, current through the circuit and voltages across the components.

Draw vector diagram, Fig. 14-10.
Add vectors to get impedance:

$$Z^2 = 200^2 + 20^2$$

$$Z^2 = 40,000 + 400$$

$$Z^2 = 40,400$$

$$Z = \sqrt{40,400}$$

$$Z = 201\Omega$$

Using the impedance value, figure current in the circuit:

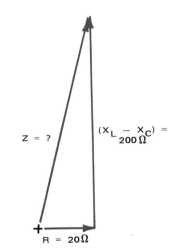

Fig. 14-10. To obtain the total impedance of the circuit shown in Fig. 14-9, draw a vector diagram and add the vectors for net reactance and resistance.

$$I = \frac{E}{Z}$$

$$I = \frac{150}{201}$$

$$I = .75A$$

Find voltage across each component:

$$V_L = I \times X_L$$

$$V_L = .75 \times 275$$

$$V_L = 206V$$

$$V_C = I \times X_C$$

$$V_C = .75 \times 75$$

$$V_C = 56.25V$$

$$V_R = I \times R$$

$$V_R = .75 \times 20$$

$$V_R = 15V$$

Using methods for adding vectors and Ohm's Law, we have taken an LCR circuit and solved for the current through the circuit and the voltage across each component in the circuit.

RESONANCE

In analyzing circuits that contain both an inductor and a capacitor, the net reactance of the two can be found by subtracting the capacitor's reactance from the inductor's reactance. A good question to ask is "What happens when the reactance of the capacitor equals the reactance of the inductor?"

You can see that the net reactance of the circuit is zero, Fig. 14-11. Also, the impedance of the circuit is equal to the resistance of the resistor in the circuit. *In an LCR circuit, when the reactance of the capacitor equals the reactance of the inductor, the circuit is called a "resonant" circuit.*

For example, our last circuit had a .219 henry inductor, a 10.6 microfarad capacitor and a 20 ohm resistor in series fed by a 150 volt, 200 Hz signal. To pose this problem of a resonant circuit, we will leave

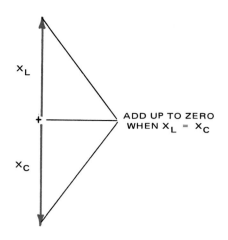

Fig. 14-11. Resonance occurs when inductive reactance (X_L) equals capacitive reactance (X_C). Using the "ladder" method for solving net reactance, the result is zero.

the voltage of the applied signal at 150 volts, but change the frequency to 104.5 Hz. See Fig. 14-12. Then, we will analyze the circuit step-by-step:

$$X_L = 2\pi fL$$

$$X_L = 2 \times 3.14 \times 104.5 \times .219$$

$$X_L = 143.7\Omega$$

$$X_C = \frac{1,000,000}{2\pi fC}$$

$$X_C = \frac{1,000,000}{2 \times 3.14 \times 104.5 \times 10.6}$$

$$X_C = \frac{1,000,000}{6956.5}$$

$$X_C = 143.7\Omega$$

Net reactance $= X_L - X_C$

Net reactance $= 143.7 - 143.7$

Net reactance $= 0\Omega$

Since $X_L = X_C$, we say that this circuit "resonates" at a frequency of 104.5 Hz.

Carry on and find the impedance of the circuit at resonance and the voltages developed across the inductor and the capacitor.

Fig. 14-12. This sample resonant circuit has a net reactance of zero. Also solve for impedance, current through the circuit and voltage across the components.

$$Z^2 = (\text{net reactance})^2 + R^2$$

$$Z^2 = 0^2 + R^2$$

$$Z = R = 20\,\Omega$$

$$I = \frac{E}{Z}$$

$$I = \frac{150}{20} = 7.5\,A$$

$$V_L = I \times X_L$$

$$V_L = 7.5 \times 143.7$$

$$V_L = 1078V$$

$$V_C = I \times X_C$$

$$V_C = 7.5 \times 143.7$$

$$V_C = 1078V$$

$$V_R = I \times R$$

$$V_R = 7.5 \times 20$$

$$V_R = 150V$$

RESONANT FREQUENCY

At the resonant frequency of 104.5 Hz, the voltages across the inductor and the capacitor are much larger than at other frequencies. For example, compare voltages at a frequency of 104.5 Hz with voltages at 200 Hz.

Frequency	Voltage	
(Hz)	V_L	V_C
104.5	1078	1078
200	206	56.25

Actually, at resonant frequency, the voltages across the inductor and the capacitor are at their highest value. See Fig. 14-13. Note how quickly the voltage drops off as we get farther from resonant frequency.

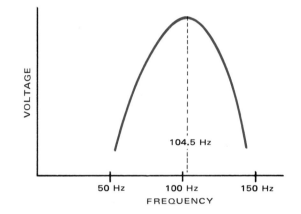

Fig. 14-13. Chart shows voltage across individual components in the circuit at different frequencies. Voltage is at a maximum at the resonant frequency of 104.5 Hz.

TUNING

The most common and useful way of using resonance is in radio circuits. The circuit shown in Fig. 14-12 is resonant at a frequency of 104.5 Hz. You might say that this circuit is "tuned" to 104.5 Hz.

Therefore, when you turn the dial on your radio to listen to your favorite station, you are tuning it to the frequency where it is resonant, Fig. 14-14.

CHANGING CAPACITANCE IN A TUNED CIRCUIT

If we change the value of the capacitance in a tuned circuit, we will find that the circuit is no longer resonant at the same frequency. To experiment, change the value of the capacitor from 10.6 microfarads to 20 microfarads, Fig. 14-15. *Remember, when the capaci-*

Fig. 14-14. The tuning control on a radio knob adjusts a variable capacitor to tune the circuit to a frequency that is resonant. (Technics)

CHANGE FROM
10.6 μ F TO
20 μ F

L = .219 H
UNCHANGED

RESONANT FREQUENCY = ?

Fig. 14-15. By changing the value of the capacitor in Fig. 14-12, capacitive reactance changes. Therefore, the circuit will not resonate.

tance changes, so does the capacitive reactance. Since the inductor remains the same, X_c no longer equals X_L, and the circuit will no longer resonate at this frequency.

Work the following formulas to find the frequency at which this new circuit will resonate. Remember, $X_L = X_c$.

$$X_L = X_c$$

$$2\pi fL = \frac{1}{2\pi fC} \quad \text{(f is resonant frequency)}$$

$$2 \times 3.14 \times f \times .219 = \frac{1,000,000}{2 \times 3.14 \times f \times 20}$$

$$1.38 \times f = \frac{1,000,000}{125.6 \times f}$$

$$1.38 \times f = \frac{7962}{f}$$

Next, multiply both sides by f:

$$1.38 \times f \times f = 7962$$

$$1.38 \times f^2 = 7962$$

$$f^2 = \frac{7962}{1.38}$$

$$f^2 = 5770$$

$$f = \sqrt{5770}$$

$$f = 76 \text{ Hz}$$

This circuit analysis proves that if we change the capacitor from 10.6 microfarads to 20 microfarads, we can make the circuit resonate at a frequency of 76 Hz. Therefore, if we want to tune a circuit to a certain frequency, all we have to do is change the value of the capacitor. NOTE: You can do the same thing by changing the value of the inductor.

TUNING A RADIO

To see how tuning works, take a look at the tuning circuit of a radio, Fig. 14-16. The antenna picks up small voltages from radio waves transmitted through the air by many different stations. Each of these stations sends out waves at a different frequency. NOTE: The antenna is shown as an inductor because most modern radio antennas are wound in a coil. Other types of antennas are found on cars, planes, and ships, Fig. 14-17.

The purpose of the tuning circuit is to make the circuit resonant at the desired frequency. For example, if your favorite radio station broadcasts signals at a frequency of 680 kHz, you would adjust the capacitor in the tuning circuit until the circuit resonates at 680 kHz. The radio would then be "tuned" to receive your station's signal.

At the same time, small voltages whose frequency is 680 kHz develop very large voltages across both antenna and the capacitor. These voltages are amplified by other components of the radio to give you your favorite program.

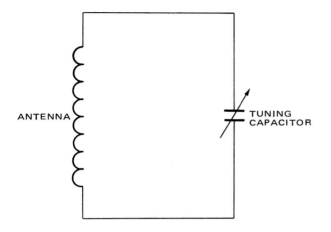

Fig. 14-16. In a simplified tuning circuit, radio waves are picked up by the antenna and the capacitor is tuned to a station's assigned broadcasting frequency.

A

B

Fig. 14-17. A—Ocean freighters use many types of electronic communication devices. B—A close-up of the freighter shows the radar, sonar, and communications antennas.

VARIABLE CAPACITORS

"Tuning" usually is performed by varying the capacitor in the circuit, rather than the inductor. This is done because it is relatively easy to make a variable capacitor.

Fig. 14-18 shows a typical variable capacitor. It is made of a number of metal plates attached to a shaft called a "rotor." Another set of plates called the "stator" is attached to the frame of the capacitor. Air is generally used as the dielectric (insulating) material.

When the rotor shaft is turned, Fig. 14-18, the plates on the rotor move between the plates on the stator. As the rotor is turned farther, more area of the rotor plates is exposed to the stator plates. You recall from Chapter 4 that the greater the area of the plates, the higher the capacitance. To increase the capacitance, then, you have to turn the rotor so that a larger area of the plates overlap.

When a capacitor is used in a radio, the rotor shaft is extended through the front cover. A tuning control is attached to the shaft to move the pointer on a dial marked for many different frequencies.

Fig. 14-18. Typical variable capacitor. Metal plates are tuned by a dial to vary the amount of capacitance in the circuit.

METAL LOCATOR PROJECT

You can build a simple metal locator by attaching a search coil to a wooden handle and connecting the coil to a circuit board and parts. Used in conjunction with a "tuned" transistor radio, the metal locator will detect coins, keys, watches and other metal objects lost in sand, dirt or grass.

Fig. 14-19. Metal locator utilizes a shop-made search coil and circuit board mounted on a wooden handle. This device works in conjunction with a transistor radio to signal the location of hidden metal. (Project by Ed Belliveau)

Study Figs. 14-19 and 14-20. Then, obtain the following items and assemble them according to the construction procedure given.

No.	Item
1	9V battery.
1	680 pF capacitor.
1	.001 μ F capacitor
1	NPN silicon transistor (general purpose).
1	5 K potentiometer.
1	1 K resistor.
1	4.7 K resistor.
1	SPST switch.
1	Coil made from 30 ft. No. 26 wire.
1	Wooden handle (broken hockey stick, etc.).
1	1/4 in. plywood disk, 6 in. in diameter.
2	1/4 in. plywood disks, 7 in. in diameter.
	Circuit board.
	Hookup wire, AWG 20.

CONSTRUCTION PROCEDURE

To build the metal locator:

1. Using 1/4 in. plywood, cut out one 6 in. disk and two 7 in. disks.
2. To make the coil form for the search coil, glue the three disks together (small coil in the middle).
3. Glue the handle to the disks.
4. Wind 30 ft. No. 26 wire on the coil form and wrap the lead wire up the handle, Fig. 14-19.

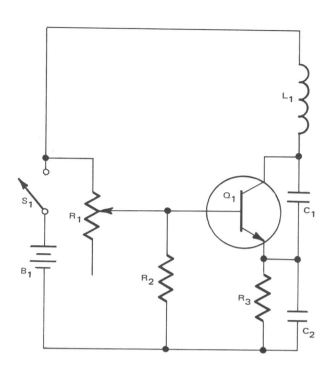

Fig. 14-20. Schematic for metal locator. B_1—9V battery. C_1—680 pF capacitor. C_2—.001 mF capacitor. L_1—inductor (search coil). Q_1—transistor. R_1—5 K potentiometer R_2—1 K resistor. R_3—4.7 K resistor. S_1—SPST switch.

5. Build circuit as shown in Fig. 14-20. Mount parts on a perforated board and solder all connections. Q_1 can be any general purpose transistor.
6. Connect search coil lead wires to circuit board.
7. Tape circuit board and 9V battery to handle.

PUTTING THE PROJECT TO WORK

To use the metal locator:
1. Place metal locator on surface to be tested.
2. Turn on transistor radio and tune it to a high frequency station. Tune it slightly off the station, yet still audible.
3. Turn on the metal locator and move the volume control until you can hear a squeal from the radio.
4. If no squeal is heard, repeat step 2 at the next lower station.
5. Then, repeat step 3.
6. Keep doing this until you find the frequency with the loudest squeal.
7. Pass the coil slowly over the area to be searched. As the coil passes over buried metal, the inductance of the coil will change. This, in turn, will change the frequency of the squeal and tell you where to start digging for your metal you located.

SUMMARY

Using the memory aid "ELI the ICE man" is an easy way to remember whether the voltage leads or lags in inductive and capacitive circuits. With this aid you will find it easier to solve problems where you have to use vector addition.

In an LCR circuit, if the reactance of the capacitor equals the reactance of the inductor, the circuit is said to be in resonance. At that frequency the voltage across the inductor and capacitor is at its highest level.

You can "tune" a radio by changing the value of a variable capacitor. The purpose of tuning a circuit is to make it resonate at the frequency you desire.

KEY WORDS AND TERMS

LCR circuit   Total impedance
Resonance   Tuning

TEST YOUR KNOWLEDGE

Do not write in this book. Write your answers on a separate sheet of paper.

1. What do the letters LCR stand for in an electrical formula?
2. If you added the voltage drops across the components in a reactive circuit, your result would be different than the voltage of your power supply. Why?
3. When the capacitive reactance equals the inductive reactance, we have a condition where the circuit is said to be in _____.
4. An antenna usually is shown in a circuit schematic as a _____ or an _____.
5. What happens when we tune a circuit in a radio?
6. In a resonant circuit, X_L will be equal to _____.
7. When a circuit is at a resonate frequency, will the voltage across individual components be at a maximum or minimum?
8. What is the formula for finding impedance (Z) of a circuit with one inductor and one resistor?
9. In a series RL circuit containing one inductor and one resistor, if $X_L{}^2$ is equal to 9 and R_2 is equal to 216, what is the value of Z? Show your work.
10. *True or False?* In an LCR circuit, when the reactance of the capacitor equals the reactance of the inductor, the circuit is called a resonant circuit.

11. Complete the following list by using the base unit for each element of the circuit.
    _____ a. Resistance
    _____ b. Impedance
    _____ c. Power
    _____ d. Capacitance
    _____ e. Current
    _____ f. Frequency
    _____ g. Inductance
    _____ h. EMF
    _____ i. RMS

ACTIVITIES

1. Find as many different kinds of radio coils as you can. Does the size or cost of a radio change the number of coils used? Why?
2. Take apart an old television set. Separate the various components into piles. How many different components are used? What are their range of sizes?
3. There was some talk that TV sets emit X-rays. Where do these rays come from and how are people watching TV protected from these rays? How did the rays get out of the TV set?
4. What are the sizes of the tuning capacitors used in radios?
5. Make a diagram of the tuning circuits used in a radio. What are the values for each?
6. Why do most radios use variable capacitors instead of variable inductors for tuning?
7. Does each city in the U.S. use the same set of frequencies for radio transmission? Are any of them the same or are they all different? Would the distance between cities make any difference which frequencies are used?
8. There are some nights when you can pick up radio stations hundreds of miles away from your home. How is this possible? Why does it happen at night? Why does it happen only on certain nights?
9. What agency of the government controls radio stations and the use of frequencies? Why must there be some type of control?
10. What international agency controls radio station frequencies when other countries are involved?
11. How would you go about learning how to operate a "ham" radio station? Who assigns call letters?

15 Filters

LEARNING OBJECTIVES

After studying this chapter, you will be able to:
- Explain the difference between a band pass filter and a bandstop filter.
- Draw a chart which shows what happens to the component voltages at resonance.
- Describe how to design a "high pass" filter.
- Describe how to design a "low pass" filter.
- Calculate the Q of a circuit.

In Chapter 14, we looked at LCR circuits and found that they can be used as tuning circuits in radios. Tuning, however, is just one of the many different ways we can make use of LCR circuits.

In this chapter, we will make a close study of LCR circuits and see how they are used to filter out unwanted frequencies.

The circuit shown in Fig. 15-1 is a series LCR circuit. As an experiment, it would be interesting to chart what this circuit would do if a voltage of one millivolt of seven different frequencies were applied to it. The results of this experiment are worked out for you in Fig. 15-2.

As you can see from the chart, the resonant frequency of the circuit is 1000 kHz. Note that at resonant frequency, the impedance (Z) of the circuit is at a minimum, and it is equal to the resistance in the circuit. Also, at resonance, voltage across the inductor and the capacitor is at a maximum.

Fig. 15-3 shows how the current through the circuit changes with frequency. The curve in Fig. 15-4 indicates voltage across the inductor. It illustrates, maximum voltage at the resonant frequency of the circuit

Fig. 15-1. This series LCR circuit is used as a filter. It has a resonant frequency of 1000 kilohertz (kHz) as indicated in the chart in Fig. 15-2.

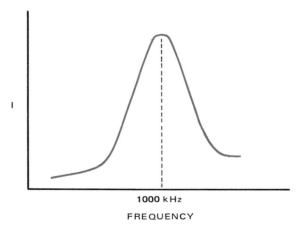

Fig. 15-3. Current flow curve shows how current through a series LCR circuit changes with frequency.

VALUE OF ELEMENTS IN CIRCUIT

		E	X_L (Ω)	X_C (Ω)	R (Ω)	Z (Ω)	V_L (μV)	V_C (μV)
	400 kHz	1 mV	360	2250	10	1890	190	1190
	600 kHz	1 mV	540	1500	10	960	562	1562
	800 kHz	1 mV	720	1125	10	405	1777	2777
FREQUENCY	1000 kHz	1 mV	900	900	10	10	90,000	90,000
	1200 kHz	1 mV	1080	750	10	330	3272	2273
	1400 kHz	1 mV	1260	640	10	620	2032	1032
	1600 kHz	1 mV	1440	560	10	880	1636	636

Fig. 15-2. Chart based on the LCR circuit in Fig. 15-1 lists values of elements under the applied voltage of 1 millivolt at various frequencies.

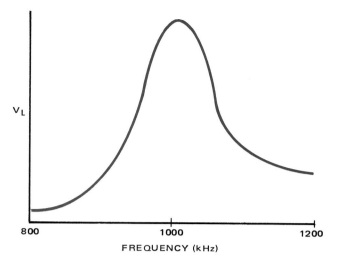

Fig. 15-4. Voltage curve shows how voltage across an inductor in a series LCR circuit reaches a maximum at the resonant frequency of the circuit.

and very small voltages at frequencies far from the resonant frequency. This information can be very useful. All you have to do is to choose the proper values of inductance (L) and capacitance (C) in order to make the circuit resonate at the frequency you desire.

BAND PASS FILTER

If we use a circuit to separate different frequencies, this action is called "filtering." If we use a circuit to filter out frequencies above and below the resonant frequency, this circuit is called a "band pass" filter. The effect of this type of circuit is shown in Fig. 15-5.

Fig. 15-5. "Band pass" filter allows only a narrow band of frequencies very close to the resonant frequency to pass through the circuit.

BANDSTOP FILTER

A "bandstop" filter, on the other hand, stops any frequencies very close to the resonant frequency from passing through the circuit. *Remember, then, that the band pass filter allows a narrow band of frequencies to pass; the bandstop filter prevents a narrow band of frequencies from passing.*

We would use a bandstop filter if we wanted to make sure that one certain frequency would not get into a given circuit. For example, the frequency of the alternating current in your home is 60 Hz. This frequency lies in the audio range, which falls between 20 Hz and 20,000 Hz. If, by chance, any small voltages at this frequency did "sneak" into a radio circuit, they would produce an annoying humming sound at the speaker.

The amplifier shown in Fig. 15-6 illustrates the use of a bandstop filter. The amplifier has been protected against any 60 Hz voltage getting into its input because the LCR circuit has been "tuned" to 60 Hz. It works like this: The input impedance of the amplifier is about 1000 ohms. That is, any signal coming into the

Fig. 15-6. The part of this circuit shown in color is a "bandstop" filter designed to intercept a signal at 60 Hz frequency before it gets to the amplifier.

amplifier "sees" a resistance of 1000 ohms. If any 60 Hz signals get to terminals A and B, these signals will travel through the 10 ohm path and very little current will flow into the amplifier. Signals at any other frequency "see" a high impedance through the filter circuit and flow directly into the amplifier instead of the 10 ohm path.

In the amplifier circuit shown in Fig. 15-6, we have made a bandstop filter, using the same components as in Fig. 15-1 (L, C and R). This filter circuit will stop any frequencies close to 60 Hz from entering the system.

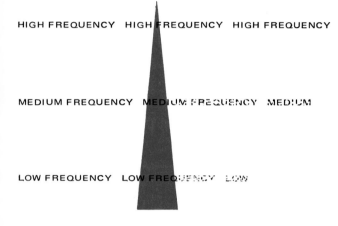

HIGH FREQUENCY HIGH FREQUENCY HIGH FREQUENCY

MEDIUM FREQUENCY MEDIUM FREQUENCY MEDIUM

LOW FREQUENCY LOW FREQUENCY LOW

Fig. 15-7. The idea behind a "high pass" filter is to make up a circuit that will pass a high frequency signal only.

HIGH PASS FILTER

A "high pass" filter is a circuit that will allow only high frequencies to pass through it. See Fig. 15-7. Any low frequencies that try to pass through this type of circuit will be attenuated (reduced in amplitude). A very simple high pass filter can be made using only a capacitor, Fig. 15-8.

In order to understand how a high pass filter works, you have to remember how capacitors and inductors behave at different frequencies. Note in Fig. 15-8 that as frequency gets higher, the reactance of the capacitor gets lower.

If we wanted to pass high frequencies and stop low frequencies from getting to our load resistor, we would use a capacitor whose reactance was very high. Suppose we have a load resistor with a value of 100 ohms. If we want to stop frequencies lower than 500 Hz from getting through, all we have to do is pick a capacitor whose reactance will be higher than the value of the load resistor when the frequency is under 500 Hz.

Fig. 15-8. This "high pass" filter will filter out almost all of the low frequency (200 Hz) signal. Only about one-tenth of the voltage will get through to the load resistor.

Suppose the capacitor has a capacitance of .8 μ f. If a signal with a frequency of 200 Hz enters the filter, the value of X_C will be:

$$X_C = \frac{1,000,000}{2\pi fC}$$

$$X_C = \frac{1,000,000}{2 \times 3.14 \times 200 \times .8}$$

$$X_C = 995\Omega$$

To keep the numbers simple, we will say that X_C is equal to 1000 ohms. Also, suppose that the signal applied to the circuit has an amplitude of one volt and a frequency of 200 Hz. How much of that voltage gets to the load resistor (R_L)?

Using Ohm's Law to solve this problem, first find the current in the circuit:

$$Z^2 = X_C{}^2 + R_L{}^2$$
$$Z^2 = (1000)^2 + 100^2$$
$$Z^2 = 1,000,000 + 10,000$$
$$Z^2 = 1,010,000$$
$$Z = \sqrt{1,010,000}$$
$$Z = 1005\Omega$$

$$I = \frac{E}{Z}$$
$$I = \frac{1}{1005}$$
$$I = .00099A \ (.99 \ mA)$$

Then, check and compare the voltages across the capacitor (V_c) and load resistor (V_R):

$$V_c = I \times X_c$$

$$V_c = .00099 \times 1000$$

$$V_c = .99V$$

$$V_R = I \times R$$

$$V_R = .00099 \times 100$$

$$V_R = .099V$$

Most of the voltage at this frequency has been dropped across the capacitor. Only about one-tenth of the voltage will reach the load resistor.

By circuit analysis, then, we have found that low frequencies are "attenuated" or cut down by a high pass filter. Next, we will see what is happening in this circuit at a high frequency. In this setup, we will use the same filter. However, we *will change* the frequency of our signal to 5000 Hz, Fig. 15-9.

Now, analyze this circuit and see how much of the signal gets across the load resistor (R_L):

$$X_c = \frac{1,000,000}{2 \times 3.14 \times 5000 \times .8}$$

$$X_c = \frac{1,000,000}{25,120}$$

$$X_c = 40\,\Omega$$

Now, find the impedance of the circuit:

$$Z^2 = 40^2 + 100^2$$

$$Z^2 = 1600 + 10,000$$

$$Z^2 = 11,600$$

$$Z = \sqrt{11,600}$$

$$Z = 108\,\Omega$$

Then, figure the current:

$$I = \frac{E}{Z}$$

$$I = \frac{1}{108}$$

$$I = .0093A$$

Finally, calculate the voltages across the capacitor and load resistance:

$$V_c = I \times X_c$$

$$V_c = .0093 \times 40$$

$$V_c = .37V$$

$$V_R = I \times R$$

$$V_R = .0093 \times 100$$

$$V_R = .93V$$

Note that if the frequency of the signal is 5000 Hz, we will get .93 volts across the load resistor. This is almost

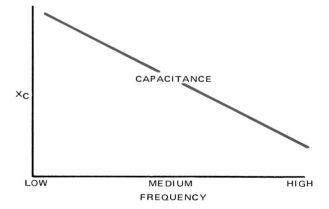

Fig. 15-9. As the frequency of the signal gets higher, capacitive reactance goes down. Therefore, a capacitor of the proper value can be selected to filter out the right range of frequencies.

Fig. 15-10. Using the same "high pass" filter shown in Fig. 15-7, but with the signal at high frequency (5000 Hz), much more of the signal will get through to the load resistor.

all of the signal which was applied, Fig. 15-10. In other words, this circuit has passed a frequency of 5000 Hz.

IMPROVED HIGH PASS FILTER

If you want to improve on the last circuit, add an inductor in parallel with the load resistor, Fig. 15-11. Without going into actual numbers, you can see the results.

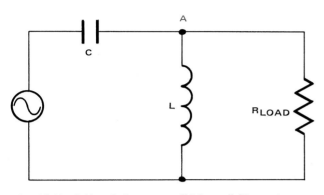

Fig. 15-11. Add an inductor to a "high pass" filter to improve performance. At low frequency, most of the voltage will be dropped across the capacitor and inductor. At high frequency, most of the voltage will get through to the load resistor.

At high frequencies, capacitive reactance (X_C) is very low. This means that most of the signal will get through the capacitor (C) to point A. From A, the signal "sees" two possible paths to follow, either by way of the inductor (L) or through the load resistor (R_L). Since inductive reactance (X_L) goes up as frequency rises, Fig. 15-12, inductive reactance will be

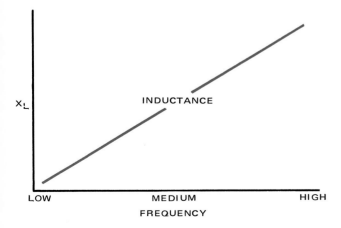

Fig. 15-12. Inductance is low at low frequencies and increases at high frequencies. This characteristic makes an inductor suitable for use in a "low pass" filtering circuit.

very high. Therefore, most of the signal will take the easier path and go through the load resistor and develop voltage across it.

If we connect low frequency voltage to the filter shown in Fig. 15-11, X_C will be very high and most of the signal will be dropped across X_C. The small amount of signal that does get to point A now has a choice of going through R_L or through X_L, which is very low at low frequencies. Therefore, most of the signal will go through X_L, and very little will develop across R_L.

The filter just explained is the normal type of high pass filter. The values of the capacitor and inductor will depend on the frequency you want to pass and on the size of the load resistance. In later courses, you will learn how to design your own filters.

LOW PASS FILTER

A low pass filter is a circuit that will allow only low frequencies to pass through it. In order to make up a low pass filter, simply interchange the location of the inductor and capacitor in a high pass circuit. Compare the high pass filter in Fig. 15-11 with the low pass filter in Fig. 15-13.

Note in Fig. 15-13 that if a low frequency is applied to the low pass filter, it will:
1. "See" a low value of inductive reactance (X_L).
2. "See" a high value of capacitive reactance (X_C) in parallel with the load resistor (R_L).

This means that low frequency signals will pass through the filter to the load resistor.

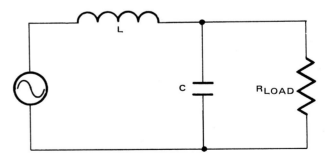

Fig. 15-13. In this "low pass" filtering circuit, the inductor allows low frequencies to pass, while the capacitor blocks passage. Most of the voltage passes through the load resistor.

High frequency signals, on the other hand, "see" a high value of inductive reactance. Therefore, the small amount of signal that does get by X_L will pass through the low value of X_C instead of through the load resistor (R_L). The high frequency signals are blocked.

POWER SUPPLY FILTER

Some devices, such as hi-fi amplifiers and television sets, need a source of high voltage direct current. A power transformer usually is used, Fig. 15-14, to step up the 120 volts found in your home. A device called a "rectifier," Fig. 15-15, also is used to change the ac voltage to dc voltage.

POWER TRANSFORMER

Fig. 15-14. A power transformer is used in this stereo power amplifier. (McIntosh Laboratory, Inc.)

You will learn more about rectifiers in Chapter 16. All you need to know now is that after the ac has passed through the rectifier, it is called "pulsating direct current." See Fig. 15-16. While the rectified current is dc, the "ripple" at the top of the waves acts like ac. If this ac ripple gets into the amplifier section, it could cause an annoying hum.

RIPPLE

In order to get rid of the ac ripple, a capacitor, Fig. 15-17, usually is added to the power supply output. When the ripple rises to its peak value point A in Fig. 15-18, the capacitor charges to the peak value of the

Fig. 15-15. A rectifier converts ac voltages into dc voltages.

output voltage. When the ripple starts to drop in value (point B), the capacitor discharges through the load resistor and helps keep the voltage across R_L at or near the peak value of the direct current. This cycle is repeated every time the pulsating current rises and falls.

The output of this circuit is dc with only a small amount of ripple, Fig. 15-19. What the circuit has done is to filter out the ac ripple from the pulsating dc. This is the most common type of filter used in power supplies. Fig. 15-20 shows other, slightly different forms of filters which do the same type of power supply filtering.

BANDWIDTH AND Q

When we looked at band pass and bandstop filters, we found that these filters would pass or stop a narrow band of frequencies around the resonant frequency (f_R) of the circuit. Now we will find the biggest factor that affects bandwidth, called the "Q" of the circuit.

PULSES OF DIRECT CURRENT AT TOPS OF SINE WAVES

Fig. 15-16. When the rectifier changes alternating current to pulsating direct current, an "ac ripple" is formed on the top of the sine waves.

Fig. 15-17. A capacitor is the most common form of filter used in power supplies. When ac is changed to dc, the capacitor helps filter out the "ac ripple." (Fisher Radio)

WHAT THE CAPACITOR WILL DO TO THE POWER SUPPLY OUTPUT

Fig. 15-18. The charging (A) and discharging (B) of the capacitor serves to filter the "ac ripple" from the pulsating dc.

UNFILTERED RIPPLE

FILTERED RIPPLE

REFERENCE LINE

REFERENCE LINE

Fig. 15-19. This filtered ripple results from the action of the capacitor shown in Fig. 15-18. Note how the highs and lows of the unfiltered and filtered ripples coincide.

L TYPE FILTER

π TYPE FILTER

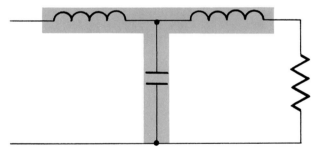

T TYPE FILTER

Fig. 15-20. Special types of power supply filters are shown. Basically, they are named for the arrangement of components in the circuit.

The Q of the circuit is defined as the ratio of the reactance of an inductor or capacitor to circuit resistance. Therefore, the value of Q can be found by dividing the reactance of the inductor at resonant frequency by the resistance in the circuit:

$$Q = \frac{X_L}{R}$$

As the formulas will prove, the higher the value of Q, the narrower the band of frequencies around the resonant frequency, Fig. 15-21.

The value of Q is very useful. If we know both the Q value and the resonant frequency of a circuit, we can find the width of the band of frequencies that is passed

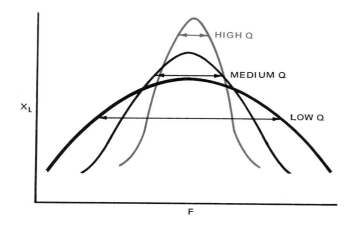

Fig. 15-21. These curves show the varied effects of "Q" at resonant frequency. Note that the higher the "Q" value, the narrower the bandwidth will be.

or stopped. The bandwidth, Q and the resonant frequency (f_R) are related by the following formula:

$$BW = \frac{f_R}{Q}$$

Take a look at a sample circuit. Fig. 15-22 shows a band pass filter. See if you can find what band of frequencies is passed by this filter. Suppose that the resonant frequency is 10 kHz and the inductive reactance (X_L) is 500 ohms at this frequency:

$$Q = \frac{X_L}{R}$$

$$Q = \frac{500}{10}$$

$$Q = 50$$

RESONANT FREQUENCY = 10 kHz
$X_L = 500\,\Omega$

R = 10 Ω

L

C

Fig. 15-22. Sample circuit illustrates the use of a "band pass" filter designed to pass a narrow band of frequencies around the resonant frequency of the filter.

Once we have found the value of Q, we can figure out the bandwidth of the filter:

$$BW = \frac{f_R}{Q}$$

$$BW = \frac{10,000}{50}$$

$$BW = 200\,Hz$$

This means that the filter will pass a 200 Hz band of frequencies whose center frequency is the resonant frequency of the filter, Fig. 15-23. To state this another way, the filter will pass frequencies from 9900 Hz to 10,100 Hz. The idea of bandwidth and Q is important in radio circuits, as you shall see as you continue your study of electronics.

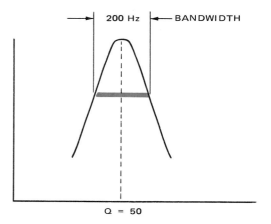

Fig. 15-23. The "band pass" filter shown in Fig. 15-22 will pass this narrow band of frequencies. Note that the center frequency is the resonant frequency of the circuit.

SMALL STROBE LIGHT PROJECT

Build a simple strobe light, Fig. 15-24, and freeze the motion of any mechanism that turns 60 times per second. Under the flashing light, the rotating part will appear to be standing still. NE 2P and five percent tolerance resistors may be difficult to obtain in some locations.

Build the small strobe light from the following parts:

No.	Item
1	HEP R0053 diode.
1	GE NE 2P neon lamp.
1	16 K resistor (R_1).
1	110 K resistor (R_2).
1	110V ac lamp cord.
	Connecting wires.

Assemble the parts and make the connections shown in the schematic in Fig. 15-24.

Use the strobe light in a dimly lit room. Hold it close to the motor, fan, clock, or whatever rotating unit you want to check. Be careful. If you get too close to moving parts, an accident may occur.

Fig. 15-24. Schematic gives the arrangement of components in a shop-made strobe light. D_1, Diode, I_1 Neon lamp, R_1 and R_2, resistors.

SUMMARY

The use of a circuit to separate different frequencies is known as filtering. Filters can be used to control which frequencies are allowed to pass and which ones are blocked. The action that they perform provides the name for the filter. These names include band pass, bandstop, high pass, and low pass filters.

You could use a filter to control voltage and to prevent damage to speakers. A filter can be used to prevent unwanted noise from being amplified in a stereo system. Filters can also be used to reduce the ripple of a power supply.

The "Q" of a circuit is defined as the ratio of the reactance of an inductor or capacitor to the circuit resistance. Knowing the value for Q is useful in finding which frequencies can be passed or blocked by a filter.

KEY WORDS AND TERMS

Attenuate	Low pass filter
Bandstop filter	Pulsating direct current
Bandwidth	Q
Filtering	Ripple
High pass filter	

TEST YOUR KNOWLEDGE

Do not write in this book. Write your answers on a separate sheet of paper.

1. At the resonant frequency, the impedance of an LCR circuit is at _____ value.
2. What do you call a filter circuit that is used to stop one certain frequency?
3. Define what is meant by ripple.
4. One way to cut down on ripple is to use _____.

5. Match the following:
   a. Passes low frequencies
   b. Passes high frequencies
   c. Stops a group of frequencies
   d. Passes a group of frequencies
      1. Bandstop filter
      2. Low pass filter
      3. Power supply filter
      4. High pass filter
      5. Band pass filter
6. In an inductive circuit, the voltage _____ the current.
7. Draw the symbols for the following:

Ammeter	Buzzer
Antenna	Ground
Electrolytic capacitor	Incandescent lamp

8. What is the range of frequencies that can be heard by the human ear?

ACTIVITIES

1. How does a radio station transmit frequencies? Why can't a message be heard as it goes through the air to a radio receiver?
2. What is the range of hearing for other animals?
3. Why is it possible to hear radio signals coming from the moon easier than from some spot on earth which is only a few thousand miles away?
4. What are the bands that surround the earth and block radio signals called? Where are they located?
5. What are microwave signals? How are they transmitted?
6. How is it possible for the telephone company to use the same wire for more than one conversation? How is it possible that you can sometimes hear other voices when you are talking to someone on the telephone?
7. In some cities, you can pick up the audio from a local TV station on the radio. How is this possible?
8. All countries do not generate 60 Hz power for use in the home. Which ones do and which ones do not? What would happen if you took an electrical appliance designed for 60 Hz to a country operating at 50 Hz? What would happen if you used a 50 Hz electrical appliance in a country that uses 60 Hz?
9. How do ultrasonic machines work? How are they able to do things like welding without creating all the heat found in normal welding operations?
10. How do you determine the amount of inductance for a coil of wire? If you wanted a certain inductance, how would you determine how much wire is needed? What determines the size of cores used?
11. What kind of fire extinguisher should be used on electrical fires? Why?
12. Why are so many electrolytic capacitors used in filtering circuits?

16 Diodes

LEARNING OBJECTIVES

After studying this chapter, you will be able to:
- Identify diodes and rectifiers.
- Determine the polarity of a diode and identify its anode and cathode.
- Explain the concept of a PN junction.
- Draw a full wave rectifier circuit and show the direction of flow through its leads.
- Discuss the methods of protecting diodes when soldering them into a circuit.

As we move along in this course from electricity to basic electronics, we will study solid state devices. Solid state is a term given to electronic components that have replaced vacuum tubes. These include diodes, transistors, SCRs (silicon controlled rectifiers) and many others.

Basically, solid state devices do one of three things. They stop the flow of electrons, start the flow of electrons, or control the amount of electron flow.

In this chapter, we will cover diodes. *A diode is a solid state device usually designed to permit electron flow in one direction and block flow from the other direction.*

Due to the fact that there are quite a few different types of solid state devices and that new ones are being discovered every day, some people have trouble understanding how they work. To help solve this problem, some companies publish manuals showing the symbols for each device. They also publish graphs that explain what each component can do and what amounts of current and voltage can be used without overloading the device.

OVERLOADS

Overloads ruin many solid state devices. To help you visualize what happens, consider a chain on a swing set that is strong enough to support a child. If this same chain is used to pull a car out of a ditch, the chain will break.

Both the chain and the solid state device can be loaded only with what they are designed to carry. Remember, even a fuse can carry only so much load before it will open. The big difference is that fuses are made to be replaced. Solid state devices usually are more expensive and much more difficult to replace.

DIODES AND HOLE FLOW

The first solid state device we will cover is the diode. Its symbol is shown in Fig. 16-1. To get a better idea of how diodes work, think back to the flow of electrons explained in Chapter 1. If necessary, review the electron theory before continuing with this chapter.

DIODE SYMBOL

Fig. 16-1. The symbol for a diode is used in drawings to show where the diode is located in the circuit.

Solid state devices, including diodes, work on the principle of *hole flow.* Hole flow is in the opposite direction of electron flow. To help you understand the principle, hole flow is demonstrated with marbles instead of electrons in Fig. 16-2.

Note in Fig. 16-2 that as a marble moves to the right, it leaves a hole to the left. Then, the next marble moves up to fill the hole. This, in turn, leaves a hole in place of the second marble. As this action continues, you can see that the marbles (electrons) are moving to the right. At the same time, however, the hole is moving to the left. This is the hole flow we will be referring to whenever we discuss solid state devices.

In earlier chapters, we mentioned the use of rectifiers or diodes. Many people think that these are two different names for the same thing. Actually, there is a difference between them, but it is really just a matter of

Diodes

MOVE MARBLE X TO THE RIGHT

MOVE MARBLE Y TO FILL SPACE

MOVE MARBLE Z TO FILL SPACE

Fig. 16-2. Marbles may be used to show the concept of moving electrons. Marbles (electrons) move to the right; "hole flow" is to the left.

how much current they will carry without burning up. A diode usually is thought of as carrying low current, while a rectifier generally means high current.

I.C. SAYS:

"When you hear the term 'diode,' you should think of current in the milliamp range. A 'rectifier' usually means current in the amps range."

Both diodes and rectifiers allow flow in only one direction. To understand how this is possible, you need to study the function of a "PN junction." See Fig. 16-3.

PN JUNCTION

A diode is made of P type material and N type material. Most people think of the P material as

positive. The N material, as you may have guessed, stands for negative. A PN junction, then, is the line of separation between P and N material in a semiconductor (diode, in this case). See Fig. 16-3.

In order to get electron flow across a diode, the electrons must travel through the P and N material. This function can be related to water trapped behind a dam, Fig. 16-4. When the water reaches a certain high level, it can be "run out" through gates put there for that purpose.

You may recall that this was the way water power was used to generate electricity. With this setup, the water can only travel out through the gates. It cannot go backward. When the water is at a level lower than the gates, it cannot flow in either direction. A diode acts almost the same way. *When a certain level of electron flow is reached, it can pass through the diode.*

However, to understand how a diode works, you must know more about the PN junction. If we wanted to put P material and N material together, we could fuse them in special ovens. However, to make it easy,

Fig. 16-3. PN junction is the line of separation between the positive and negative materials that makes up a diode.

Fig. 16-4. Water flowing out through the gates of the Wallace Dam can be compared with current flow (one way only) through a diode. (Georgia Power Co.)

just think that both materials are heated and stuck together, Fig. 16-5. This is somewhat similar to the way you would solder two components together.

FUSED TOGETHER
AT THIS POINT

Fig. 16-5. Positive and negative materials must be fused together to form a diode.

BIASING

Once our P and N materials are put together, we will want to get current flowing in the circuit, Fig. 16-6. To do this, we will need some type of power supply. A battery with the polarities shown in Fig. 16-7 would be a good source of power. By connecting the N material to the negative side of the battery and the P material to the positive side of the battery, we will get current flow.

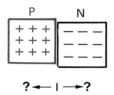

Fig. 16-6. Once formed, the diode is ready to pass current (I) in one direction only. Which way will it flow?

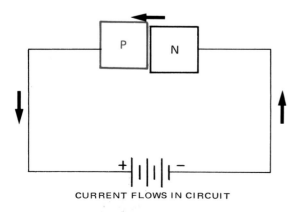

CURRENT FLOWS IN CIRCUIT

Fig. 16-7. When a battery is connected to the diode, positive to P material and negative to N material, current will flow.

Then, since like charges repel, Fig. 16-8, the *electrons* in the N material are repelled toward the junction. On the other side of the diode, the *holes* (plus signs) in the P type material are repelled toward the junction. When these actions occur, the electrons and holes meet at the junction and current flows through the diode. This is what is known as "forward biasing" of a diode, which is just another way of saying that the diode *will* pass current. Also, as you might guess, we can do just the opposite to stop the flow.

Fig. 16-8. With this setup, electrons at right are repelled toward the PN junction. At the same time, "hole flow" at the left is toward PN junction.

REVERSE BIAS

To reverse bias the diode, Fig. 16-9, put the positive terminal of the battery to the N material. Also, hook up the negative terminal of the battery to the P material. This will draw electrons and holes away from the junction. When this happens, we cannot get any current flow through the diode. You will soon see that it is possible to get flow in either direction if we put a high enough voltage on the diode. In some cases, you will find there are diodes made just for that purpose. Other times, this will ruin them.

PEAK INVERSE VOLTAGE

Current going through a diode when it is forward biased is written I_f. Voltage is written V_F. A diode, however, has two important ratings. One is the current in the forward direction (I_f). The second is the amount of voltage that it can take in the reverse direction without being damaged. This reverse, or inverse, voltage is called the "peak inverse voltage," which is written

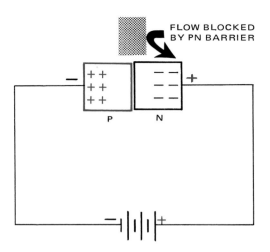

Fig. 16-9. When a battery is connected to the diode, negative to P material and positive to N material, current flow is blocked (reverse bias).

PIV. These ratings differ for all the different kinds of diodes. To show what the ratings are, many people plot them on a graph, Fig. 16-10.

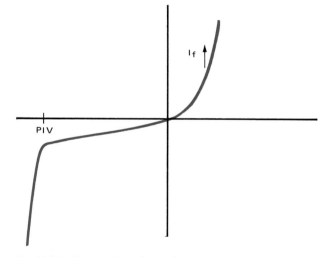

Fig. 16-10. This graph is plotted from two important ratings of a diode, peak inverse voltage (PIV) and forward bias (I_f).

GRAPHING

In plotting a voltage and current graph for diodes, Fig. 16-11, the line going from left to right (on the horizon) is called the "horizontal axis." The line going up and down is called the "vertical axis." Voltage is shown on the horizontal axis; current is shown on the

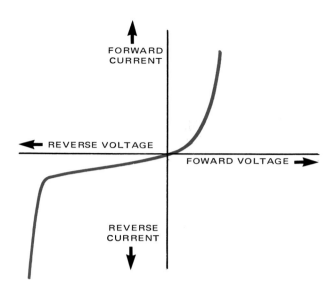

Fig. 16-11. Forward and reverse current and voltage values for a diode can be plotted on a graph.

vertical axis. By studying the plotted curves, you can tell how much voltage and current each diode can stand without being ruined.

DIODES IN SERIES

Some circuits use two diodes (rectifiers) in series, Fig. 16-12. If one of these diodes has a rating I_f equal to 3 amps, and the second diode has a rating I_f equal to 1 amp, what is the safe amount of current that you could pass through the diode? Note that one of the diodes can handle only 1 amp. If we tried to pass 3 amps through it, this diode would be ruined. Therefore,

Fig. 16-12. Series-connected diodes will pass an amount of current that is equivalent to the diode of the lowest rating.

217

figure that two diodes in series can handle current equivalent to the diode with the lower rating.

Next, take these same diodes and look at their PIV, Fig. 16-13. Also consider their PIV in series. Bear in mind that when two diodes or rectifiers are connected in series, their PIV is the sum of the two. In this case, our PIV will increase to 900 (600 + 300).

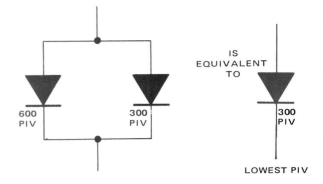

Fig. 16-15. Diodes connected in parallel will have peak inverse voltage equivalent to the diode with the lower PIV rating.

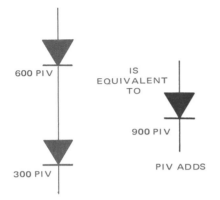

Fig. 16-13. "PIV adds" when diodes are connected in series.

DIODES IN PARALLEL

If we hooked those same 1 amp and 3 amp diodes in parallel instead of in series, we would get different results. The I_f value for the parallel hookup would add up to 4 amps, as shown in Fig. 16-14. This means that if there is a need for more current than a given diode can take, we can hook two diodes in parallel to handle the current load.

Looking at the PIV for this parallel hookup, Fig. 16-15, you can see it now has the rating of the diode

with the lower value. Anytime we hook two diodes in parallel, the hookup can handle more current, but we must watch for low PIV. *If the circuit voltage is higher than the PIV rating, the diode will pass current in the reverse direction.* Relating this to the dam we discussed earlier, it is as if the water is pumped back up to the top of the dam.

SYMBOL POLARITY

The symbol for a diode, Fig. 16-16, is labeled plus and minus. The minus side is known as the "cathode." The plus side is called the "anode." You might ask, "What difference does it make?" It *is* important because not all diodes or rectifiers are marked with a plus or a minus.

Fig. 16-16. Diode symbols should always be drawn with polarity labels in mind. The wide end of the symbol faces the direction of foward bias.

However, by using an ohmmeter, you can find out which end of the diode is cathode and which is anode. With this information, you can put the diode into the circuit the right way. Otherwise, you might hook the diode the wrong way and block current flow.

DIODE POLARITY

If a diode is not marked for polarity, hook the positive lead from the ohmmeter to one end of the diode and the negative lead to the other end. See Fig. 16-17. If you get a low resistance reading, you are

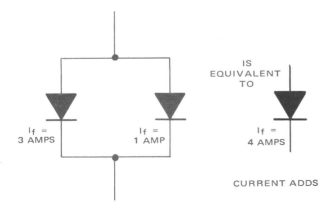

Fig. 16-14. "Current adds" when diodes are in parallel.

forward biasing the diode. Polarity is correct. Mark a minus sign on the end of the diode hooked to the negative lead of the ohmmeter. Mark a plus (anode) sign on the other end of the diode.

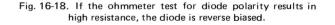

Fig. 16-17. To check polarity, make an ohmmeter test across the diode. Low resistance indicates that diode is forward biased.

If the test reading shows high resistance, Fig. 16-18, you are reverse biasing the diode. Polarity is incorrect. Simply reverse the lead connections and retest for forward biasing. Then, mark the diode ends for correct polarity.

It is important when making ohmmeter tests that you know which of the terminals is plus and which is minus. Although the outside of the meter is marked with a plus and minus, this polarity might not be correct when compared with the battery. The safest way to find out is to open the back of the meter and see where the leads from the battery are connected (plus to plus, minus to minus).

Fig. 16-18. If the ohmmeter test for diode polarity results in high resistance, the diode is reverse biased.

MEASURING RESISTANCE

Diodes do not have a fixed resistance. Resistance will change, depending on the amount of voltage put on the diode. To help you understand this reaction to applied voltage, simply measure three or four different diodes for their resistance value at various voltages. If you use a VTVM (vacuum tube voltmeter), instead of a VOM (volt ohm milliammeter), you will have more resistance scales to work with in plotting the resistance of each diode.

Fig. 16-19 shows how to connect the ohmmeter test leads across the diodes or rectifiers to make resistance tests. As you move the range selector switch from R x 1 to R x 10, you are decreasing the voltage applied by the ohmmeter to the diode. Note that each diode or rectifier has different resistance values, depending on where the range selector switch is set.

Fig. 16-19. To make resistance checks on diodes, connect ohmmeter test leads as shown and set the range selector switch to various positions given on a VTVM.

The results of resistance tests on 1N604, 1N519 and 408A diodes on all the ohmmeter ranges are plotted on the chart shown in Fig. 16-20. This chart proves that solid state devices are not fixed resistors. Therefore, current will increase or decrease, depending on the amount of voltage being applied. How much the current will change is not fixed by Ohm's Law because, in some cases, the law does not apply to solid state devices.

SMALL SIGNAL VS POWER DIODES

Under test, small signal diodes show a big difference between forward resistance and reverse resistance. Diodes used in high current circuits do not. Therefore,

	FORWARD	REVERSE	FORWARD	REVERSE	FORWARD	REVERSE
R x 1	13	∞	7	∞	10	∞
R x 10	45	∞	37	∞	72	∞
R x 100	200	∞	230	∞	560	∞
R x 1000	1100	700K	1.5K	∞	4.1K	∞
R x 10K	5K	420K	9K	ALMOST ∞	30K	∞
R x 100K		160K	50K	7 MEG	200K	ALMOST ∞
R x 1 MEG				6 MEG	1.1 MEG	70 MEG
	1N604		**1N519**		**408A**	

Fig. 16-20. Chart shows results of resistance tests made by forward biasing, then reverse biasing three different diodes.

when tests on the 408A unit resulted in only small differences in forward and reverse resistance values, it was determined to be a power type diode (rectifier). The 1N604 and 1N519 units, on the other hand, had big differences in resistance values, so they were considered to be small signal diodes. These typical differences in resistance are normal for diodes of both types. See Fig. 16-21.

POWER DIODES → SMALL RESISTANCE DIFFERENCES

SMALL SIGNAL DIODES → LARGE RESISTANCE DIFFERENCES

Fig. 16-21. Diode resistance differences help to identify power diodes and small signal diodes.

IDENTIFICATION NUMBERS

The level of electron flow depends on the size of the diode. However, there are many sizes of diodes; so many, in fact, that they are given numbers rather than names. Most diodes start with 1N, followed by other numbers. Examples include: 1N40, 1N363, 1N946 and 1N3750.

SUBSTITUTION

There are thousands of diodes used in circuits. Since many companies make diodes, there are many ways used to label them. In addition, you must be able to find a subsitute for each diode number. This is necessary because some diodes shown in circuits are not available in all electronic stores. Therefore, most companies publish a cross-reference (substitution)

catalog, Fig. 16-22. This catalog makes it easier for you to change from one diode manufacturer to another and still have your circuit work. Be aware, however, that there may be a slight difference in I_f and PIV.

I.C. SAYS:

"If you want to substitute a diode and cannot find one with values exactly as the one in your circuit, make sure that you use one with higher I_f and PIV ratings."

If you go to diodes with smaller ratings, you run the risk of ruining them with too much current or too high voltage once they are in the circuit.

COLOR CODE

Basically, diodes are made from one of two materials. One type of diode uses germanium and the other uses silicon. Germanium carries smaller amounts of current than silicon. The silicon diodes (sometimes called "rectifiers") are larger and carry heavier loads. Because of this, they even look different.

The smaller germanium diodes will often have a color code painted on the side, Fig. 16-23. This color code is the same one used for resistors. To read the code, start with 1N, followed by whatever the colors tell you "by the numbers." If the colors on our diode are brown, orange and red, Fig. 16-24, this diode is a 1N132 germanium diode. By following our resistor color code, brown is 1, orange is 3 and red is 2. You can see how this color code helps you to label diodes.

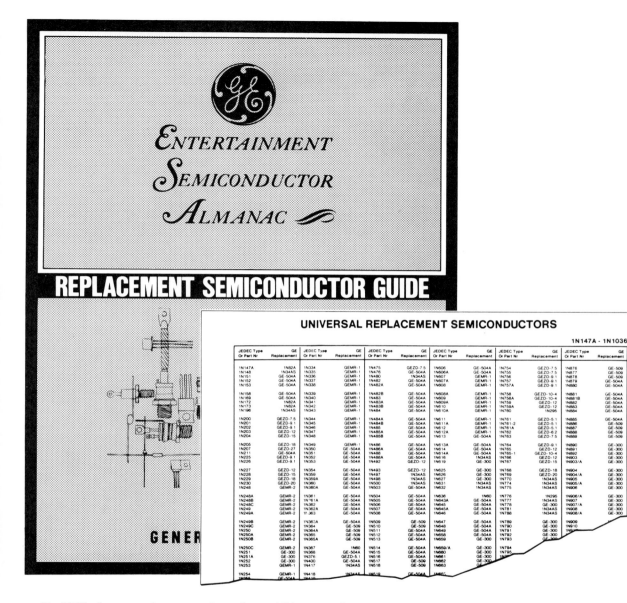

Fig. 16-22. Parts manufacturers and suppliers publish cross reference catalogs that list original equipment numbers and replacement parts numbers.

GERMANIUM DIODE

Fig. 16-23. Small germanium diodes usually have bands of color that help to identify the diodes by number.

USES

Now we will see some of the things that diodes can do when hooked into a circuit. In Fig. 16-25, we have a

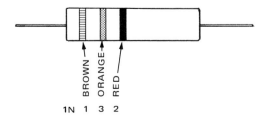

BROWN ORANGE RED

1N 1 3 2

Fig. 16-24. In this example of a diode color code, the diode number is found to be 1N132.

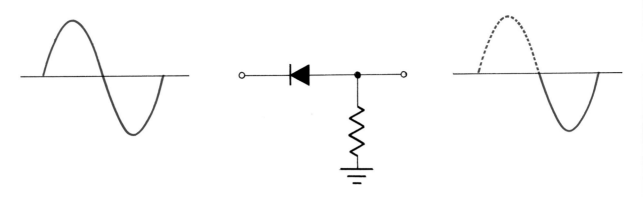

Fig. 16-25. If a diode hooked into a circuit is followed by a resistor to ground, it will "clip" off the top half of the sine wave.

diode followed by a resistor going to ground. This will cut off the top half of our sine wave and let only the bottom half through. If we reverse the direction of the diode, Fig. 16-26, we will get the top half of our sine wave and cut off the bottom half. Because each of these diodes is in series with the resistor going to ground, it will clip off one-half of the sine wave. For this reason, diodes used in this way are called "clippers."

As we go through more circuits in solid state, you will be seeing more letters used under both I and V. For example, in Fig. 16-27, the forward current through the diode in series with this resistor will result in a clipper potential (V_{CP}), which is about 0.6 volts for a silicon diode.

FULL WAVE RECTIFIER

If you change the clipper circuit shown in Fig. 16-27, by adding another diode to ground in the opposite direction, we will get a square wave. See Fig.

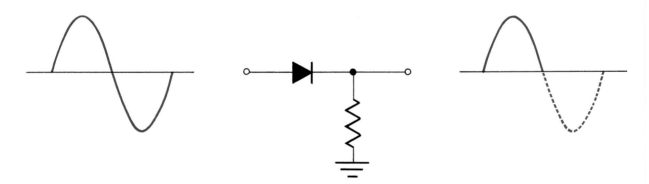

Fig. 16-26. If the diode in Fig. 16-25 is connected in reverse, it will "clip" off the bottom half of the sine wave.

Fig. 16-27. The term V_{CP} is related to drawing sine waves and writing formulas. It stands for "voltage/clipper potential."

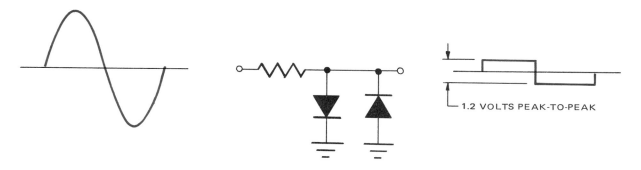

Fig. 16-28. If we make a change in Fig. 16-27 by adding another diode to ground in the opposite direction, we will get a square wave.

16-28. This double shunt clipper circuit gives us a clipped wave of about 1.2 volts peak-to-peak when using a silicon diode.

However, one of the biggest uses for diodes is found in a circuit used to change ac to dc. This circuit usually is known as a "full wave rectifier." Some people also call it a "bridge rectifier circuit." As you can see in Fig. 16-29, there are four diodes (rectifiers) connected from the secondary of a transformer. Note that this transformer has a 12.6 volts, 1.2 amp output (same type mentioned in earlier chapters). To change ac to dc, the rectifiers act in the way shown in Figs. 16-30, 16-31 and 16-32. Actually, there are hundreds of other ways in which you can use diodes in circuits.

SOLDERING

You must be very careful when installing diodes, especially germanium diodes. A soldering iron can be used to connect a diode in a circuit, but it could give

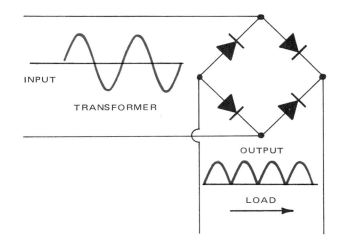

Fig. 16-30. Schematic shows full wave rectifier in a circuit. Note the direction of forward bias through the four diodes.

Fig. 16-29. This full wave rectifier (bridge rectifier circuit) uses four diodes to convert alternating current to direct current.

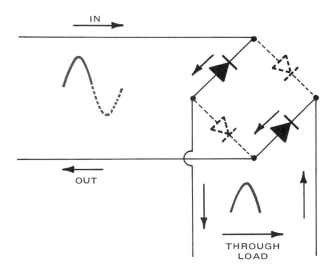

Fig. 16-31. The first half cycle of the conversion from ac to dc is illustrated. Arrows indicate current flow. Note that two diodes are blocked.

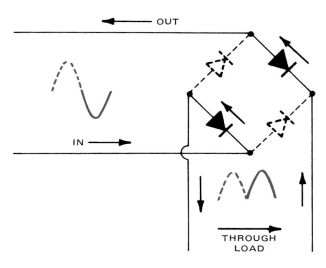

Fig. 16-32. The second half cycle of the ac/dc conversion is presented. Note blocked diodes and new path of current flow.

off enough heat to destroy the diode. To avoid this, use a heat sink (metal device that dissipates heat) between the diode and the soldered connection. This little trick will save many dollars and much time.

Even the so-called expert who tries to solder a diode connection without using a heat sink has ruined many diodes in the process. Very few packaged electronic components or plans for building circuits will warn you about this possibility of overheating the diodes. *Always use a heat sink when soldering diode connections.*

Overheating diodes or rectifiers can cause one of two things to happen:

1. It may open the diode.

   How would you know this? Remember how we measured the resistance of a diode in two directions? In one direction, we found the resistance to be very high. In the opposite direction, the resistance was very low. If your diode or rectifier is open, the resistance will be *very high (∞) in both directions,* Fig. 16-33.

2. It may short the diode.

   Again, your resistance check will prove this by measuring *low resistance in both directions.* Generally, however, when a diode connection is soldered without a heat sink, the diode will open. High currents in a circuit will do the same thing.

ZENER DIODE

Another fairly popular type of diode is one called a "zener diode." Its symbol is shown in Fig. 16-34. This type of diode is used to regulate the voltage. Fig. 16-35

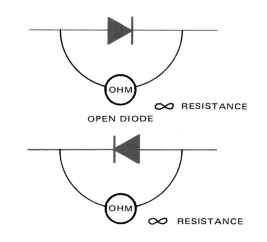

Fig. 16-33. If resistance checks with an ohmmeter indicate high (∞) resistance in both directions, the diode is open.

ZENER DIODE

Fig. 16-34. This symbol is used in drawings to represent a zener diode. Again, the wide end of the symbol faces direction of forward bias.

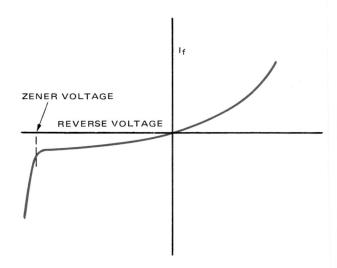

Fig. 16-35. The curve on this graph shows that reverse voltage falls sharply at zener voltage.

illustrates the reason it can be used in that way. Note that the voltage in the reverse direction reaches a point (zener voltage) where the current in the reverse direction will go to a very high level. Up until that time, the reverse current was almost constant.

As we reverse bias this zener diode, the current will remain at a low level. Finally, you will get to the point where any increase in voltage will cause the current to go way up. This "zener point" is often called the "saturation point" of the diode. Actually, the voltage level where saturation of the diode results will range from a few volts to over 400 volts.

BREAKDOWN VOLTAGE

A zener diode has two important specs (specifications):
1. Zener breakdown voltage.
2. Power rating.

You recall from Chapter 4 that power is equal to the voltage times the current ($P = E \times I$). We can use this information to find the maximum current we can use in a circuit with a zener diode. First, look up the power rating for the diode. Next, check the operating voltage of our circuit, and we can use the following formula:

$$\text{maximum current} = \frac{\text{power rating}}{\text{operating voltage}}$$

I.C. SAYS:

"Never go above the wattage that a zener diode can handle, otherwise it will be ruined."

To use the formula for finding the maximum current, assume that we have a 1 watt zener diode with a breakdown voltage of 40 volts:

$$I_{MAX} = \frac{\text{power rating}}{\text{operating voltage}}$$

$$I_{MAX} = \frac{1 \text{ watt}}{40 \text{ volts}}$$

$$I_{MAX} = 25 \text{ mA}$$

As a follow-up, you can hook a milliammeter in series with the diode to check the maximum current for a diode having this power rating.

ZENER DIODE USED AS A VOLTAGE REGULATOR

We can use a zener diode as a voltage regulator, Fig. 16-36. Note that the zener diode is used as a shunt.

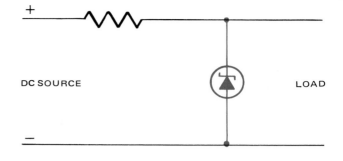

Fig. 16-36. Schematic reveals how a zener diode can be used as a voltage regulator.

That is, it is hooked up in parallel with our load. To fix the operating load, we must place the resistor ahead of the diode. This will also control the range of load current and any changes in voltage from the input without going over the power rating of the zener diode.

When voltage from the input increases, current through both the reverse biased zener diode and load will also increase. However, as the zener current increases, its resistance decreases and still more current is passed through it. See Fig. 16-37. The voltage drop across our resistor will also go up. This lets us keep the voltage across our load at an almost constant level.

If the voltage across the load should drop, the resistance of the zener would increase and keep the

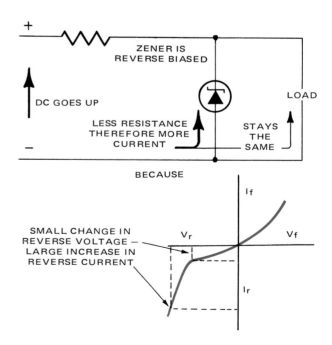

Fig. 16-37. This schematic serves to explain how a zener diode keeps constant voltage across the load.

voltage across the load almost constant. In this way, the zener diode can keep an almost constant output to the load even though the input is always changing.

CHECKING THE ZENER DIODES

You cannot test a zener diode the same way you checked other diodes. Since the resistance of a zener changes in a different way, we must use an oscilloscope to check it.

RESEARCH

There are other types of diodes besides the ones mentioned in this chapter. They have names like tunnel diode, light emitting diode, Fig. 16-38, and many others. Reashers work is always going on to find new and better solid state devices. It is this type of research that has made electronics such a rapidly moving field. In Fig. 16-39, note that LEDs are now as small as a pinhead.

Fig. 16-39. Light emitting diodes (LEDs) come in a wide variety of shapes and designs. (Hewlett-Packard)

Fig. 16-38. These symbols are used in circuit drawings to represent tunnel diodes and light emitting diodes.

SUMMARY

A diode is a device used to block the flow of electrons in one direction and permit flow in the opposite direction. Diodes are usually thought of as carrying small amounts of current, usually in the milliamp range. When carrying high amounts of current, usually in the amp range, they are called rectifiers instead of diodes.

Forward biased diodes permit the flow of electrons (reverse biasing will block the flow). The PIV of a diode tells how much voltage it can take without breaking down. When

diodes are connected in series, the maximum current should be limited to the diode with the smallest current rating. The PIV will be the sum of the two ratings. Connecting diodes in parallel will result in a higher current but lower PIV rating.

Some of the more important uses of diodes include rectifying, clipping, and voltage regulating. The latter is an important function of the zener diode. Other diodes have names such as light emitting diodes and tunnel diodes.

KEY WORDS AND TERMS

Anode	Peak inverse voltage (PIV)
Bridge rectifier circuit	PN junction
Cathode	Rectifier
Clippers	Reverse bias
Diode	Solid state
Forward bias	Zener diode
Full wave rectifier	Zener point
Hole flow	Zener voltage
Overload	

TEST YOUR KNOWLEDGE

1. A diode is identified by labeling one end the _____ and the other end the _____.
2. In order for a diode to conduct, it must be properly _____.
3. How much current will two diodes in series be able to conduct?
4. PIV stands for _____.

5. What would the color code of a IN420 diode look like?
6. Draw the symbols for a diode and a zener diode.
7. Before soldering, a diode should be protected with a _____.
8. Diodes are usually thought of as carrying current in the _____ range, while rectifiers carry current in the _____ range.
9. The anode is _____.
10. What results would you expect to get if you were to make a resistance check on a diode?
11. If a diode must be replaced, what is the best thing to do if the exact values could not be found for a replacement part?
12. Give one use for a zener diode.

ACTIVITIES

1. Obtain as many different types of diodes as possible. Label each lead. Are all of them identified the same way?
2. Why is a diode called a solid state device?
3. Take a diode apart. Can you see how it has been made? If you were to use a microscope, what other things could you see?

4. Why are there so many different types of diodes? How is a manufacturer able to control the process for making so many different types?
5. How do you know which type of diode to use in a circuit? Make a list ranging from those carrying low current to those carrying high current.
6. How does a manufacturer make diodes with glass cases? How do they get the glass around it? How are the colored bands put on the glass without breaking it?
7. Try an experiment with a couple of diodes. Measure the amount of heat it takes to ruin each type. Plot the results to show the differences.
8. How much overload current will a diode take before it is ruined? Does it make any difference whether it is silicon or germanium?
9. Using rectifiers, build a full wave bridge. How many ways can you filter the output?
10. How many different circuits can you find using zener diodes? Do they fall into any one type?
11. Take a zener diode apart. Does it look any different from a rectifier or standard type diode?
12. How much voltage is needed to break down a zener diode? How much overload will it take before it is ruined?

17 Transistors

LEARNING OBJECTIVES

After studying this chapter, you will be able to:
- Identify PNP and NPN transistors.
- Draw the direction of current flow and label the bias voltage on both types of transistors.
- Explain the concept of the Gain of a transistor and tell why it is important.
- Describe what is meant by common emitter, common base, and common collector as related to transistor circuits.
- Demonstrate how to identify the three leads on a transistor.

In this chapter, we will continue our study of solid state devices. A diode, you recall, will permit electron flow in one direction and block the flow from the other direction. *Transistors, on the other hand, are solid state devices used for switching and/or amplifying the flow of electrons in a circuit.*

Although the first transistor looks rough by today's standards, Fig. 17-1, its principle of operation is still the basic idea behind many of the solid state devices in use today, Fig. 17-2.

TRANSISTOR TYPES

There are two basic types of transistors, the *switching* type and the *amplifying* type. No matter which of the thousands of transistors available you use, they either switch or amplify. Some transistors are designed to switch *and* amplify.

SWITCHING

To help you understand what is meant by transistors that switch and/or amplify, we will use the light switches in your home as examples.

In the first example, Fig. 17-3, a light switch must be flipped in order to let the current flow to the lightbulb or to stop current flow across the switch terminals. Normally, there are only two possible results from flipping the switch: the lightbulb will light up or it will shut off. Any other result would be caused by an electrical problem.

Fig. 17-1. The first transistor was designed to "amplify" by passing electrical signals through a solid, semiconductor material.

Fig. 17-2. Today's transistors look more compact and attractive, but the operating principle is still based on the idea behind the first transistor.

ANSWER BOX PROJECT

In the second example, Fig. 17-4, switching is used in the design of an answer box. The answer box is similar to those used on television quiz shows.

By its construction, the answer box can be used to prove who pushed the button first. When a question is asked of the contestants, the first one to push the button is the one who gets the chance to answer the question.

The circuit for the answer box has a transistor connected to each of two buttons, but only one transistor can conduct at any given time. Therefore, the person with the faster finger will always go first. Even if the second person hits the

Fig. 17-3. In an everyday example of "switching" an electrical signal, a light switch must be flipped to make the bulb light up or shut off.

Fig. 17-4. This quiz show answer box is an interesting project that illustrates how transistors can switch electrical signals. (Project by Larry Wood)

button a fraction of a second later, the light will not come on.

Obtain the following materials and assemble them according to Fig. 17-5 and the construction procedure given:

No.	Item
1	6-9 volt battery.
2	6-9 volt light bulbs.
2	NPN transistors.
2	2.2K resistors.
2	Push button switches.
1	4 in. x 6 in., 18 gage steel box.
1	4 in. x 6 in. circuit board.
	Connecting wires.

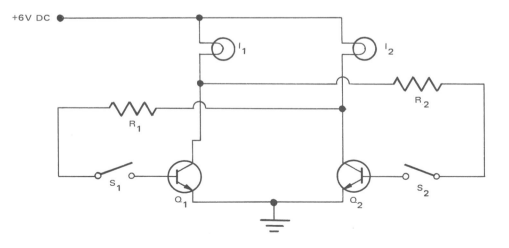

Fig. 17-5. Schematic shows hookup for answer box. Parts include: B_1—6-9V battery. $I_{1,2}$—6-9V bulbs. $Q_{1,2}$—NPN transistors. $R_{1,2}$—2.2 K resistors. $S_{1,2}$—Switches.

CONSTRUCTION PROCEDURE

To build the answer box:
1. Connect positive leads of lights, using wire or alligator clips.
2. Connect a resistor to negative lead of each light.
3. Connect each resistor to one terminal of a switch.
4. Connect other leads of switches to bases of two NPN transistors.
5. Connect emitters together; also attach a wire to the emitters, forming a ground.
6. Connect collector of transistors to point where resistor meets light of other wire (see Fig. 17-5).
7. Attach power supply's positive terminal to either light; connect negative terminal to ground.
8. Make a metal box large enough to hold circuit board and complete circuit (approximately 4 in. x 6 in. x 1 1/2 in.).
9. Drill four 5/8 in. holes in box and install lights and push buttons (see Fig. 17-4).
10. Solder all terminals on circuit board and secure board in box.

Use the answer box in conjunction with flash cards, questions from the teacher or any other quiz program. If this project is mass produced, it will be possible to have a class-wide contest. The teacher asks the questions and the students compete in pairs to guess the answers.

AMPLIFYING

In your third example of switching and amplifying, a dimmer switch, Fig. 17-6, is used in conjunction with the light bulb to demonstrate "amplification of an electrical signal." With the dimmer switch, you can turn the control knob so that the amount of light given off by the light bulb will vary from dim to very bright.

You also can turn the dimmer switch control knob to shut off the light bulb. Then, as you turn back the knob, you will reach a point where the light bulb will come on. From that point on, the more you turn the control knob, the brighter the light bulb will get.

SWITCHING APPLICATIONS

Switching transistors are used in circuits which are either "on" or "off" (similar to lighting circuit just described). These transistors are found in computers that perform "counting" operations. In counting circuits, the signal is either present or not present. There are no "in-betweens."

The computer signal can be in the form of a pit on

Fig. 17-6. In an example of "amplifying" an electrical signal, turning the dimmer switch control knob makes the bulb give off light ranging from dim to very bright.

Fig. 17-7. In a computer, information can come in the form of pulses on a magentic tape or from tiny pits on a CD like the ones shown.

a laser read compact disc or an electronic pulse on a floppy disk or magnetic tape, Fig. 17-7. This last application uses almost the same type of magnetic tape that you use in a tape recorder. Although you cannot see the pit or pulse, it *is* there.

We can take a floppy disk, for example, and run it through a disk drive, Fig. 17-8, to count the pulses. These pulses could represent people in a census, money in a account or signals sent to a turret drill, Fig. 17-9. Can you imagine drilling a piece of steel because a pulse in a disk sent the signal by means of a transistor? The signal ordered the machine to drill a hole or not to drill a hole. The transistor performed the switching operation.

Fig. 17-8. Floppy disk drives read pulses on magnetic disks. (Command Communications, Inc.)

AMPLIFYING APPLICATIONS

Amplifying transistors are used in places where the amount of signal is important. You would use this type of transistor for a stereo, where you want to amplify (strengthen) a radio signal, Fig. 17-10. Because these signals are small, they must be made larger so you can hear them over a speaker.

The amplifying transistor must be able to go from "off" through an "on" range of increasing volume, similar to increasing bulb brightness with a dimmer switch. The radio signals must go through a few transistors to increase the size of the signals. These transistors are the final power type which feed the signal into the speaker for the music or voices (audio) that we hear.

Fig. 17-9. This machining center will perform specific machining operations as ordered by the computer disk. (Mitsubishi Machine Tools)

Fig. 17-10. Amplifying transistors (circled) are used in radios to build up weak signals. (McIntosh Laboratory Inc.)

PNP AND NPN

Usually, when you hear the word "transistor," certain letters are used with it to identify the type of transistor being discussed. The first type to be considered is the PNP transistor. In working with circuit drawings, you will find that there are two ways of drawing the PNP transistor symbol, Fig. 17-11. Both symbols are in popular use, and they stand for the same device.

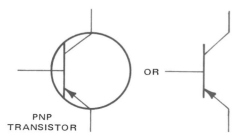

Fig. 17-11. These two PNP transistor symbols are commonly used in circuit drawings.

The second transistor for study is the NPN type. Its symbol also can be drawn two ways, Fig. 17-12. You recall that these same letters, PN, were used with reference to diodes in Chapter 16. Although the transistors are drawn as large pieces of P and N materials, Fig. 17-13, these junctions are so small that it takes a microscope to see them.

TRANSISTOR CASES

When you see transistors on circuit boards, Fig. 17-14, you will see many different kinds. Some look like small thimbles. Others have shiny metal cans. Still

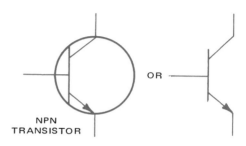

Fig. 17-12. Either of these two ways of drawing NPN transistor symbols is acceptable.

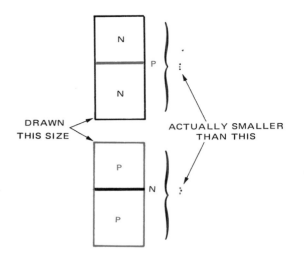

Fig. 17-13. Drawings of transistor P and N materials are much larger than the actual materials.

Fig. 17-14. Tiny black transistors are scattered about this circuit board.

others have black containers. This presents a real problem for someone just starting out in electronics. Before you can solder transistors into a circuit (using a heat sink, of course), you must identify the leads.

LEAD IDENTIFICATION (SYMBOL)

Transistor leads are known as the emitter, base and collector. If you have a PNP transistor, its leads (wires) will be labeled as shown in Fig. 17-15. The letters PNP also let you know which way the arrow is pointing. In this case, PN could mean POINTING IN.

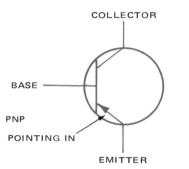

Fig. 17-15. Marking the leads on a PNP transistor symbol.

If you look at an NPN transistor, Fig. 17-16, think of NOT POINTING IN. Note also that the lead with the arrow is always the emitter. Knowing this should be a big help when you start working with transistors.

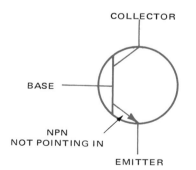

Fig. 17-16. Marking the leads on an NPN transistor symbol.

DIRECTION OF FLOW

Since a transistor can either switch or amplify, we need to know what to do to the leads so they can conduct. The first example, Fig. 17-17, uses an idea similar to the light switch. In order to turn on the light,

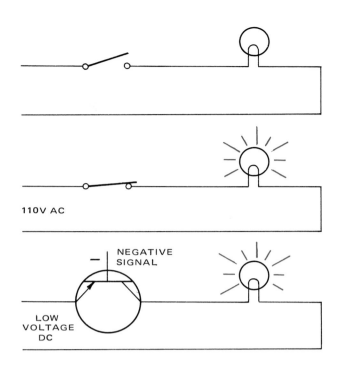

Fig. 17-17. Examples are given for various switching operations. 1—Switch open, light bulb off. 2—Switch closed, light bulb on. 3—Transistor on, light bulb on.

you have to flick the switch with your hand. If you use a PNP transistor in place of the light switch, you can do the same thing.

In order to turn on the PNP transistor, we must put a negative signal on the base. When this happens, the electrons will flow through the transistor. When working with a PNP transistor, this flow of electrons is from the collector to the emitter, Fig. 17-18. As with the light switch, we must use some outside source to allow the flow of electrons. Note that the flow of electrons from the collector to the emitter is against the direction

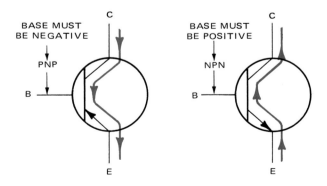

Fig. 17-18. When working with transistors, the flow of electrons is opposite the way the emitter arrow points.

indicated by the arrow on the emitter.

With an NPN transistor, we must put a positive signal on the base to make it conduct. This will let the electrons flow from emitter to collector. Again, the flow of electrons is against the direction in which the arrow on the emitter points.

LEAD IDENTIFICATION (ACTUAL)

The next thing you will want to know is how to identify the leads on an actual transistor. The top two transistors shown in Fig. 17-19 are the small signal type. The first step toward identifying them is to turn the transistor upside down so you can see the leads at the bottom. Next, try to identify the leads as emitter (E), base (B) and collector (C).

If the transistor has a small tab, it usually is made with the emitter lead closest to the tab. See Fig. 17-19. Then, going around the transistor in clockwise direction, the next lead is the base and the last lead is the collector.

If the transistor you are trying to identify is laid out in a half round shape with a flat part, Fig. 17-19, place the flat part up. In this position, the leads are arranged as emitter, base and collector in left to right order. We say "usually" because this is not always true. Some manufacturers label their leads in different ways. The safest and best way to check transistor leads is by using an ohmmeter (to be explained later in this chapter).

The third type of transistor, shown in Figs. 17-19 and 17-20, is a power transistor, with a metal plate on the back to take away the heat. In order to label these leads, lay down the transistor with the metal plate up

Fig. 17-20. Power transistors usually are the flat, plastic type, having leads on the bottom or back. The metal plate dissipates excess heat.

and away from you. Then, the left hand lead is the emitter, the middle one is the collector and the right hand lead is the base.

The other power transistor shown in Figs. 17-19 and 17-20 also must be turned upside down to identify its leads. Then, position the transistor so that the two leads are closer to the left hand side. Now, you can label them. The top lead is the emitter, the bottom one is the base. What happened to the collector? This type of transistor has its collector connected to the case. Therefore, the whole bottom of the transistor is the collector.

FLASHING LIGHT PROJECT

There are a lot of uses for a small flashing light, Fig. 17-21. Build the circuit shown in Fig. 17-22 and place it in a small box or soap dish. The flashing light can be used inside a paper mache animal and placed on a table. Halloween will give you another chance to use this flasher. Turn it on and drop it inside a cut-out pumpkin or jack-o-lantern.

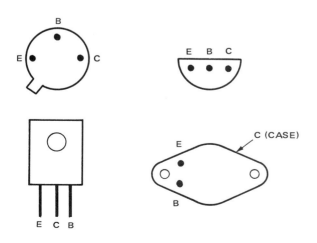

Fig. 17-19. Typical transistor shapes include: Top—Two small signal types. Bottom—Two power types. Labels are: E—Emitter. B—Base. C—Collector.

Fig. 17-21. Circuitry for a small blinking light is contained in a soap dish. (Project by Dick Butcke)

Fig. 17-22. Schematic shows hookup for a small blinking light. Parts include: B_1—Battery. C_1—Capacitor. I_1—Lamp. $Q_{1,2}$—Transistors. $R_{1,2,3,4}$—Resistors. S_1—Switch.

Obtain the following materials and assemble them according to Fig. 17-22 and the construction procedure given:

No.	Item
1	9V dc battery.
1	100-μF 15WVDC electrolytic capacitor.
1	4 1/2V dc lamp.
1	GE 2 transistor (Q_1).
1	GE 8 transistor (Q_2).
1	100 K resistor (R_1).
1	100 Ω resistor (R_2).
1	2.7 K resistor (R_3).
1	470 resistor (R_4).
1	SPST switch.
1	Perforated circuit board.

CONSTRUCTION PROCEDURE

To build the flashing light:
1. Lay out wiring of schematic on a breadboard.
2. Make sure that flasher works.
3. Transfer wiring to perforated board.
4. Solder all joints. Tape all joints that might short out flasher.
5. Place flasher in desired container.

HEAT SINK

Heat sinks are used in many solid state applications to dissipate (take away) heat from heat-sensitive areas where damage might otherwise occur. Power transistors are one of those applications.

Power transistors can carry much more current than the small signal type. However, the larger current causes extra heat, so we must do something to help the transistor get rid of it. We can do this by attaching the transistor to a heat sink shown in blue, Fig. 17-23. This is not the same kind of heat sink we used when soldering diode leads, but it does the same job. It takes heat away from the transistor so it will not burn up.

Fig. 17-23. Four transistors (center) with large metal heat sinks keep this stereo running.

Fig. 17-24 shows how to mount a power transistor and mica washer on a heat sink. To install the washer:
1. Place a small dab of silicone grease on underside of transistor.
2. Install mica washer on transistor.
3. Put a small dab of silicone grease on washer.
4. Attach assembly to heat sink.

If you use screws to fasten the assembly to the heat sink, be sure to insulate the screws with extruded fiber or plastic washers, or use nylon screws and nuts. Otherwise, the circuit will be affected when the assembly is installed.

Fig. 17-24. When installing a power transistor on a heat sink, a mica insulator must be used between the transistor and heat sink. Attaching screws also must be insulated.

PNP IDENTIFICATION

Suppose you have a transistor to install, but cannot tell whether it is a PNP or NPN type. First, make sure that you know which is the positive lead and which is the negative lead from your ohmmeter. If necessary, take off the back of the instrument and check the polarity of the battery against the lead connections (positive-to-positive, negative-to-negative).

To test the transistor for type:

1. Hook the positive lead from the ohmmeter to the base of the transistor, Fig. 17-25.
2. Connect the negative lead from the ohmmeter first to one transistor lead, then to the other.
3. If both readings show high resistance, hook the negative ohmmeter lead to the base of the transistor, Fig. 17-25.
4. Connect the positive lead from the ohmmeter first to one transistor lead, then to the other.
5. If both readings show low resistance, you have a PNP transistor.

NPN IDENTIFICATION

Suppose your ohmmeter tests show high resistance with the negative ohmmeter lead connected to the base of the transistor and the other lead is switched from transistor lead to transistor lead. See Fig. 17-26.

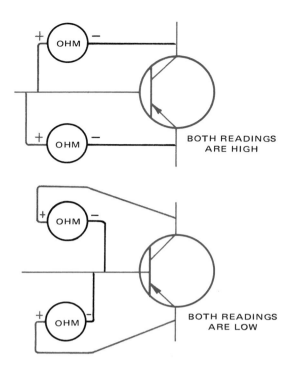

Fig. 17-25. Results of these ohmmeter tests prove that transistor is the PNP type.

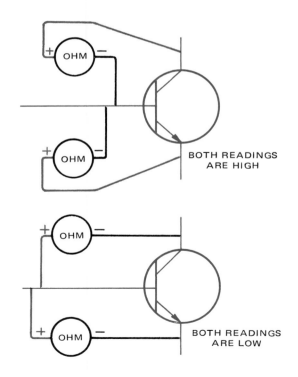

Fig. 17-26. Results of these ohmmeter tests prove that transistor is the NPN type.

Continue testing as follows:
1. Reverse the ohmmeter leads, connecting the positive lead to the base of the transistor.
2. Connect the negative lead from the ohmmeter first to one transistor lead, then to the other.
3. If both readings show low resistance, you have an NPN transistor.

GERMANIUM OR SILICON?

After you have determined whether your transistor is PNP or NPN, the next thing you need to know is whether it is silicon or germanium. Bear in mind that a germanium transistor will carry less current than a silicon transistor.

I.C. SAYS:

"Do not mix up the terms 'silicon' and 'silicone.' Silicon is an element used in making transistors. Silicone is the grease used when installing heat sinks."

A quick check can be made with an ohmmeter to determine whether a transistor is made from silicon or germanium. In the test of a PNP transistor shown in Fig. 17-27, first connect the ohmmeter negative lead to the collector and the positive lead to the emitter. With this hookup, you will get a high resistance reading from emitter to collector.

Fig. 17-27. Ohmmeter test results prove whether the PNP transistor under test is made from germanium or silicon.

Then, reverse the ohmmeter lead connections and the resistance reading will go even higher. If you can read the ohms on the meter scale, you have a germanium transistor. If the reading is in the megohms-to-infinity (∞) range, you have a silicon transistor.

To make these same checks on an NPN transistor, connect the ohmmeter leads as shown in Fig. 17-28. With the ohmmeter positive lead on the collector and the negative lead on the emitter, the resistance will be high. Switching the leads, then, will make the resistance even higher. Again, if you can read the ohms on the meter scale, you have a germanium transistor. If you cannot read the resistance value because it is near infinity, you have a silicon transistor.

Fig. 17-28. Ohmmeter test results prove whether the NPN transistor under test is made from germanium or silicon.

Do not mix up transistor tests with diode tests. Though the procedures are similar, the results do not mean the same thing. From the transistor test examples given, you can see why it is important to identify the transistor as PNP type or NPN type.

MANUFACTURING TRANSISTORS

At this point of study, you probably would like to know how transistors are made. There are many steps in their construction. Back in the 1950s, transistors were assembled by hand operation, Fig. 17-29. It was a slow process, which is why transistors were very expensive to manufacture.

Today, transistors have their start as a huge silicon rod, Fig. 17-30, grown in a special furnace, Fig. 17-31. Then, wafers are cut from the silicon ingot, Fig. 17-32, and placed in a special machine where they are polished to a mirror finish. Following this, the wafers are put into special reactors, Fig. 17-33, where controlled vapors apply very thin coatings (doping) on the wafers. These vapor coatings, "make up" the transistor, diffusing (distributing evenly) the P and N material to make

Fig. 17-29. In early 1950s, workers used hand-operated fixtures to assemble transistors. (Western Electric Co.)

Fig. 17-31. This furnace is operating at 1440 degrees Centigrade. (Motorola)

Fig. 17-30. Using modern transistor manufacturing techniques, a single silicon rod is "grown" in a special furnace. (Motorola)

Fig. 17-32. Wafers are cut from the silicon ingot by means of a diamond saw. (Motorola)

either PNP or NPN silicon transistors.

Next, the wafers are cut up and completely covered with plastic. This is called "encapsulating" the transistor. During this operation, the transistor chips are handled by vacuum pick up needles and connected to .001 in. diameter wire. See Fig. 17-34.

Then, the encapsulated transistors are put into automated testing machines. Producing semiconducting material is a very delicate process. There will be some variance in the curves produced by the transistors. Transistors are sorted into bins according to their curves. One bin handles the rejects. The testing machinery shown in Fig. 17-35 checks the electrical specifications of semiconductor parts and then sorts them into bins. They are then ready for packaging and shipment.

Fig. 17-33. After polishing, the wafers are placed into a special reactor where controlled amounts of gas vapors are applied. (Motorola)

Fig. 17-34. Casings are being applied to the semiconductors. (Motorola)

I.C. SAYS:

"Excess heat can destroy a transistor. When installing a transistor, attach a heat sink to the lead you are soldering."

Fig. 17-35. The machine automatically tests the semiconductor parts for electrical specifications. The parts are sorted into the bins below.

This brief description of transistor production helps explain why transistors must be handled with care. The PN junctions are so thin, they can be ruined very easily if you get careless.

CURRENT PATHS

Earlier in this chapter, you learned how to label the leads and identify the two types of transistors. Then, you had a quick look at a transistor manufacturing process. Now, you will want to know how to use transistors.

PNP CURRENT

If we hook a PNP transistor into a simple circuit, Fig. 17-36, we can see how the current flows. Note that there are two current paths. The first path is through

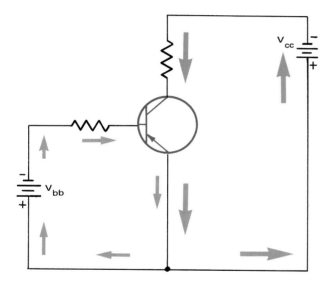

Fig. 17-36. PNP transistor circuit has two batteries and two current paths, both passing through emitter. V_{cc} path carries larger current flow than V_{bb} path.

the base and into the emitter, then back to the battery. This current usually is very small, but the amount depends on the circuit in which it is used. The resistor in this path is similar to a small load resistor. It is there to control the amount of current.

BATTERY LABELS

The battery voltage in the first path of current flow is labeled V_{bb} because it is connected to the base. We are using a system with a double set of letters to avoid

confusion with labels for voltage drops and voltages at various points in the circuit. Note that the other battery connected from emitter to collector is labeled V_{cc} for the same reason.

TOTAL CURRENT

The second path for current in Fig. 17-36 is from the collector through the emitter. This path is the main flow of current in the circuit. Note that the emitter handles the current flow from both the base and collector.

The transistor in this particular circuit is said to be forward biased because current can flow through the junctions. Forward bias means "direction of electron flow," just as it did in our study of diodes.

The amount of current in the emitter can be found by using the following formula and doing some simple addition:

$$I_e = I_b + I_c$$

This formula states that the emitter current is equal to the base current plus the collector current. For example, if the base current is 40 microamps and the collector current is 3 milliamps, find the emitter current. Using the formula, you have:

$$I_e = I_b + I_c$$

$$I_e = 40 \ \mu A + 3 \ mA$$

$$I_e = 40 \ \mu A + 3000 \ \mu A$$

$$I_e = 3040 \ \mu A \ or \ 3.04 \ mA$$

GAIN

Current flow information is really important when we get into amplifying transistors. We started this chapter by stating that the two types of transistors used are switching and amplifying. When we wish to label the amount that current has been amplified by a transistor, we call it the "gain" of that transistor.

Gain is labeled "beta" and has a letter which looks similar to a fancy capital B (β) as its symbol. The gain of a transistor is nothing more than the ratio of the collector current, I_c, and the base current, I_b:

$$\beta = \frac{I_c}{I_b}$$

Using the same current values, what is the gain for the PNP transistor in our last example? Using the formula:

$$\beta = \frac{I_c}{I_b}$$

$$\beta = \frac{3 \text{ mA}}{40 \ \mu A}$$

$$\beta = \frac{3000 \ \mu A}{40 \ \mu A}$$

$$\beta = 75$$

If you look through a transistor catalog, you will find gain or β listings from 30 to 50,000. However, the most common gain falls in the range of 30 to 200. For example, when you hear someone say that a transistor has a gain of 75, it refers to the ratio of collector current (75) to base current (1).

NPN CURRENT

If we look at an NPN transistor in use, Fig. 17-37, we will see its current paths. Note that again there are two circuits:

1. From the first battery (V_{bb}), through the emitter, the base and back to the battery.
2. From the second battery (V_{cc}) through the emitter, the collector and back to the battery.

The second circuit is the main path for current. Note in both examples, Fig. 17-36 and 17-37, that the smaller current flow is through the base of the transistor.

The base turns the transistor "on" or "off." To do this, it must receive either a negative signal (PNP) or a positive signal (NPN). These signals cause the transistor to turn on, which relates to flipping the switch to turn on the lights in your home.

Depending on how much we can amplify the signal (β), we can figure out how much current we can get through the collector to emitter safely. This relates to using the dimmer switch and turning it on full, so that your house light is as bright as you can get it.

SIGNAL FLOW

Note in Figs. 17-36 and 17-37 that the emitter is used in both the base circuit and in the collector circuit. Therefore, it is called a "common emitter circuit."

There are two other ways you can wire a transistor. One is known as "common base," the second is

Fig. 17-37. NPN transistor circuit also has two batteries and two current paths. NPN has opposite direction of current flow than PNP.

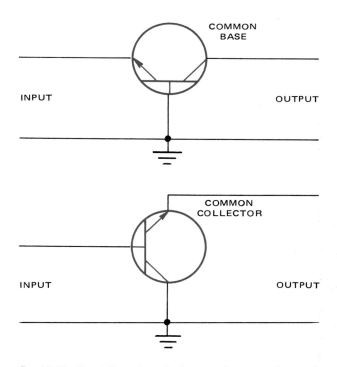

Fig. 17-38. Signal flow through the use of common base and common collector hookups are shown for an NPN transistor.

"common collector," Fig. 17-38. These terms are mentioned a lot. Now you can see why they are labeled this way. Signal flow is through one particular transistor connection which is common to both the input circuit and the output circuit of the transistor.

DATA SHEETS

The last thing we will cover on transistors is other data you might find in parts catalogs. Transistor voltages, for example, are marked as CBO, CEO or EBO. After manufacture, the transistors are tested and marked this way.

CBO, then, means voltage from collector to base with the emitter open, Fig. 17-39. The letter missing in the label is the lead that is open.

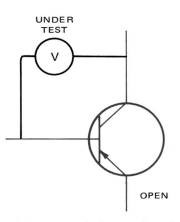

Fig. 17-39. Voltmeter test indicates voltage from collector to base with the emitter open. This function is listed as V_{CBO} under transistor voltages on data sheets.

In the case of CEO, which letter is missing? Since B is missing, this means that there is collector to emitter voltage with the base open. See Fig. 17-40.

The last marking, EBO, is emitter to base voltage with the collector open. See Fig. 17-41.

Gain (β) is also listed in catalogs, along with operating temperature, cutoff frequency and collector cutoff current (I_{CBO}) at some collector-to-base voltage (V_{CB}).

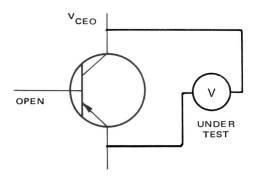

Fig. 17-40. This voltmeter test shows voltage from collector to emitter with the base open (V_{CEO}).

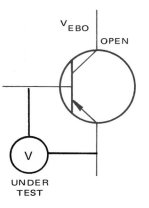

Fig. 17-41. Final voltmeter test reveals voltage from emitter to base with the collector open (V_{EBO}).

You will begin to recognize these letters in circuit drawings as you get a little deeper into electronics. Some catalogs also tell you the type of case the transistor comes in. The shapes we used to illustrate how to find the labels for our leads are just four of the many case types. There are many others, Fig. 17-42.

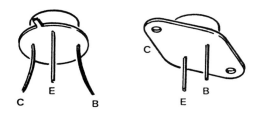

Fig. 17-42. Transistor cases come in a variety of shapes and leads arrangements. Two common case designs are shown.

SUMMARY

Transistors have two basic functions, switching and amplifying. Switching transistors can be found in areas where they must change from ON to OFF thousands of times in one second. Amplifying transistors are used to increase the strength of a very small signal.

The two types of transistors are the PNP and the NPN. The middle letter of each type gives the clue as to what is needed to bias the transistor. The N in the PNP requires a negative signal while the P in the NPN requires a positive bias signal. An ohmmeter can be used to determine an unknown type (PNP or NPN) of transistor by checking for bias voltage.

Transistors were once assembled by hand and were very costly to produce. Production today is more complicated but completely automated and more cost effective.

KEY WORDS AND TERMS

Amplifying transistor

Base

Collector

Emitter

Encapsulating

Gain (β)

NPN transistor

PNP transistor

Power transistor

Switching transistor

Transistor

TEST YOUR KNOWLEDGE

Do not write in this book. Write your answers on a separate sheet of paper.

1. The two basic functions of transistors are _____ and _____.
2. Draw the symbols for PNP and NPN transistors. Label each one for type.
3. Label the three leads on each transistor drawn in answer to question 2.
4. The lead of the transistor that has the arrow is the _____.
5. "Doping" is a term used to describe _____.
6. When a transistor is completely coated with plastic, it is said to be _____.
7. "Beta" is a term used to describe the _____.
8. What is meant by the term EBO in a parts catalog for semiconductors?
9. *True or False?* All silicon transistors have the same "Beta," and all germanium transistors have different "Betas."
10. Which type of transistor, silicon or germanium, will carry more current?

ACTIVITIES

1. Take apart NPN and PNP transistors. Is there any difference in construction between the two types?
2. Find as many different shapes of transistors as you can. Identify the lead location and name for each type.
3. Solder a couple of transistors without using heat sinks. How much does it take before they are ruined? Do the leads discolor in any way? Can you "see" when they are ruined?
4. Visit a plant or try to get a film that shows how a transistor is encapsulated. How is the process done? How do they identify which type of transistor is inside the plastic? Are they processed in batches or one at a time?
5. Why do manufacturers give guarantees on solid state components? Do they last longer than those with tubes?
6. You often hear that if a solid state device is going to fail, it will do so in the first 30 days. If not, if will last for years. Why?
7. Find some circuits that have common emitter, base, and collector wiring. Are there any advantages for each type?
8. Make a list of the properties listed in a replacement catalog. What do each of the items mean or stand for? Why are there so many different categories?
9. Communications satellites are affected by the altitude. Some have solid state devices which were ruined by *things* in the atmosphere. How is that possible?
10. You often see a weather report given where clouds are shown on a radar screen. What causes the blips on a radar screen? How can you tell clouds from airplanes?
11. Holography has become very important in science. What is it? How does it work? What can you do with it?
12. How is it possible to send communications messages to submarines? Does it make any difference if they are under ice?

18 Relays and Switches

LEARNING OBJECTIVES

After studying this chapter, you will be able to:
- Identify a relay and its contacts.
- Draw a circuit containing relays and explain how the circuit operates.
- Explain the numbering system used in relay circuits.
- Draw the symbols for the four types of normally open and normally closed contacts and explain their operation.
- Design a circuit using fuses, relays, limit switches, solenoids, and correctly number the various components.

There are times when electrical equipment must be set up so it will operate in a known sequence. Suppose a manufacturing sequence is: drill a hole, move the piece, and insert a resistor in the hole. One way to control the sequence is through the use of relays and switches. A relay is an electrical switch designed to operate in a controlled "on" or "off" sequence. It will pass on a signal (relay an electrical message) when you make the switch open or close. For that reason, you will find a large number of relays being used as industrial controls.

RELAYS

A relay controls a large flow of current using a low voltage-low current signal. That signal is controlled by an operator pushing a button or from another electrical device. Basically, a relay is a magnetic switch. It consists of a coil and a plunger. Connected to the plunger are contact points, Fig. 18-1. When current passes through the coil, a magnetic field is created. The field moves the plunger causing the contact points to close or open, depending on the situation. If the plunger contacts close, a large current will pass through the contacts without affecting the relay coil.

The circuit that the relay controls is called the load circuit. This circuit is closed or opened by the contacts. A control circuit is used to operate the relay. This control circuit consists of a power source which supplies electricity to the relay coil and some device to turn the control circuit on and off. Most often, a push button is used, Fig. 18-2.

Fig. 18-1. Typical industrial relays.

Fig. 18-2. Control circuit, when closed, energizes the coil, which closes the contacts to complete the load circuit.

A relay can have from one to twelve sets of contacts, each of which can complete a load circuit. The contacts can be either "normally" open or "normally" closed. Normally refers to their condition when no current is flowing through the coil. The industrial symbols for a simple relay and its contacts are shown in Fig. 18-3A.

The power to the coil (control circuit) usually comes from a transformer, although it could come from any power source. The coil and power source must be matched in their voltage level. Thus, a 110 volt ac coil must be attached to a 110 volt power source. A 24 volt dc coil must be energized by a 24 volt dc circuit. For dc current, the main power supply must be rectified. A simple ac circuit with a relay is shown in Fig. 18-3B. A simple dc circuit with a relay is shown in Fig. 18-3C. Most of the remaining discussion will deal with ac circuits, although the same concepts will apply to dc. The only difference in the circuit would be in the components selected. Some of them will have to be matched to the operating dc voltage level.

Energizing the coil of the relay requires completing its control circuit. Therefore, some method of turning the circuit "on" and "off" is needed. An easy way to do

this is to place a pushbutton in the circuit. Also, if an electrical overload should occur, there must be a way to protect the circuit. Therefore, you should install a fuse in the circuit. To be safe, most companies install fuses on each side of the power supply. A schematic of a circuit with a relay is shown in Fig. 18-4.

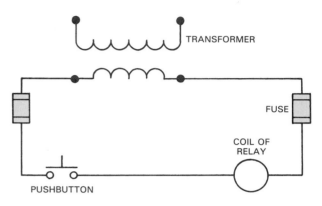

Fig. 18-4. Fuses protect the control circuit.

When the control circuit is complete (which energizes the coil), you may hear a click. This noise is caused by the plunger being pulled in by the magnetic field. The contacts attached to the plunger hit stationary contacts to complete the load circuit. Also available are sealed relays. A sealed relay has its coil and contacts encased in a plastic box. The box prevents dirt or other particles from getting in between the opening and closing contacts. You may not hear the contacts click in a sealed relay.

As stated earlier, a relay can have more than one set of contacts which are controlled by the same coil. Also, these contacts may be normally open or normally closed. "Normally" refers to their status when no voltage is applied to the coil. When the relay energizes, the normally open contacts will close and the normally closed contacts will open. In other words, all contacts switch their position, Fig. 18-5.

With a continuity tester, you can check the position of the contacts to see whether they are normally open or closed. This check is done when the relay is sealed and you cannot see the position of the contacts. It is also done to check whether the contacts are making the proper connection. First, make sure that no power passes through the contacts. Then place the tester leads to each terminal to see if the contacts are open or closed. You can also test the contacts directly on an unsealed relay. Place one lead of the tester on the stationary contact and the other on the plunger contact.

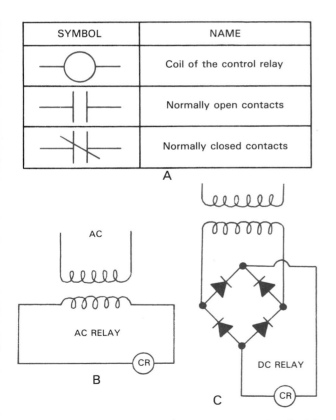

SYMBOL	NAME
	Coil of the control relay
	Normally open contacts
	Normally closed contacts

A

AC

AC RELAY

CR

B

DC RELAY

CR

C

Fig. 18-3. A—Symbols for coil and contacts for a relay. B—AC circuit with relay. C—Rectified dc circuit with relay.

Fig. 18-5. Two or more sets of contacts may be controlled by the same coil. A—Coil not energized. B—Energizing the coil closes the normally open contacts and opens the normally closed contacts.

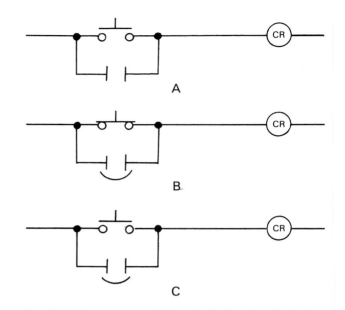

Fig. 18-6. Designing a method to hold closed a circuit. A—Pushbutton and normally open set of contacts. B—Pushing the button energized the circuit and closes the contacts. C—Releasing the start button does nothing since the circuit is complete through the contacts.

HOLDING CONTACTS

Contacts will only retain their "changed" position while the coil is energized. Suppose you are using a pushbutton to complete the control circuit. What happens just as soon as you release the button? Obviously, the circuit will be de-energized and the relay will drop open. The term drop open is used because once the magnetic field is lost, gravity or a spring will make the plunger fall, thus opening those contacts which had closed.

There is a way to get around the problem of holding in a pushbutton. A normally open set of contacts can be connected in parallel with the pushbutton. When the pushbutton is pressed, the relay coil will energize and close the contacts. Since the contacts are now closed, you have a parallel path to the coil which will stay energized even if you release the pushbutton. The circuit would now look like the one shown in Fig. 18-6.

Once the pushbutton is released, the contacts will "hold in" the circuit of the relay. For this reason, when contacts are used to hold in a part of the circuit, they are given the nickname "holding" contacts. However,' the circuit now has another problem. There is no way to de-energize the relay.

STOP BUTTON

Most machines have magnetic controls. The pushbuttons are usually labeled "start" and "stop" because that is their function in the circuit. The holding contacts are placed only in parallel with the start button. Placing the holding contacts across both buttons would make the circuit useless. The start button is almost always a normally open pushbutton. The circuit is completed by pushing the normally open pushbutton. When that happens, the holding contacts will also close, allowing you to let go of the start button.

To open the circuit, push down on the normally closed pushbutton labeled stop, Fig. 18-7. This breaks current flow through the control circuit. All normally open contacts will then return to their open position, including the holding contacts. Once this happens, the relay is de-energized and the load circuit is open.

Fig. 18-7. Stop button to break circuit held by holding contacts.

NUMBERING

At some point, you may wish to add a second relay to the circuit. To identify the various relays, it is best that you number them. Usually they are numbered from top to bottom. However, this system of numbering is not always used. You can either place the number in front of the "CR" or behind it. However, you should be consistent with your circuit diagram. The relays in Fig. 18-8 are labeled 1CR and 2CR.

The circuit is easier to follow if every horizontal line is given a line number. Refer to Fig. 18-8. Does the normally closed contact in line 4 belong to the 1CR or the 2CR relay? As the schematic is drawn, there is no way of telling. There is a way to make it easier for the electrician to follow the circuit. The contacts can also be numbered in two ways, by location or relay number.

If you pick up a relay and look at it, the contacts are numbered from left to right and top to bottom. There are also two terminals for the coil. The relay 1CR

diagramed in Fig. 18-9 is shown with eight contacts; six are normally open and two are normally closed. Those normally open numbered 1, 2, 3, 4, 6, and 7. Contacts 5 and 8 are normally closed. Thus, if you were to connect a load circuit to the number 4 contacts of relay 1CR, you would be wiring a set of normally open contacts in the circuit. When the coil is energized, those contacts would close and the load circuit would be complete.

Labeling the contact on the diagram as 1CR-4 tells the electrician to use the fourth set of contacts. It also specified relay 1CR for the particular load circuit being connected, Fig. 18-10.

There is also a way of labeling the relay to show where the contacts are being used. This is done by placing a set of numbers on the drawing beside the coil. Fig. 18-11 shows relay 8CR. The numbers to the right of 8CR tell you on what line of the schematic the contacts are being used. They also show whether the contacts are open or closed. The line under the number 48 tells you that those contacts are normally closed.

Fig. 18-8. Numbering relays long lines of a schematic.

Fig. 18-10. Labeling contacts within a schematic.

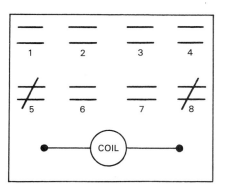

Fig. 18-9. Labeling contacts of a relay.

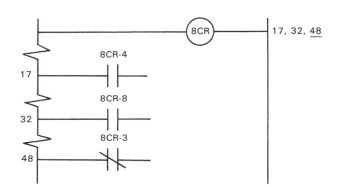

Fig. 18-11. Locating contacts by placing their line numbers next to the coil.

Notice that this system does not tell you which of the contacts are being used. Also, it does not specify how many contacts there are in the relay. You must still label each contact.

Why would you use only three sets of contacts on a relay which might contain eight? There are several possible answers. First, the five remaining contacts are either not needed or are not being used in that circuit. If the relay is placed in another circuit, other contacts can be used.

Second, when machine builders construct a specialized machine, they try to use as many standardized parts as possible. Usually the relay panel for a machine has already been built by an electrical contractor. The relay panel is then simply bolted to the machine where it is needed. An electrician attaches the wires to the needed contacts. Third, the remaining contacts can be used later as spares. They can be used if the contacts in use are destroyed or welded together by accidental arcing.

TIMED RELAYS

Another type of relay is called a timed relay. It will provide a time delay, often as long as one minute, before the contacts change position. The contacts can be normally open or normally closed. The industrial symbol for the coil of a timed relay looks just the same as the symbol for a control relay. The only difference is in the letter used to identify it. A timed relay is identified by the letter T (meaning timed), Fig. 18-12. The number of the relay can be placed either in front of or behind its R code. Thus TR1 and 1TR could refer to the same relay. However, always use consistent labeling when diagraming a schematic.

TIMED CONTACTS

Timed relays have two types contacts; normally open and normally closed. Another feature of timed

relays is that the contacts can either time open or time close. Thus, the four possible positions for timed relay contacts are:
1. Normally open, timed closed.
2. Normally open, timed open.
3. Normally closed, timed open.
4. Normally closed, timed closed.

These are separated from regular contacts by their symbols. The symbols for timed contacts tell you whether the contacts are normally open or normally closed. They also tell you the direction in which the contacts are being timed with an arrow head, Fig. 18-13.

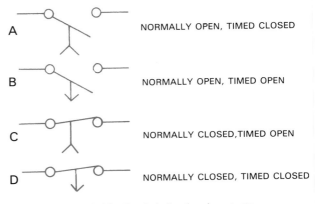

Fig. 18-13. Symbols for timed contacts.

As mentioned earlier, both the timed and untimed contacts can be either normally open or normally closed. Gravity or springs are used to hold them in either the open or closed position.

NORMALLY OPEN, TIMED CLOSED

A normally open, timed closed contact will be open when no current is passing through its control circuit. However, when the coil is energized, the contact will not close immediately. Rather, it will start timing before it closes, Fig. 18-14. You can set the amount of time it takes to close simply by turning an adjustment screw. After the timer reaches the preset time, the contacts will close. They will remain closed until current to the coil of the relay is switched off. When the control circuit is opened, the contacts will open immediately. These contacts do NOT time back open.

An example of the use of a normally open, timed closed contacts is its use in a burglar alarm system. Connect switches to the doors and windows. When the

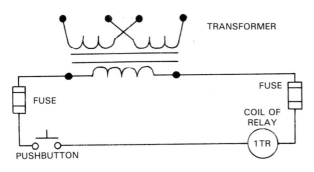

Fig. 18-12. Timed relay in a circuit.

door is opened, the switch closes, completing the control circuit of the relay. This energizes the coil of the relay. The normally open, timed closed contacts start timing to give the homeowner time to turn off the alarm. After the time is up and a burglar has not turned off the system, the contacts close, completing the load circuit. This circuit could automatically dial the policy, ring a bell, sound a siren, or turn on the lights. All of these alarm features could be wired in as part of the load circuit. Note that normally open contacts are used in the control circuit while timed contacts are used in the load circuit. The load circuit will be used to trigger the alarm.

The circuit can be made so that the only way to deactivate the alarm is to turn a key in a control box. This prevents the burglar from closing the door and thus deactivating the control circuit. Remember the concept of a start and stop button on a relay mechanism. Use a key lock as the stop button to break the control current. After the alarm has sounded, you must use the key to turn it off.

You must use also the key to deactivate the alarm once it is triggered. Remember, the relay is timed a certain amount. When you open the door after arriving home, the relay contacts begin timing because the coil of the relay is energized. You have only a preset amount of time to get inside with your key to deactivate the control box. Normally this control box would be hidden so that it could not be easily seen by an intruder coming into the building.

NORMALLY OPEN, TIMED OPEN

The second type of normally open contacts is the normally open, timed open contacts. The symbol for these contacts is shown in Fig. 18-13B. When the control circuit is energized, the contacts close immediately. Remember the direction of the arrow tells you the direction of the timing. Since the arrow points down the contacts time only in that direction. The contacts remain closed as long as there is power to the coil of the relay. As soon as the circuit is opened, the timing of the contacts begins. The contacts remain closed as long as they are timing, Fig. 18-15. When the time set on the

Fig. 18-14. Normally open, timed closed contact before and after coil is energized.

Fig. 18-15. Normally open, timed open contact closes immediately when coil is energized. Then it times open when the coil is de-energized.

relay finally runs out, the contacts open. They stay open until the relay is energized again and the process repeats itself.

NORMALLY CLOSED, TIMED OPEN

Normally closed, timed open contacts are closed when no power passes through the control circuit. As soon as power is applied to the control circuit, the contacts remain closed but start timing. When the preset time has elapsed, the contacts will open and remain open until the control circuit is de-energized, Fig. 18-16. The symbol for these contacts is shown in Fig. 18-13C.

NORMALLY CLOSED, TIMED CLOSED

The last type of timed contact is the normally closed, timed closed contact. Its symbol is shown in Fig. 18-13D. The contacts are closed in the de-energized

Fig. 18-16. Normally closed, timed open contacts time open when the coil is energized.

(normal) condition. When the power is applied to the coil of the relay, it will be energized. When that happens, the contacts open instantly. They remain open until the coil is de-energized. Then, the contacts begin their timing sequence, Fig. 18-17. After the preset time has elapsed, the contacts close and remain closed until the coil is energized again.

NORMAL
CONDITION

OPEN
INSTANTLY

TIMING
CLOSED

Fig. 18-17. Normally closed, timed open contact open immediately when the coil is energized, but then time closed when the coil is de-energized.

TIMED CONTACTS IN A CIRCUIT

Now that you have seen the four types of timed contacts, see how they work in a circuit, Fig. 18-18. This is only a portion of a circuit. It shows lines 16, 17, and 18. Before the circuit is energized the contacts in line 16 are closed, in line 17 they are open, and in line 18 they are open.

When the circuit is energized (power step 1), relay 2CR also is energized. This closes the contact in line 18 almost instantly, energizing the relay TR3 (power step 2). The contacts in line 17 are open at this point.

After the amount of time set on the relay is reached, the contacts in line 17 close (power step 3). That energizes relay 1CR. When that happens the normally closed contacts on line 16 open instantly. This in turn de-energizes relay 2CR (power step 4). When that happens, the contacts in line 18 open instantly, dropping relay TR3 (power step 5). When that happens, the contacts in line 17 open instantly dropping relay 1CR (power step 6). This in turn closes the contacts in line 16, (power step 7) and the whole process is ready to repeat itself.

ELECTRONIC RELAYS

In addition to standard electromagnetic relays, there are a series of electronic relays. They are used to switch on and off either ac or dc circuits. The dc electronic relay is usually designed around a semiconductor device called an SCR. Once it is turned on, it remains on until the current falls to zero. The ac electronic relay is usually designed around another semiconductor device called a TRIAC. It is triggered on or off with a small current (up to 20 ma) on one of its three leads. The SCR or TRIAC may be found as separate components or they can be mounted as part of a printed circuit board. Since relays are nothing more than switches, even transistors can be used as electronic

SCHEMATIC	DESCRIPTION
16 1CR-3 2CR 18 17 TR3-4 1CR 16 18 2CR-6 TR3 17	**No Power**
16 1CR-3 2CR 17 18	**Power Step 1** Relay 2CR energizes.
18 2CR-6 TR3	**Power Step 2** Contact 2CR-6 closes and relay TR3 energizes.
17 TR3-4 1CR	**Power Step 3** Contact TR3-4 closes after a preset time and relay 1CR energizes.
16 1CR-3 2CR	**Power Step 4** Contact 1 CR-3 opens and relay 2CR de-energizes.
18 2CR-6 TR3	**Power Step 5** Contact 2CR-6 opens again (they were closed in Step 2) and relay TR3 de-energizes.
17 TR3-4 1CR	**Power Step 6** Contact TR3-4 opens again (they were closed in Step 3) and relay 1CR de-energizes.
16 1CR-3 2CR	**Power Step 7** Contact 1CR-3 closes again (they were opened in Step 4) and relay 2CR energizes. (Cycle repeats back to Power Step 1.)

Fig. 18-18. An example application of timed contacts in a circuit.

relays for switching small current devices. Others may be used as a trigger for a device carrying several hundred amps.

SWITCHES

In addition to relays there are other ways to control electrical circuits. Rather than timing a circuit, it can be controlled through the use of switches. Switches are made to open and close by the movement of a machine or a part moving on a conveyor (limit switches). Other switches are controlled by pressure of a liquid or a gas (pressure switches) or the height of a liquid (float switches). Still others are designed to control the "on" and "off" movement of a hydraulic or pneumatic fluid (solenoid). In spite of all their differences, all these devices are merely "on" or "off" switches used for controlling a circuit.

LIMIT SWITCH

A limit switch contains an electrical contact which is either normally open or normally closed. The limit switch usually is triggered by some outside mechanical source. It is not activated by magnetism. The trigger source can be a machine component, the workpiece, an operator, or a number of other possibilities. The symbol for a limit switch is shown in Fig. 18-19.

To illustrate an example use of a limit switch, suppose you had a conveyor belt on a production line. The conveyor was carrying a product to be packed in boxes. You could station three opertors on each side of the belt and have them pick up the product as it came down the conveyor belt, Fig. 18-20A. Suppose one of the operators is absent, you might slow down the production line so the other five could keep up with the product. If you did not slow it down, the conveyor belt would dump the product off the end of the production line.

One way to prevent that from happening is to use a limit switch. Place it near the end of the conveyor and connect its contact to the drive motor for the belt. When product hits the switch, the contact will open and the circuit will stop the conveyor belt, Fig.18-20B. As soon as the product is removed from the switch, the contact will close and the belt will start moving again. To see how this is connected in a circuit electrically, look at Fig. 18-20C. The limit switch contacts are normally closed. When the circuit is energized, relay 3CR will close the contacts in line 8. This action completes the circuit to drive the motor. As long as the limit switch is closed, the conveyor will continue to move.

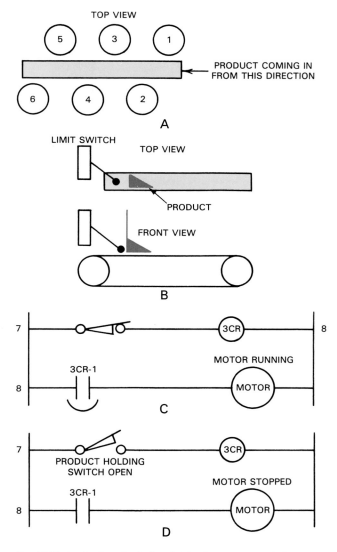

Fig. 18-20. Application of a limit switch to stop a conveyor belt. When a product hits the switch, the circuit is opened, stopping the motor.

When the product hits the switch, Fig. 18-20D, the contacts in line 7 open, thus opening the circuit to relay 3CR. This in turn will drop the contacts in line 8 which stops the conveyor motor.

On a schematic, the symbol for a normally open limit switch appears as shown in Fig. 18-21. Remember, gravity or a spring holes the contacts open. Therefore, the symbol is drawn below the terminals. The switch must be triggered by some mechanical object exerting pressure on it. When that happens, the contacts will close to complete a portion of the circuit. When used in series with other contacts, all of them must be closed to complete the circuit.

Fig. 18-19. Limit switch symbol.

Fig. 18-21. Normally open limit switch symbol.

Fig. 18-22. Using normally open and normally closed limit switches in combination to control high and low speed motor windings.

A limit switch can have a normally open and normally closed set of contacts connected together mechanically. This will insure that if one set of contacts is open, the others will be closed. However, it does not allow both sets to be open or closed at the same time. This type of limit switch is shown in a circuit with a dashed line connecting the two contacts, Fig. 18-22.

The limit switch in Fig. 18-22 is being used with a two speed motor having high speed and low speed windings. You do not want to energize both windings together. Therefore, with the limit switch in this position, the low speed winding (line 75) will be in the circuit. When the limit switch in line 74 is tripped, its contacts will close and those in line 75 will open. This will energize the high speed windings on the motor. At the same time the open contacts in line 75 will de-energize the low speed windings.

PRESSURE SWITCH

Another common device found in a circuit is called a pressure, or vacuum, switch. Its contacts can also be either normally open or normally closed, Fig. 18-23. Rising or falling pressure is used to activate the switch which closes or opens its contacts.

An example of use of a pressure switch can be found on an air compressor. A normally closed pressure

NORMALLY
OPEN

NORMALLY
CLOSED

Fig. 18-23. Symbols for pressure switches.

switch is installed on the air tank. When the air compressor pump is turned on, the motor will continue to run until the pressure is high enough to activate the pressure switch. At that time, the contacts on the pressure switch open, stopping the motor. Without other protective devices, if the pressure switch fails, the motor would continue to run. This would eventually rupture the tank or harm the pump.

FLOAT SWITCHES

A pressure switch used with a ball float (float switch) is activated mechanically by a rising or falling water level. For example, suppose you have a pump transfer water from a well to a storage tank. How does the pump know when to start? A float which sits inside the storage take is attached to the arm of the switch. When the water level drops, the float drops, moving the arm, and closing the switch. This will complete the circuit to the pump which then delivers more water, Fig. 18-24.

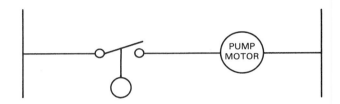

Fig. 18-24. Symbol for a float switch.

SOLENOID

A large number of electrical systems are tied in with hydraulic (oil) or pneumatic (air) control units. These units are used to move conveyors, cylinders, and other components through the use of directional valves. One method of controlling a valve is through the use of a solenoid. A solenoid is similar to a relay in that it has a coil and plunger. However, it does not have contacts. When the control circuit is energized, the magnetic field of the coil pulls in the plunger. The plunger might be connected to a movable spool inside a valve. When the plunger and spool is shifted by the solenoid, oil or air can pass through the valve and into the lines.

The solenoid will have two symbols depending on where it is found. In a hydraulics or pneumatics circuit, it is drawn as the symbol shown in Fig. 18-25A. When used in an electrical circuit, the solenoid is shown as the symbol in Fig. 18-25B. In electrical uses, the solenoid

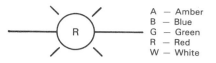

Fig. 18-26. Symbol for a light.

Fig. 18-25. A—Solenoid symbol and example use in a hydraulics or pneumatics circuit. B—Solenoid symbol and example use in an electrical circuit schematic.

would control some component such as "clamps." A label is drawn near the solenoid symbol to show what is being controlled.

Notice that soleniod of the circuit in Fig. 18-25B has two contacts, as well as a fuse. The two contacts from the same relay and fuse are used as a safety precaution. If one set of contacts weld together because of arcing, you still have control over the solenoid by the second set. The fuse will protect the solenoid in case of an overload.

GROUND DETECTION

There must be some system for protecting the relay controls from unwanted short circuits. Relays are used on large machines or assembly line electrical systems. For that reason most companies do not want to shut a machine down and lose production. They would rather run the machine for a few hours with a short or unwanted ground. When the production shift is over, the maintenance electrician is sent in to correct the fault. Obviously, there must be some method to tell when a short or ground exists. That method is called a ground detection system. It utilizes two lights in conjunction with an intentional ground. The symbol used for lights is shown in Fig. 18-26. The letter in the symbol tells the

color of the light. The ground detection circuit would normally be found on the last line of the schematic and is shown in Fig. 18-27.

The voltage drop across each light would be one-half of the circuit voltage. Therefore, when there is no unwanted ground both lights will be burning at half brilliance. However, when a ground occurs, one light will go out and the other will burn at full brilliance. Suppose you had an unwanted ground occur on the left side of the line. The left amber light would go out and the right one would light at full brilliance, Fig. 18-28.

Fig. 18-27. The circuit is intentionally grounded between lamps so both will light.

Fig. 18-28. An unintentional ground causes one lamp to go out and another to burn at full brilliance.

SUMMARY

A relay is a device used to transfer an electrical signal to open or close switches. The switches are called contacts in a relay and may be either normally open or normally closed. Normal means the position of the contact when the coil of the relay is in the de-energized state. The contacts can also be made to open or close after a preset amount of time.

Other devices used in relay circuits include fuses, limit switches, pressure switches, float switches, solenoids, and other devices. To protect the circuits from shutting down at an unwanted time, ground detection circuits are built into some relay circuits.

KEY WORDS AND TERMS

Float switch
Holding contact
Limit switch
Normally closed, timed closed contact
Normally closed, timed open contact
Normally open, timed closed contact
Normally open, timed open contact
Pressure switch
Relay
Solenoid
Timed relay
Vacuum switch

TEST YOUR KNOWLEDGE

Do not write in this book. Write your answers on a separate sheet of paper.

1. The diagram below shows a description of relay 13CR. What would the numbers next to the relay tell you?

2. Note the circuit below. What is needed to energize the relay coil 5CR?

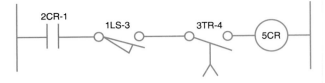

3. Based on the information on relay circuits, troubleshoot the three situations discussed about the circuit schematic below. What would be your conclusions? Move the voltmeter leads to the test points indicated and observe the reading or lack of voltage.
   a. Voltage between test points 36 and 39 but not between test points 37 and 39.
   b. Voltage between test points 48 and 39, 41 and 39, but not between test points 42 and 39.
   c. With contact 3CR-1 in line 432 open: voltage between test points 36 and 39 but not between test points 36 and 38.

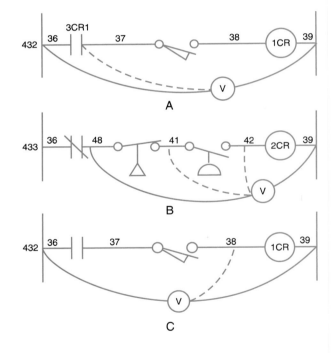

19 Integrated Circuits and Other Solid State Devices

LEARNING OBJECTIVES

After studying this chapter, you will be able to:

- Name several different kinds of Field Effect Transistors and describe how they work.
- Draw the symbols for JFETs, MOSFETs, and SCRs.
- Explain how to turn an SCR on and off.
- Draw two of the different symbols for Integrated Circuits.
- Create a chart which depicts the Truth Table and explain how knowing binary will help you quickly check the various input and output levels.

In the last chapter, we studied transistors. Now, we will look at some of the other types of solid state devices, how they are constructed, how they function, and how they are used.

FIELD EFFECT TRANSISTORS

A field effect transistor (FET) is another solid state device that will do many things that a transistor does. FETs usually are made from a small block of silicon called the *channel*.

In Fig. 19-1, for example, a chunk of N type silicon is used as the channel. Then, a small piece of P type material is attached to the side of the channel to form a P-N junction. The P type material is called the *gate*. Finally, two leads are added at either end of the channel. These are known as the *source* and the *drain*.

The P-N junction of the FET is very similar to the type of junctions you dealt with in the last two chapters. Fig. 19-2 illustrates a completed field effect transistor.

Looking back to Chapter 17, you could compare the *source* as the FET with the *emitter* of a transistor, the *drain*

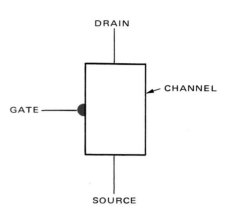

Fig. 19-2. A completed FET is shown with the channel made from a block of silicon. Gate material and leads are attached.

Fig. 19-3. In comparing transistor and FET leads, note that the emitter, base, and collector of the transistor equals the source, gate, and drain of the FET.

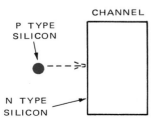

Fig. 19-1. A field effect transistor (FET) consists of a block of silicon, to which a small piece of P type material is attached.

with the *collector*, and the *gate* with the *base*, Fig. 19-3. Unlike the transistor, however, the FET is not made of PNP or NPN junctions, Fig. 19-4. Instead, it is made from a solid piece of N material with P materials as its gate. It also could have been made from a solid piece of P material with N material as its gate. See Fig. 19-5.

Why the FET does *not* work on the junction idea will be explained later.

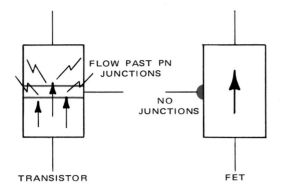

Fig. 19-4. Comparing flow of electrons past the PN junction of a transistor with flow through the channel of the FET.

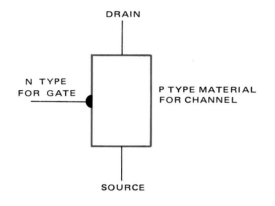

Fig. 19-5. Making the FET from P type material combined with N type material to serve as the gate.

TYPES OF FETS

There are several types of FETs.
1. Junction field effect transistors.
   a. JFET — N channel.
   b. JFET — P channel.
2. Metal oxide semiconductor field effect transistors.
   a. MOSFET — N channel.
   b. MOSFET — P channel.

As indicated, both JFETs and MOSFETs can be made of either N type material or P type material.

JFET

We will examine the JFET first, Fig. 19-6. Note that we have another gate on the opposite side of the channel and the two gates are tied together. In this way, we can use the gates to block the flow of electrons through the channel.

The input circuit is from the gates to the source, and the output circuit is from the source to the drain,

Fig. 19-6. With zero input on the FET, current output is high because nothing is blocking the flow through the channel.

Fig. 19-6. In order to let the FET conduct, we must not block the flow of electrons. This is a fact because the FET is made from a solid piece of material. The FET does not require biasing to make it conduct (as a conventional transistor does). Instead, the gates are used to block the flow of electrons, Fig. 19-7. As the gates are made more negative, fewer electrons can flow from source to drain.

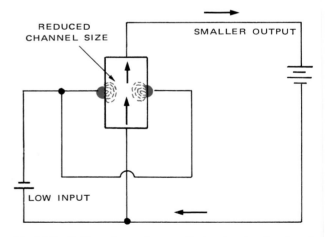

Fig. 19-7. Putting a low voltage on the input makes the size of the channel smaller and reduces output current.

DEPLETION LAYER

With voltage applied to the gates of the JFET, a depletion layer is set up in the channel. This layer resists or opposes the flow of electrons through the channel. Fewer electrons can get past the depletion layer than when no signal was put on the gates. Then, when increased voltage is applied to the gates, current in the output circuit drops to a very low value. Finally, when the voltage on the gates reaches a high negative value, the depletion layer extends all the way across the channel, Fig. 19-8. The electrons cannot flow and the current falls to zero.

Note that we used voltage on the gates to stop the flow of current. With FETs current does not flow across a junction as it does with conventional tran-

Fig. 19-8. Increasing voltage on the input sets up a depletion layer that blocks the flow of current through the channel.

Fig. 19-9. Symbols are shown for N channel and P channel JFETs. Only the arrow changes direction.

Fig. 19-10. Diffusing two P type strips on a substrate of N type material for a MOSFET.

sistors. Therefore, there is much less noise with FETs. This characteristic makes them very useful in amplifer circuits. Since there is little noise on the input, it means there is less noise amplified at the output.

Although we have shown the JFET as an N channel (made of N type material), we could have used P type material. In this case, the JFET would work with polarities being just the reverse of N channel usage.

The symbols for N channel and P channel JFETs are shown in Fig. 19-9. The only difference between these two symbols is the direction in which the arrow points.

MOSFET

The metal oxide semiconductor FET (MOSFET) is similar to the JFET. The major difference is in how they are made. With a MOSFET, Fig. 19-10, a piece of N type material (substrate) is used. On it, two P type strips are diffused. One of the strips will become our source, and the other becomes our drain. Between them, the P channel is diffused. This layer, shown in Fig. 19-11, is not as thick as the first two.

NOTE: The drawings in Figs. 19-10, 19-11 and 19-12 are meant to give you some idea how a MOSFET

Fig. 19-11. Diffusing the P channel between the two P type strips of a MOSFET.

is made. Do not think that this is what a MOSFET would look like if you took one apart. The diffused layers on the substrate are very thin and are measured in microns (only a few thousandths of an inch thick).

Looking at an end view of the MOSFET in Fig. 19-12, a thin film of dielectric (insulating) material is grown over the channel. On top of this, another film is deposited to complete the gate of the MOSFET. The

Fig. 19-12. Finished MOSFET showing gate, drain, source and channel. The dielectric creates a capacitor between the gate and the channel.

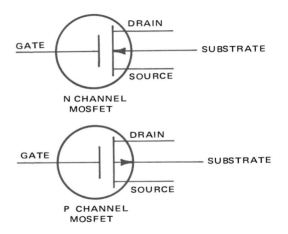

Fig. 19-13. Symbols are shown for N channel and P channel MOSFETs. The substrate is the block of material on which the various parts were diffused.

last layer applied is metal, which is why the unit is called a "Metal Oxide Semiconductor FET."

The dielectric separates the metal from the channel. Since it acts as an insulator, this particular FET is also called an IGFET (Insulated Gate Field Effect Transistor). In a MOSFET, then, the gate is separated from the channel by a dielectric. As you recall from Chapter 4, when two conductors are separated by an insulator, you have a capacitor. The small capacitor in a MOSFET can be damaged very easily by spikes (sudden, unintended pulses of electricity) and even static charges. Even the capacitance of your body or stray voltages when soldering can ruin a MOSFET. For this reason, manufacturers ship them with their leads shorted.

I.C. SAYS:
"Use extreme caution when working with a MOSFET. Solder all other components first and save the MOSFET until last. Use heat sinks and avoid touching the leads. Your body capacitance can ruin them. Ground all sources of static electricity before contacting a MOSFET."

There is a whole series of MOSFETs. No attempt will be made to describe all of them. However, it *is* important to know that P type material (instead of N type) could have been used in our example of how a MOSFET is made. Again, they would operate with opposite polarities. The N channel MOSFET which we used in our example has a symbol with the arrow pointing in, Fig. 19-13. The P channel MOSFET has its arrow pointing out.

To make our N channel MOSFET conduct, hook it up the same way you hooked up the JFET. See Fig. 19-6. As the gate is made more negative, the current between the source and drain will again decrease because of the depletion region, Fig. 19-7. The main

difference between the JFET and MOSFET is that the MOSFET has an extremely high input impedance; much more than the JFET.

Once the FET has been made, it is placed in a small plastic or metal case with three leads. The completed FET looks just like a transistor. In fact, the only way you can tell some of them apart is by looking up the code numbers printed on them. These numbers usually can be found in a semiconductor data book.

ADVANTAGES OF THE FET

The main advantage that FETs have over conventional transistors is the fact that any signal trying to enter the FET "sees" a very high impedance. Fig. 19-14 shows a FET used as an amplifier connected to a radio tuning circuit. When you tune in a station, the tuning circuit will develop the signal voltages of that station. These voltages, in turn, will be amplified by the FET, which uses a small voltage at the gate to control a large current through the channel.

If you think back to Chapter 15, you will recall that we studied the "Q" of a resonant circuit. We found that a high Q circuit has a narrow bandwidth. If you attach a low resistance in parallel with the resonant circuit, it will lower the Q of the circuit and make the bandwidth much wider.

However, if the bandwidth of the tuning circuit of a radio is made too wide, you might pick up the signals from two stations at once. FETs help avoid this because they have a very high input impedance. So high, in fact, that when you attach a FET to a tank (parallel resonant) circuit, the Q of the circuit shows little effect.

Fig. 19-14. Using the FET in a circuit to amplify the radio signal.

SILICON CONTROLLED RECTIFIERS

Another solid state device found in the electronics field is the silicon controlled rectifier (SCR). This device usually is used in circuits where the current is very high. You will find SCRs in circuits carrying as much as 4000 amps.

By using an SCR, it is possible to switch a circuit thousands of times in one second. Consider the fact that during one cycle of a 60 Hz sine wave, there are 16,667 microseconds. See Fig. 19-15. Since the SCR can be switched in about one microsecond, it can be used to switch high current circuits in extremely short periods of time. This makes the SCR very valuable in switching circuits.

TURNING ON THE SCR

The symbol for an SCR, Fig. 19-16, looks like a diode symbol except that it has one additional line. This line is known as its "gate." The anode and cathode are the same as for a diode.

Since the SCR looks like a diode and is turned on like a transistor, many people say it is a combination of both of them. However, there is one big difference. To turn on the SCR, the gate must be given a pulse that is positive with respect to the cathode. Once it is turned on, the SCR will conduct from cathode to anode. Then, comes the difference. *If you open the circuit to the gate, the SCR will keep on conducting.* Removing the gate current does nothing.

Therefore, the SCR is like a latching switch. Once it is triggered, it remains on as long as there is current

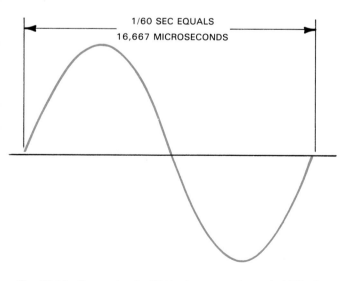

Fig. 19-15. One cycle of a 60 Hz sine wave takes only 1/60 of a second. This is equal to 16,667 microseconds.

Fig. 19-16. Symbol is shown for the SCR. It looks the same as the diode symbol except that another lead known as the "gate" is added.

flowing through it. Only a short pulse to the gate was needed to make it conduct.

TURNING OFF THE SCR IN DC CIRCUITS

Most SCRs need less than 20 milliamps to keep them turned on. One way to turn off the SCR is to lower the load current to a value of less than 20 milliamps. There are many ways to do this. One way would be to use a switch, Fig. 19-17, in the load circuit.

Fig. 19-17. To turn off the SCR in a dc circuit, wire a normally closed switch in series with the SCR. Opening the switch will shut off the SCR.

If the load is drawing a heavy current (200 amps or more), it will cause a heavy arcing when you open the switch. However, if the circuit is carrying small current, this would not be a problem.

A second way to turn off the SCR (open the circuit) is to wire a push button switch in parallel to the SCR, Fig. 19-18. When the switch is closed, the SCR is shorted out and will stop conducting. When the push button is released, the gate must be triggered again to turn on the SCR.

Fig. 19-18. Another way to turn off the SCR in a dc circuit is by wiring a normally open push button switch in parallel with the SCR. Pushing down the button while the SCR is conducting will short it out.

TURNING OFF THE SCR IN AC CIRCUITS

When an SCR is used in an ac circuit, it is an easy matter to switch it off. Actually, the SCR will automatically shut off during each negative alternation (half cycle) when the current from the positive alternation falls to zero. Therefore, it must be triggered "on" every positive alternation. This is not a problem, however, all that is needed is another pulse at the gate.

Since the SCR can be controlled anywhere on the positive alternation, it has many uses in circuits that control heavy currents. You can trigger the SCR early in the cycle, Fig. 19-19, by sending a pulse to the gate at that time. If you want to delay its firing, the SCR can be pulsed "on" later in the alternation.

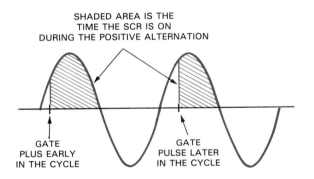

Fig. 19-19. There are over 8000 microseconds in a 60 Hz signal during one alternation. Since the gate can be pulsed anywhere in the positive alternation, the SCR will conduct for as much of the positive half cycle as you wish.

There are over 8000 microseconds in one half cycle of a 60 Hz signal. Since only a short time is needed to trigger the SCR, it can be turned on anytime during the positive alternation. For this reason, SCRs are used in motor speed control circuits, switching circuits, lighting controls and welding circuits.

POWER TOOL SPEED CONTROL PROJECT

You can build the speed control unit shown in Fig. 19-20 as a valuable exercise in working with ac circuits having resistors, rectifiers and SCRs. Then, with the twist of a knob, you can vary the speed of any series universal (brush type) motor that draws less than 400 watts. This is the type of motor found in most drills, table saws, hand grinders and sewing machines.

CAUTION: Do not use the speed control unit for other types of motors.

This speed control will let you slow down your tools

when working with different kinds of material. Suppose you tried to drill holes in a piece of steel and your drill bit squealed and burned. This indicates that your drill is running too fast, so install the speed control and slow it down.

Fig. 19-20. Power tool speed control. Top. Finished project. Bottom. Assembled components. (Project by Jim Shelton)

To build the speed control unit, obtain the items given in the parts list and assemble them according to the construction procedure given.

No.	Item
2	Motorola HEP 162 silicon rectifiers.
1	2.5K resistor, 5 watts (R_1).
1	500 ohm potentiometer, 2 watts (R_2).
1	1.5K resistor, 1/2 watt (R_3).
1	SPST switch, 5 amps.
1	Motorola HEP 302 silicon controlled rectifier.
1	Aluminum heat sink for SCR, 3 1/2 x 1 1/2 in.
1	Three prong panel mount ac receptacle.
1	Three wire grounded line cord.
1	Aluminum minibox, 3 in. x 4 in. x 5 in. Connecting wiring and cord strain relief.

CONSTRUCTION PROCEDURE

To build the power tool speed control:
1. Discard the insulating washers furnished with the SCR, then install SCR on heat sink. See Fig. 19-21.
2. Apply a thin coat of heat sink compound to surface of minibox that will contact top of heat sink.
3. Mount heat sink/SCR assembly in minibox. Make a direct electrical connection between minibox and heat sink, but do not overtighten nut.
4. Mount and connect other components, Fig. 19-20. Make certain that rectifiers and other parts do not short-circuit against bottom half of minibox. The receptacle is wired to insure against incorrect connection which could be a safety hazard.
5. Connect line cord.

Fig. 19-21. Schematic for power tool speed control: $D_{1,2}$—Silicon rectifiers. $R_{1,3}$—Resistors. R_2—Potentiometer. S_1—SPST switch. SCR—Silicon controlled rectifier. SO—Receptacle.

Fig. 19-22. Color organ with an SCR. Left. Finished project. Right. Circuitry inside case. (Project by Ed Belliveau)

Be sure to use a three wire grounded line cord and three prong panel mount socket to prevent electrical shock in case the insulation within the power tool should break down. Also see that your bypass switch and wiring are able to carry at least 5 amps ac.

After you have completed the speed control unit, plug the line cord of the control unit into a 110 volt ac receptacle. Plug your power tool line cord into the panel mount socket of the control unit. You should be able to control the speed of the power tool up to 70 percent of maximum speed. If you need full speed, simply flip the bypass switch.

COLOR ORGAN PROJECT

Do you want to experiment with SCRs? The color organ shown in Fig. 19-22 is an easy-to-build project that uses one SCR. Within it, you are able to vary the

brightness of a low wattage bulb in keeping with changes in the audio level from your radio.

You can mount the simple circut, Fig. 19-23, in any handy plastic box and use a knob on the outside to control the potentiometer. Obtain the following items:

No.	Item
1	Plastic box, approximately 3 in. x 6 in. x 1 1/2 in.
1	Circuit board, about 2 in. x 5 in.
1	Audio output transformer.
1	5K potentiometer.
1	Control knob.
1	1K resistor.
1	.001 μF capacitor.
1	SCR.
1	110 volt receptacle.
1	Lamp cord with plug.
	Connecting wiring.

CONSTRUCTION PROCEDURE

To build the color organ:
1. Mount transformer, resistor, capacitor and SCR on circuit board, Fig. 19-22.
2. Place board in plastic box.
3. Install receptacle in plastic box.
4. Install potentiometer and control knob.
5. Attach lamp cord and connecting wiring, Fig. 10-23.
6. Solder connections.

The transformer output, as usually used, will be the input for this circuit.

Connect the audio input side of the transformer into the speaker of your radio. Connect the lamp cord for a low wattage bulb into the receptacle in the side of the

Fig. 19-23. Schematic for color organ: C_1—Capaciator. R_1—Potentiometer. R_2—Resistor. SCR—Silicon controlled rectifier.

plastic box. Plug your color organ lamp cord into a 110 volt receptacle. Turn on the radio and watch the results.

If you want to experiment further, mount the lamp behind different colored plastic sheets. You can even make a four-sided, four-color lamp for this use.

There are a number of other color organ circuits you can build. Some will have six to eight transistors. To decide which one you should build, consider the cost of how fancy you want to make your color organ.

OTHER SOLID STATE DEVICES

Another type of transistor you may work with is called a "phototransistor," Fig. 19-24. The base of this type of transistor is right underneath a tiny lens. As the amount of light through the lens changes, the current

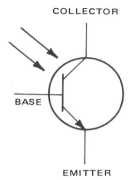

Fig. 19-24. The phototransistor is activated by light.

through the transistor changes. The only difference between the phototransistor and a conventional transistor is the fact that the light on the base controls current flow in a phototransistor. As you recall, current on the base of a conventional transistor controls current flow in the emitter-collector direction.

A "light emitting diode" (LED) is a semiconductor device that gives off a tiny bit of light when current flows through it. Because a LED is a diode, current will flow only when it is forward biased. The symbol for a LED is shown in Fig. 19-25.

The main use of LEDs is in the display of numbers in test instruments or calculators, Fig. 19-26. The LEDs are arranged in seven-segments, Fig. 19-27. When the proper voltages are applied to the LEDs, one or more of the segments will light up to form a number. For example, if five of the segments are forward biased, they will form the number 3. Small bulbs could be used, but LEDs are much cheaper and can be turned on and off thousands of times without failing.

LIGHT EMITTING DIODE

Fig. 19-25. Symbol for a light emitting diode (LED).

Fig. 19-26. On-vehicle computer uses LEDs for digital readouts. (National Semiconductor)

Fig. 19-27. LEDs in seven segments can be used to display all numbers from 0 to 9.

INTEGRATED CIRCUITS

In reading electronics magazines, no doubt you have seen a large number of projects that use integrated circuits (ICs). An IC is a circuit containing resistors, transistors and capacitors made very small, then placed in a compact package, Fig. 19-28.

THICK FILM CIRCUITS

Certain types of ICs are made by reducing the size of a circuit, attaching a number of terminals and encas-

Fig. 19-28. A hard plastic case protects the complex circuitry of the integrated circuit.

ing the entire circuit in a plastic package. Fig. 19-29 shows the various steps involved in making this "thick film" type of integrated circuit:

1. Material which is to be the "frame" or "substrate" for finished IC.
2. Flat wires called "conductors" are deposited on substrate. These will be wires for circuit.
3. An insulating glaze or film is put over conductors.
4. Layers of carbon are deposited on film. These will become resistors in the circuit. Values are set by erasing bits of carbon until we have the right amount of resistance.

5. Leads are added and conductors are "tinned." This means that conductors are covered by a layer of solder to allow them to carry more current.
6. Small transistors and diodes are added to circuit.
7. Whole circuit is coated with plastic and marked so that it can be identified.

Fig. 19-30 shows some "thick films" before they have been coated with plastic.

ADVANTAGE OF INTEGRATED CIRCUITS

The main advantage of integrated circuits is that so much electronic circuitry can be put in a very small package, Fig. 19-31. There are many ICs today that contain a whole AM radio. To make it work, all you need to do is attach an antenna, a battery and a speaker. The IC alone is smaller than a book of matches and the price is just a few dollars.

STEPS IN MAKING AN IC

Another type of integrated circuit is made from a single block, or wafer, of silicon. First, a circuit drawing is made much larger than the finished circuit. This is done so that the drawing can be reduced and still maintain accurate spacing between parts. No part of any line can be allowed to touch another line. If if did, some part of the circuit would be shorted out.

Fig. 19-29. Steps are shown in making thick film integrated circuits.
(Centralab Electronics Div. of Globe-Union, Inc.)

Fig. 19-30. Some thick film integrated circuits are shown before encapsulation.
(Sprague Electric Co.)

Fig. 19-31. This circuit board has over 70 integrated circuits.
(Autonetics Div. of North American Rockwell)

Next, a camera is used to reduce the drawing. The camera in Fig. 19-32 can reduce a drawing down to 400 times smaller than original size. It can shrink lines down to .0001 in. This allows several hundred completed circuits to be put on a piece of silicon 1 1/4 inches in diameter, see Fig. 19-33.

MONOLITHIC IC

Special furnaces (similar to those used for making transistors) add the impurities (N and P), Fig. 19-34, to make the completed unit. Integrated circuits manufactured by this process are called "monolithic" ICs, because they are made from a single piece of silicon (mono means one). Since IC are so small, the only way to see what the circuit looks like is to use a microscope, Fig. 19-35.

Before shipment, ICs are checked on a special

Fig. 19-32. A special reducing camera is used in making integrated circuit drawings much smaller in size. (The Boeing Co.)

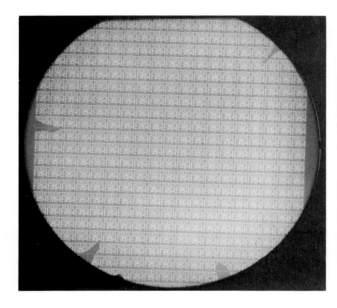

Fig. 19-33. A silicon wafer is filled with integrated circuits. This 1 1/4 in. diameter wafer holds several hundred circuits. (Sprague Electric Co.)

Fig. 19-35. Assembly worker examines an IC with a microscope. (Electronics Group Div. of Northern American Rockwell Corp.)

Fig. 19-34. Special molecular beam epitaxial growth systems are used to deposit layers of gallium arsenide, P or N materials on integrated circuits. (Rockwell International)

machine. The one shown in Fig. 19-36 can test hundreds of ICs in a single day. This once was a very difficult job. Now, it is a simple matter of hooking up the IC and automatically checking it. Since the IC is such a small part, it is very important that its circuit works properly.

IC SIZE

You may wonder why integrated circuits are so low priced when they are so hard to manufacture. It is because the manufacturer makes ICs by the thousands. Special machines produce ICs so fast and so accurately that the price can be kept quite low.

The development of ICs looks promising. Their small size and low price mean that you will be seeing

Fig. 19-36. This special testing machine automatically tests ICs and prints the results so circuit performance can be analyzed. (The Boeing Co.)

more and more of these circuits in the next few years. Because they are so small, ICs can be used where, in the past, even a single component would not fit. The IC shown in Fig. 19-37 has over 100 transistors on it. Think of some of the places where it can be used. Hearing aids, for example, are an ideal IC application.

Fig. 19-37. This integrated circuit containing 100 transistors, resistors and diodes is interconnected by the etched pattern of the printed circuit. It is small enough to pass through the eye of a needle. (Western Electric Co.)

Researach has made all these solid state devices possible. The discovery of the transistor, for example, really sparked the growth we have in electronics today.

IC SYMBOLS

Several of the symbols for integrated circuits are shown in Fig. 19-38. Because the actual circuit inside the container is so complex, circuits are rarely drawn. Instead, a circuit will give you a symbol and some numbers. Other times, they will tell you what the IC can do, such as the 3 input AND gate and the 3 input OR gate. With this information, you can wire the IC into the circuit to do what you want. You can imagine the time it would take to draw the circuit for the IC having 100 transistors that you saw earlier.

Most integrated circuits are made up of electronic components such as transistors. However, because of their size and the way they are made, ICs cannot be repaired. Many of these electronic parts are completely sealed (encapsulated) inside a small plastic box. Any attempt to open the box will ruin the parts inside. ICs are made this way because the manufacturer does not want you to repair them. Also, it is faster to unplug a particular IC and replace it with a new one.

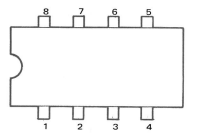

Fig. 19-38. IC symbols used in circuit drawings have many different shapes, rather than forming true electrical schematics.

THE "AND" SYMBOL

The "AND" unit is one of several types of solid state devices which make up the "insides" of an IC. The AND symbol, Fig. 19-39, is used in a circuit where all inputs must be present to get an output. To get an output from the AND, therefore, you would need inputs at A "and" B "and" C. You can see why the AND deserves its name.

A simple circuit can be used to show how the AND symbol might be used. Suppose you wanted to have one portion of a circuit where three things HAD TO TAKE PLACE BEFORE the next step would occur. See Fig. 19-40. Based on this diagram, the machine operator must perform the following three steps before the machine can start moving safely:
1. Close the switch for input A.
2. Turn the selector switch to terminal 3 for input B.
3. Use the push buttom switch for input C.

Fig. 19-39. The three input AND is shown here.

There must be signals at all three inputs before we can get an output. Once all three steps have been taken, the machine will safety start moving. If any one of the three safety steps is left out, the machine will not move. If we made a table of inputs to see if an output resulted, we would have the following:

	INPUT		OUTPUT
A **SPST** **SWITCH**	**B** **SELECTOR** **SWITCH**	**C** **PUSH BUTTON** **SWITCH**	**D** **MACHINE** **MOVES**
No	No	No	No
No	No	Yes	No
No	Yes	No	No
No	Yes	Yes	No
Yes	No	No	No
Yes	No	Yes	No
Yes	Yes	No	No
Yes	Yes	Yes	Yes

The table gives all possible ways in which we could complete the circuit. It is only when we have inputs at all three locations (last line) that we will have a circuit.

TRUTH TABLE

The table just shown can be drawn in several ways. Rather than using NO and YES to tell us that an input was present, we could use a 0 (zero) and a 1 (one). The 0 would mean that the signal was absent. The 1 would mean that the signal was present. This would be similar to having a switch. When it is OFF, it would be labeled 0. When the switch is turned ON it would be labeled 1. If we were to use 0 and 1, our table would make up in the manner shown on the following page:

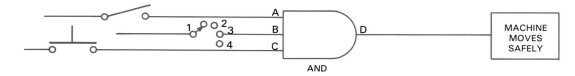

Fig. 19-40. Three things must be done to the input (A,B, and C) of this "AND" to get the output (D), which will result in the machine moving safely.

INPUT			OUTPUT
A SPST SWITCH	B SELECTOR SWITCH	C PUSH BUTTON SWITCH	D MACHINE MOVES
0	0	0	0
0	0	1	0
0	1	0	0
0	1	1	0
1	0	0	0
1	0	1	0
1	1	0	0
1	1	1	1

This is known as a "TRUTH TABLE." It tells us what must be done to the inputs in order to get an output.

BINARY

The location of various 0 and 1 combinations on the lines of the truth table are listed in a specific order. They are placed there based on a system of counting called "Binary," meaning two states. This is necessary because parts of many electronic circuits can only be in one of two possible states. They can only be OFF or ON.

If only the numbers 0 and 1 can be used, how can we get to 2, 3, 4 or a higher number? There is an easy way of doing this while still using the binary counting system. Since binary only uses a 0 or a 1, a number must spill over into the next column just as it does in our conventional numbering system. When we count . . . 6, 7, 8 and finally reach 9, the next number spills over to the left. This adds a second column which we call "tens." Thus, our next numbers would be a 10, 11 and so on:

$$8$$
$$9$$
$$10$$
$$11$$

As you can see from this example, we had to add another column when we went beyond nine in our conventional numbering system. The same is true in the binary system. However, since we can only use 0 or 1, the spillover into the next column will occur much sooner:

$$0 = 0$$
$$1 = 1$$
$$10 = 2$$
$$11 = 3$$
$$100 = 4$$
$$101 = 5$$
$$110 = 6$$
$$111 = 7$$

If the next number is added to this list, it would result in having to add a fourth column. Since we are only using devices with three inputs, it will not be necessary to add that fourth column. However, the binary counting system does continue, using the same method shown.

When several AND units are used together, they are normally found packaged inside of an IC, Fig. 19-41. Each of the input and output leads are wired to one of the pins on the outside of the unit. To help you identify the location of each lead, the manufacturer will include a diagram of the IC in the package. Normally, this same diagram is not shown on the outside case of the IC. However, each integrated circuit will have some type of identification mark to help you locate the first pin on the unit. For example, when the notch on the model shown in Fig. 19-41 is positioned to the left, the number 1 lead will be at the bottom left of the IC. The remaining numbers are read counterclockwise.

THE "OR" SYMBOL

The next symbol we will look at identifies the "OR" unit, Fig. 19-42. To get an output from the OR, there must be an input on at least one of its leads. In other words, to get an output in Fig. 19-42, there must be an input at either A "or" B "or" C. Again, you can see why the OR deserves its name.

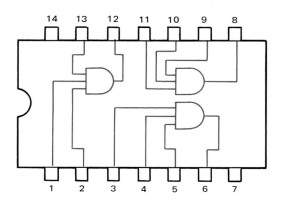

Fig. 19-41. Three AND units are wired up inside of this IC.

Fig. 19-42. The three input OR unit is shown here.

The truth table for the OR is shown in the following way:

INPUT			OUTPUT
A	B	C	D
0	0	0	0
0	0	1	1
0	1	0	1
0	1	1	1
1	0	0	1
1	0	1	1
1	1	0	1
1	1	1	1

Any time there is an input on one of the OR leads, an output will be present. The only time that there is not an output from the OR is when signals are missing from every input lead.

A whole series of solid state symbols is handled in the same manner. These are known as "LOGIC" symbols. Many of them have a TRUTH TABLE or some type of chart to tell you what must be done to get an output.

THE INVERTER

The symbol for the inverter may be shown in several ways, Fig. 19-43. As with the other logic symbols discussed so far, the inverter does what its "name" implies. The inverter will "invert" or change the signal which comes into it. Thus, if a 0 is used on the input lead, the output will be 1. If a 1 is placed on the input lead, the output will go to a 0. The truth table for the inverter is shown in the following way:

INPUT	OUTPUT
0	1
1	0

As you can see, the inverter is a very simple logic device.

The circle part of the symbol, Fig. 19-43, is where the reversing of the input will take place. The triangle is used in some circuits to represent the circuit itself. At other times, you will find that only the circle is shown. This is important because you may find the inverter being used in both ways. You may find the inverter (as a circle) being used on the input lead to either the OR or the AND unit, Fig. 19-44. Used in this way, it will invert only that signal coming in on that input lead.

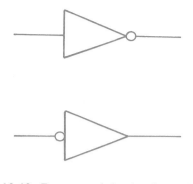

Fig. 19-43. Two ways of showing the symbol for an INVERTER.

Fig. 19-44. An INVERTER being used on one of the input leads to an AND, another being used on one of the input leads to an OR.

THE "NAND" SYMBOL

When the inverter is added to the output of the AND, you will end up with the "NAND" symbol, Fig. 19-45. Note that only the circle portion of the inverter is being used as part of this symbol.

The truth table for the NAND is shown in the following way:

INPUT			OUTPUT
A	B	C	D
0	0	0	1
0	0	1	1
0	1	0	1
0	1	1	1
1	0	0	1
1	0	1	1
1	1	0	1
1	1	1	0

The only way to stop the output of the NAND (make it go to 0) is to have all the inputs at 1.

THE "NOR" SYMBOL

When the inverter is combined with the OR, you will end up with the "NOR" symbol, Fig. 19-46. Again, only the circle portion of the inverter symbol is being used to form the NOR.

The truth table for the NOR is shown in the following way:

INPUT			OUTPUT
A	B	C	D
0	0	0	1
0	0	1	0
0	1	0	0
0	1	1	0
1	0	0	0
1	0	1	0
1	1	0	0
1	1	1	0

The only way to get an output from the NOR is to have all the inputs at 0. When A, B and C are all 0s, the output will be at 1. Anytime a signal is fed into one of the input leads, the output will go to 0.

Although there are a large number of other solid state logic devices (flip-flops, shift registers, counters, etc.), these are the only ones which will be covered here. A whole course can be devoted to logic circuits alone. However, with the symbols shown, you can form some of the simple circuits found in many of the electronics magazines. A few examples of logic symbols being used in circuits are shown in Fig. 19-47. Their inputs and outputs have been labeled to show how each of the logic symbols work as part of that circuit.

Fig. 19-45. A NAND is the combination of the AND along with an INVERTER. It is called a Not AND by some people.

Fig. 19-46. The NOR is a combination of the OR with an INVERTER.

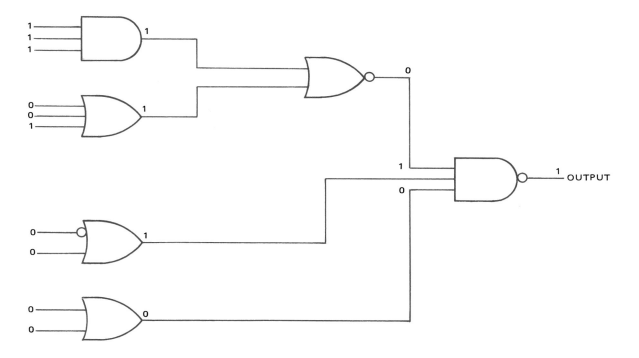

Fig. 19-47. A circuit using AND, OR, INVERTER, NOR, and NAND units are shown with typical results.

PRINTED CIRCUITS BOARDS

When it is not necessary to make the circuit as small as an IC, you can make your own printed circuits. Simply obtain a board, lay out the circuit, mount your transistors and capacitors and solder them into position.

To make the printed circuit, start with a special board coated with copper. Lay out the circuit you wish to make, using special ink or tape, Fig. 19-48. This is necessary because of the etching process used in making the circuit board. In this process, chemicals will "eat away" the copper that is not covered with ink or tape. If the ink does not protect the copper, there is no way to make the circuits.

Put the ink on the copper in the shape that you want your finished conductors to take. Most of these conductors are a series of paths which will act as wires for your circuit. The next important step is to lay out each component exactly where you want to locate it. Once the copper is removed, it is difficult to make repairs.

Fig. 19-48. Special tape is used to cover the copper clad on this printed circuit board. You can even mark you name on the board with special ink as this student did.

ETCHING THE PC BOARD

When you finish your printed circuit board layout, the next step is to remove the copper from the places where it is not wanted. This is done by placing the PC board in chemicals that will etch (eat away) unwanted copper, Fig. 19-49. Therefore, the copper that you need to form your circuit must be covered with a layer of material that will resist being etched away. Once the copper is etched, wash it off, remove the tape or ink, clean it, drill the holes, and you have your finished PC board, Fig. 19-50.

Fig. 19-49. Students etching a printed circuit board to remove the unwanted copper. (Hickok Teaching Systems, Inc.)

UNDERCUTTING

The PC board is left in the chemicals only until the uncovered areas of copper are etched away. Do not leave the board in the solution too long or the conductors will be "undercut." See Fig. 19-51. Undercutting occurs when the chemicals start to etch away the copper under the protective coating. This, in turn, will cause an open conductor (will not carry current). In some cases, the conductor will crack easily and open the path to the component.

When you have a good printed circuit board, you can solder the parts into your circuit. The big advantage of the PC board system is that it gets rid of a lot of wires. It also decreases the size of your circuit, so that it will fit in a smaller package or chassis box.

OTHER PROJECTS

Now that you have covered the basics of electricity and electronics, consider advanced studies in this field. The projects presented throughout this text have been kept simple and directly related to the subject area of the chapter in which they

Fig. 19-50. After the ink is removed from the etched printed circuit board, only the copper that the ink protected is left on the board.

Fig. 19-52. Automatic photo enlarger controller unit (at left) and sensor (at right) work together to properly time the exposure of the enlarged print. (Project by Bruce Swail)

FINISHED
PC BOARD

PROTECTIVE MATERIAL TO
PREVENT ETCHING AWAY
THE COPPER

INSULATED
BOARD

GOOD—COPPER NOT
ETCHED AWAY UNDER
THE PROTECTIVE INK

BAD—COPPER
IS UNDERCUT

Fig. 19-51. Close-up views show two conditions of a finished PC board. The undercut copper was left in the etching solution too long.

appeared. If you are interested in building more complicated projects, page through the various electricity and electronics magazines and paperback project books that are available. They contain helpful information and excellent projects to further your knowledge and improve your circuit-building ability.

Fig. 19-52, for example, shows a typical advanced IC project. The photo enlarger pictured is controlled automatically by a shop-built timing controller unit and a sensor that picks up the reflected light of the enlarger. The sensor then signals the controller and a built-in timer IC times the exposure.

The automatic photo enlarger controller project will allow you to select the proper exposure time and cut down on wasted photo paper. This particular project is just one of hundreds described and illustrated in magazines and books devoted to the field of electricity and electronics.

SUMMARY

The Field Effect Transistor (FET) uses a solid piece of N type material or P type material for its main body. When the electrons flow, (no voltage on its gate), there is less noise with this device than with a regular transistor. For this reason, FETs are often used in amplifier circuits.

The Silicon Controlled Rectifier is designed to carry heavy current. To turn on the SCR, the gate must be given a pulse that is positive with respect to the cathode. Once it is turned on, a very small current (less than 20 milliamps) is needed to maintain current flow through the device.

An Integrated Circuit (IC) is a device made up of a few or as many as thousands of transistors, resistors, and capacitors in a very small body. The pins of the IC are numbered in schematics. The numbers help identify which leads are to be used as inputs or connected to output devices. Through the use of Truth Tables, the AND, OR, NAND, NOR, and inverter input and output signals on IC's can be tracked. These chips are widely used in computers and many other electronic devices. In fact, ICs are the heart of most electronic devices in use today.

KEY WORDS AND TERMS

AND
Binary
Channel
Depletion layer
Drain
Field effect transistor (FET)
Gate
Insulated gate field effect transistor (IGFET)
Integrated circuit (IC)
Inverter
Junction field effect transistors (JFET)
Light emitting diode (LED)
Metal oxide semiconductor field effect transistors (MOSFET)
Monolithic
NAND
NOR
OR
Phototransistor
Silicon controlled rectifier (SCR)
Source
Thick film
Undercut

TEST YOUR KNOWLEDGE

Do not write in this book. Write your answers on a separate sheet of paper.

1. Draw the symbol for the AND.
2. Show the TRUTH TABLE for the AND.
3. What are the two basic steps in making a printed circuit board?
4. *True or False?* An integrated circuit can contain at least five transistors as part of its circuitry.
5. A thick film circuit is made of deposited resistors. How are the diodes and transistors added to the circuit?
6. What is an LED?
7. What do the letters MOSFET stand for?
8. What must be done to turn on an SCR?
9. What must be done to turn off an SCR?
10. Draw the symbol for the OR GATE.
11. Make a TRUTH TABLE for the OR GATE.
12. The copper on a printed circuit board may be _____ if it is left in the etching solution too long.
13. The input circuit for a JFET is from _____ to the _____.

ACTIVITIES

1. How is the copper clad attached to the printed circuit board material? How can it be put on one side only, or on both sides?
2. Make a list of the different types of solid state devices. How many can you find? Show the symbols for each one.
3. How many different sizes of SCRs are there? What is the minimum amount of current they will carry? What is the maximum current?
4. What are some of the uses for lighting emitting diodes?
5. If you were given a number on an IC, how can you tell what it will do? Does each manufacturer label them in a different manner? How do you know where to start counting for each lead?
6. Solid state LOGIC symbols are different for different companies. How do you know which one to follow and use? Are some of the symbols the same for different companies?
7. Make a list of at least 10 different LOGIC symbols. Does each have a TRUTH TABLE?
8. Make a printed circuit board with your own personalized symbol or name. How do you tell which company made a printed circuit board? Do they use special symbols?
9. You sometimes hear the words *consumer products* being used in the electrical field. What does this mean?
10. What are majority and minority carriers?
11. Where do you find unijunction transistors being used?
12. If you were to increase the temperature surrounding a transistor, how would it affect operation? Does the heat found in foundries or other industrial plants affect the operation of the transistor? What effects does space travel have on the transistor?

20 Computers

LEARNING OBJECTIVES

After studying this chapter, you will be able to:
- Identify the main parts of the computer and their function.
- Explain the purpose of using ASCII with a keyboard.
- Describe the differences between a floppy disk and a CD ROM.
- Describe how data are sent long distances over phone lines or by satellite.
- List the main types of computer software programs and describe their function.

Many items that are used to create computers have been discussed in previous chapters. These items include: a power supply (transformer and bridge rectifier), integrated circuits, PC boards, and electrical connectors.

With these and some other items, you can build a computer. A number of computer stores sell the individual pieces of a computer. Assembling a computer yourself saves you the labor cost involved and reduces the price of the completed machine. Knowing how the pieces fit together can also save on repairs.

A *computer* is a device that takes in information, processes it, and displays the results for the user. The information going into the computer is called *input*. The results are called *output*. The person running the computer has many choices on how to supply the input and how to display the output.

Commonly used input devices include: keyboards, light pens, disk drives, modems, and magnetic tape drives. The most used output device is a monitor, a computer screen that displays the output. However, there are many other output devices that a computer uses. Some devices work as both input *and* output devices. Disk drives, magnetic tape drives, and modems are input and output devices.

TYPES OF COMPUTERS

There are three classes of computer that are distinguished by size and speed. Mainframes are the largest and most powerful. Universities and very large industries may use these computers. Minicomputers are the next step down. They are still fixed machines, but they have smaller memories and slower processing speeds than mainframes. Microcomputers, or personal computers, make up the final category. Personal computers, notebook or laptop computers are common in businesses, homes, and schools. Rapid changes in computer technology have diminished the differences between the three classes.

For most consumers, the personal computer has more capability than they will ever need. The two types of personal computers that dominate the market are the Macintosh (or Mac) and the IBM (or an IBM clone).

The major differences between these two machines are their operating platform and their microprocessor. The Mac operates using the concept of a desktop with folders located on it, a very visual method. The IBM operates with a screen and a disk operating system (DOS), which displays everything with words. To run a program under DOS, the computer operator had to type a command to make it operate. More recently, many IBM users switched to a graphics screen using Windows. Instead of typing in the commands, all that was needed was a double click of the mouse on the icon. An icon is a small figure that represents a program that can run using the Windows program. This icon system is very similar to double clicking folders on the Mac's desktop system. There is much less of a difference between today's two systems than those used only a few years ago.

The second difference between the two machines is in their microprocessors. Since the Mac worked on a graphics design, the ICs had to work in a different manner. IBM machines were designed to handle words. Graphics use a lot more of a computer's memory. This means there were differences in speed, how files were shown on the screen, and the way files were saved to memory. Many of the other components inside the two types of computers are very similar.

TRANSISTORS, BINARY CODE, AND THE COMPUTER

The heart of a computer is the transistor. You recall that a switching transistor has only two states, on and off. By using many of these transistors, a computer operator can solve math problems or write to a monitor. Since the transistors have only two states, the computer uses a binary code. You will also recall that binary in our math system only uses a series of 0's and 1's. The 0 is the off condition while 1 is the on position. This makes it a perfect match for the OFF or ON state of the transistor.

Binary numbers were discussed in Chapter 19. A table is provided here for review.

Base 10	Binary
0	0
1	1
2	10 carry to the next column
3	11
4	100 another carry
5	101
6	110
7	111
8	1000 another carry
9	1001
10 carry in base 10	1010
11	1011
12	1100
13	1101
14	1110
15	1111
16	10000 another carry

A binary 1 is also called a "bit" (Binary digIT).
- The numbers 2 and 3 (in base 10) use two bits (in binary).
- The numbers 4, 5, ,6 and 7 (in base 10) use three bits (in binary).
- The numbers 8, 9, 10, 11, 12, 13, 14, and 15 use four bits.

You will reach five bits for the number 16. Notice that a carry in the next binary column occurs each time the number in base 10 doubles; 2, 4, 8, 16, and so on.

COUNTING

ICs use transistors to create logic gates. Transistors are used to create the logic gates found inside Integrated Circuits. However, late model computers can manage binary numbers in lengths of up to 32 bits at one time. You will hear that microprocessors such as the 486 and Pentium are 32 bit processors. What this means is that they can handle 32 bits at once. The biggest base 10 number that can be contained in 32 bits is the number 4,294,967,296. Thus, a 32 bit computer can add and subtract a number that large in a single operation. This is part of the reason why computers are able to do math problems so much faster than we can.

The transistors form AND, OR, NOR, NAND, and other solid state logic devices described in Chapter 19. These logic devices are used in computers.

When adding, subtracting, multiplying, and dividing larger numbers, computers use shortcut systems that are fairly complex. Placing a group of over 200 transistors in an IC package allows chip builders to create "half adders." By combining logic devices into adders and up/down counters, a computer can process blocks of data at one time. This and devices such as math coprocessor chips speed up the process of doing math problems ten or twenty times. Math coprocessor chip are discussed later in this chapter.

Today's chip manufacturers are able to put as many as 1.5 million transistors on a single IC. That is why computers are getting faster and faster, while at the same time their size continues to shrink. There are all kinds of hand-held computers being manufactured today. Some are in the form of calculators. Some store dates and addresses. Still others are made in the form of games.

PARTS OF A COMPUTER

If you look inside the case that contains the inner workings of a computer, you will see many items you have already studied, Fig. 20-1. These items include transformers, capacitors, diodes, transistors, and ICs. Some computers run on vac power, some run on dc power, and some can be run from either source. Desktop machines are normally plugged into an ac outlet. These will be the main type of computer discussed. Portable computers use batteries, a dc source of power.

A close look inside a computer shows that the line cord to the computer brings in 110 volts ac. The IBM computer has a power supply connected to that cord, Fig. 20-2. The power supply converts the 110 vac to several levels of dc needed to operate the solid state devices. Five volts dc is needed to operate most of the devices inside the case.

Fig. 20-1. How many of these components can you identify?

Fig. 20-2. Inside the metal casing of the power supply is a large power transformer. This transformer steps down the 110 Vac coming from the outlet.

Fig. 20-4. This mouse allows the computer to respond to slight hand movements.

There are three main categories of items that make up a computer.

- Input devices.
- Central processing devices.
- Output devices.

INPUT DEVICES

"Input devices" are used to bring information into the computer. Some important input devices are:

- Keyboard, Fig. 20-3.
- Mouse, Fig. 20-4.
- Tape drive, Fig. 20-5.
- Modem, Fig. 20-6.
- Scanner, Fig. 20-7.
- Light pen, Fig. 20-8.
- Tablet, Fig. 20-9.
- Disk drive, Fig. 20-10.

Fig. 20-5. Computer tape drives are often used as backup storage for very large files.

Fig. 20-3. The keyboard for a computer is very similar to the keyboard of a typewriter. Do you see any differences?

Fig. 20-6. Modems allow computers to communicate through phone lines.

Fig. 20-7. Scanners use optics to "read" pages of text and graphics. This material is then stored in a magnetic form in the computer. (Ricoh Corp., Peripheral Products Division)

Fig. 20-10. This computer has both a 3.5 inch disk drive and a CD-ROM drive. (Jerrie Hulsey)

Fig. 20-8. Light pens are often found in industry. (IBM)

The keyboard, mouse and disk drive are three of the most popular input devices and deserve some attention. Although disk drives are discussed under input devices, they, like tape drives and modems, are both input and output devices.

KEYBOARD

The keyboard is one of the main input devices for the computer. At first sight, the keyboard appears to be a fairly simple device. In truth, all of the keys are being scanned by the central processing unit (CPU) hundreds of times every second. When a key is pressed, a signal is sent to the CPU. Combinations of keys, such as SHIFT and the Y key, are also used to send signals. In this case, the keyboard creates capital letters.

Every one of the numbers and letters in our alphabet is designed to be read through the use of special codes. A keyboard is designed so that each letter sends one of these codes when one of its keys is pressed. Since a computer operates using transistors, number codes are needed to spell out a letter. Each letter on the keyboard is assigned a specific code number, Fig. 20-11. The code is called "ASCII" (American Standard Code for Information Interchange). There is an ASCII code number for a capital F and a different one for a lowercase f. As you touch the keyboard in different combinations (shift and f) or just the letter f, an electronic signal is sent out. This letter f signal is stored in the computer's temporary memory and at the same time is displayed on the computer's monitor.

MOUSE

The "mouse" is another important input device for the computer. The shape of the first mouse and its connecting wire earned this device its name, Fig. 20-12. With the

Fig. 20-9. Tablets are not used much in the home computer market, but are often found in industry. (Kurta)

Digit KEY	Binary	ASCII CODE	Digit KEY	Binary	ASCII CODE
0	00110000	48	V	01010110	86
1	00110001	49	W	01010111	87
2	00110010	50	X	01011000	88
3	00110011	51	Y	01011001	89
4	00110100	52	Z	01011010	90
5	00110101	53	(	01011011	91
6	00110110	54	\	01011100	92
7	00110111	55	)	01011101	93
8	00111000	56	^	01011110	94
9	00111001	57	-	01011111	95
:	00111010	58	,	01100000	96
;	00111011	59	a	01100001	97
<	00111100	60	b	01100010	98
=	00111101	61	c	01100011	99
>	00111110	62	d	01100100	100
?	00111111	63	e	01100101	101
@	01000000	64	f	01100110	102
A	01000001	65	g	01100111	103
B	01000010	66	h	01101000	104
C	01000011	67	i	01101001	105
D	01000100	68	j	01101010	106
E	01000101	69	k	01101011	107
F	01000110	70	l	01101100	108
G	01000111	71	m	01101101	109
H	01001000	72	n	01101110	110
I	01001001	73	o	01101111	111
J	01001010	74	p	01110000	112
K	01001011	75	q	01110001	113
L	01001100	76	r	01110010	114
M	01001101	77	s	01110011	115
N	01001110	78	t	01110100	116
O	01001111	79	u	01110101	117
P	01010000	80	v	01110110	118
Q	01010001	81	w	01110111	119
R	01010010	82	x	01111000	120
S	01010011	83	y	01111001	121
T	01010100	84	z	01111010	122
U	01010101	85			

Fig. 20-11. Pushing the various keys will send these ASCII code numbers to the computer.

Fig. 20-12. The computer mouse derived its name through its form, not its function.

wire as a *tail,* it looked just like a mouse. The main reason for using a mouse is to speed up movement of the cursor on the screen. The mouse is intended for use with pull-down menus found on many computer programs. In some programs it is used to locate starting and ending points of lines used for making drawings. This pointing method is commonly used in computer-aided design (CAD) programs.

The ball on the underside of the mouse is connected in such a way that its mechanical movements are turned into electrical signals. You recall that a potentiometer does the same thing. The more the mouse ball moves, the greater the electrical signal. The design of the mouse allows for horizontal, vertical and diagonal pointing.

DISK DRIVES

Once data in the form of letters, numbers or graphics, are created, they must be saved so they may be used at a later date. The contents of a computer's memory that change as you work are stored in an area called "random access memory (RAM)." When the computer is shut off, everything stored in RAM is lost. Other, more permanent, ways for storing data are needed. Saving your data can be done several ways. The most common ways to save data are on a floppy disk or a hard drive. Both of these drives are input and output devices.

HARD DRIVES

The hard drive is a storage location inside the computer for files that you use repeatedly, Fig. 20-13. A hard drive's size is given by the number of *bytes*. One byte contains eight bits of information. Think of a hard drive as a container. The larger the container, the more it will hold. Containers can come in pint, quart, gallon, or liter sizes. Hard drives come in 20, 40, 60, 120, 200 *megabytes* (MB) and even larger sizes. Older hard drives came in 120, or 200 megabytes (MB) sizes. Newer drives have sizes in the gigabyte range. Mega means million, therefore megabyte means million bytes. Giga means billion, therefore gigabyte means billion bytes. A 2.4 gigabyte hard drive holds 2,400,000,000 bytes of information.

Fig. 20-13. A computer's hard drive allows speedy access to large files. Files that would need the space of many floppy disks easily fit on a hard drive. (IBM)

Fig. 20-14. Read/write heads hover over the hard disk. Their sufaces do not touch. (IBM)

A brand new hard drive must be formatted the first time it is used. A new computer disk is similar to a new video tape. All of its magnetic particles are scattered in random order. "Formatting" is the process of aligning the magnetic particles on the disk in a pattern so that information can be stored. The formatting process is done by the read/write head, Fig. 20-14. This head consists of a coil that is hung just above the surface of the hard disk. Since the coil is wrapped with wire that carries a current, an electromagnet is created. As the hard drive spins, the coil induces a voltage on the magnetic particles.

A large hard drive is made up of several disks stacked one above the other. There is just enough space between the disks for the read/write head to pass between them. This is why damage to the hard drive can result if it is handled in a rough manner. If a computer is dropped, the read/write head could scratch the disk surface. With such small spaces involved, you can see why the hard drive is made as a sealed unit. Wires going in and out of the drive provide a way for the data to be read from and stored on the disks.

Once information is written to the disk, the read portion of the head can sense the polarity of the magnetic particles. Sensing takes place by induction. No part of the read/write head touches the disk.

Information is easier to find on a hard disk than that on a tape. To get to a song on the end of a tape, you must play the whole tape or use fast forward. A hard disk is divided into concentric circles called "tracks." Each track is then divided into a series of "sectors," Fig. 20-15. As

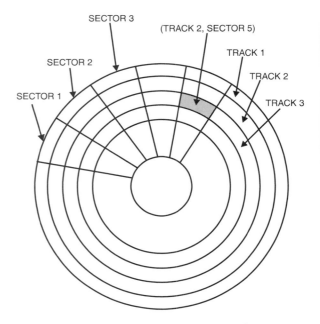

Fig. 20-15. Disks are divided into tracks and sectors.

the disk spins, the read/write head senses the information on the tracks. It can sense magnetic particles in one or two revolutions.

FLOPPY DRIVES

Information can also be stored on a *floppy drive*. There are a number of different sizes of floppy drives. The 3.5 in., 1.4 meg., and 5.25 in. sizes are the most common, Fig. 20-16. The numbers refer to the size of the floppy disk that fits inside the drive. A floppy disk is a hard plastic protective case with a flexible plastic disk inside. The disk is coated with magnetic material so that it can store computer data. A 3.5 in. disk typically can hold 1.4 MB of information. The 5.25 in. disk can hold 1.2 MB of data.

Again, formatting and writing information is done with the read/write head. The disk is divided into sectors and tracks just the same way as was done with the hard drive. Some 5.3 in. disks will hold two megabytes or more. This is possible because newer methods permit closer spacing of tracks and sectors.

Floppy drives are usually found inside the case of the computer. However, they can also be mounted outside the case. When the drives are mounted outside the case they are called "external disk drives." Other devices also may be mounted outside of the case. This is done for convenience, to reduce heat or because of the limited space available inside the computer.

How you save a file depends on the program you are running. In many cases, a pull-down menu of commands includes the word SAVE. By selecting that word with your mouse, the computer will save your file. In other programs you may have to type Y for YES to SAVE and hit the return key.

Fig 20-17. Backing up your work is extremely important.

Important work should be saved on two different floppy disks. Saving on two disks is the smart thing to do in case one of them is somehow damaged. Saving your work twice is called making a "backup," Fig 20-17. Some people believe they are safe once their work is saved on a computer's hard drive. However, problems may arise that cause the hard drive to "crash" (another name for fail). If a crash occurs, there is a good chance that all the information you stored on your hard drive will be lost.

CD-ROM DRIVES

Many files and programs used today contain a tremendous amount of information. A method of storage was needed to easily load and access this data. The "CD-ROM" (Compact Disk Read Only Memory) drive was able to meet this need, Fig. 20-18. The amount of data contained in one CD can fill some hard disks. A single CD-ROM can store as much as 650 megabytes. If all the files on one CD were placed on 1.4 MB floppy disks, they would fill more than *450 disks.*

The CD-ROM drive is different from a computer's hard and floppy drives. While hard and floppy drives are input and output devices, CD-ROM drives are only input devices. The information on the CD cannot be changed by the drive or the computer operator.

CDs are used to hold large programs. A full set of encyclopedias, world history facts, games, clip art, and music or recorded sounds are stored on CD-ROM. Information is read off the CD and loaded into RAM memory. There it can be used by the operator or stored on a hard disk of floppy disk for later use. None of the information taken off the CD is saved back to that CD. It is read-only data.

Information on a CD is not stored in a magnetic form. Instead it consists of digital data etched into the disk as a

Fig 20-16. A 3.5 in. floppy disk and CD-ROM drive have been installed on this computer.

series of pits and flat areas, or lands, Fig. 20-19. The data is read off these lands and pits by a laser beam. The different values of reflected light are converted to voltage levels using a light sensing diode. These voltages represent 1's and 0's. The 1's and 0's are the digital signals that the computer uses for data entry.

CENTRAL PROCESSING DEVICES

The "central processing unit (CPU)" takes the input, manages it, stores it and saves it. The CPU also provides the dc power to operate the computer. The parts that make up the CPU include:

- Case, Fig. 20-20.
- Motherboard, Fig. 20-21.
- Cards that control input and output devices, Fig. 20-22.
- Power supply.
- Battery.

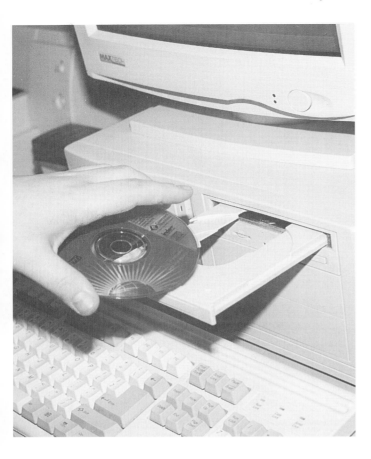

Fig. 20-18. It is easy to load a disk in the CD-ROM drive. The drive can also be used to play your favorite music CD while you are working on the computer. Some musical CDs even contain graphics that can be displayed on your computer screen.

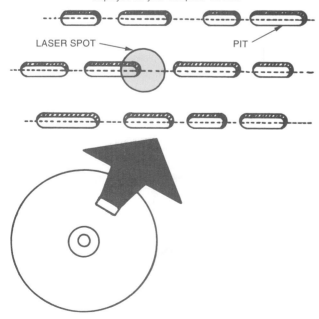

Fig. 20-19. Data on a CD is stored in microscopic lands and pits.

Fig. 20-20. A hard plastic case houses all the computer's electronics.

Fig. 20-21. The motherboard is the home for all of the components of the CPU.

Fig. 20-22. The card on the left is a sound board. The card on the right controls a CD-ROM drive.

MOTHERBOARD

Did you remember that the power supply converts 110 Vac to five Vdc? Low voltage dc is needed to power the IC's found inside the computer. Most of these IC's are located on the motherboard, Fig. 20-23. The "motherboard" is the master printed circuit board usually found on the lower part of the case. This board holds elements such as the basic input/output system (BIOS), memory in the form of CMOS and SIMM's chips and the math coprocessor.

The "CMOS chip" contains the memory that keeps track of settings on the computer. It tracks how many drives are on the machine, which chips are being used, calendar settings and many other functions. Since the computer must keep track of these elements even while it is turned off, the CMOS uses power from a small battery mounted on the motherboard, Fig. 20-24. Without this battery, all stored settings would be lost when the computer is shut off.

SIMMs are groups of chips that make up computer RAM. Some machines use SIPPs chips for their memory storage. Other computer manufacturers use a private brand of chip sets. Memory is generally installed in increments of 4, 8, 16 MB, or more. When purchasing a computer, most users prefer that it have at least 16 MB of RAM. This is the minimum needed to run many current computer programs. Newer programs are driving the minimum size RAM up to 8, 16, 32 MB, and even higher amounts of memory.

"Math coprocessor chips" are added to a motherboard to increase the computer's speed in calculating. Data processing routines such as sorts and math manipulations, or any process that uses large batches of material, run much faster with a coprocessor installed, Fig. 20-25.

Fig. 20-24. Personal computers have a small battery in their CPU. This allows the computer to keep track of date, time and some setup features.

Fig. 20-23. The motherboard contains IC chips and slots for add-on devices.

Fig. 20-25. Math coprocessor chips are small but powerful tools.

Some data processing operations can be sped up as much as 20 times when using a math chip in a computer.

In addition to the chip sets, the motherboard also has a group of edge card connectors mounted on it. The disk drive controller card, serial and parallel ports and video card are plugged into these connectors. Since the motherboard holds all these items, you can see how it gets its name.

CARDS

The CPU is used to control the output of the computer. Inside the CPU you will find a group of "cards" installed in slots, Fig. 20-26. These slots provide the power for the cards. The design of the cards make electrical connections possible without soldering. The cards simply plug into a matching slot.

Cards are commonly used for a serial port, a phone modem, a printer, a plotter and disk drives. Most of these cards are installed on their edges because of the small surface space available. Edge card connectors also allow heat to escape more easily from inside the case.

The disk drive controller card allows data to be sent to and received from the hard disk. Information in the computer is processed and sent to the hard drive through electrical paths that lead to the edge card connectors. From there the data is routed by the BIOS to the spot on the hard drive that is selected for storage. At the same time, the "file allocation table (FAT)" marks the location by cluster, track and sector. The FAT serves as a map to where the data is found on the hard drive. Without the FAT it would be impossible to find any of your stored data.

Fig. 20-27. Plugs attached to the card slots provide a convenient method to receive and send input and output.

Cards plugged into the serial and parallel ports extend out the back of the computer case. The end coming out of the case has a plug or receptacle mounted to it, Fig. 20-27.

Serial ports typically have 9 or 25 pins. "Serial ports" get their name because bits travel down the wire in serial fashion, one bit at a time. A serial port is used to connect a mouse or an external modem to a computer. The serial port is also known as the communications port or as an RS-232 port.

Computers are also equipped with "parrellel ports." Parallel ports typically have a receptacle with 25 holes in it. The parallel port is usually connected to a printer. The wires in the parallel port can transmit eight bits or more at one time. This increase in speed allows the computer to transmit much more information to a printer than is possible using a serial port.

OUTPUT DEVICES

For a computer to be useful, you must be able to receive output in response to your input. "Output devices" are used to take information out of the computer. They include:

- Monitor, Fig. 20-28.
- Plotter, Fig. 20-29.
- Printer, Fig. 20-30.
- Modem.
- Disk drive.

COMPUTER MONITORS

The computer monitor is the most used output device. There are a number of different technologies used in monitors. By far the two most common technologies are

Fig. 20-26. Computers are designed with several open card slots. Notice how the lower edge of this card makes the electrical connection by plugging it into the motherboard.

Fig. 20-28. Monitors are the most used output device. This monitor is the cathode ray tube type.

Fig. 20-30. Printers create a hard copy from computer files.

Fig. 20-29. Plotters reproduce mechanical drawings in fine detail. (Hewlett Packard)

Fig. 20-31. There are only three electron guns in a color monitor. They can produce thousands (millions on newer monitors) of colors.

the cathode ray tube (CRT) and liquid crystal display (LCD). Monitors for desktop computers mainly use CRT's. Laptop machines use LCD screens.

The CRT screen on your desktop computer works very similar to the screen on an oscilloscope. The colors seen on the CRT are produced using three color guns. Each gun shoots a beam of electrons at the inside of the CRT. One gun shoots a red beam, one shoots a green beam and one shoots a blue beam, Fig. 20-31. The CRT screen is coated with phosphor, which lights up when struck by the beam of electrons. Since the color guns shoot the three primary colors, they can be mixed to create different hues. For example, mixing red and blue will create purple. Screens can display hundreds, thousands and, with the latest equipment, even millions of colors. The different colors are created by changing the combinations and intensity of the electron stream. Only the correct combinations of red, green and blue will produce the desired results.

The color on the screen is made up of small dots of the three colors. The smaller the dot pattern, the sharper the color. You can use a magnifying glass and see this dot pattern on the screen. It takes thousands of these dots to fill the screen as it creates the picture. The dots that make up the picture are called "pixels." They are arranged in a grid pattern across the screen. A screen with a grid of 640 pixels across and 480 pixels down is made up of a total of 307,200 pixels. The number of pixels is often referred to as the "resolution" of the display. The more pixels a screen has, the smoother looking an image it can produce. High resolution screens are able to produce graphics with resolution that rivals an actual photograph.

MODEMS

Sometimes it is important for computer users to share information. People who are separated by large distances use the phone lines and computer "modems," Fig. 20-32. Both sending and receiving computers use an electronic card with a built-in phone jack. The card can either be inside the computer's case (internal modem) or outside the case (external modem). The card has the ability to send and receive signals over phone lines.

The problem that a modem faces is in its data transfer. A computer is a digital device; data is in the form of 0's and 1's. Phone lines are designed to transmit analog signals; signals of varying voltage such as sine waves. The sending modem must change the computer's digital data to an analog signal. This is known as modulating a signal. The receiving modem demodulates, or changes the signal back into digital data. This process of MOdulation and DEModulation is how the MODEM gets its name.

TRANSFER RATES

Modems are built to operate at different speeds. The speed at which data is transferred is given in bits per second (bps). The speed is called the "baud rate" for the modem. Common speeds include 1200, 2400, and 9600, 14,400, 28,800, and 56,000 bps. Early models transmitted at much slower speeds. A 2400 bps modem can transmit data at twice the speed of a 1200 bps modem. A 28,800 bps modem will transmit at 24 times the speed of a 1200 bps modem. When paying phone bills the baud rate becomes very important. If a file takes 30 minutes to transfer with a 1200 bps modem, it will take 15 minutes with a 2400 bps modem and slightly more than one minute with a 28,800 bps modem.

NETWORKS

When a group of computers are connected together, a "local area network (LAN)" is used. The main task of a LAN is to share data between machines without mixing up that data. This task is accomplished by having one main computer storing the programs and data. This main computer is called the "file server." The other computers which are linked to the file server are called "nodes." The main task of the network is to be sure that the server sends data to the requesting node and not to the other machines. The big advantage of using a network is that the nodes do not have to be equipped with as much equipment as the file server. A node does not need a hard drive. This reduces the cost of those systems with large numbers of nodes.

Networks are wired together using phone lines, twisted pair and fiber-optic cable. A special card must be

Fig. 20-32. Shown are an external modem and an internal modem. Both of these modems operate at 14,400 bits per second.

installed in each of the nodes for proper signal transfer. The number of nodes possible and how they are connected into the network affects the speed of the system. The choice of the network pattern is dictated by which system will be the most efficient. Some of the most common choices are Star, Token Ring, and Bus networks. The choice of network may also be determined by the cost of the installation.

EXAMPLE OF HOW A COMPUTER WORKS

The workings of a computer are not difficult to understand. Running through the steps a computer takes can aid in the understanding of the computer itself. The steps that follow assume the computer, keyboard, monitor, and printer are hooked up properly. The main steps are shown in the order listed below. Steps taken by the computer are in italics.

- Power cord is plugged into a 110 Vac outlet and the computer is turned ON.
- *Power supply converts 110 Vac into 5 Vdc needed to operate the transistors and ICs.*
- *Computer goes through a BIOS (Basic Input/Output System) self check to be sure that all internal systems are in working order. This is a check of the computer's hardware. ROM (read only memory) chips control the process in the self check.*
- *The next step is the boot-up operation (internal loading process) using the CPU (central processing unit). The computer reads the hard disk for files that control the computer's software. These files tell the computer which programs to load and the path on which they can be found.*

At this point, the computer stops and waits for instructions from the operator or loads windows with a batch command that was written into the startup process.

- Instructions are typed on the keyboard or selected with a mouse to load a program into RAM memory by the operator, Fig. 20-33.
- *The keys send electrical impulses to the computer's motherboard. At the same time, they show up on the computer monitor.*
- *The typed commands force the read head to search the hard drive for the program needed.*
- *Once found, the program is read and loaded into RAM (random access memory).*

The computer waits for instructions.

- Data is keyed into the program. Some programs require that you select fonts, spacing, and other setup features at this time.
- *The keys send electrical impulses to the computer's motherboard. The program in RAM acts on the data.*

Fig. 20-33. The four rows of chips on the left contain the RAM memory of this computer.

- Information should be saved to the hard disk or floppy disk every 15 minutes. Saving this often prevents you from losing much work should a power outage occur.
- *The save command causes the write head to select the sectors on the disk that are available for storing information.*
- When you are finished entering data in the program, make the final save to disk.
- To print out needed data, select the routine that is needed by the program.
- *Data from a disk, hard drive, or RAM is spooled to the printer for transfer to paper.*
- When printing is completed, use the quit routine required by the program. Some quit routines are needed to prevent damage to the program or the data files.
- Shut off the computer. All files and data that were stored in RAM are erased when the machine is turned off.

SOFTWARE

"Software" is a creation of instructions and data that is fed into a computer. There are thousands of kinds of software sold. These programs include games, utilities, self-help programs, personal software, history, and many, many others.

PROGRAMMING

Programmers create thousands of programs for computers. Some keep track of schedules on a built-in calendar while others record golf scores. Regardless of the programs used, each had to be designed by an inventor (or a group of inventors). The inventors use some type of programming code to build their programs. If you were to read the code it would look like some strange language. Though the code will look strange to you, you must remember what it is designed to do. The code is being read by a computer, not by people. Each line of code is a set of commands or messages for the computer. A code may tell the computer to do math functions, another many tell the computer to put sounds out to a speaker, still other codes create graphics for the viewer.

Programmers decide what code to use to get the desired result. Older programs were written in BASIC, Fig. 20-34. Engineers who dealt with problems that involve the use of many formulas often used COBOL or FORTRAN. Later programmers developed code for Assembler, C, and Visual Basic just to mention a few. When robots were used in dangerous or labor saving jobs, they were programmed using M codes and G codes.

VERSIONS

When a program is first developed it is given a name, such as AutoCAD, and a number 1.0. The number signifies which "version" you have. After the program is in use, the developer continues to make changes so that it will work better or faster. The program is then assigned a new number such as AutoCAD Rel. 2.0. Rel. 2.0 means release 2.0. After minor changes, the program might be renumbered AutoCAD Rel. 2.2. As major improvements are made, another release number is given such as Rel. 3.0. Sometimes a change might never be released to the public. Those numbers are skipped over. There are some programs whose versions are release 12, 13 and higher.

When using a software package, it is important to know which version of the program you have got. It is important because with some programs you cannot create a file with a later version and run it on an earlier release. Most files created on early releases, however, will run on later releases.

PROGRAMS IN BUSINESS

Programs used in most businesses include word processing, spreadsheets, data bases and communications packages. Each of these programs is designed to make a task easier to accomplish and cut down a company's time and cost.

WORD PROCESSING

Most books, letters, newspapers, magazines and other print media are produced by using a "word processing" program. Word processors are designed to make writing easier. Some of the major names in word processing are Word Perfect, Microsoft Word, Ami Pro, Wordstar, PFS Pro Write and Displaywrite.

The main task of a word processor is to get words printed onto paper. The main task for writers is making sure the words make sense to the reader. If a document is filled with errors, it is very difficult for the reader. Errors can almost be eliminated through some of the features of word processing programs. Features like a dictionary, a spell checker and even a grammar checker are built into word processing programs. When you have trouble finding the right word to use, many programs offer a thesaurus for your convenience.

In addition to making corrections easier, word processing programs can make documents more visually appealing. Word processors allow you to change margins, tabs and fonts. They easily produce bold and italic letters. They can underline, shadow and even change the size of letters, Fig. 20-35. All these features make reading a document easier.

Most writers will tell you that word processing programs have improved their articles. Instead of just turning in an article after the first draft, writers keep making changes in flow and content. With these programs, authors can move words, lines, paragraphs or even a full page with a few keystrokes. This feature allows writers to create a draft and keep making moves until they are satisfied with the finished document.

```
10 For X = 1 to 10
20 Next X
30 If Y < 20 then goto 10
40 If Y > 300 then goto 290
50 Print
60 ....
70 ....
80 ....
90 (Other lines of code are written until end of program)
```

Fig. 20-34. Several lines of code in BASIC.

Regular text	**Bold text**	Underlined text
12 point	10 point	
Times font	Helvetica font	Courier font

Fig. 20-35. Word processing programs allow you to alter the way text appears.

The ability of the program to make changes is due to the construction of the hard disk and computer RAM. Information stored in RAM can be moved at will. Since RAM is temporary storage, data can be placed in a block, moved and the new order saved. Several versions of a story can be saved to the hard drive and compared against one another. The best version is then selected and turned over to the editor for publication.

DESKTOP PUBLISHING

Another important type of program is called "desktop publishing." This is also called "electronic publishing." Desktop publishing allows a writer to put text in multiple columns, add graphics, and even blend the text into or around the graphics. In addition, the column width can be made narrow or wide with just a few keystrokes. Readers have trouble following lines when column widths get too large, Fig. 20-36. Columns can be made so all the letters line up on the left, on the right, or on both sides. This process is called "justification." It is done to make text easier to read and understand.

Some of the major names of desktop publishing programs are Aldus Pagemaker, Finesse, Publish It!, Express Publisher and PFS: First Publisher. These desktop publishing programs can bring in text from nearly all the word processing programs.

Desktop publishing programs can even import files created with different word processing programs. To make this task easier, the files are often converted into their ASCII codes. ASCII, as discussed earlier, is the universal electronic code for text. All letters, numbers and punctuation marks can be recognized by their ASCII code numbers. Importing the author's work as an ASCII document is simple and quick work for any desktop publishing program.

The main problem with importing ASCII codes is with the document itself. Although the letters, numbers and punctuation transfer correctly, there are some features that may be lost as they are imported. Tabs, margins and special characters can be lost when the files are converted from their ASCII codes. For this reason, text which is to be converted to ASCII should be kept in simple blocks. Avoid changing tabs, margins and columns several times in the body of the document.

Graphics created by a wide variety of programs can also be imported into desktop publishing files. This means that the writer can bring almost any type of photo, drawing or piece of artwork into their document.

Graphics and text can be brought into the computer by using a scanner. A "scanner" works much like a copying machine. Instead of producing a hard copy, the scanner produces an *electronic* copy. This copy is stored in the computer. It can be changed by the operator as needed. With the endless combination of text and graphics, a writer can create any desired story for the reader to enjoy.

SPREADSHEETS

One way to make data easier to read is through the use of spreadsheets. A "spreadsheet" is a document laid out in the form of a grid. All the numbers you want to display can be seen using a series of columns and rows, Fig. 20-37. Some of the major names for spreadsheet programs are Lotus 1-2-3, Microsoft Excel, Quattro Pro and Allways.

With a spreadsheet, data can be placed in columns and rows. Numbers can be set into formulas, added, subtracted, multiplied or divided. They can be displayed and printed in the form of graphs, pie charts, bar graphs and other shapes, Fig. 20-38. The major advantage of using a spreadsheet is the ability to play *what if* with the data. You can display one budget and compare it against a second one with some of its numbers changed. *What if*

Fig. 20-36. Desktop publishing allows the creation of multiple short columns on a page.

Sample Spreadsheet Budget				
	Jan	Feb	Mar	Apr
Salary	1200	1200	1200	1200
Car Payment	240	240	240	240
Gasoline	68	72	91	88
Licenses	48	0	0	0
Savings	100	100	100	100
Rent	288	288	288	288
Balance	456	500	481	484

Fig. 20-37. Spreadsheets are a very popular business tool.

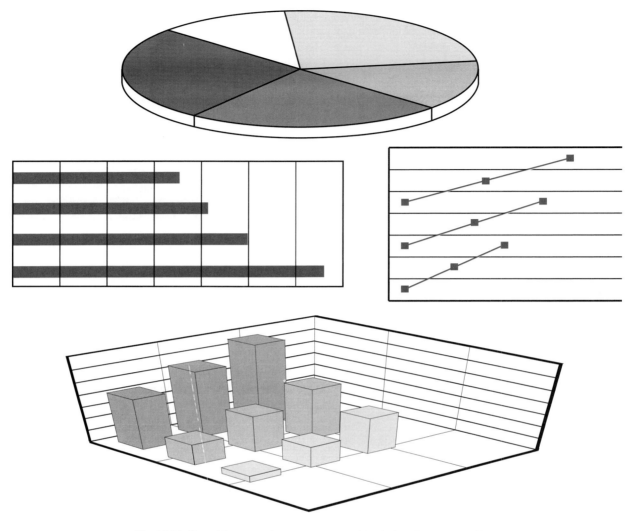

Fig. 20-38. Spreadsheets produce attractive graphic displays in a variety of forms.

more products are sold, their prices increase or the cost of materials increase can all be compared. Computers do all the calculations in just a fraction of the time required to do it by hand or with a calculator. Hours of work can be done in seconds using a spreadsheet.

DATABASES

A "database" is a collection of information that can be sorted for easy use by the person viewing the data. The phone book is a manual database. The phone book contains a list of people with their phone numbers and addresses. It is sorted in alphabetical order by last name and by city. Computer databases are used by the police to sort out car owners. License numbers are placed in a computer in alphabetical and numerical order for fast

identification. Retail stores inventory their products or customers using a database. Some of the major names for database programs are dBase, Access, Paradox, Foxbase, and RBase.

Keeping an address book is a simple form of a database. Each item on which data is kept is called a "field." Some fields would be:

- Last name.
- First.
- Address.
- City.
- State.
- Zip.
- Home phone.
- Work phone.
- Birthday.

Therefore, Last name is a field, City is a field and Birthday is a field. When all of the above fields are grouped together on each person you produce a "record." If you put together a series of these records on all your friends, you form your database. Computer databases allow you to do a search by field. The records may be sorted under the Last name or any other field. A database will allow you to find all people in a state of your choice. Or, if you wished to know if anyone was born on Feb. 28th, you could have the computer search and sort through the Birthday field.

A database can be used to store hundreds of pieces of information on thousands of different subjects. Banks store data on the payment history, savings and checking accounts and car and house loans of their customers. Similar data is stored by publishers, car manufacturers, airline companies and nearly all other major businesses. Computers permit in-flight adjustments to the flight of space vehicles through the use of information in their database.

COMMUNICATIONS PROGRAMS

Computers have created the need for a new type of communications. With so much data being stored, the need arose to transfer this data from one computer to another and to do it quickly. This rush is necessary because of the speed required to compete in some businesses. Some of the major names for communication programs are ProComm Plus, Smartcom, Carbon Copy Plus, PC Anywhere and LapLink.

One example of the use of this technology is in the newspaper business. The Wall Street Journal sends information from New York to California daily. They use a computer to send data to a satellite that then transmits it back to earth in California. Once it arrives, the transmitted stories are put into a West Coast version of the Wall Street Journal. Previously, the Wall Street Journal had to print the newspapers in New York and ship them to the West Coast. Stories would be old news before they were read because shipment might take two or three days. Using communications programs, time was reduced to a matter of minutes. All the stories in the paper are now up-to-date because of satellite communications.

Most communications programs do not use satellites to link computers. Phone lines are the common link between machines. Modems make communication between computers an easy matter. First, both computers are hooked up to telephone lines. One of the slots on the motherboard is used for this purpose. The back of the modem card sticks out of the case. It has two phone connectors, Fig. 20-39. One is for the line from the phone wall outlet. The other is for a telephone when the modem

Fig. 20-39. Modern modems have two phone connectors. This allows you to use your telephone without disconnecting your modem.

is not in use. Modem use also requires a communications program. Both the sending and receiving computers need software to talk to each other.

Suppose you wanted to connect to a second computer on the other side of town. The second computer operator would start running its communications software package. One of the options of the program is to place that machine in "host mode." The host computer waits in that condition until a call is received from your machine. When your software dials the host computer's number, the two machines are electronically connected.

If you were to listen to the modem signal on your telephone, you would hear a high pitched squeal. That noise is the modem equivalent of the voices we hear on the phone. Once connected, the rate of data transfer between the two machines must match so they can understand each other. The speeds 14,400 and 28,800 bps are commonly used transfer rates.

PROGRAMMABLE LOGIC CONTROLLERS

Robotics in the workplace brought about an entirely new industry that used computers. Instead of just being used to count, computers were needed to program thousands of different motions. Currently, robots are used to paint car bodies, weld metal pieces travelling down assembly lines and even tasks as simple as squirting out a precise amount of glue. Programming is required no matter how simple or complex the task, Fig. 20-40.

Many of the robots just described use a "programmable logic controller (PLC)" to control their motions. PLC's use many of the elements of computers mentioned

Fig. 20-40. This robot has been programmed to perform a welding operation. (Motoman)

earlier in this chapter. The name PLC describes what the controller is used to accomplish. *Programmable* means some type of code is entered into a computer. *Logic* means there are a number of on and off combinations used with various motion devices. *Controller* means it is the brain that controls the motions of the robot.

A PLC could be used with a robot that sorts out pieces of material by length. It could also serve in a "computer integrated manufacturing (CIM)" cell. CIM is a term that is used to describe a group of machines which are put together to produce a finished product. The group might include a milling machine, robot, conveyor belts, measuring devices and sorting racks. Raw materials would enter at one end and a finished product would come out the other end. A block of plastic might be changed into an artificial hip socket in a CIM cell. Most large manufacturing companies use CIM cells to produce their products. Engineering and technical schools have entire courses designed around the use and setup of PLC's.

SUMMARY

Regardless of the computer or program used, the signals that move back and forth consist of bits of data traveling through transistors and integrated circuits. Even as programs get more and more complex and the speeds

increase, the concepts still remain the same. Transistors trigger on and off as they are biased to switch from one mode to another.

Computers got more complex as integrated circuits became smaller and more complex. Changes were brought about by improvements in the electronics industry. As transistors got smaller, IC's got smaller. Smaller sizes meant less heat and improved computer performance.

Through the use of lasers, optics and finer controls over spacing, electronic devices will get smaller and faster. The smaller they get, the less heat they generate and the process continues. Computers that took up as much space as a house have been replaced by those that fit on a desk. Desktop machines are being replaced with portable versions. Portable machines are being replaced with those that you can carry in the palm of your hand. The cycle of miniature devices continues in the electronics field.

More powerful software has been developed to match each improvement in a computer's hardware. Word processing programs, desktop publishing, spreadsheets, databases and communications programs have made large differences in the business world. Programmable logic controllers have had the same effect in industry.

Computers

KEY WORDS AND TERMS

ASCII
Backup
Baud rate
Bit
Byte
Card
CD-ROM
Central processing unit (CPU)
CMOS chip
Computer
Computer integrated
  manufacturing (CIM)
Crash
Database
Desktop publishing
Electronic publishing
External disk drive
Field
File allocation table (FAT)
File server
Floppy disk
Floppy drive
Formatting
Half adder
Hard drive
Host mode
Input
Input device
Justification

Local area network (LAN)
Math coprocessor chip
Megabyte (MB)
Modem
Monitor
Motherboard
Mouse
Node
Output
Output device
Parallel port
Pixel
Programmable logic
  controller (PLC)
Random access memory
  (RAM)
Read only memory
  (ROM)
Record
Resolution
Scanner
Sector
Serial port
Software
Spreadsheet
Track
Version
Word processing

TEST YOUR KNOWLEDGE

Do not write in this book. Write your answers on a separate sheet of paper.

1. If you opened the case that makes up a computer, what electrical and electronic components would you see?
2. What level and type of voltage is needed to operate most of the devices inside the case of a computer?
3. Output devices are used to bring information out of the computer. List three of the devices.
4. Define the following abbreviations.
  a. BIOS -
  b. ROM -
  c. CPU -
  d. RAM -
5. The heart of a computer is the _____, which has only two states, on and off.
6. What is the binary number for 14?
7. Explain what is meant by a bit.

8. What is the ASCII code (American Standard Code for Information Interchange) and why is it used?
9. The information stored on a CD-ROM is not magnetic. Describe its makeup and how data is read off the disk
10. What is the function of the CMOS chip in a computer? Where does it get power?
11. The speed that data is transferred using a modem is called the _____.
12. What are five of the most commonly used computer programs in businesses?
13. The major advantage of using a spreadsheet on a computer is the ability to play *what if.* What does that mean?

ACTIVITIES

1. Open the case of a central processing unit with the power off. Observe the items inside. Make a sketch and label the various components.
2. Make a spreadsheet of the various components that make up a total computer system in column A. List the prices for each of the items in column B. Type TOTAL at the bottom of column A. Use a formula to calculate the total in column B. Does the total cost of the items exceed the cost of an assembled computer? Why?
3. Create a database of names (last, first), addresses (city, state, zip), phone numbers (home, work), and birthdays for all your friends. When it is completed, try some sample sorts for last name, phone number, state, etc., to see how sorting works.
4. Make a list of some of the programming languages available to you. Study the code from one of the Programming books you have in your school or library. Write a simple program and make it operate. If you cannot do this, try one of the programs you can find in a computer magazine
5. Ask your teacher or a friend if you can have a useless computer chip to take apart. Using a great deal of care, see if you can remove the plastic cover and the circuitry. What did you learn from doing this task?
6. Try to locate a number of computer bulletin boards in your city or state. Do any of the bulletin boards (national or state) you found have toll-free numbers? What are some advantages of becoming a user of this type of service?
7. Compare the cost and advantages of at least five word processing programs using a spreadsheet. Based on the items in your spreadsheet, which one of the programs would you buy? Why?
8. There are several other codes in use besides binary including octal and hex. Where would these codes be used? Create a chart using the same digits to compare these codes. What are some of the advantages of using different code systems?

9. What are some of the numbers of the chips used in Macintosh computers? Compare them to those used on IBM computers (286, 386, 486) for speed and cost. What does it take to run IBM files on a Mac? What does it take to run Mac files on an IBM? Are there any machines that run both systems?

10. Create a one page brochure that includes graphics using a desktop publishing program. Use 8 1/2 in. by 11 in. sheets of paper for this tasks and design its finished size to be 8 1/2 in. high by 5 1/2 in. wide. Next, create an eight page brochure using the same program and process. Fold up a mock brochure for the latter task. How are the pages laid out so that the page numbers follow in the correct order?

11. Describe how a laptop computer can be made so much smaller than one that sets on a desk. Make a list showing the cost of different laptop computers. Which one has the highest price and which has the lowest price? How would you account for this difference? Is the most expensive of these computers a better machine? Why or why not?

12. A computer is used to send a signal to a space satellite. If the message is being sent to a person in another country on the opposite side of our planet, how long does it take the message to arrive? If the message is being sent to a space probe in orbit around Mars, how long would it take for the message to arrive?

21 Fiber Optics

LEARNING OBJECTIVES

After studying this chapter, you will be able to:
- Diagram the process used by fiber optics to transmit electrical signals.
- List the advantages of fiber optics compared with copper wire.
- List the problems and disadvantages of fiber optics compared with copper wire.
- Compare and contrast the size and weight of fiber optics vs. copper wire.

Fiber optics is becoming the standard method for transmitting data and voice communications. *Fiber optics* refers to communicating with light pulses transmitted through a solid glass fiber the thickness of a human hair. The fiber is surrounded by a *silicone coating,* then a *buffer jacket,* then *strength members,* and finally a *polyurethane jacket,* Fig. 21-1. These layers protect the glass fiber from damage. They also prevent the light pulses from escaping from the fiber wall. Unlike the fragile glass found in most windows, the glass used for fiber optics is strong, yet flexible enough to bend.

FIBER OPTICS TECHNOLOGY

An electrical signal cannot be transmitted along a piece of glass fiber. This is because glass is an insulator. However, a glass fiber can carry messages by using pulses of light. To do this, electrical signals are first changed (digitized) into binary code and then sent to a *transmitter.* The *on* and *off* binary electrical signals are used to trigger either a light emitting diode (LED) or laser diode. The output of either diode is pulses of light known as *photons.* These pulses are transmitted through a length of glass fiber to a receiver, Fig. 21-2.

When the photons reach the receiver, they strike an *optical detector.* The detector senses the light pulses and converts them back into an electron flow. Two devices are commonly used in the detector to make this change. They are the PIN (Positive Intrinsic Negative) diode and the APD (Avalanche Photo Diode) diode. Both diodes convert the energy of the photons back into electrons. This digital code is either transformed into analog signals for sound transmission or left as digital code for computer applications.

Fig. 21-1. Fiber optics cables consist of glass fiber surrounded by protectice layers.

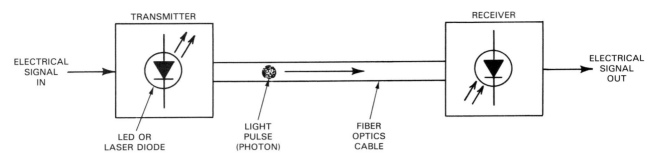

Fig. 21-2. Electrical signals converted to photons by a transmitter. The photons travel along the glass fiber until they are detected by the receiver and converted back into electrical signals.

When the photons must travel distances longer than 50 to 60 kilometers, they must pass through a *repeater station*. The station boosts the strength of the signal to prevent loss of any part of the message. Electrical signals sent on copper wire must pass through a repeater every one to two kilometers.

A glass fiber can carry more than one signal at a time. In fact, 50,000 voice messages can travel at the same time through a single glass fiber. This is done using a time shift which produces signals at different frequencies. When they reach the receiver, the signals are separated without losing any of the information being transmitted. The processes involved are known as *modulation* and *multiplexing*. These processes save large amounts of money by reducing cable cost and installation labor costs.

Fig. 21-3. These two data transmission devices carry the same amount of information. A—Typical fiber about the thickness of a human hair. B—Cable consisting of several hundred copper wires.

FIBER OPTICS' ADVANTAGE OVER COPPER WIRE AND RADIO WAVE TRANSMISSION

Glass fibers have various advantages over copper wire and radio wave transmissions. These include the number of signal transmissions, resistance to electrical and atmospheric interference, and reduced signal loss.

SIGNAL TRANSMISSIONS

A cable with only 12 glass fibers can carry about the same number of signals as 900 pairs of copper wire. That same copper cable would be 3 in. in diameter and would weigh 16,000 pounds per kilometer. The fiber optics cable would be 3/8 in. in diameter and would weigh only 132 pounds per kilometer, Fig. 21-3. With this size and weight advantage, fiber optics can reduce some of the expense of laying the larger copper cable.

ELECTRICAL AND ATMOSPHERIC INTERFERENCE

Another advantage of fiber optics and light pulses over copper wire and electron flow is that glass fibers are not affected by lightning. Since there is no electrical charge in a light pulse, it is immune to electrical surges caused by lightning. Also, lightwaves are not affected by electromagnetic fields found around power lines. This is very important, especially when sending computer data which if not received exactly as it was sent could result in costly errors.

Some of the same advantages hold true for fiber optics over radio transmissions. Radio transmissions, such as standard broadcast, microwave, and other frequencies, are very sensitive to weather and atmospheric conditions. Sun spots, clouds, and electrical storms can all cause a great amount of signal loss. On the other hand, glass fibers are immune to these conditions, except for those which damage the cable itself.

SIGNAL LOSS

Over distance, the resistance of copper wires causes a loss in the signal. This is why copper wire systems require a repeater station every one to two kilometers. On the other hand, there is less light lost in a single strand of glass fiber 30 kilometers long than there is through a single pane of window glass. This holds true for any weather condition or the location of a fiber close to any type of electomagnetic field. The exact signal loss is about 0.5 decibles per kilometer. This is why a fiber optic transmission needs to be repeated only every 50 to 60 kilometers.

On the other hand, radio frequencies can travel distances much farther than a signal using optics transmission. Yet, as mentioned earlier, radio waves are subject to atmospheric interference.

PROBLEMS WITH FIBER OPTICS

The photon (light signal) travels inside the glass fiber optics material. The speed of light in a vacuum is about 300,000 kilometers per second. This is equal to about one foot per nanosecond. However, the speed of a photon is reduced inside a glass fiber. This loss in speed is often caused by minute impurities in the glass.

The early fiber optics systems had problems with glass purity and water absorption in the glass fibers. They made the signal losses too high for efficient communication. However, by 1984, silica glass fibers were made that suffered losses of only 0.5 decibels per kilometer. There are still some problems caused by impurities and deflection of light inside the glass fibers. Researchers are still working to reduce the impurities in the fibers which hinder light travel.

The Light Emitting Diode (LED) must be placed at a perfect 90° angle with the fiber. If it is even a slight angle off, some of the emitted light bounces off the walls of the glass fiber, Fig. 21-4. This lessens its speed and reduces the signal. If the light pulses are sent into the fiber at too much of an angle, they can bounce through the edge of the fiber and are lost. New coating materials are being developed to prevent some of this loss from around the fiber.

To join two cables together, a technician makes a splice. The connecting fibers must line up exactly if they are to retain good light transmission. A bad connection can cause the light pulses to diffuse or even be lost.

Another problem can be caused when the fiber must be bent. Although the fiber is flexible to some degree, bending causes signals on the inside of the fiber to travel faster than on the outside. This causes what is known as *signal attenuation* (loss of signal strength). Technicians laying the cable or making splices must know the maximum amount the cable can be bent. If the glass fibers were damaged *during manufacture or installation,* the light will be diffused and the cable will be useless.

Fig. 21-4. Light flows through the center of the fiber cable. Light trying to escape is reflected back toward the center.

FUTURE FOR FIBER OPTICS

Fiber optics has made great strides since the term was first introduced in the 1950s. Refinements in the silica glass fiber during the 1970s brought the signal loss down to about 20 decibels per kilometer (it is now 0.5). Finally, in 1977 the first commercial fiber optics system was placed into service by AT&T Bell Research.

Even now, researchers are working on replacing glass fibers (having a life span of 100 years) with plastics and fluoride glass compounds having much greater life spans. These new materials also have less problems with signal losses caused by distance and bending of the cable.

In addition to the fiber itself, researchers are working on LED transmitters and optical receivers capable of over 1,000,000,000,000,000 (one quadrillion) pulses a second. This research will greatly increase the number of transmissions that can be carried over a single fiber. It will also reduce the size of the cable still further.

SUMMARY

Fiber optics consists of thin strands of glass fiber. They are used to transmit photons across a greater distance than is possible with electrical signals on a copper wire. Greater distances between repeater stations are possible with fiber when compared to those required when using copper lines.

There are a number of advantages for using fiber. These include the ability to transfer signal information without the problems of copper caused by lightning. Another is the large reduction in the size and weight of fiber compared to copper. Major problems of using fiber include the difficulty in bending and matching alignment when splicing.

KEY WORDS AND TERMS

Avalanche photo diode (APD)
Fiber optics
Modulation
Multiplexing
Optical detector
Photon
Positive intrinsic negative (PIN) diode
Repeater station
Signal attenuation

TEST YOUR KNOWLEDGE

Do not write in this book. Write your answers on a separate sheet of paper.

1. *True or False*? A glass fiber can carry an electrical charge.
2. Describe the two purposes of the protective layers around the fiber.
3. A _____ or _____ is used to create the light pulses (photons) needed to carry a message through the fiber.
4. The optical detector located at the receiver may be either a _____ or _____.
5. Explain how the purity of the glass used in fiber optics can affect data transmission.
6. List two advantages which fiber optics have over copper cable.
7. A repeater is used to boost a signal traveling long distances. A light pulse is boosted every _____ kilometers, whereas an electrical signal must be boosted every _____.
8. The technical term for signal loss is _____.
9. List three problem areas which can hinder the effectiveness of fiber optics.

22 Power Supplies and the Oscilloscope

LEARNING OBJECTIVES

After studying this chapter, you will be able to:
- Identify the ac/dc input and output voltages of four different types of power supplies.
- Explain the difference between a regulated and unregulated power supply.
- Describe the functions of the various parts of an oscilloscope.
- Demonstrate how to connect an oscilloscope into a circuit.
- Draw several different Lissajous figures and explain what they tell you about the frequencies being compared.

Solid state devices and the basic principles of electronics were covered in the last four chapters. In this chapter, we will cover two related and very important areas of electricity and electronics, power supplies, and oscilloscopes.

First, every circuit you have worked with had some type of power supply to provide for the flow of electrons. Therefore, in the first half of this chapter, we will discuss some of the various power supplies that are available.

Second, many of your circuit tests were made with meters. However, some of the values you tried to measure would last for only a fraction of a second on the dial of a conventional meter. With this in mind, the second half of this chapter is devoted to methods of checking these circuits with a high speed meter called the *oscilloscope*.

TYPES OF POWER SUPPLIES

There are many different types of power supplies used in the electricity and electronics field. The name power supply tells you that we must have some way of supplying power to many types of circuits. Since there are so many different means of supplying power, we will cover only the more common types you will find in beginning circuit work.

BATTERIES

The simple battery is one type of power source that people often forget. Yet, it has many advantages that some expensive power supplies do not have:

- The battery is easy to hook up in most simple circuits. There are many different types of clips available for holding it in place on the back of a circuit or on the chassis.
- There is no need to take along adapters and plugs when you want to connect the battery.
- You are not forced to depend on having a nearby electrical outlet if you want to use your circuit.
- When the life of the battery is used up, you can buy a new one for a low cost.

Sometimes a battery will not suit your circuit's needs. When this happens, an alternate power supply is necessary. This means you will use ac or dc produced by rectifying an ac signal—at increased cost. The more you want a power supply to do—or the greater the number of different voltages you want it to produce—the more it will cost.

TRYING OUT A NEW POWER SUPPLY

You can get various types of power supplies by buying a preassembled one or building your own. If you decide to build it yourself, be very careful when installing the solid state devices. Watch the polarity. If you hook up a diode or rectifier the wrong way, certain things could happen—including failure of the device. The same is true for transistors, electrolytic capacitors, and many other components.

I.C. SAYS:
"Here is a warning worth repeating. Make sure you check and recheck the polarity of your circuit when building any power supply. Otherwise, wrong polarity can ruin some of these solid state devices."

After the power supply has been assembled and wired, test it by applying the voltage in easy steps. *Do not bring it up to full voltage right away and hope that everything is wired right.* By increasing the voltage in easy steps, you can make a series of checks to be sure that each area being tested is satisfactory. By doing it this way, you can correct any problems that come up without ruining other parts of the circuit.

Again, remember to use heat sinks when soldering. If you use rectifiers in the circuits, mount them on a heat sink if needed. Also, use silicone grease between the high power transistor and its insulating washer.

Finally, install a fuse in the power supply circuit. Fusing the circuit has saved experts a lot of expense just because they used common sense ahead of time. Mistakes are possible no matter how many times you check your circuit. A fuse may not always prevent damage, but it will help when you get careless.

THE 120V AC POWER SOURCE

Looking at common types of power supplies, batteries rank first. The second most common type of power supply is the 120 volt ac found at your wall outlets. This ac voltage is used to drive motors, light lamps and operate heaters.

As with batteries, many people overlook the 120 volt ac "convenience outlet" as a source of power. Actually, batteries and ac outlets are called "power sources" rather than power supplies.

Power supplies, on the other hand, usually are classified into four different types (with examples):
1. dc in, dc out (converters).
2. dc in, ac out (inverters).
3. ac in, ac out (step up or step down transformers).
4. ac in, dc out (regulated or unregulated power supply).

CONVERTERS

The first type of power supply on our list has a dc input and gives a dc output. It is known as a "con- verter" because it converts dc from one level to another. With a simple converter circuit, you can convert the 6 volt dc of a battery to 125 volts.

Most converter circuits use two transistors, Fig. 22-1. This is known as an "oscillator circuit." The two transistors are said to oscillate or switch back and forth.

When a converter is connected to the primary of a transformer, it will produce what the transformer "sees" as ac. If you connect the secondary of the transformer across a full wave bridge, it will produce dc output. At this point, however, all you need to know is that a converter will change one level of dc to another level of dc. Shortly, you will see that many things can be done to the output.

INVERTERS

The second type of power supply on our list has dc for an input and gives an ac output. It is known as an "inverter" and works much the same way as the converter. However, when dc is changed to ac in the inverter, it is not necessary to rectify the output of the transformer, Fig. 22-2. With the inverter, it is possible to get a square wave out of the output of the transformer. The voltages and currents you are working with will determine the size of the resistors, capacitors and other components.

LINE REGULATORS

The third type of power supply has an ac input and an ac output. It is called a "line regulator" or "voltage changer." Its main purpose is to change ac from the input to either a higher or lower voltage on the output.

CONVERTER TYPE POWER SUPPLY

Fig. 22-1. A converter circuit uses two transistors that switch back and forth to create ac at the transformer input. Output is changed back to dc at a different level than the power source.

INVERTER TYPE POWER SUPPLY

Fig. 22-2. An inverter circuit is similar to the converter circuit except that the ac created by the two transistors remains ac on the output.

You recall from the chapter on transformers that this was done with a step up or step down transformer. If you want a higher voltage, use a step up transformer. If you want a lower voltage, use a step down transformer.

AC TO DC

The fourth type of power supply has an ac input with a dc output. Because ac to dc is the most common type, we will cover it in more detail than any of the others.

The ac to dc type of power supply can be either:
1. Regulated.
2. Unregulated.

REGULATED POWER SUPPLIES

A regulated power supply, Fig. 22-3, is one which will maintain a constant output voltage or current. The output is constant, even though there may be a change in the line voltage, output load or temperature of the air around the device (ambient temperature). An unregulated power supply on the other hand, will not keep the voltage or current constant.

The regulated type of power supply would seem to have a big advantage over the unregulated type. You would think that everyone would use the regulated type. However, the regulated type of power supply costs much more than the unregulated type.

UNREGULATED POWER SUPPLIES-HALF WAVE

The easiest type of power supply to understand is one which will give us a half wave rectified output, Fig. 22-4. If we connect one diode or rectifier in a circuit, it will give us pulsating dc since only one alternation can get to our load. The other alternation is biocked because it is the wrong polarity.

Fig. 22-3. A high voltage regulated power supply will produce a constant output voltage regardless of load changes. (Heath Co.)

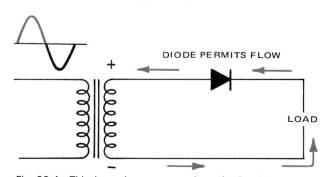

Fig. 22-4. This is a sine wave used as the input to an un-regulated power supply. On the first half cycle, electrons flow through the diode because it has correct bias voltage.

You recall that a diode must be biased with the correct polarity before it will allow electrons to flow. In Fig. 22-4, you can see that the first half cycle will pass the electrons. On the second half cycle, Fig. 22-5, they are blocked. This results in a wave that is dc but pulsing on and off every half cycle, Fig. 22-6.

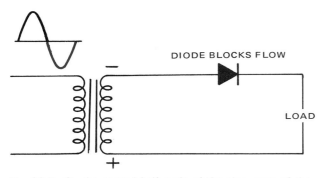

Fig. 22-5. On the second half cycle of the sine wave of the unregulated power supply, the diode is not biased correctly and will block the flow.

Fig. 22-6. Pulsating dc comes from the power supply because the negative half cycle of the sine wave is blocked.

POWER SUPPLY FILTER

There are ways to help reduce this pulsating action or "ripple." One way is to wire a capacitor in parallel with the load, where it serves as a filter (see Chapter 15). In this way, the capacitor will charge during the first half cycle, Fig. 22-7. The first pulse of dc will also pass through the load. The second half cycle is when the diode will not conduct electrons. At this time, the capacitor will go to work. Instead of falling to zero, the

Fig. 22-7. With a capacitor added to the circuit shown in Fig. 22-4, we get flow through the diode, and the capacitor is charged on the first half cycle.

capacitor will discharge. See Fig. 22-8.

During the second half cycle, the load "sees" a continued flow of electrons in the same direction as during the first half cycle. And, the flow of electrons from the capacitor will not run out before the next half cycle begins. Remember that the time needed for a capacitor to discharge is about five RC time constants. As it starts to discharge, another charging action will follow, keeping the capacitor almost fully charged.

Fig. 22-8. As the sine wave falls, the capacitor will discharge through the load until the diode is again biased to conduct.

The charging and discharging actions of the capacitor will result in a wave similar to the one shown in Fig. 22-9. Note that the output of this power supply is much higher than the one without the capacitor. The capacitor takes away some of the pulsing that results from using only one diode. The "ripple" will be less, but you cannot eliminate it with this type of power supply.

PULSATING DC WITH REDUCED RIPPLE
RESULTS FROM USING CAPACITOR

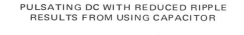

Fig. 22-9. By using a capacitor in our power supply circuit with one diode, we will eliminate part of the sine wave, reduce ripple and raise the output.

CENTER TAP TRANSFORMER

One way to reduce the power supply output ripple is to install a transformer using a center tap. Then, if you add a second diode, the first half cycle will take the path shown in Fig. 22-10. The load will "see" the first half cycle as a pulse. The second half cycle will also pass a pulse. See Fig. 22-11.

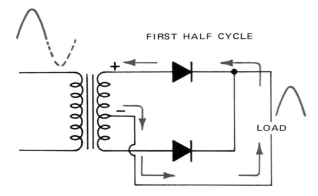

Fig. 22-10. By using a center tap transformer with two diodes, we will get the path of flow shown in this schematic for the first half cycle of the sine wave.

Fig. 22-11. Working with the circuit set up for Fig. 22-10, this is the second half cycle of the wave. Note that we have used only one half of the transformer voltage for each half cycle.

Using two diodes will give you a real advantage. Now, it is possible to get both half cycles through the load. This means there will be much less "ripple." There no longer will be a large gap to be filled by a discharging capacitor.

If a capacitor is used in this circuit, Fig. 22-12, the output ripple will be very small. The capacitor will discharge for a shorter period of time. The output wave would be much smoother if you saw it on an oscilloscope.

You might think that this center tap transformer type of power supply would be the best one to make. However, it has problems too. The biggest problem can be seen by looking at the circuit. Note in Figs. 22-10 and 22-11 that each alternation used only one-half of the transformer. This means that only half of the voltage is useful at any one time. If 6 volts are needed, the transformer must give 6 volts from each side to center, Fig. 22-13. The full 12 volts could not be used.

Fig. 22-12. Placing a capacitor in the circuit with a center tap transformer with two diodes will give us a power supply with very little ripple.

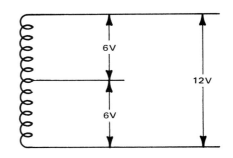

Fig. 22-13. Output voltage from a center tap transformer is one half of the total output.

FULL WAVE RECTIFIERS

There *is* a way that the full output of the transformer can be used. First, look at just one half cycle, Fig. 22-14. There, we are using two diodes to pass electrons through the load. Pay close attention to the direction of electron flow through the load. On the second half cycle, Fig. 22-15, we can use two other diodes. The direction through the load is not changed. Full transformer output can be used.

If we have a 12 volt transformer, the full 12 volts will be supplied to the load. This is an advantage, but it means that we must use four diodes. You recall that we worked with four diodes in an earlier chapter. The finished power supply, Fig. 22-16, is our full wave bridge rectifier. You can buy this bridge rectifier as an

Fig. 22-14. With two diodes connected to the power supply circuit, note how the first half cycle of flow passes through the load. Also note the direction of flow.

Fig. 22-15. By using two other diodes in the Fig. 22-14 circuit, flow through the load is maintained in the same direction on the second half cycle of flow.

assembly rather than buying four separate diodes. This power supply can be filtered to further smooth out and almost eliminate the ripple.

POWER SUPPLY SIZE

Power supplies, Fig. 22-17, are available in quite a range of sizes. Some small types can produce 30 volts and up to five amps. Plants in industry use much larger power supplies. Industrial units must provide the power needed for:
1. High frequency heating.
2. Annealing furnaces used to soften metals.
3. Large industrial controls for giant spot welders.
4. Hardening the surfaces of metals and gears.
5. Huge presses for stamping out automobile sheet metal parts.

There are many other places where large power supplies are needed. Many of those used in industry are operated around 460 volts, Fig. 21-18. Most important, however, is that the voltage must be controlled.

Fig. 22-16. Putting all four diodes or a full wave bridge rectifier into the Fig. 22-14 circuit will result in full transformer dc output through the load.

Fig. 22-17. Small power supplies will deliver 30 volts and up to 5 amps. (Interplex Electronics, Inc.)

Fig. 22-18. Large industrial power supplies often are mounted on I beams. This one operates at 460 volts. (Pillar Corp.)

INDUSTRIAL POWER SUPPLIES

With large changes on the output, unregulated power supplies lose control. Often, therefore, large and small power supplies are regulated. In some cases, the voltage is controlled within plus or minus one percent. Others must do even better.

Fig. 22-19 shows the inside of a 300 kW, 3 kHz power supply. Over a dozen semiconductor devices are built into it. These large units are water cooled to aid in getting rid of the heat that is created during loading. In this way, they are able to run much longer without overheating. Water cooling is also very important when it comes to regulation. Both large and small power supplies can be regulated to control the output within close tolerances.

FEEDBACK

There are several ways to regulate the output of a power supply. Most regulation works on the idea of "feedback." Feedback is a simple idea. For example, we may ask "How tall are you?" Your answer would be feedback. You would be giving information back to us. *Feedback is information being fed back to the source.*

Fig. 22-19. Arrow points to one of 15 water-cooled SCRs used in this power supply unit to keep the heat down.

Suppose that transformer output is 2 amps. If we added 1 more amp to the load, it would climb to 3 amps. If this information could be relayed to the input, it would be known as feedback.

Feedback is used in regulated power supplies. This means that more circuitry must be added to the power supply. As a result, costs will go up.

Among other things, feedback is used to tell the input when the output load increases or if more heat is being generated at the output. This is important because one of the main reasons for using a regulated power supply is to control the output. In many cases, controlled output is needed because a change in 1 or 2 volts can turn on a transistor or SCR. You recall that an SCR carrying 200 amps can be affected by a change of only a few volts.

There are many other uses for regulated power supplies. However, there is one main point to rememeber: *regulated power supplies control the output by using feedback to the input.* In this way, we can maintain close control of the output voltage.

POWER SUPPLY PROJECT

A 12 volt power supply, Fig. 22-20, seems to be the one most needed for use in the home. This need came about when car tape players became popular. Many people wanted to remove them at night for use in playing tapes at home. Therefore, a good 12 volt supply was needed.

Here are plans for a power supply that can be built at a reasonable cost. The amount of filtering could be improved, but it is not really necessary. No voltage regulator is needed. Tape players are regulated for constant speed.

The circuit has been laid out for you, showing diode type of construction, Fig. 22-21. Keep the leads short and compact so that the assembly can be placed in a

Fig. 22-20. This power supply unit can be used to power car tape players in the home. (Project by Bill Martinez)

Fig. 22-21. Schematic shows hookup for power supply for home use. $C_{1,2}$—Electrolytic capacitors. F_1—Fuse. S_1—Switch. T_1—110/12V transformer.

small case. Buy a bridge rectifier or use four separate diodes. Use whatever capacitors you can find to make up the capacitance to around 6000 μF. Note that they are electrolytic capacitors.

Obtain the following parts and assemble them according to the construction procedure given.

No.	Item
1	110/12 volt transformer.
2	Bridge rectifier or four diodes.
2-3-4	Electrolytic capacitors to total 6000 μF at 25 WVDC.
1	SPST switch.
1	Fuse.
1	Line cord and plug.
1	Case.
2	Output terminals.

CONSTRUCTION PROCEDURE

Assemble the parts and hook up the circuit as shown in Fig. 22-21.
1. Lay out parts and determine size of case.
2. Mark positions of switch, output terminals and other attachments on case.
3. Drill all holes in case.
4. Bend case to shape. Paint it or cover it with contact paper.
5. Mount parts in case.
6. Wire circuit according to Fig. 22-21.
7. Install fuse in series with transformer primary.
8. Add decals to front of case.

THE OSCILLOSCOPE

The oscilloscope, Fig. 22-22, is a testing instrument designed to give a technician a lot of information about circuits. Most people just call it a "scope."

There are many types of scopes. A common type used by those beginning the study of electronics is shown in Fig. 22-22. Most scopes, however, have the same basic parts and will read the same basic values in a circuit.

Fig. 22-22. Typical oscilloscope used for taking measurements in electronic circuits. (Michael Murray)

CATHODE RAY TUBE

The heart of all scopes is the cathode ray tube (CRT), Fig. 22-23. The CRT makes it possible for you to see what the circuit is doing.

The inside face (screen) of the CRT is coated with phosphor. Since phosphor will give off a glow when an electron beam strikes it, this glow will be seen on the screen. Your eyes will see the glow for a short time, even after the electron beam has moved. This is called "persistence of vision." It is the same thing that lets you see a picture on a TV screen instead of a bunch of dots and lines.

Persistence of vision also takes the flicker out of movies. As you know, a movie is really a group of still pictures being run through a projector. It is this per-

Fig. 22-23. This cathode ray tube (CRT) is ready for installation in a scope. Note its many parts.   (Hewlett-Packard)

sistence of vision that makes it possible for the electron beam to move across the screen and show up as a line to your eyes.

The scope is nothing more than a voltmeter. It will however, measure voltage changes during a fraction of a second. This makes it very valuable for use in checking circuits that have a pulse lasting just a fraction of a second. See Fig. 22-24.

Fig. 22-24. Technician uses an oscilloscope to check a fast pulse circuit.   (Hewlett-Packard)

Take a pencil and move it quickly across the surface of a pool of water. Note that you will create a line which quickly disappears. If you start at point 1 and draw a line to point 2, this will take a certain amount of time. If you draw a line to point 3, a little further on, it will take a little longer. This is the same way that a scope works, Fig. 22-25. It takes a certain amount of time to move a beam from the left to the right side of the screen. Therefore, the horizontal axis of the scope is used to show the amount of time.

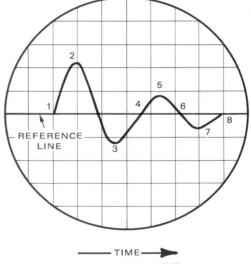

Fig. 22-25. The points along the line being traced out by a scope can have many different shapes.

Often you hear someone ask how tall a mountain is, or how deep a lake is. What they really want to know is "how high" or "how deep" it is with respect to the ground at sea level. In other words, they are using the ground as a reference axis. A scope does the same thing. Earlier you saw traces of sine waves and many of them also had a reference line. This reference line gives us the point from which we judge the value of our voltage.

GRATICULE

The screen of the scope, then shows us the time on the horizontal axis and the voltage on the vertical axis, Fig. 22-26. The horizontal axis is also called the X-axis. The vertical axis is also called the Y-axis. These graphs are very similar to police lie detectors, sales graphs

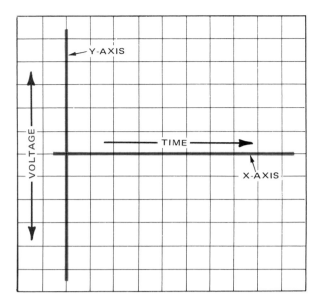

Fig. 22-26. The horizontal axis on a scope screen shows the time. The vertical axis shows the voltage.

showing profits or losses, or medical records of patients with heart trouble.

To help make measurements on a scope, a graticule is mounted on the front of the CRT. See Fig. 22-27.

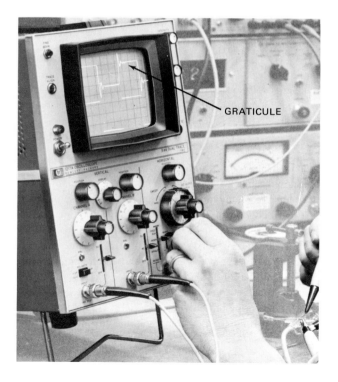

Fig. 22-27. A graticule is placed in front of a CRT to make it easier to read scope traces. (Hewlett-Packard)

The graticule has a series of lines on the order of graph paper. The horizontal spaces help us measure the amount of time needed (time interval). The vertical space gives us information about the voltage.

DEFLECTION PLATES

Inside the CRT are groups of deflection plates, Fig. 22-28. *Deflection plates make the trace move on the screen.* You recall that an electron has a negative charge. Therefore, the electron beam is nothing more than a stream of electrons.

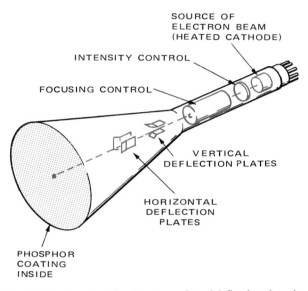

Fig. 22-28. Location of various controls and deflection plates inside a cathode ray tube.

The electrons come from the electron gun, which is in the small end of the tube. They are forced to travel down the length of the tube toward the screen. The tube is a big glass envelope with a vacuum inside.

As the beam travels down the tube, it will pass between two sets of deflection plates. *Remember, unlike charges attract.* If the negatively charged electron beam passes between a set of plates, it will be attracted to one of the plates if it has a positive charge. Because of the high speed of the beam, it will move toward or be deflected toward the positive plate. The beam can be bent up or down. See Fig. 22-29. The amount of deflection depends directly on the amount of voltage put on the plates. If you had a small voltage, the deflection will be small. A large voltage will cause a large deflection.

The first set of plates are the vertical deflection plates. They will move the beam up and down on the screen. The second set of plates are the horizontal deflection plates. They cause the beam to move sideways on the screen. If you turn the horizontal or vertical centering dials on the scope, you will see how they move the beam.

Fig. 22-29. The electron beam can be deflected by changing the charge on the deflection plates. This attracts the beam and moves it on the screen of the CRT.

INTENSITY CONTROL

By adjusting a control, you can stop the beam from appearing on the face of the CRT. The scope shown in Fig. 22-22 has an intensity control. You can make the beam very bright by turning this control one way, or you can make the beam disappear by turning it in the opposite direction.

To see how this intensity control works, first place a wire screen (grid) in front of the beam so you can control it. Then, put a small negative charge on the screen. Some of the beam will be blocked and will therefore, be less bright (less intense). If you put a strong negative charge on the wire screen, you can block the beam completely. See Fig. 22-30. This is true because like charges repel. The grid also helps to focus the beam when we are not blocking it.

I.C. WARNS:

"If you make the beam very bright, you can damage the face of the CRT. The beam must be moving across the face of the screen. If not, you will burn the phosphor. This will show up as a dark, burned spot on the face of the CRT."

Burned phosphor will not disappear; the CRT is ruined. To avoid this problem, turn down the intensity of the beam or take the beam out of focus when it is not moving on the screen.

FOCUS

The beam is focused by another dial on the front of the scope. Focusing the scope is similar to using a magnifying glass to focus sunlight down to a pinpoint

Fig. 22-30. By putting a high negative charge on the control grid, you can block the electron beam.

size. If you were to focus the spot of sunlight on your hand, you would burn yourself. This is the same thing that happens to the phosphor of the scope with a finely focused beam.

Again, when using the scope, move the beam across the face of the CRT so that it will not build up enough heat to burn the phosphor. Also, when the scope is on but not being used, turn down the intensity and/or put the beam out of focus.

PRECAUTIONS

Scopes usually have two types of power supply. One carries medium amounts of current at about 300 volts dc. The other carries low currents at over 1000 volts dc. With this in mind, do not take the protective metal case off the scope. Only those who know how to handle and repair scopes know where these voltages are present. See Fig. 22-31.

Fig. 22-31. Scopes and other electronic equipment have some complicated circuits. Do not work on this equipment until you know where to look for voltage levels that may be dangerous. (Hewlett-Packard)

Another caution concerns the CRT, which has a vacuum inside its glass housing. Any CRT or picture tube on a television receiver should be handled with extreme care. Either of these tubes can cause severe cuts and injury if dropped or broken. The chemical coating inside the CRT adds to this hazard. It can cause problems of infection to cuts from the broken glass. Technicians working with these tubes use a special technique to release the vacuum very slowly. Do not try it unless you are given proper instructions on how to do it safely.

SCOPE HOOKUPS

There are a number of buttons, dials and jacks on the front of a scope. Each is used to make certain types of measurements. The jacks are used for plugging in test leads, Fig. 22-32. Then, by connecting these test leads to the circuit, the technician is able to operate the scope and see the results under test.

Some scopes even have two beams so that you can compare two different signals at one time. Each time new features are added to a scope, the more the test results can tell you. This is why scopes come in so many different sizes and shapes.

STORAGE SCOPES AND CAMERAS

Some scopes even have the ability to read one cycle, then store the trace on the CRT. These are called "storage scopes." By using a storage scope, the technician is able to study very high speed signals. It also will let you decide which specific pulse you would like to study. These scopes cost much more than standard models.

Some companies make cameras, Fig. 22-33, so that you can take a picture of the CRT. This is not the same as a storage scope. However, it does provide a way in which you can compare different traces at different times. With it, you can make pictures to show other people if the need arises.

Fig. 22-33. Camera used to take pictures of traces that appear on the CRT. (Hewlett-Packard)

PROBES

Besides the test leads, probes can be used with a scope, Fig. 22-34. There are several types of probes, so the one that you use will depend on the type of circuit being tested. Commonly used probes include:
1. Low capacitance probe.
2. RF probe.
3. Demodulator probe.
4. High impedance probe.

Basically, all probes attach to jacks on the front of the scope. Then, they can be held to the circuit or attached to it. When the probes are attached, Fig. 22-35,

Fig. 22-32. This technician is using a test lead to pick up a signal from a circuit and take a measurement with a scope. (Autonetics Div. of North American Rockwell)

Fig. 22-34. Typical probe used to make checks on circuitry with an oscilloscope. (Heath Co.)

Fig. 22-35. By attaching the probe to a circuit, the technician is free to make adjustments on the scope.   (Hewlett-Packard)

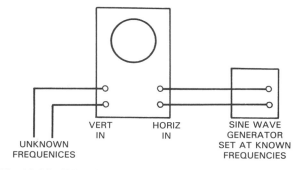

Fig. 22-36. Using the socpe and sine wave generator to find unknown frequencies. Lissajous figures will help give the results.

the technician is free to make adjustments by means of controls on the scope. There are times, however, when you are only looking for voltages or certain wave-shapes. Then, you will just touch the probe to the circuit and go on to the next test point.

MEASURING UNKNOWN FREQUENCIES

The number of things you can measure by using a scope is almost endless. For example, a scope can be used for the measurement of unknown frequencies. To do this, you will need to use a sine wave generator in addition to the scope.

The sine wave generator is an instrument marked off with frequencies which you can set. This check is made by using the known frequency of the sine wave generator to find the value of the unknown frequency, Fig. 22-36. It is often used when working on television receivers.

LISSAJOUS FIGURES

To check for an unknown frequency, you must know about "Lissajous figures." These are a group of figures of various shapes named in honor of the French scientist Lissajous. He discovered that these figures

could be developed in several ways. However, we are interested in using them to measure frequencies.

We can demonstrate how Lissajous figures help us find unknown frequencies. First, hook up the scope to the sine wave generator and to the unknown frequency as shown in Fig. 12-21. Then, adjust the sine wave generator until a figure appears on the scope.

Suppose the figure on the scope is a circle. Next, draw a right angle and place it by the figure on the scope, Fig. 22-37. Place it so that the left side of the figure touches the vertical line. Next, set it so that the horizontal line touches the bottom of the figure. Actually, you do not need to draw the right angle because of the graticule on the scope. Finally, count the places where the figure touches each line.

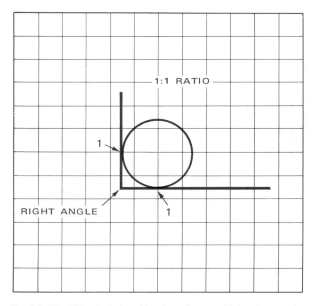

Fig. 22-37. This circle is a Lissajous figure which tells you that the two frequencies being measured are equal. The figure touches each line in one place.

RATIOS FOR LISSAJOUS FIGURES

Our circle in Fig. 22-37 touches the horizontal line in one place, and it touches the vertical line in one place. Therefore, it has a 1 to 1 ratio. This means that the unknown frequency is equal to the frequency of the sine wave generator.

Suppose that our Lissajous figure touched the horizontal line in two places, Fig. 22-38. Now, we have a 2 to 1 ratio. Therefore, the vertical input to the scope would be twice the frequency of the horizontal input signal. This means that our unknown frequency is twice the frequency of the sine wave generator. If the generator had been set on 300 Hz, the unknown frequency would be 600 Hz.

$$\text{Unknown frequency} \times \text{Points touching vertical line} = \text{Known frequency} \times \text{Points touching horizontal line}$$

Therefore: Unknown frequency x 1 = 300 Hz x 2
Unknown frequency = 600 Hz

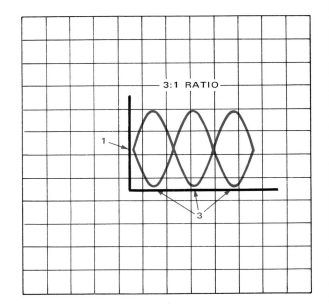

Fig. 22-39. In a 3 to 1 ratio Lissajous figure, the figure touches the horizontal line in three places and vertical line in one place.

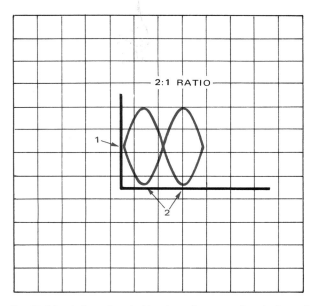

Fig. 22-38. A 2 to 1 ratio Lissajous figure touches horizontal reference line in two places and vertical line in one place.

If we had a 3 to 1 ratio, Fig. 22-39, the unknown frequency would be three times as large as the known frequency. If our sine wave generator had been set at 400 Hz, our unknown frequency would be equal to 1200 Hz:

Unknown frequency x 1 = Known frequency x 3
Unknown frequency   = 400 Hz x 3
Unknown frequency   = 1200 Hz

All the Lissajous figures do not end up with high ratios on the horizontal axis. Some will have the greater number touching the vertical axis, Fig. 22-40. In this case, the ratio is 1 to 3. From this, it is easy to figure out what the unknown frequency would be.

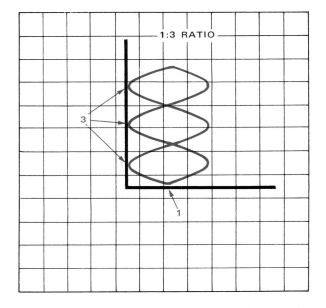

Fig. 22-40. In a 1 to 3 ratio Lissajous figure, the figure touches the horizontal line in one place and vertical line in three places.

GETTING READABLE RATIOS

In many cases, you will get figures that touch the horizontal axis and vertical axis several times and end up with ratios of 3 to 5, 4 to 6 or some other combination. At this point, you will have trouble counting the number of spots where the figures touch the horizontal and vertical lines. Then, your best bet is to adjust the sine wave generator to different frequencies until you can get a ratio that is easy to read.

In some cases, the figures will tend to turn slowly. When this happens, the sine wave is not adjusted so that the ratio reads in whole numbers. The Lissajous figure may turn in either direction. It still means the same thing. Again, the best solution is to change the known frequency until you get a figure that is easy to read. If this is not possible, you will have to try some other method used to check for unknown frequencies.

PRACTICE USING SCOPE

The use of Lissajous figures is just one example of what a scope can do for you. There are many other uses possible. However, it is best to check on the manufacturer's suggested hookup for any check you wish to make.

Each company makes their scope a little different from the others. The only way to really learn how to hook them up and take readings is through practice. Too often people see the scope and are afraid to use it. Some companies have scopes in their electrical shop just collecting dust.

Once you learn how to read a scope, you will have one of the best tools available for checking circuits and correcting faults. A scope can save many hours of troubleshooting when used by people who know how to read them.

SIGNAL TRACER PROJECT

Do you need a small signal tracer to help find trouble spots in audio systems? You can build this project, Fig. 22-41, quickly and easily. Basically, it amplifies minute signals that can be heard on the earphone. As you probe the circuit, the point where you lose the sound is where your problem is.

Obtain the following parts and assemble them according to the construction procedure given.

No.	Item
1	9 volt battery.
1	0.0022 μF capacitor (C_1).
2	2.0 μF electrolytic 15 volt capacitors (C_2, $_3$).

1	IN38B diode.
1	2N464 transistor.
1	1.2 megohm resistor.
1	2 megohm potentiometer with SPST switch, or substitute an SPST slide switch.
1	Probe and alligator clip.
1	Battery clip hookup.
1	Earphone and earphone jack.
1	Chassis box and perfboard.
	Miscellaneous hardware and wiring.

Fig. 22-41. This shop-made signal tracer project will help in troubleshooting audio systems. Top—Finished project. Bottom—Assembled parts. (Project by Mike O'Berski)

CONSTRUCTION PROCEDURE

To build the signal tracer:

1. Lay out the probe lead and battery lead, earphone jack, and potentiometer or slide switch to determine correct hole size and hole locations in cover of chassis box.
2. Drill holes and mount parts in cover.
3. Mount parts on perfboard as shown in Fig. 22-41.
4. Connect all parts in circuit, Fig. 22-42. Observe correct polarity and make mechanically sound connections.
5. Solder all connections.
6. Coat all soldered connections with a heavy layer of non-conductive material. The circuit must be insulated from the metal box when the cover is installed.

To use the signal tracer, plug in the earphone lead and turn on the switch. Clip the input ground lead to the chassis of the audio system to be tested. Probe the circuit with the "hot" lead, starting at the input audio stage. Adjust the potentiometer, or slide switch, until you hear a very small audio signal. Then, using the probe, work your way toward the speaker until the problem area is pinpointed by the complete loss of sound. Do not leave the power "on" when the unit is not in use. It may damage the transistor.

SUMMARY

Converters, inverters, and step up or step down transformers have numerous uses. There will be times when the current and voltage of these devices must be precisely controlled. This may be done with a regulated power supply. Generally speaking, the more control you have with a power supply the greater the cost of that power supply.

You can get very accurate readings of electrical signals through the use of meters. However, if you wish to see two or three cycles of that signal, the oscilloscope is the instrument to use. It is a high-speed device capable of examining a 60 Hz signal (or other frequencies) so it appears to have stopped. Once they are stopped, you can examine any portion of that cycle. This operation can be captured through the use of a storage scope. The waves captured with the storage scope will appear on the phosphorus screen as though they were frozen.

Scopes can be equipped with a series of tools or other equipment to make measurements easier. Probes and cameras can be attached or a sine wave generator can be connected with leads. The latter is used to help find unknown frequencies of the device being tested.

KEY WORDS AND TERMS

Cathode ray tube (CRT)	Lissajous figures
Center tap	Oscillator circuit
Converter	Persistence of vision
Deflection plate	Power source
Electron gun	Power supply
Feedback	Regulated power supply
Graticule	Storage scope
Inverter	Unregulated power supply
Line regulator	Voltage changer

Fig. 22-42. Schematic signal tracer includes: B_1—Battery. C_1—Capacitor. $C_{2,3}$—Electrolytic capacitors. D_1—Diode. Q_1—Transistor. R_1—Resistor. R_2—Potentiometer or slide switch.

TEST YOUR KNOWLEDGE

Do not write in this book. Write your answers on a separate sheet of paper.

1. Which of the following power supplies is also known as a converter?
   a. dc in, dc out.
   b. dc in, ac out.
   c. ac in, ac out.
   d. ac in, dc out.
2. Which of the following is also known as an inverter?
   a. dc in, dc out.
   b. dc in, ac out.
   c. ac in, ac out.
   d. ac in, dc out.
3. What is a regulated power supply?
4. A half wave rectifier will produce a _____ wave.
5. One way to reduce the ripple in a wave is through the use of _____ or _____.
6. How many diodes are used in a full wave bridge rectifier circuit?
7. How many diodes are needed in a full wave rectifier that uses a transformer with a center tapped secondary winding?
8. Explain the advantage of a full wave rectifier.
9. What is a graticule?
10. *True or False?* An unknown frequency can be found on a scope with the use of a sine wave generator and Mossimbique figures.
11. As the electron beam moves down the length of the CRT, it is moved up, down, or sideways by _____.
12. In order to make some measurements possible on an oscilloscope, it is necessary to connect _____ to the input leads.

ACTIVITIES

1. Find out the best and safest method to release the vacuum from a CRT or picture tube from a TV receiver.

2. How is the electron beam on a scope generated? Why does it move toward the front of the CRT? How fast does the beam move?
3. You may have heard the word "astigmatism" when dealing with scopes. What is it? How does it affect the scope?
4. Make a list of the different types of probes used with a scope. Tell the advantages of each.
5. What types of power supplies do you work with? Are they regulated or unregulated power supplies? Why do you use that particular type? What does a good regulated power supply cost? What does an unregulated power supply cost?
6. How did Lissajous make his discovery? How did he use it?
7. How many different types of jobs can be found which require electrical or electronics experience? What do these jobs pay? Does an electrical engineer know how to use all electrical equipment? What does this person do that is different from what a technician does?
8. What kind of background does a person that wires homes have? Must the work be inspected? By whom? Why?
9. What is the difference between a dual trace and a dual beam scope?
10. How is it possible for a scope to retain the image on the CRT after only one sweep? How does a camera mounted on a scope catch the speed of the trace on scopes other than storage scopes?
11. What is the price range for various types of scopes? What do some of the accessories cost?
12. Why are some electronic calculators so much more expensive than others?
13. How does the memory on a calculator work? How is it able to add and subtract?
14. How does a digital clock work? What makes it *not* count over 12 hours or 24 hours?
15. What is a Schmitt trigger? How is it used?

23 Career Opportunities

LEARNING OBJECTIVES

After studying this chapter, you will be able to:
- List five areas of employment opportunity in the electricity/electronics field.
- Describe the training requirements for a number of electrical and electronics related positions.
- Explain the differences between the responsibilities of different electrical and electronics work assignments.
- Compare the types of work performed in various jobs.
- Discuss what job you feel most closely matches your aptitude.

Some people think that job opportunities in the electricity and electronics field are changing too fast. Consider, however, that changes are the main reason why so many jobs are available in this field. Changes in electricity and electronics have resulted from new demands of the world around us. For example, the need to store large amounts of information for later recall led to the development of computers.

In another example, people in countries around the world wanted to be warned about storms to prevent disasters. They no longer wanted to be at the mercy of the weather. If they knew in advance about the coming of a hurricane or tornado, many lives could be saved. Weather satellites now in use provide us with that early warning information.

This same need created many other jobs in research, development, and communications.

FIVE AREAS OF OPPORTUNITY

Jobs in electricity and electronics can be broken down into five general areas of career opportunities: construction workers, maintenance workers, technicians, engineers,

Fig. 23-1. This new substation was constructed to meet the needs of a growing community.

and supervisors. To get any of these jobs, you need to start preparing early. The more you know about electricity and electronics, the better and higher paying jobs you can get.

The first area of opportunity we will look at is construction, Fig. 23-1. This includes workers who build hundreds of the items we use every day. They do the wiring in our homes, factories, and schools. Their work gives us the electricity we have grown to depend on in our everyday living.

CONSTRUCTION WORKERS must have the skills to be sure that all wiring is safely installed. To help ensure this, cities enforce local safety codes and the National Electrical Code. All building wiring is done according to these codes, Fig. 23-2. CHIEF ELECTRICAL INSPECTORS are sent out by the city to approve the wiring before it is put in service.

The construction area of electricity and electronics also includes jobs for ASSEMBLERS. These workers wire and solder various components for television sets, stereos, printed circuit boards, computers, industrial controls, citizen band (CB) radios, airplanes, and many other electronic devices.

Fig. 23-3. A quality control inspector tests a radar system. (Autonetics Div. of North American Rockwell, Inc.)

Assemblers must be able to identify many electronic components and install them into circuits. Once the parts are installed, quality control inspectors check out the finished work. Inspectors, Fig. 23-3, put the wired circuits through a series of tests. Some circuits are so small that they have to be inspected under a microscope, Fig. 23-4.

MAINTENANCE WORKERS

Once the products have been built, we must have a group of qualified maintenance workers to maintain them. Those doing maintenance work must have skill and knowledge, Fig. 23-5. They are the ones who keep so many of our home appliances in good operating condition. MAINTENANCE WORKERS are the service workers who fix our dishwashers, ranges, computers, stereos, and televisions.

Another group of maintenance workers are needed to keep TV and radio stations broadcasting. They keep the transmitters working day after day. Other groups in communications fix CB radios, aircraft communication systems, and all the telephone and microwave equipment that most of us rarely see.

Trained persons are needed to keep our large and small manufacturing firms running. Although schools can provide the basic necessary training, many companies have their own training programs that focus on their specialized equipment.

Fig. 23-2. An electrician is in the process of pulling lengths of wire into place as part of a new construction project. (Georgia Power Co.)

Fig. 23-4. Inspectors put integrated circuits through tests to be sure they will work before being installed in a circuit. (Sprague Electric Co.)

Many companies set up training programs with the cooperation of the employees of the Federal government. An APPRENTICE has to go through an On-the-Job Training (OJT) program, Fig. 23-6. Usually, this is combined with special classes or self-study courses at home. It takes about 8000 hours (four years) to complete the program.

Fig. 23-5. A journeyman maintenance worker uses some of his skill and knowledge to check an aircraft component. (Autonetics Div. of North American Rockwell)

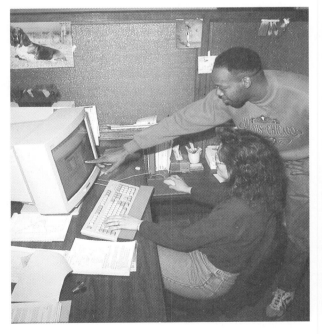

Fig. 23-6. This part of on-the-job training is performed at the direction of the instructor. Next, the employee will practice the task just learned.

Upon finishing the training, the person is granted JOURNEYMAN ELECTRICIAN status. With the journeyman card, an ELECTRICIAN has an advantage when job hunting is necessary. Every company knows that this job hunter has had at least four years of planned electrical training.

A number of companies have set up another kind of television transmission called closed circuit television (CCTV), Fig. 23-7. The companies use CCTV to help them troubleshoot the equipment in their plants. First, they make video tapes, then play them back for viewing. When troubleshooting high-speed equipment, the tapes are played back in slow motion. Skilled maintenance workers are needed to keep this type of equipment operating.

Fig. 23-8. Technicians with the ability to read scope traces and digital pulses on an oscilloscope are in high demand by industry. (Hewlett-Packard)

Fig. 23-7. Using a closed circuit television (CCTV) setup to troubleshoot high-speed machinery. The tape is played back later to look for faults with machine operation. (Guide Div., General Motors Corp.)

TECHNICIANS

A TECHNICIAN, Fig. 23-8, is specially trained to keep the manufacturer's equipment running. Generally, the basic training is done by a vocational technical school or community college. In addition, some companies send their technicians to programs set up by their equipment suppliers.

Once trained, the job of the technician is to work with existing equipment. But, the job involves more than that. A technician also works with engineers to

help design and build even better and better machines. To do this, a technician must be able to work with hands and mind, Fig. 23-9. If you do become a technician, you must continue to keep up to date. Each new component discovered and built by the electronic companies must be understood. You might be able to use them in new machine designs.

New components may make it possible for you to design faster and more accurate machines. Millions of dollars are saved by companies whose technicians can make their production operations faster and more accurate.

Technicians may be found working in the following places:

1. Electronically controlled steel mills.
2. Automotive electronics design departments.
3. Laboratories.
4. Electronic companies such as Hewlett-Packard, Texas Instruments, Bell Laboratories, General Electric and Westinghouse.

These are only a few of the hundreds of places that need the help of skilled technicians. Some companies need between three and ten technicians for every engineer they have on their payroll.

Fig. 23-9. Job opportunities are growing for people having electricity/electronics training. Here, an engineer and a technician are running operational tests on an electronic device. (Autonetics Div. of North American Rockwell)

ENGINEERS

Many of the recent discoveries in the electronics field have come about because of the work of ENGINEERS, Fig. 23-10. Engineers usually have gone through a four year college training program. Since they must have this training, engineers get more responsibility and higher pay than the first three job opportunities mentioned.

Engineers design and follow the building of new equipment until it is finally installed. They must make sure that it will run with the least amount of problems. Once the equipment is in operation, the engineers usually assign technicians to keep it running.

However, if a major problem should occur after installation, the engineers are called back. Then, they must redesign or find a better way of doing that operation.

People who go into engineering must have a good math and science background. This is necessary because so much of the work of an engineer is abstract, Fig. 23-11. They have to be able to visualize things before putting them on paper.

Engineers must have a good understanding of all the principles of physics, electronics and English. You can imagine what would happen if an engineer was not able to write a report on a new discovery so that people could understand it. Even the smartest engineer would be of little value to the company if no one understood what he said or wrote.

SUPERVISORS

Probably the highest paying job in the field of electricity/electronics is that of a SUPERVISOR, Fig. 23-12. A supervisor must have knowledge and skills related to construction, maintenance, technical and engineering responsibilities.

Fig. 23-10. Engineers run a software package through a series of tests.

Fig. 23-11. Engineers use math in every aspect of their job.

Fig. 23-12. Management and supervisory people with electronic knowledge are needed in research and development, training, and operations. Here a supervisor is checking the operation of motion simulator which recreates the visual and physical forces in a real submarine. (Rockwell International)

The supervisor has the added responsibility of making sure that others do their jobs right. Most supervisors have handled a great variety of work assignments. Only in this way could you gain the skill and knowledge needed to supervise efficiently.

Supervisors also gain the skill needed through a lot of study. They read technical and management reports and keep up to date on new discoveries. They attend conferences, national meetings, and seminars. Supervisors have to write hundreds of reports each year and they must be skilled in handling people.

Fig. 23-13. Will you have the skills needed to handle a key job in electricity/electronics? This technician is checking the time, temperature, and force needed by an injection molding machine. (Guide Div., General Motors Corp.)

Once new equipment is built and installed, more job opportunities are present, Fig. 23-13. People having the skills needed are the ones who will get the best jobs. These skills and choice jobs will not be handed to you. You must work and work hard to earn them.

Typical jobs in electricity and electronics include:

Construction workers
- Assembler
- Checker
- Sorter
- Inventory clerk

Maintenance workers
- Adjuster
- Repair specialist
- Aircraft electrician
- Home appliance service specialist
- Industrial electrician

Technicians
- Office machine service specialist
- Sound technician
- Radio operator
- Field technician
- Computer repair specialist
- CCTV maintenance specialist

SEEKING EMPLOYMENT

DETERMINING YOUR CAREER PATH

Early in your schoolwork, you should begin the process of identifying your career path. This process can be started as early as the sixth grade. It should continue through grades 6, 7, 8, and during high school. Each year of your schooling begins the process of narrowing down your selection. Career counselors can help you through this process. They can identify the things you like to do and those things you do well.

It is important that you like your job. Nothing is worse than hating to go to work each day. A person who hates to be "locked up in a building" should explore careers where the majority of the work is performed outside, Fig. 23-14. People who prefer not to be out in the sun, should examine careers that keep you indoors the majority of the time.

SELECTING COURSES

Once you have selected an area of interest, and narrowed it down to a cluster of related careers, you should begin selecting courses that will advance you toward your goal. You must prepare yourself for the future.

For example, you can't be an engineer without taking math and science classes. Consider taking pre-algebra and

Fig. 23-14. Building bridges involves a great deal of planning and construction. After the design is completed, many people are needed to work outdoors on the actual construction.

algebra in the seventh and eighth grade. In that way, you can take high school math classes in geometry, trigonometry, statistics, and calculus. These courses will go a long way in preparing you for solving engineering related problems in college. Select those courses that help you build toward your chosen career, Fig. 23-15.

COMPLETING SCHOOL ASSIGNMENTS

As you complete your school assignments, Fig. 23-16, explain them to others. This process will sharpen two skills. First, if you can explain your work to others, you will get a better understanding of what you have accom-

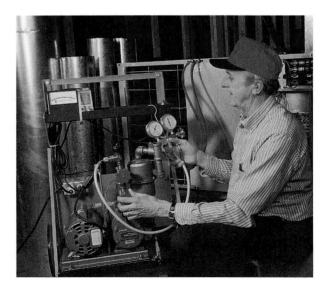

Fig. 23-15. A heating, ventilation, and air conditioning (HVAC) technician should have a good knowledge of math and science. (Georgia Power Co.)

Fig. 23-16. Do all the lab work that is assigned. It will help sharpen your skills.

plished. "You know something if you can teach it to others." Second, explaining the process to others will enhance your communication skills. Employers want people with good communication skills.

IDENTIFYING POSSIBLE EMPLOYERS

Once you have begun the process of learning the required skills for your chosen career, start looking at local employers. Do they hire part-time people? Do they have temporary summer positions where you could see what it's like working in the field firsthand? Some businesses will hire apprentices who are still in high school, Fig. 23-17. This is an excellent way to check out the career field of your choice. Try to work in your chosen field as early as possible.

Next, start making a list of the companies that you are interested in. You can get help at your local library. If you have a specific city in mind and are not able to travel there, the chamber of commerce office usually has useful information. Get as much information about these companies as

Fig. 23-17. To become a certified electrician, apprentices must dedicate themselves to learning and practicing their new skills. Working with experienced electricians will help you develop proper and safe work habits. (Georgia Power Co.)

possible so that you can have considerable knowledge about a company *before* you apply for a job.

APPLYING FOR THE JOB

Once you are ready to seek employment, prepare a resume and apply for the job. If you are blindly seeking a position (not responding to an ad), obtain the name of the person responsible for hiring, usually the human resources director. You will be able to personalize your cover letter and make a good impression. Make sure that the spelling and grammar are correct. Stress your strengths and the type of employment you are seeking. No company can match you to their openings if they don't know the kind of work you want.

Depending on where the company is located, either mail your resume and letter or deliver it in person. Many companies will accept faxed resumes and will provide a fax number or e-mail address.

PREPARING FOR THE INTERVIEW

Study the information that you collected about the company before you go for an interview. Learn as much as possible ahead of time so that you can prepare a list of questions. These questions should provide you with the list of items that are important to you. You will want to know about their scheduled working hours, medical and dental programs, educational reimbursement programs, salary, and many other items. Make a list of these items in their order of importance to you. Put them on a 3×5 card and put it in your pocket. Have it handy when you start your interview.

When you are called for an interview, wear clothes that will not embarrass you. Be dressed in clean, neatly pressed clothing and freshly polished shoes. Even if you are not seeking an office job, you should dress professionally. Remember that you only have one chance for a first impression, make it a good one. Soon after the interview, write a short note thanking them for granting you an interview.

ACCEPTING OR REJECTING THE EMPLOYMENT OFFER

If you are offered a job and decide not to accept it, be sure to notify the employer in a timely manner. Give them reasons you cannot accept their offer. If it is the pay, hours, or you have taken other employment, let them know. As the saying goes, "don't burn your bridges behind you." At some future date you might wish to go back.

If you wish to accept the offer, let them know as soon as possible. Waiting too long to accept may give the appearance that you really were not interested. Be courteous.

WORK PERFORMANCE

Employers expect to hire workers who have basic skills in reading, writing, and mathematics, Fig. 23-18. They also want people with other traits that make them good employees. Some of these traits are listed below:

- Punctual and dependable.
- Honest and responsible.
- Productive and takes pride in his/her performance.
- Refrains from drinking alcohol prior to and during work.
- Does not use illegal drugs and willingly participates in drug-screening program.
- Practices safe working habits in the interest of themselves as well as that of co-workers.
- Respectful of other employees and refrains from offensive behavior.

You will continue to learn new skills and knowledge as you gain more and more experience. Your willingness to develop these skills can often determine whether or not you'll receive opportunities for advancement.

Some of the areas on which you should focus include:

- Your willingness to work as a member of a team, Fig. 23-19.

Fig. 23-18. Workers in a nuclear power plant have a great deal of responsibility. Due to the strict regulations that govern nuclear power plants, personnel often have to complete daily reports in an accurate and timely manner. (Georgia Power Co.)

Fig. 23-19. Teamwork often makes a difficult job easier and safer. This team of workers is positioning the control rods in a nuclear reactor. One person could not safely do the job alone. (Georgia Power Co.)

- The ability to develop and improve skills pertaining to new or unique tasks.
- The improvement of problem-solving abilities.
- Your ability to communicate with supervisors, co-workers, clients, and customers.
- Willingness to share your knowledge and assist others when possible.

CHANGING EMPLOYERS

As you gain knowledge and experience, you may need to change jobs if you are seeking advancement. Before leaving your place of employment, however, you should do some research before you begin looking. New opportunities can be found in newspapers, magazines, trade journals, employment agencies, and even on the Internet.

It is customary to provide your employer with at least two weeks notice. A new employer should be understanding as they would expect the same courtesy. Prospective employers will also respect your right to privacy and will not contact a present employer unless you give them permission to do so.

You should also be courteous and respectful to your present employer. Their reference can be very important when you are changing jobs. As stated earlier, it is better to leave with all of your bridges intact.

CAREER ADVANCEMENT

The person who stops learning will create a dead end for their career. If you refuse to remain current, you will be left behind. For instance, making phonograph records was a huge business that dwindled with the introduction of the cassette tape. The introduction of compact discs had an even greater effect on cassette production in an even shorter period of time.

As in business, changes in technology can occur very quickly in a global economy. Intel is a company that makes millions of dollars each year producing integrated circuits. This business did not even exist a few years ago. If you are going to advance you must be willing to continue to learn. This will make it possible for you to adapt as new discoveries are perfected. The person who cannot adapt will fall by the wayside in a technological society.

PLANNING FOR RETIREMENT

When we are young, we often do not focus on our financial future. The thought of retirement is not a prevalent thought. However, the quality of life at the end of your working career will depend on how well you plan for your retirement. Millions of people put off saving for their retirement until it is too late. You should develop a plan as soon as you start working. Put a small percentage of your earnings in a stock plan, into mutual funds, individual retirement accounts (IRAs), or other savings programs.

The value of money over a long period of time will grow at a remarkable rate. If you wait "until you can afford it," you will never be able to retire comfortably. The time value of money can be seen if you double the value of a penny every day for one month. Granted, you will not get that kind of a return, but you can retire as a millionaire by investing about 5% of your gross salary every payday. Get some professional advice on how to accomplish this goal. It is easier than you might think. If you wait until you are 40 years old, the goal becomes very difficult if not impossible. Start saving for your retirement now while you are still young.

SUMMARY

There are five general areas of opportunity in the electricity and electronics field: construction, maintenance, technician, engineer, and supervisory. Each one of these areas encompasses a variety of positions. Entrance into any of these areas can begin through education and apprenticeships.

Career planning begins early in your life. Through the help of your family, instructors, and counselors, you can begin planning your career path while you are in junior high and high school.

This chapter provides a partial list of the thousands of different jobs that are available in the electricity and electronics field. Many of the jobs of the future don't even exist today and many of today's will be replaced. If you wish to participate in this change, you must be prepared to keep up with advancements through reading, studying, and research. Remember, you are the only one who can prepare yourself for the future.

Electricity and Basic Electronics has introduced you to a fast growing field full of career opportunities. If you want a place in the electricity and electronics field in the future, begin working toward that goal now.

KEY WORDS AND TERMS

Apprentice
Assembler
Chief electrical inspector
Closed circuit television (CCTV)
Construction worker
Electrician
Engineer
Journeyman electrician
Maintenance worker
On-the-job training
Quality control inspector
Supervisor
Technician

TEST YOUR KNOWLEDGE

Do not write in this book. Write your answers on a separate sheet of paper.

1. List the five general areas of career opportunities in the electricity and electronics field.
2. Chief electrical inspectors are sent out by the _____ to approve wiring before it is put into service.
3. _____ must be able to identify many electronic components and install them into circuits.
   a. Quality control inspectors
   b. Assemblers
   c. Construction workers
   d. Maintenance workers
4. An apprentice has to go through a(n) _____ program.
5. CCTV stands for _____.
6. Career planning should begin _____.
   a. after you receive your college degree
   b. as early as junior high
   c. when you are eighteen
   d. None of the above.
7. *True or False?* Once you are finished with school, you will never have to take any courses.
8. Being _____ and dependable are important traits for an employee to possess.
9. When leaving a place of employment, it is customary to give _____ notice.
   a. one week
   b. two weeks
   c. four weeks
   d. three days
10. Career advancement can often depend on your willingness to _____.

Reference Section

This chapter contains reference information to aid you in your study of electricity and electronics. Included are formulas in common use, dozens of symbols, scientific notation, color codes for resistors and diodes, frequency bands, metric prefixes, twist drill sizes and decimal equivalents.

FORMULAS IN COMMON USE

Ohm's Law for dc circuits

$$I = \frac{E}{R}$$

$$E = IR$$

$$R = \frac{E}{I}$$

$$P = IE$$

$$I = \frac{P}{E}$$

$$E = \frac{P}{I}$$

$$R = \frac{E^2}{P}$$

$$P = I^2 R$$

$$I = \sqrt{\frac{P}{R}}$$

$$E = \sqrt{PR}$$

$$R = \frac{P}{I^2}$$

$$P = \frac{E^2}{R}$$

Ohm's Law for ac circuits

$$I = \frac{E}{Z}$$

$$E = IZ$$

$$Z = \frac{E}{I}$$

$$P = EI \cos \theta$$

$$I = \frac{P}{E \cos \theta}$$

$$E = \frac{P}{I \cos \theta}$$

$$Z = \frac{E^2 \cos \theta}{P}$$

$$P = I^2 Z \cos \theta$$

$$I = \sqrt{\frac{P}{Z \cos \theta}}$$

$$E = \sqrt{\frac{PZ}{\cos \theta}}$$

$$Z = \frac{P}{I^2 \cos \theta}$$

$$P = \frac{E^2 \cos \theta}{Z}$$

$$\cos \theta = \text{power factor}$$

Resistance

In Series $R_T = R_1 + R_2 + R_3$

In Parallel $\dfrac{1}{R_T} = \dfrac{1}{R_1} + \dfrac{1}{R_2} + \dfrac{1}{R_3}$

Two Resistors in Parallel

$$R_T = \frac{R_1 R_2}{R_1 + R_2}$$

Equal Resistors in Parallel

$$R_T = \frac{R}{N}$$

R = any one resistor
N = number of resistors in parallel

Capacitance

In Parallel $C_T = C_1 + C_2 + C_3$

In Series $\dfrac{1}{C_T} = \dfrac{1}{C_1} + \dfrac{1}{C_2} + \dfrac{1}{C_3}$

Two Capacitors in Series

$$C_T = \frac{C_1 C_2}{C_1 + C_2}$$

$$Q = CE$$

Q = coulombs
C = farads
E = volts

Inductance

Inductors in Series

$$L_T = L_1 + L_2 + L_3$$

Inductors in Parallel

$$\frac{1}{L_T} = \frac{1}{L_1} + \frac{1}{L_2} + \frac{1}{L_3}$$

Two inductors in Parallel

$$L_T = \frac{L_1 L_2}{L_1 + L_2}$$

Coupled Inductance (Fields Aiding)

Series $\quad L_T = L_1 + L_2 + 2M$

Parallel $\quad \dfrac{1}{L_T} = \dfrac{1}{L_1 + M} + \dfrac{1}{L_2 + M}$

Coupled Inductance (Fields Opposing)

Series $\quad L_T = L_1 + L_2 - 2M$

Parallel $\quad \dfrac{1}{L_T} = \dfrac{1}{L_1 - M} + \dfrac{1}{L_2 - M}$

M = Mutual Inductance

Mutual Inductance

$$M = K \sqrt{L_1 L_2}$$

K = coefficient of coupling

Reactance

$$X_L = 2 \pi fL \qquad X_C = \frac{1}{2 \pi fC}$$

Resonance

$$f_r = \frac{1}{2 \pi \sqrt{LC}} \quad \text{or} \quad \frac{.159}{\sqrt{LC}}$$

$$L = \frac{1}{4 \pi^2 f_r^2 C}$$

$$C = \frac{1}{4 \pi^2 f_r^2 L}$$

$$2 \pi = 6.28 \qquad 4 \pi^2 = 39.5$$

Impedance

$$Z = \sqrt{R^2 + X^2}$$

where $X = X_L - X_C$

Power Factor

$$P_{true} = EI \cos \theta \qquad P_{apparent} = EI$$

$$PF = \text{Power Factor} = \cos \theta$$

Time Constants

R (in ohms) x C (farads) = t (in seconds)

$$t \text{ (secs)} = \frac{L \text{ (in henrys)}}{R \text{ (in ohms)}}$$

Peak, RMS and Average ac Values

$$E_{rms} = E_{peak} \times .707 \qquad E_{peak} = E_{AV} \times 1.57$$

$$E_{peak} = E_{rms} \times 1.41 \qquad E_{rms} = E_{AV} \times 1.11$$

$$E_{AV} = E_{peak} \times .637$$

Wavelength

$$\lambda = \frac{3 \times 10^8}{f} \text{ meters} \qquad f = \frac{3 \times 10^8}{\lambda} \text{ cycles}$$

Conductance

$$G = \frac{1}{R} \qquad R = \frac{1}{G}$$

G (in siemens)

Figure of Merit Q

$$Q = \frac{X_L}{R_L}$$

Gain

$$db = 10 \log \frac{P_{out}}{P_{in}}$$

$$db = 20 \log \frac{E_{out}}{E_{in}}$$

$$db = 20 \log \frac{I_{out}}{I_{in}}$$

ELECTRICAL AND ELECTRONIC SYMBOLS

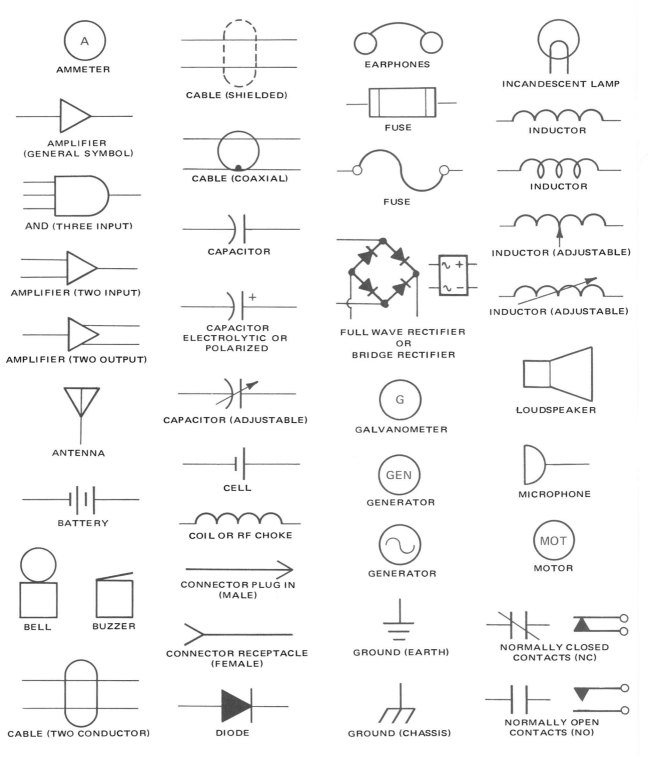

AMMETER

AMPLIFIER
(GENERAL SYMBOL)

AND (THREE INPUT)

AMPLIFIER (TWO INPUT)

AMPLIFIER (TWO OUTPUT)

ANTENNA

BATTERY

BELL   BUZZER

CABLE (TWO CONDUCTOR)

CABLE (SHIELDED)

CABLE (COAXIAL)

CAPACITOR

CAPACITOR
ELECTROLYTIC OR
POLARIZED

CAPACITOR (ADJUSTABLE)

CELL

COIL OR RF CHOKE

CONNECTOR PLUG IN
(MALE)

CONNECTOR RECEPTACLE
(FEMALE)

DIODE

EARPHONES

FUSE

FUSE

FULL WAVE RECTIFIER
OR
BRIDGE RECTIFIER

GALVANOMETER

GENERATOR

GENERATOR

GROUND (EARTH)

GROUND (CHASSIS)

INCANDESCENT LAMP

INDUCTOR

INDUCTOR

INDUCTOR (ADJUSTABLE)

INDUCTOR (ADJUSTABLE)

LOUDSPEAKER

MICROPHONE

MOTOR

NORMALLY CLOSED
CONTACTS (NC)

NORMALLY OPEN
CONTACTS (NO)

Reference Section

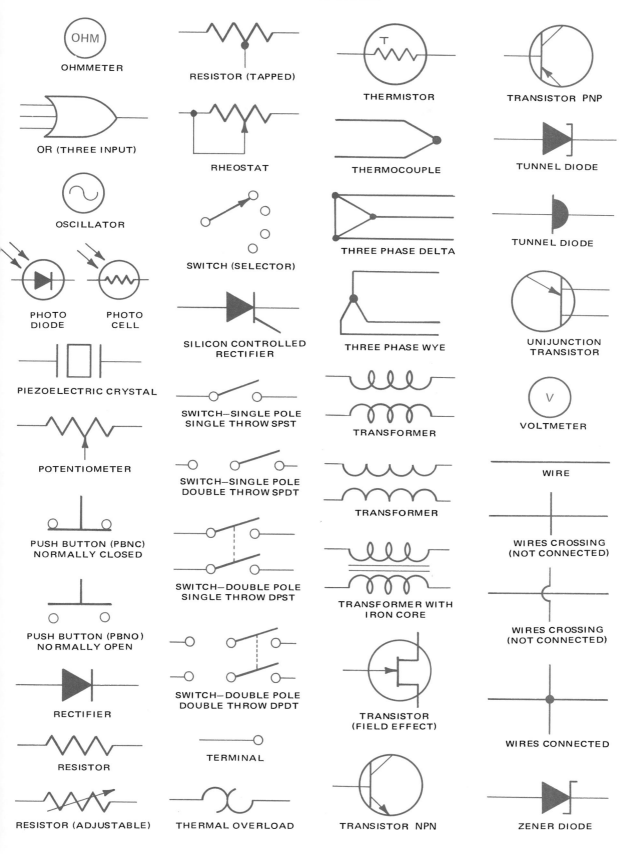

OHMMETER

RESISTOR (TAPPED)

THERMISTOR

TRANSISTOR PNP

OR (THREE INPUT)

RHEOSTAT

THERMOCOUPLE

TUNNEL DIODE

OSCILLATOR

SWITCH (SELECTOR)

THREE PHASE DELTA

TUNNEL DIODE

PHOTO DIODE

PHOTO CELL

SILICON CONTROLLED RECTIFIER

THREE PHASE WYE

UNIJUNCTION TRANSISTOR

PIEZOELECTRIC CRYSTAL

SWITCH—SINGLE POLE SINGLE THROW SPST

TRANSFORMER

VOLTMETER

POTENTIOMETER

SWITCH—SINGLE POLE DOUBLE THROW SPDT

TRANSFORMER

WIRE

PUSH BUTTON (PBNC) NORMALLY CLOSED

SWITCH—DOUBLE POLE SINGLE THROW DPST

TRANSFORMER WITH IRON CORE

WIRES CROSSING (NOT CONNECTED)

PUSH BUTTON (PBNO) NORMALLY OPEN

SWITCH—DOUBLE POLE DOUBLE THROW DPDT

TRANSISTOR (FIELD EFFECT)

WIRES CROSSING (NOT CONNECTED)

RECTIFIER

TERMINAL

WIRES CONNECTED

RESISTOR

RESISTOR (ADJUSTABLE)

THERMAL OVERLOAD

TRANSISTOR NPN

ZENER DIODE

329

SCIENTIFIC NOTATION

You probably noticed that some numbers used in formulas are very small and some are very large. When you have both small numbers and large numbers in the same formula, that formula can be very difficult to use in solving problems. To make these numbers easier to multiply and divide, a method called "scientific notation," or "engineer's shorthand," has been devised. It is a fast way of working out problems, based on being able to move the decimal point either to the left or to the right. Here is how it works:

10^2 is read as 10 squared and is the same as 10 x 10 (10 times 10), and it is equal to 100. Therefore, 10^2 = 100.

10^3 is read 10 cubed or 10 to the third power. It is the same as 10 x 10 x 10. Therefore, 10^3 = 1000.

10^4 = 10 x 10 x 10 x 10 or 10,000.

10^5 = 10 x 10 x 10 x 10 x 10 or 100,000.

EXPONENTS

An "exponent" is a mathematical symbol that indicates the power of a given number. In our first example of scientific notation, the exponent is 2. This means that 10^2 is 10 to the second power, and that 10 is to be multiplied by itself.

In our second example, 10^3 is 10 to the third power and number 10 is to be multiplied by itself twice. Likewise, 10^4 is 10 to the fourth power, and 10^5 is 10 to the fifth power. Note, too, that the exponent tells you the number of zeros after the 10 has been multiplied.

10^2 = 1 followed by 2 zeros or 100.
10^3 = 1 followed by 3 zeros or 1000.
10^4 = 1 followed by 4 zeros or 10,000.
10^5 = 1 followed by 5 zeros or 100,000.

POSITIVE EXPONENTS

If you want to change a large number by scientific notation, you can do it by moving the decimal point. For positive exponents (10^2, 10^3, etc.), you would move the decimal point to the left. Moving it to the left will increase the exponent by one for every digit the decimal point is moved. Here, for example, is how you would change a resistor rated at 120,000 ohms by using scientific notation:

120,000 ohms = 1.2×10^5 ohms

We have moved the decimal point five places to the left as follows:

120,000 with the decimal point moved one place to the left would be

120,000 = 12,000 x 10

120,000 with the decimal point moved two places to the left would be

120,000 = 1200 x 10^2

120,000 with the decimal point moved three places to the left would be

120,000 = 120 x 10^3

120,000 with the decimal point moved four places to the left would be

120,000 = 12 x 10^4

Finally, 120,000 with the decimal point moved five places to the left would be

120,000 = 1.2×10^5

Note, too, that each time we moved the decimal point, the exponent increased by one digit.

Try another example. Change 6700 ohms by using scientific notation:

6700 ohms = 6.7×10^3 ohms

Note that we moved the decimal point three places to the left, and the exponent over the 10 is 3.

NEGATIVE EXPONENTS

If you want to change a small number by scientific notation, you can do it by moving the decimal point to the right. The only difference in this method is that you will go to negative exponents (10^{-2}, 10^{-3}, etc.).

For example, change .00013 amp by using scientific notation:

.00013 amp = 1.3×10^{-4} amp

We have moved the decimal point four places to the right as follows:

.00013 with the decimal point moved one place to the right would be

$$.00013 = .0013 \times 10^{-1}$$

.00013 with the decimal point moved two places to the right would be

$$.00013 = .013 \times 10^{-2}$$

.00013 with the decimal point moved three places to the right would be

$$.00013 = .13 \times 10^{-3}$$

Finally, .00013 with the decimal point moved four places to the right would be

$$.00013 = 1.3 \times 10^{-4}$$

Try another example. Change .000006 amp by scientific notation:

$$.000006 \text{ amp} = 6 \times 10^{-6} \text{ amp}$$

Since we moved the decimal point six places to the right, the exponent is -6. The following table will help you see both methods of moving the decimal:

1,000,000,000	=	1×10^{9}
100,000,000	=	1×10^{8}
10,000,000	=	1×10^{7}
1,000,000	=	1×10^{6}
100,000	=	1×10^{5}
10,000	=	1×10^{4}
1000	=	1×10^{3}
100	=	1×10^{2}
10	=	1×10
1	=	1
1×10^{-1}	=	.1
1×10^{-2}	=	.01
1×10^{-3}	=	.001
1×10^{-4}	=	.0001
1×10^{-5}	=	.00001
1×10^{-6}	=	.000001
1×10^{-7}	=	.0000001
1×10^{-8}	=	.00000001
1×10^{-9}	=	.000000001

MULTIPLYING BY SCIENTIFIC NOTATION

Once you are able to convert with exponents, multiplying and dividing numbers by scientific notation is much easier. *To multiply, you add exponents. To divide, you subtract exponents.*

Study the following examples that show how to multiply numbers by scientific notation:

$$6000 \times 60,000$$

First, convert to scientific notation.

$$(6 \times 10^{3}) \times (6 \times 10^{4})$$

Adding the exponents gives

$$(6 \times 6) \times 10^{7}$$

because 3 plus 4 equals 7, and this is equal to

$$36 \times 10^{7} \text{ or}$$

moving decimal point one place to left equals

$$3.6 \times 10^{8} \text{ or}$$

moving decimal point eight places to right equals

$$360,000,000.$$

If you want to multiply numbers by scientific notation and one exponent is plus while the other is minus, you still add the components. For example:

$$6000 \times .0006$$

First, convert to scientific notation.

$$(6 \times 10^{3}) \times (6 \times 10^{-4})$$

Adding the exponents gives

$$(6 \times 6) \times 10^{-1}$$

because +3 and -4 equals -1, and this is equal to

$$36 \times 10^{-1} \text{ or}$$

moving decimal point one place to left equals

$$3.6$$

If you want to multiply numbers by scientific notation and both exponents are minus, you still add the exponents. For example:

.0006 x .006

First, convert to scientific notation.

$(6 \times 10^{-4}) \times (6 \times 10^{-3})$

Adding the exponents gives

$(6 \times 6) \times 10^{-7}$

because -4 plus -3 equals -7, and this is equal to

36×10^{-7} or

moving decimal point seven places to left equals

.0000036

DIVIDING BY SCIENTIFIC NOTATION

When dividing numbers by scientific notation, you subtract exponents. Be careful when the signs are different. They may give you a problem if you are not paying attention. Try these examples:

120,000 ÷ 400

First, convert to scientific notation.

$$\frac{120,000}{400} = \frac{12 \times 10^4}{4 \times 10^2}$$

Since it is easier to divide 12 by 4, you would not change the 120,000 to 1.2×10^5. By subtracting the exponent in the denominator (numbers below line) from the exponent in the numerator (numbers above line) you get

$$\frac{12 \times 10^2}{4}$$

because 10^4 minus 10^2 equals 10^2. Remember, you are subtracting exponents. Then, 12 is divided by 4 to get

3×10^2 or

moving the decimal point two places to right equals

300.

If you want to use scientific notation to divide numbers with negative exponents, you still subtract the exponents. For example:

.00012 ÷ .004

First, convert to scientific notation.

$$\frac{12 \times 10^{-5}}{4 \times 10^{-3}}$$

When you subtract a negative number, it becomes

$$\frac{12 \times 10^{-2}}{4}$$

because the negative exponent (-3) in the denominator becomes positive, and this is equal to

3×10^{-2} or

moving decimal point two places to left equals

.03

From these various examples, you can see that scientific notation, gives you a fast way of multiplying or dividing very large numbers or very small numbers.

RESISTOR COLOR CODE

SECOND DIGIT

FIRST DIGIT

TOLERANCE

NUMBER OF ZEROS

THIS EXAMPLE:

COLOR	DIGIT				
BLACK	0	RED	VIOLET	RED	SILVER
BROWN	1	2	7	00	± 10%
RED	2		2700 Ω ± 10%		
ORANGE	3		2.7K Ω ± 10%		
YELLOW	4				
GREEN	5				
BLUE	6				
VIOLET	7				
GRAY	8				
WHITE	9				
GOLD	5%				
SILVER	10%	} TOLERANCE			
NONE	20%				

TWIST DRILL SIZES AND DECIMAL EQUIVALENTS

DRILL	EQUIVALENT	DRILL	EQUIVALENT	DRILL	EQUIVALENT	DRILL	EQUIVALENT
.1 mm	.003937	38	.101500	B	.238000	33/64	.515625
.25 mm	.009842	37	.104000	C	.242000	17/32	.531250
80	.013500	36	.106500	D	.246000	13 1/2 mm	.531495
79	.014500	7/64	.109375	E 1/4	.250000	35/64	.546875
78	.016000	35	.110000	6.5 mm	.255905	14 mm	.551180
1/64	.015625	34	.111000	F	.257000	9/16	.562500
77	.018000	33	.113000	G	.261000	14 1/2 mm	.570865
.5 mm	.019685	32	.116000	17/64	.265625	37/64	.578125
76	.020000	3. mm	.118110	H	.266000	15 mm	.590550
75	.021000	31	.120000	I	.272000	19/32	.593750
74	.022500	1/8	.125000	7. mm	.275590	39/64	.609375
73	.024000	30	.128500	J	.277000	15 1/2 mm	.610235
72	.025000	29	.136000	K	.281000	5/8	.625000
71	.026000	3.5 mm	.137795	9/32	.281250	16 mm	.629920
70	.028000	28	.140500	L	.290000	41/64	.640625
69	.029200	9/64	.140625	M	.295000	16 1/2 mm	.649605
68	.031000	27	.144000	7.5 mm	.295275	21/32	.656250
67	.032000	26	.147000	19/64	.296875	17 mm	.669290
1/32	.031250	25	.149500	N	.302000	43/64	.671875
66	.033000	24	.152000	5/16	.312500	11/16	.687500
65	.035000	23	.154000	8. mm	.314960	17 1/2 mm	.688975
64	.036000	5/32	.156250	O	.316000	45/64	.703125
63	.037000	22	.157000	P	.323000	18 mm	.708660
62	.038000	4. mm	.157480	21/64	.328125	23/32	.718750
61	.039000	21	.159000	Q	.332000	18 1/2 mm	.728345
1. mm	.039370	20	.161000	8.5 mm	.334645	47/64	.734375
60	.040000	19	.166000	R	.339000	19 mm	.748030
59	.041000	18	.169500	11/32	.343750	3/4	.750000
58	.042000	11/64	.171875	S	.348000	49/64	.765625
57	.043000	17	.173000	9. mm	.354330	19 1/2 mm	.767715
56	.046500	16	.177000	T	.358000	25/32	.781250
3/64	.046875	4.5 mm	.177165	23/64	.359375	20 mm	.787400
55	.052000	15	.180000	U	.368000	51/64	.796875
54	.055000	14	.182000	9.5 mm	.374015	20 1/2 mm	.807085
1.5 mm	.059055	13	.185000	3/8	.375000	13/16	.812500
53	.059500	3/16	.187500	V	.377000	21 mm	.826770
1/16	.062500	12	.189000	W	.386000	53/64	.828125
52	.063500	11	.191000	25/64	.390625	27/32	.843750
51	.067000	10	.193500	10 mm	.393700	21 1/2 mm	.846455
50	.070000	9	.196000	X	.397000	55/64	.859375
49	.073000	5. mm	.196850	Y	.404000	22 mm	.866140
48	.076000	8	.199000	13/32	.406250	7/8	.875000
5/64	.078125	7	.201000	Z	.413000	22 1/2 mm	.885825
47	.078500	13/64	.203125	10 1/2 mm	.413385	57/64	.890625
2. mm	.078740	6	.204000	27/64	.421875	23 mm	.905510
46	.081000	5	.205500	11 mm	.433070	29/32	.906250
45	.082000	4	.209000	7/16	.437500	59/64	.921875
44	.086000	3	.213000	11 1/2 mm	.452755	23 1/2 mm	.925195
43	.089000	5.5 mm	.216535	29/64	.453125	15/16	.937500
42	.093500	7/32	.218750	15/32	.468750	24 mm	.944880
3/32	.093750	2	.221000	12 mm	.472440	61/64	.953125
41	.096000	1	.228000	31/64	.484375	24 1/2 mm	.964565
40	.098000	A	.234000	12 1/2 mm	.492125	31/32	.968750
2.5 mm	.098425	15/64	.234375	1/2	.500000	25 mm	.984250
39	.099500	6. mm	.236220	13 mm	.511810	63/64	.984375
						1	1.000000

DIODE COLOR CODE

Crystal diodes can be marked according to the EIA color code, which is the same code used with resistors. The color bands start from the cathode end with the numbers following the 1N prefix. For example, the diode in the drawing is a 1N462.

There are a number of other ways of coding diodes. Some companies will use other letters and numbers. If you want to be sure of the code, use the reference catalog of the company that made the diode in question.

BLACK	0
BROWN	1
RED	2
ORANGE	3
YELLOW	4
GREEN	5
BLUE	6
VIOLET	7
GRAY	8
WHITE	9

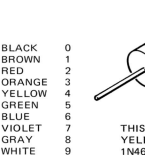

THIS EXAMPLE:
YELLOW 4 BLUE 6 RED 2
1N462

FREQUENCY BANDS

ABBREVIATION	DESCRIPTION	FREQUENCY
VLF	VERY LOW FREQUENCY	LESS THAN 30 kHz
LF	LOW FREQUENCY	30 TO 300 kHz
MF	MEDIUM FREQUENCY	300 TO 3000 kHz
HF	HIGH FREQUENCY	3 TO 30 MHz
VHF	VERY HIGH FREQUENCY	30 TO 300 MHz
UHF	ULTRA HIGH FREQUENCY	300 TO 3000 MHz
SHF	SUPER HIGH FREQUENCY	3 TO 30 GHz
EHF	EXTREMELY HIGH FREQUENCY	30 TO 300 GHz

METRIC PREFIXES

PREFIX	ABBREVIATION	MULTIPLE	
TERA	T	10^{12}	1,000,000,000,000
GIGA	G	10^{9}	1,000,000,000
MEGA	M	10^{6}	1,000,000
KILO	k	10^{3}	1000
HECTO	h	10^{2}	100
DEKA	da	10	10
DECI	d	10^{-1}	0.1
CENTI	c	10^{-2}	.01
MILLI	m	10^{-3}	.001
MICRO	μ	10^{-6}	.000001
NANO	n	10^{-9}	.000000001
PICO	p	10^{-12}	.000000000001

Reference Section

STANDARD ABBREVIATIONS

A	ampere	max	maximum
ac	alternating current	MHz	megahertz
AF	audio frequency	mega	one million
AFC	automatic frequency control	mmf	magnetomotive force
AGC	automatic gain control	μA	microampere
AM	amplitude modulation	μF	microfarad
b	base	μH	microhenry
c	capacitor, collector	$\mu\mu$F	micromicrofarad
C	Celsius, coulomb	μV	microvolt
CRT	cathode ray tube	mA	milliampere
CT	center tap	mH	millihenry
cw	continuous wave	mV	millivolt
dB	decibel	mW	milliwatt
dc	direct current	min	minimum
DPDT	double pole, double throw	MOSFET	metal oxide semiconductor field effect transistor
DPST	double pole, single throw		
DTL	diode transistor logic	NC	normally closed
e	emitter	NO	normally open
E	voltage	OP AMP	operational amplifier
emf	electromotive force	osc	oscillator or oscilloscope
f	frequency	P	power
F	Fahrenheit, farad	pF	picofarad
f_r	resonant frequency	PF	power factor
FET	field effect transistor	PIV	peak inverse voltage
FM	frequency modulation	pot	potentiometer
G	conductance	R	resistance or resistor
gnd	ground	RC	resistance capacitance
H	henry	rf	radio frequency
hf	high frequency	rms	root mean square
hp	horsepower	rpm	revolutions per minute
Hz	hertz	SCR	silicon controlled rectifier
I	current	SPDT	single pole, double throw
IC	integrated circuit	SPST	single pole, single throw
if	intermediate frequency	spkr	speaker
IGFET	insulated gate field effect transistor	sw	switch
JFET	junction field effect transistor	t	time
kHz	kilohertz	uhf	ultra high frequency
kΩ	kilohm	VOM	volt-ohm-milliammeter
kV	kilovolt	VTVM	vacuum tube voltmeter
KWH	kilowatt hour	V	volts
L	inductance	W	watts
LCR	inductance, capacitance, resistance	X	reactance
LED	light emitting diode	X_C	capacitive reactance
lf	low frequency	X_L	inductive reactance
M	mutual inductance	Z	impedance

Dictionary of Terms

A

Absolute Maximum Supply Voltage: The most voltage that can be applied to a circuit without the danger of causing permanent change to the characteristics of that circuit.

Absolute Minimum Resistance: The resistance between the wiper and the end terminal of a potentiometer when the wiper is moved to the point where you would expect to get the lowest resistance.

Absolute Temperature: Temperature measured from a point called absolute zero, usually defined as 0 K (Kelvin) or –273C (Celsius), 0 R (Rankine) or –460 deg. F (Fahrenheit).

Absolute Zero: (Same as above.)

AC (ac): Abbreviation for alternating current.

Accelerating Electrode: A conductor element in a cathode ray tube used to increase the speed of electrons or ions toward the anode.

Accelerator: A device used to give a high velocity to charged particles such as electrons or protons. It is used in scientific research to study the structure of the atom.

Acceptor: An impurity used in semiconductors. It accepts electrons from other atoms and creates what is called a "hole" in the structure of the crystal.

Acceptor Circuit: A circuit tuned to a single frequency or said to be "at resonance." Therefore, it will accept signals at the resonant frequency.

AC Circuit Breaker: A device used in an ac circuit to allow current flow and open the circuit when a fault occurs or an overload is put on the circuit.

AC Coupling: Connecting one ac circuit to another ac circuit by using a capacitor. This allows the ac passage but blocks the dc signals.

AC/DC (ac/dc): Equipment made so that it can be operated from either an ac or a dc power source.

AC Generator: A device called an "alternator," used to change mechanical energy to alternating current.

Achromatic: A term used to mean black and white television.

AC Power Supply: One which gives an ac output voltage. Some may give a whole range of ac output voltages from which you can choose.

AC Transducer: A device which is activated by an ac signal or produces an ac signal. In the case of an ac input, the output could be some other form of energy such as pressure or light. These same things, pressure or light, could be used as inputs to produce the ac signal output.

Adapter: A device used to change a receptacle, such as a plug, so that it can be used in another way. For example, an adapter which allows a sander with two prongs and a ground to be plugged into an outlet which does not have a ground outlet.

Address: A way of telling the specific location on a tape or drum of a computer so that a piece of information can be located in the storage memory.

Adjacent Channel: The frequency band just above or below the one to which you refer.

Adjustable Resistor: One which has the resistance wire partly exposed so that the user can move the lug from one position to another when a different resistance value is needed.

ADP: Abbreviation for automatic data processing.

AF: Abbreviation for audio frequency.

Aging: Applying a voltage to devices such as capacitors, diodes, etc., until their characteristics level off to a constant value.

AIEE: Abbreviation for American Institute of Electrical Engineers.

Air Capacitor: One in which air is the insulating material between its plates.

ALGOL: Short for ALGOrithmic Language in computer language.

Align: To adjust tuned circuits so that you get the maximum signal response.

Alkaline Cell: One that uses an electrolyte that gives the cell more capacity than the standard zinc-carbon cell. Electrolyte is potassium hydroxide.

Alligator Clip: A spring-loaded metal clip used to make temporary electrical connections.

Alnico: An alloy made from ALuminum, NIckle, CObalt and iron, used in making magnets.

Alpha: The emitter-to-collector current gain of a transistor. It is taken from the Greek letter α.

Alpha Cutoff Frequency: Frequency at which the current gain of the transistor drops to 0.707 of its maximum gain.

Alpha Particle: An electrically charged particle given off by many radioactive materials.

Alternating Current (ac): A flow of electrons which regularly reverses its direction of flow.

Alternator: A device used to convert mechanical energy into electrical energy in the form of an alternating current.

Alumina: A ceramic used as substrates (supporting material) in thin film circuits. It is used because it can withstand high temperatures and has little effect on the circuit.

AM: Abbreviation for amplitude modulation.

American Standard Code for Information Interchange (ASCII): A number code assigned to each of the keys of the computer.

Ammeter: An instrument used to measure current in ac or dc circuits.

Ammeter Shunt: A low resistance conductor placed in parallel with the meter movement to avoid possible damage to meter when measuring high currents.

Amp: Abbreviation for ampere.

Ampere (A): The unit of measure for current based on the flow of one coulomb per second past a given point. Also, one volt across one ohm of resistance causes a flow of one ampere.

Ampere-Hour: A current of one ampere flowing for one hour. It is a term used to tell the amount of energy a battery can give before it has to be recharged.

Ampere-Turn: Unit used to describe the magnetomotive force produced by a coil. It is found by multiplying the number of turns of wire in the coil by the current flowing in the coil.

Amplification: A term used to describe the increase in current or voltage from one side to the other side of a device. A transistor, for example, can amplify (increase) the current from base to collector.

Amplifier: A device that takes a small input signal and converts it to a much larger output signal.

Amplitude: The amount of change in a quantity, such as a sine wave.

Amplitude Modulation (AM): A way of changing the waveform of a signal by impressing it on a carrier frequency. This is done so that it is possible to have different radio stations broadcast at different frequencies and not have them all found at one point on a dial.

AM Receiver: A device used to change amplitude modulate signals into audio frequencies.

Analog Computer: An automatic electronic calculating machine where both the input and output signals are constantly varying, such as measuring the amount of rotation, temperature change, speed change, etc. (as opposed to a digital computer).

AND Circuit: An electronic circuit where all the inputs must be present to get an output.

Angle of Deflection: The amount that an electron beam in a cathode ray tube is bent with respect to its normal position.

Angle of Lag: The angle between the voltage and current vectors of an ac circuit.

Angstrom: Unit of measurement for the wavelength of light. It is equal to one ten thousandth of a micron.

Annealing: Process of heating material, such as copper, and cooling it so that it becomes softer.

Anode: The positive electrode or terminal.

Anode Terminal: The terminal of a diode that is positive with respect to the other terminal (cathode) when it is forward biased.

Antenna: Part of a radio receiver used to "catch" the radio waves from the transmitter or from space. In the case of the transmitter, it is that part which is used to radiate the signal into space.

Antenna Cores: Ferrite cores used for radio antennas.

Antimagnetic: Material that will not remain in the magnetic state, such as copper, brass and other nonferrous alloys.

Apparent Power: The product of the current times the voltage in a circuit where the two reach their peaks at different times.

Appliance: Equipment used in the home, such as radios, television sets, toasters and dryers.

Arc: An electrical discharge between two points having different electrical potentials.

Armature: The moving part of a motor or generator, and the vibrating part of a buzzer or relay.

Armature Wire: Soft wire used for winding coils.

Armored Cable: Two or more insulated wires inside a flexible metal covering, protecting them from damage.

ASA: Abbreviation for American Standards Association.

Asbestos: An insulating material.

Assembly: The complete unit made up of various individual parts.

Astable: Not stable. A device that has two states and constantly alternates between them, usually at some specific rate.

Astable Multivibrator: A circuit that switches back and forth between two stable states.

Atmospheric Noise: The crackle heard in radio reception caused by atmospheric interference.

Atom: The smallest particle that makes up an element.

Atomic Fission: Splitting the nucleus of an atom of material such as uranium.

Atomic Number: The number of protons in the nucleus of an atom.

Atomic Weight: The weight of the protons and neutrons in the nucleus of an atom.

Attenuation: The drop in amplitude of a signal from one point to another during its transmission.

Attenuator: A network of resistors that reduces the amplitude of a signal without too much change in the frequency.

Audible: Sound that can be heard by the human ear.

Audio: Frequencies from 20 to 20,000 hertz, which is roughly the range that can be heard by the human ear.

Audio Frequency (AF): The number of complete cycles per second within the range that can be heard by the human ear.

Audio Frequency Transformer: An iron core electrical device used to transfer signals from one circuit to another or for impedance matching.

Automatic Circuit Breaker: A device used to open a circuit automatically when an overload occurs. It can be reset manually after the problem is fixed.

Automatic Frequency Control (AFC): A circuit that automatically maintains the frequency of an oscillator within certain limits

Automatic Gain Control (AGC): A circuit which maintains the output volume of a receiver even though the strength of the signal it receives is always changing.

Automation: A method of automatically controlling machines in the manufacturing process, without having people involved.

Autotransformer: An electrical device with only one winding that acts as both the primary and secondary circuit to step up or step down the voltage.

Auxiliary Circuit: A circuit which is not the main circuit.

Avalanche: A condition where the current in the reverse direction builds up very quickly as electrons flow past a junction.

Avalanche Breakdown: The rapid passing of electrons through a diode in the reverse biased direction, but usually without ruining the diode.

Avalanche Diode: A diode that has the ability to break down in the reverse direction when a specified point is reached. For this reason, it is often used to regulate voltage. A zener diode.

Average Voltage: Value of alternating current or voltage of a sine wave found by dividing the area from 0 to 180 deg. of one cycle by the distance along the X axis. It is equal to 0.637 times E_{max}.

Avionics: Short way of saying AVIation electrONICS.

AWG: Abbreviation for American Wire Gage which is a way of measuring the diameter of wire.

Axial Leads: Leads coming out of the ends of a resistor or capacitor rather than out from the side of the device.

B

B: The symbol for the base of a transistor.

Back to Back: When two semiconductors are connected in opposite directions to control current without rectifying it. One semiconductor conducts for one half cycle, the second conducts for the other half cycle.

Backup: Making a copy of a computer program or file for use in the event of failure of original file or disk.

Balance: A way to control the volume from each speaker in a stereo system.

Balanced Bridge: A circuit that is adjusted so that its output voltage is zero.

Balanced Circuit: One which has both sides electrically balanced to some reference point.

Ballast Resistor: A resistor in series with the load used to keep the current constant even though the line voltage is changing.

Banana Jack: A socket which will take a special plug shaped like a banana yet make a good electrical connection.

Banana Plug: A male connector that fits into a banana jack.

Band: A part or range of frequencies which falls between two defined limits.

Band Elimination Filter: A filter that passes frequencies on either side of the band, but not the one which it is designed to stop.

Band Pass Filter: A filter that will pass one band yet decreases inputs of a higher or lower frequency.

Band Reject Filter: See Band Elimination Filter.

Bandwidth: The frequency limits of a given waveband for transmitting a modulated signal.

Bare Conductor: A wire not covered with any insulation.

Bar Magnet: A piece of metal in the shape of a bar which holds its magnetism.

Barrier: Something which acts as an insulator between circuits or prevents the flow of electrons. In some cases, it will act as a block to the passage of electrons until they reach a certain level.

Barrier Voltage: The minimum potential difference necessary to cause current flow through a PN junction.

Base: The control region of a transistor, which blocks or allows flow between the emitter and collector.

Basic Input/Output System (BIOS): Used as the interface between an operating system and the software so it can access the hardware of the computer.

Bass: The low audio frequency sound range.

Batch Process: A way of making groups of resistors, capacitors, etc., at the same time.

Bat Handle: The lever on a toggle switch, which is shaped like a baseball bat.

Battery: Two or more cells connected to deliver a dc voltage.

Battery Acid: The electrolyte in a storage battery.

Battery Charger: Device used to take the ac from an outlet and convert it to dc for increasing the charge of a storage battery.

Baud Rate: Speed of transmission for computer information being sent over phone lines.

Beam: Electromagnetic radiation concentrated so that it is focused in one direction.

Beam Current: That part of the electron stream that is focused on the screen of a cathode ray tube.

Beat: The rhythmic increase and decrease of amplitude which result from the combination of two waves at different frequencies.

Beat Frequency: A frequency produced when two different frequencies are combined. There are two beat frequencies. One is equal to the difference between them. The other is the sum of the two frequencies.

Bell Transformer: A small iron core transformer used to step down the primary voltage to operate doorbells and chimes.

Bench Test: A test conducted in a shop or laboratory rather than in the home.

Beta: The Greek letter β, used to specify the current gain from base to collector in a transistor.

Beta Particle: An electrical charge given off by radioactive material.

Bias: Voltage applied to a transistor or diode to block passage or allow the flow of electrons in the device.

Bias Current: The current through the base-emitter junction of a transistor used to set its operating point.

Bidirectional Antenna: One which has a maximum response in only two directions.

Bimetallic Strip: A strip formed by welding two dissimilar metals together. It is often used in temperature sensing.

Binary: A numbering system that uses only the numbers 0 and 1.

Binary Code: System using 0 and 1 or OFF and ON as a code.

Binary Digit (Bit): In the binary numbering system, a character which is either a 0 or a 1.

Binding Post: A device used for making electrical connections.

Bistable Multivibrator (Flip Flop): A circuit that has two stable states and can be switched back and forth.

Bit: Abbreviation for binary digit.

Bits Per Second (bps): A measure of the speed of data transfer such as that of a modem.

Black Box: A method used to describe a circuit where you only want to know about its inputs and outputs but are not concerned about how and what makes up the individual parts of the circuit.

Bleeder Resistor: A resistor used to discharge a capacitor after its circuit has been deenergized, to stabilize voltages or to draw a fixed amount of current.

Block Diagram: A way of showing how a circuit acts by representing its parts in blocks and explaining them, instead of using the components of the circuit.

Blocking: Putting a high voltage bias on a transistor to stop current from flowing.

Blow: The act of opening a circuit, usually because of too high a current.

Boot-up: The internal loading process at start-up of the computer.

Braided Wire: A wire made up of many strands that are woven together.

Breadboard: To put the components together on a temporary circuit so that it can be checked before soldering.

Breakdown Voltage: The voltage that causes a big change in the characteristics of a diode.

Bridge Rectifier: Using four rectifiers to convert ac to full wave rectified dc.

Broadcast Band: The band of frequencies from 535 to 1700 kilohertz from which AM radio stations broadcast.

Brush: A piece of graphite or carbon used to make the electrical connection on the commutator of a motor.

Bulk Eraser: A piece of equipment used to degauss or erase the magnetic fields that are found on a piece of audio tape or video tape.

Bus Bar: A heavy copper plate or bar usually used in factories to carry high current or to provide a common connection between three or more circuits.

Button: A container that holds the granules in a carbon microphone.

BX Cable: A flexible metal tube which houses two or more pieces of insulated wire.

Bypass Capacitor: One which provides a low impedance ac path around some part of the circuit.

Bypass Filter: One which provides a low attenuation path around some part of the circuit.

Byte: Eight bits.

C

C: The symbol for a capacitor, carbon or coulomb.

Cable: Two or more conductors insulated from one another, but in the same covering.

Calibrate: To set up a piece of equipment by comparing it to some standard (something with a known fixed value).

Call Letters: A fixed set of letters assigned to transmitting stations by the government.

Cannibalization: Taking parts off a similar piece of equipment so that at least one piece can be kept in operation.

Capacitance: The electrical characteristic which permits the storage of electrical energy in the electrostatic field between two conductors. The amount of charge that can be stored by a capacitor as measured in farads.

Capacitive Reactance: Opposition to any change in voltage between two conductors having capacitance. It is measured by the formula X_c equals $\frac{1}{2}\pi fc$.

Capacitor: Two conductors separated by an insulator or dielectric used to store an electrical charge.

Capacitor Start Motor: An induction motor that has a capacitor wired in series with its windings for easier starting.

Capstan: A part of a tape recorder used to pull the tape at a constant speed so the recording and playback speeds are always constant.

Carbon: A black material used in resistors and brushes because of its special ability to conduct electricity.

Carrier Wave: A single frequency wave which when it is modulated by a transmitting station is used to send information over the air.

Cartridge: The removable part of a phonograph pickup.

Cartridge Fuse: A glass covered fuse with metallic ends for connecting it in the circuit you wish to protect.

Cathode: The general name for any negative electrode such as the negative side of a diode or electrical cell.

Cathode Ray Tube (CRT): A tube used in television sets and oscilloscopes where the electron beam is capable of being deflected to produce a visible pattern.

CATV: Abbreviation for community antenna television.

Cat Whisker: A small pointed wire used to make contact on the surface of a semiconductor.

CCW: Abbreviation for counterclockwise.

CDI: Abbreviation for capacitive discharge ignition.

Cell: A single power unit, such as those used in flashlights, which will produce electrical energy to supply power to operate a circuit.

Celsius Scale: Temperature scale based on water freezing at 0 C and boiling at 100 C. It is also called the "centigrade scale."

Center Tap: An electrical connection in the center of a resistor or winding of a transformer.

Central Processing Unit (CPU): Unit that controls all the operations of the computer. Also called the microprocessor.

Ceramic: An insulating material capable of withstanding high temperatures.

Characteristic Curve: A graph showing how the values change for some component or circuit.

Charge: The amount of electrical energy stored in a capacitor or battery.

Charged Particle: An extremely small piece of matter which has a negative or positive electrical charge such as an ion, electron or proton.

Charger: A device used to change ac to dc for the purpose of increasing the electrical charge of a battery.

Chassis: The framework, such as a sheet metal box, upon which components are mounted or attached in building an electrical circuit.

Chassis Ground: An electrical connection to the metal frame or chassis that holds the circuit.

Chatter: The unwanted and repeated opening and closing of electrical contacts.

Chip: A single piece of material on which all the parts of an integrated circuit are found.

Choke: An inductor.

Choke Coil: An inductor used to limit the flow of alternating current.

Chopper: A device used to interrupt a beam of light at regular intervals.

Circle Cutter: A tool used to cut holes in a panel or chassis.

Circuit: An electrical path having a power source, load and conductors to carry current.

Circuit Breaker: A device that automatically opens a circuit when its current carrying ability has been exceeded.

Circular Mil: The cross-sectional area of a round wire having a diameter of 0.001 in.

Closed Loop: A circuit where the output is being fed back to the input. In this way, the output can be constantly compared and checked so that changes can be made automatically.

CMOS: Integrated circuit that keeps track of all the settings of the computer such as date, time, amount of RAM and other elements.

Coaxial Cable: A transmission wire completely surrounded by a second wire, which is insulated from the first. This is done so that the inner wire is protected from external magnetic fields.

Coil: Wrapping a number of turns of wire on a coil form or an iron core.

Coil Form: An insulating support for a coil, made from plastic, paper or other insulating material.

Cold: Another way of saying that the circuit is disconnected or that the wire is not carrying current.

Collector: One of the leads on a transistor.

Collector Junction: The point between the collector and base of a transistor.

Color Code: A way to identify the value of components by reading the color patches on the body of the component in a specified order.

Common Base Amplifier: A transistor amplifier where the base is common to both the input and output circuits.

Common Collector Amplifier: A transistor amplifier where the collector is common to both the input and output circuits.

Common Emitter Amplifier: A transistor amplifier where the emitter is common to both the input and output circuits.

Commutation: A method of converting ac to dc in a generator by using a pick off system that will reverse itself every half cycle.

Commutator: A group of bars providing connections between armature coils and brushes.

Compact Disk Read Only Memory (CD-ROM): A digital information storage device consisting of platter etched to create pits and lands to hold data.

Comparison Bridge: A special circuit used to balance voltage by means of a four-part circuit arrangement that will give a zero error signal when balance exists.

Component: A single part used in a circuit or a series of parts that are considered to work together as a piece of the complete circuit.

Component Layout: Method of placing all parts to be used in the circuit on a chassis to make them fit and work the best possible way.

Computer: An automatic electronic machine that performs calculations.

Computer-Aided Design (CAD): Computerized system used to create or modify a plan or design.

Computer-Integrated Manufacturing (CIM): A system that uses machines and computers working together to create the desired product.

Condenser: Term used by auto mechanics for a capacitor.

Conductor: Any item or material which is used to carry current; a wire.

Conduit: Specially built tubing used to hold wire and protect it from damage.

Connection: The point where two or more wires or components are tied together electrically.

Connector: A device used to make a mechanical or electrical connection.

Constant: A fixed value that does not change.

Constant Voltage Power Supply: A power supply which is regulated so that the voltage does not change when it is loaded.

Contact: A current-carrying part of a switch or relay that is capable of opening and closing to allow current flow.

Contact Bounce: Repeated opening and closing of relay contacts when they should be closed. This is caused by springs and is similar to the bouncing of a rubber ball on a floor.

Continuity: An unbroken path for electron flow.

Continuity Test: An electrical check to see if a part of the circuit has a completed path for electron flow.

Convergence: Focusing the electron beams of a cathode ray tube to a single point.

Copper Losses: Heat losses or I^2R losses in motors, generators and transformers that result from the resistance of the copper wire.

Core: The magnetic material inside a relay, coil or transformer used to increase the strength of the magnetic field. Also magnetic material inside coils of an electromagnet.

Coulomb: The quantity of electricity that will flow past a point in a circuit as measured in one second when the current is maintained at one ampere. It is also represented by 6.24×10^{18} electrons.

CPS: Abbreviation for cycles per second, now known as hertz.

Crash: Term used to describe the mechanical or electrical failure of a hard drive on a computer.

Crimp: To crush a connector around a wire to make an electrical connection.

Crossover: The point on a print where two conductors insulated from one another pass each other.

CRT: Abbreviation for cathode ray tube.

Crystal: A piece of material that will vibrate at one special frequency determined by the way it is cut. It is used in certain types of radio work.

Crystal Diode: A diode formed by a small semiconductor crystal and cat whisker. They form the PN junction of the diode.

Current: The flow of electrons through a conductor, measured in amperes.

Current Amplification: Ratio of current at output to current at input. Amplification takes place when the ratio is greater than 1, which tells you that the output is higher.

Current Density: The amount of current that passes through a given cross-sectional area.

Current Limiting Resistor: A resistor put in a circuit to limit the current to some specified value.

Cutoff: The point where the emitter base junction of a transistor is reverse biased or has zero bias, and there is no collector current.

Cycle: The change in an alternating wave from zero to a positive peak to zero to a negative peak and back to zero. This is the sine wave normally seen for an ac cycle.

D

Dampen: To progressively lower the amplitude.

Dampening: A method of making the pointer on a meter come to rest instead of overshooting the value of the reading and constantly going back and forth until it finally stops.

D'Arsonval Movement: A meter where the movement is supported on jeweled bearings between the poles of a permanent magnet. When current is passed through the movement, a pointer attached to a small spring will rotate to indicate the amount being measured.

dB: Abbreviation for decibel.

DC Transducer: A device that will convert a mechanical signal into a dc output.

DCWV: Abbreviation for direct current working voltage. It is the rating found on capacitors which tells the maximum continuous voltage that can be applied.

Dead: Said of a part of a circuit that is not carrying current. This term applies to a circuit that usually carries current.

Dead Short: A path for current which bypasses the load and, therefore, has almost no resistance and very high current.

Debug: To troubleshoot and correct problems in a piece of equipment when it is first being set up.

Decade Box: A box that contains a group of precision resistors, capacitors or coils wired to a series of switches for use in substituting many values in circuits. It is used for temporary connections into circuits.

Decay: A slow drop in the value of a quantity.

Deci: A prefix which means one-tenth.

Decibel: A unit to give the relative increase or decrease in power.

Decimal Code: A code which uses a scale of numbers from 0 to 9.

Decimal to Binary: Changing a decimal code number written in a scale from 0 to 9 to a binary code number which uses a scale of 0 to 1.

Decoupling Network: A group of chokes, resistors and/or capacitors placed in some circuits to stop them from harmful coupling between one another.

De-energize: To disconnect a device from its power supply.

Deflection: To bend the electron beam in a cathode ray tube so that it gives a pattern on the face of the tube.

Deflection Plates: Two pairs of parallel electrodes inside a cathode ray tube used to change the electron beam in either a horizontal or vertical direction.

Degausser: A device used to demagnetize taped signals. Also, another device found in television sets to reduce magnetic fields which are not wanted because of the effect they have on the picture tube.

Degradation: The gradual lowering of quality.

Delta Connection: The terminal connections in a three phase electrical system which are in the shape of a triangle similar to the Greek letter delta.

Demodulator: A device used to separate the original wave which was joined to a carrier wave for purposes of transmitting.

Depletion Region: The region in a reverse biased semiconductor where there is a lack of electrons and holes at its junction.

Depolarization: A way of removing the hydrogen gas bubbles that try to form inside a primary cell.

Derate: To reduce the rating of the voltage, current or power of a device so that its reliability will be improved when subjected to higher temperatures.

Detector Probe: A device used with a vacuum tube voltmeter or oscilloscope to analyze the signals of certain waves.

Detune: To change the value of a tuned capacitor or inductor that was at the resonant frequency.

Diac: A two-lead alternating current semiconductor that will conduct when its breakdown voltage is reached. It has properties of both diodes and transistors.

Diagram: A schematic or print used to show the function or sequence of a circuit.

Dicing: The process used to saw a formed crystal wafer into blanks.

Dielectric: The insulating material between the plates of a capacitor.

Difference in Potential: The voltage difference between two points in a circuit.

Differential Amplifier: A special circuit that will work when there is a difference between the two voltages or currents at the inputs to two transistors.

Diffused Junction: A junction formed in a semiconductor by adding impurities at a high temperature.

Diffusion: A way of adding impurities such as boron and arsenic to a semiconductor material by using heat and special containers so that it can be controlled to very small values.

Digital Computer: A device which operates on, and records in terms of, numbers which are represented by a series of pulses.

Digital Voltmeter: A meter which gives voltage readouts in numbers instead of by means of a pointer moving on a scale.

Diode: A semiconductor device that has a PN junction. Usually, it is thought of as allowing electron flow in one direction and blocking flow from the other direction. However, there are some special types which do not work that way.

Diode Transistor Logic (DTL): A type of circuit that uses diodes as inputs to control or activate the transistor outputs.

DIP: Abbreviation for dual in-line package, a type of integrated circuit.

Dip Soldering: A way of soldering the bottom of a printed circuit by floating it on a molten pool of solder. This method is used when the components have been mounted on the top.

Direct Current (dc): The flow of electrons in only one direction.

Direct Current Generator: A device that converts mechanical energy into dc electrical energy. Brushes pick up energy from a rotating armature.

Discharge: The release of energy stored in a battery or a capacitor.

Disconnect: To unplug or break the power to an electrical circuit.

Discrete Component: Parts such as resistors, capacitors, etc., which are made up prior to being installed into circuits or on printed circuit boards.

Disk Operating System (DOS): Commands and files for IBM computer designed to provide the messages that tell the computer how to perform its functions.

Display: The visual part of a signal seen on the cathode ray tube.

Dissipation: Losing electrical energy in the form of heat.

Distortion: The unwanted change in a signal caused by some outside source.

Donor: The impurities added to semiconductors because they give up electrons.

Dope: To add impurities to semiconductors in a controlled way.

Double Pole Double Throw Switch (DPDT): A switch with two terminals that can be connected to one of two other pairs of terminals, depending on how it is thrown.

DPDT: Abbreviation for double pole, double throw switch.

Double Pole Single Throw Switch (DPST): A switch with two terminals that can be connected to or disconnected from another pair of terminals, depending on how it is thrown.

DPST: Abbreviation for double pole, single throw switch.

Drain: The part of a field effect transistor which corresponds to the collector of a transistor.

Drift: The unwanted change in the voltage of a power supply over a period of time.

Dry Cell: A cell which produces electricity through chemical means. It is commonly called a "battery."

DTL: Abbreviation for diode transistor logic.

Duplex: Two-in-one, such as two wires in one cable, two receptacles in one outlet, or transmitting and receiving at the same time.

Duty Cycle: The amount of time a device is "on," as opposed to the time it is "off" or in idle condition.

DV/DT: Actually: $\Delta V / \Delta t$; the change in voltage with respect to time.

Dynamometer: A device used to measure the power output or a rotating machine.

E

E: The symbol for electromotive force. Also, the symbol for the emitter of a transistor.

E Core: The shape of the laminations used in building some types of transformers.

Eddy Currents: Currents that are induced in a body. In transformers, these currents usually circulate in the iron and copper windings and produce unwanted heat.

Edison Base: The screw base used for electric lamps.

Effective Value: In ac sine wave voltages, it is 0.707 times the peak value and is the heat equivalent of the same amount of dc. Also see RMS.

Efficiency: The ratio of the output of a device to its input.

EHF: Abbreviation for extremely high frequency.

EIA: Abbreviation for Electronic Industries Association.

Electric Eye: Another way of saving photoelectric cell.

Electric Motor: A device used to convert electrical energy into rotating mechanical energy.

Electrical Discharge Machining: A way of removing metal from a part with a controlled spark in a dielectric.

Electrical Load: A device which is the resistive part of a circuit.

Electrical Noise: Unwanted electrical energy in a circuit, usually caused by some other source.

Electrode: A part of a battery. Also, a piece of metal used in electroplating. A terminal of an electrical component that gets an electrical signal into or out of that component.

Electrolyte: The paste in a dry cell. Also, the fluid in a storage battery or material found in an electrolytic capacitor.

Electrolytic Capacitor: A capacitor made with an aluminum positive plate, electrolyte as a negative plate and a thin oxide layer on the aluminum as the dielectric. Its great advantage is larger capacitance from a smaller package.

Electromagnet: A temporary magnet which has magnetism only when current is passing through a coil of wire.

Electromagnetic Induction: Electromotive force is generated in a conductor as an expanding and collapsing magnetic field causing electrons to flow.

Electromotive Force (emf): The force that causes electricity to flow because a difference in potential exists between two points.

Electron: A negatively charged particle which orbits the nucleus of an atom.

Electron Beam: A narrow stream of electrons forced to move in a certain direction.

Electron Microscope: An electrical instrument used to magnify a sample of a material over 300,000 times larger so that you can see how it is made up.

Electronic Flash: A source of controlled light used by photographers to take pictures. Commonly called a "strobe."

Electronic Industries Association (EIA): A trade association in the electronics industry.

Electroplate: A method used to deposit a thin layer of metal on the surface of an object.

Electroscope: An apparatus with gold leaves used to demonstrate charges.

Electrostatic Charge: The electric charge stored by a capacitor.

Element: A substance that cannot be divided into simpler substances by chemical means. It is composed of protons, electrons and neutrons.

emf: Abbreviation for electromotive force.

Emitter (E): The lead of a transistor shown with the arrowhead on it.

Empirical: Information that can be found by actual measurement or observation.

Encapsulation: The protective coating of plastic put around fragile electrical and electronic components.

Energized: Connected to a source of voltage. Also, called "hot" or "live" by many people.

Energy: That which is capable of producing work.

Energy Conversion: To change energy from one form to another.

Entrance Cable: The large power line that brings electricity into a building from an outside power line.

Epitaxial Process: A method by which semiconductor devices are made by depositing a thin layer of single crystal material on a substrate (supporting material). This is done by using a vapor and controlling both the resistance and thickness of the material being deposited.

Equivalent Circuit: A way of taking a complicated circuit and finding out what it is like in a simpler, more easy to understand version that is the same electrically.

Etched Printed Circuit: A way of making printed circuits by using a chemical to dissolve the copper from a specially made insulating board.

Excitation Current: The current caused by applying voltage to the field windings of a motor.

Exothermic: Heat being produced, usually the result of a chemical reaction.

Exponent: A mathematical symbol which indicates the power of a given number.

Extremely High Frequency (EHF): The range of frequencies from 30 to 300 gigahertz (10^9).

F

F: Symbol for a fuse. Also, abbreviation for Fahrenheit and farad.

Face: The front part of a meter that shows the readings.

Fade: The very slow lowering of a signal's amplitude.

Fahnestock Clip: A spring device used for making temporary connections in electrical circuits.

Failure Rate: The average number of parts that will fail in a given period of time.

Farad (F): The unit of capacitance that is the result of a charge of one coulomb producing a difference in potential of one volt.

Fault: A defect or break in a line. Also, a problem with an electrical circuit.

FCC: Abbreviation for Federal Communications Commission, a body which regulates all electrical communication systems in the United States.

Feedback: Transferring voltage from the output of a circuit back to its input. Also, information being fed back to the source.

Female: The recessed part of a device into which another part (male) fits.

Ferrite: An iron type material used for cores because it is easy to magnetize and it demagnetizes very rapidly.

Ferrite Antenna: An antenna found in radios. Its coil is wound around a ferrite core.

FET: Abbreviation for field effect transistor.

Field Effect Transistor (FET): A semiconductor device that conducts from one terminal called the "source" to another terminal called the "drain" when a voltage is applied to a third terminal called a "gate."

Field Magnets: Electromagnets used to make up the magnetic field of motors, generators and other electrical devices.

File Allocation Table (FAT): The internal memory map of where all the files are stored on the computer's hard drive.

File Server: Master computer used in a network application.

Film Resistor: A resistor made from a very thin layer (film) of material deposited on an insulated form.

Filters: Circuit networks made from resistors, capacitors and inductors. They are used to block or reduce the amplitude of specific bands of frequencies.

Finite: Having a fixed limit.

Fishpaper: An insulating paper used to wrap coils and transformer windings or other conductors which are close together to protect against a possible short.

Fission: Splitting the nucleus of an atom.

Flat Pack: A rectangular integrated circuit in a flat package.

Flip Flop: A multivibrator circuit having two stable states and the signal is switched back and forth between them.

Floating: A condition when a device is not grounded.

Floppy Disk: A portable source for saving and reading information on a computer.

Floppy Drive: The slot on a computer in which floppy disks can be inserted for purposes of writing and reading information.

Flux: A material used in soldering to clean the surface of any oxide so that a good connection will result.

Flux Density: Number of lines of flux per cross-sectional area of a magnetic circuit.

FM Band: The band of frequencies from 88 to 108 MHz.

Format: The process of aligning all the magnetic particles on a computer disk prior to saving data to that disk.

Forward Bias: The voltage applied to a PN junction so that it conducts.

Free Electrons: Electrons that circulate among the atoms of a substance without being tied to any particular atom.

Frequency: The number of complete cycles per second as measured in hertz.

Frequency Modulation (FM): A system of radio transmission where the amplitude of the carrier remains constant but the frequency is varied.

Fuse: An electrical device put in a circuit to protect against overloading. Current above the rating of the fuse will melt the fusible link and open the circuit.

Fusestat: Trade name for a time delay fuse.

Fusetron: A fuse that allows short periodic overloads without blowing.

G

Gain: The ratio of the output ac voltage to the input ac voltage. Common examples also include current gain or power gain.

Galvanometer: A meter used to measure very small amounts of current.

Ganged Capacitors: Two or more variable capacitors mounted on the same shaft and varied by turning one knob.

Gate: One of the leads on a FET or SCR. Normally used to control current through the device when it is properly biased.

Gauss: Unit of measure for magnetic flux density equal to one line of magnetic flux per square centimetre.

Generator: A device used to convert rotating mechanical energy into electrical energy.

Germanium Diode: A two terminal semiconductor device made from germanium (a brittle, grayish-white metallic element).

Gigahertz (GHz): A term used to represent 10^9 cycles per second.

Graticule: A calibrated screen placed at the face of a cathode ray tube of an oscilloscope for measuring purposes.

Grid Dip Meter: A test instrument for use in measuring resonant frequencies, detecting harmonics and checking relative field strength of signals.

Grommet: A rubber washer used to prevent a wire from touching exposed metal on a chassis.

Ground: The voltage reference point in a circuit.

Growler: A device used to locate short-circuited coils by setting up a magnetic field. It makes a growling noise when a short is present.

H

H: Symbol for Henry.

Half Adder: Integrated circuit used for processing data using in counting on a computer.

Half Cycle: The interval required for the travel of 180 deg. on a sine wave.

Half Wave Rectification: A pulsating dc produced by passing only one half of a sine wave.

Ham: An amateur radio operator.

Hard Drive: Storage area for data or files used with a computer.

Harmonic Frequency: A frequency which is a multiple of a fundamental frequency.

Harness: Wires and cables which are tied together for easier handling.

Heat Loss: The loss of electrical energy in the form of heat.

Heat Shrink: A type of tubing placed over bare wire for insulation. It will shrink in diameter when heat is applied to it.

Heat Sink: A metal base on which semiconductor devices are mounted to help dissipate heat. Also, a device used when soldering components to stop them from overheating. It usually is placed between the component and the joint being soldered.

Henry (H): The unit of measure for inductance. A coil has one henry of inductance if an EMF of one volt is induced when the current through the inductor is changing at the rate of one ampere per second.

Hertz (Hz): The unit of measure for frequency which is equal to one cycle per second.

Heterodyne: The process of combining two signals of different frequencies to obtain two other frequencies: the sum frequency and the difference frequency.

High Fidelity (Hi-Fi): The sound output of an amplifier and loudspeaker combination, which is a reasonably true reproduction of the quality of the original sound.

High Frequency (HF): The frequency band from 3 to 30 megahertz.

High Tension: Wires carrying voltages as high as several thousand volts.

High Voltage Probe: A probe used for measuring high voltages. Therefore, it has a high internal resistance.

Hipot: A device which has high voltages and is used for testing insulation breakdown or leakage of transformers.

Hole Flow: The idea that a positive charge carrier in a P type material will attract electrons which, when combined, will form new holes. It is similar to the idea that a flow of positive charges will exist in a semiconductor.

Hollerith Code: The code used when holes are punched into an 80 column card. The holes represent numbers and letters for use in keypunch machines.

Hologram: A way of recording three dimensional images on a two dimensional film plate through the use of lasers.

Hood: The shield placed over the front of an oscilloscope to make it easier to see the image on the CRT.

Horsepower (hp): The unit of power equal to 746 watts: 33,000 ft. lb. per minute or 550 ft. lb. per second.

Host Mode: Modem setup so that another computer can call in on phone lines for the purpose of sharing its files and data.

Hot: Connected to a source of power; energized.

hp: Abbreviation for horsepower.

Hybrid: A circuit made up of thin film and discrete integrated circuits.

Hydroelectric: Producing electricity by water power.

Hydrometer: A device used to measure the specific gravity of the electrolyte in a storage battery.

Hysteresis Loop: A curve used to show flux density when the magnetic force is increased and decreased.

I

I: Symbol for current. Also, abbreviation for indicator.

IC: Abbreviation for integrated circuit.

IEEE: Abbreviation for Institute of Electrical and Electronic Engineers.

IF: Abbreviation for intermediate frequency.

IGFET: Abbreviation for insulated gate field effect transistor.

Impedance: The total opposition which a circuit offers to the flow of alternating current at a given frequency. It is the combination of resistance and reactance.

Impregnated Coils: Coils of wire completely covered with electrical varnish or epoxy to protect them from vibration and moisture.

Impurity: Material such as boron or arsenic which is added to semiconductor material in order to make P and N material.

Increment: A small change in the value of something.

Induced Current: Current which flows in a conductor because of a changing magnetic field.

Inductance: That property of a circuit or device which opposes any change in current through it. Its symbol is L.

Inductive Reactance: The opposition of an inductor to a changing current. Its symbol is X_L.

Infinity: A number larger than any other number which can possibly exist. Its symbol is ∞.

Input: The current, voltage or power applied to a circuit.

Insulated Gate Field Effect Transistor (IGFET): A specially made diffused transistor which has very high input impedance and an insulated gate.

Insulated Wire: A conductor covered with any nonconducting material.

Integrated Circuit (IC): A circuit made from transistors, resistors, etc., all placed in a package smaller than the traditional transistor and sometimes called a "chip."

Interference: Any disturbance, natural or otherwise, that interferes with the reception of signals.

Interlock Circuit: A circuit which will not activate until after one or more other actions have taken place. Often, these actions are made to occur in a certain sequence by means of relays. This prevents accidental activation of the circuit.

Intermediate Frequency (IF): It is the difference frequency obtained by beating the incoming signal against the local oscillator frequency.

Intermittent: Something that occurs at intervals and not in a regular pattern.

Internal Resistance: The resistance within a source of voltage such as that within a transformer primary.

International Morse Code: A system that uses dots and dashes for signals.

Interpolation: The method used to find a value between two known values.

Ion: An electrically charged atom.

IR Drop: The voltage drop across a resistor when current is flowing through it.

Iron Constantan: A combination of two metals used in thermocouples.

Isolation Transformer: An electrical device used to link, by magnetic means, one or more parts of isolated circuits.

J

Jack: A socket for plugging in a wire.

JFET: Abbreviation for junction field effect transistor.

Jogging: A way of inching a motor by quickly pushing the start and stop buttons in rapid succession.

Joint: The connection of two wires.

Joule: The work done by a force of 1 newton acting through a distance of 1 meter.

Jumper: A short piece of wire used to eliminate or bypass portions of a circuit temporarily.

Junction Diode: A PN junction diode that will conduct more easily in one direction than it will in the opposite direction.

Justification: Controlling the left and/or right margins of columns of letters so they are aligned.

Jute: A fiber used to cover an electrical cable.

K

k: Abbreviation for kilo.

Keeper: A piece of metal put over the ends of a magnet to keep it from being demagnetized.

Kelvin Scale: A temperature scale using absolute zero at −273C.

Keypunch: A machine used for punching holes into cards or paper tape as information.

kHz: Abbreviation for kilohertz.

Kilo (k): Prefix used to represent 1000.

Kilowatt Hour: The amount of energy supplied by 1000 watts for one hour.

Kirchhoff's Laws: 1–At any junction in a circuit, the algebraic sum of the currents around any closed loop is zero. 2–In a simple circuit, the algebraic sum of the voltage around the circuit is zero.

Knockout: The removable slug in the side of an electrical box.

Kraft Paper: An electrical insulating material.

kV: Abbreviation for kilovolt.

kVA: Abbreviation for kilovolt ampere.

kW: Abbreviation for kilowatt.

L

L: Symbol for a coil or inductance.

Lag: The property of an ac circuit where the current reachers its peak value later than the voltage. In a purely inductive circuit, it does this 90 deg. later than voltage and is said to "lag" the voltage by 90 deg.

Laminated: Made in layers or stacked together, such as cores in a transformer.

Lamp: A device which produces light.

LASCR: A light activated silicon controlled rectifier (SCR), which has its gate activated by a light source.

Laser: Light amplification by stimulated emission of radiation, which is a device that takes incoherent light and produces a very narrow, highly intense beam of coherent light.

Lattice: The way the atoms are arranged in semiconductor material.

Law of Magnetism: Like poles repel, unlike poles attract.

Layout: The way the parts are positioned on a chassis as shown on a diagram.

LCD: Abbreviation for liquid crystal display.

LED: Abbreviation for light emitting diode.

Left Hand Rule: Grasp a conductor carrying current with your left thumb pointing in the direction of current flow and your fingers will show the direction of the magnetic field.

Lenz's Law: Induced emf in any circuit is always in the opposite direction of the effect that produced it.

Leyden Jar: A special kind of construction for experimentation, using a jar and metal foil. It was the original device used to study capacitors.

Light Emitting Diode (LED): A PN junction diode that emits light when it is biased in the forward direction.

Limit Switch: A device used to make and break electrical circuits by tripping a switch that is part of the body of this device.

Line Cord: A cord which is plugged into an outlet to provide power to a device.

Line Drop: The voltage loss in a power transmission line as measured between two points.

Line Frequency: The frequency which is supplied by the power source.

Lines of Force: The flux lines given off by an electric field. Also, the magnetic field surrounding a current-carrying device.

Liquid Crystal Display (LCD): The type of screen found on most portable computers that use a technology designed to keep it flat and narrow.

Lissajous Figures: The patterns produced on the screen of an oscilloscope by changing the amplitude and phases of sine waves and feeding those to the horizontal and vertical inputs of the scope.

Live: A current-carrying member of a circuit, electrically hot.

Load: The device that is being driven by the source of power. It absorbs the power from the supply voltage and converts it to heat, light, etc. It is the resistance connected across a circuit that determines the current flow and energy used.

Local Area Network (LAN): Tying several computers together to a master computer called a server so that all users share common software and files.

Lodestone: A substance which is naturally magnetic as it occurs in nature.

Logic: A method of using the symbols AND, OR and NOT to represent complex circuit functions.

Loop: A closed electrical circuit or path.

Loss: The dissipation of energy without any useful work.

Low Capacitance Probe: One type of test probe used with an oscilloscope.

Low Pass Filter: A filter that allows all frequencies below a predetermined frequency to pass frequencies higher than the predetermined frequency.

Lug: Terminal that is soldered or crimped on the end of a wire so that it can be attached to some part of a circuit.

M

M: Abbreviation for meg. Also symbol for mutual inductance.

mA: Abbreviation for milliampere.

Magnet: A substance, such as iron or steel, which attracts magnetic material. In its natural state, it is called "lodestone."

Magnet Keeper: A bar of iron that is put across the poles of a horseshoe magnet when not in use to prevent the magnet from being demagnetized.

Magnetic Circuit: The complete path the lines of flux follow from the north pole to the south pole and through the magnet to the north pole.

Magnetic Deflection: Using a magnetic field to bend the electron beam inside an oscilloscope.

Magnetic Field: The area around a magnet in which the effects of magnetism are felt.

Magnetic Flux: All of the magnetic lines surrounding a magnet. The symbol is phi (Φ).

Magnetic Pickup: A phono cartridge that uses magnetism to produce an electrical output. It is connected to the stylus.

Magnetic Saturation: A condition that exists in a magnetic material when a further increase in magnetizing force produces very little increase in flux density.

Magnetism: The invisible force that attracts certain materials such as steel.

Magnetomotive Force (mmf): The force that produces the flux in a magnetic circuit.

Magnitude: The size or numerical value assigned to a quantity.

Mainframe: Large powerful computer used in business and industry to store and process information.

Maintenance: The process of keeping equipment repaired and/or in good working order.

Majority Carriers: The principal charge carriers in a doped semiconductor. These are the holes in a P type material and the electrons in an N type material.

Manual: Hand operated. Also, the book of instructions that explains how to operate or repair a piece of equipment.

Maser: Amplification by stimulated emission of radiation; microwave.

Mask: A thin piece of material used in the process of making semiconductor devices.

Masonite: A trade name for compressed material used in the construction of electrical panels.

Math Coprocessor: Integrated circuit used to speed up the computing ability of a computer.

Matrix: A coding system for putting signals in a grid-shaped network so they can be found when needed by a computer. Similar to the way dates are put on a calendar.

Meg: Abbreviation for megohm.

Mega: Short way of saying "one million."

Megahertz (MHz): One million hertz.

Megger: An ohmmeter used for making very high resistance measurements.

Megohm (MΩ): One million ohms.

Melt: The molten semiconductor material from which the basic crystal ingots are formed.

Mercury Battery: A special battery which gives an almost constant output for its entire life.

Mercury Switch: A special switch that has mercury in it. As the switch is opened or closed, the mercury moves so that it breaks or makes the circuit.

Mesa Transistor: A transistor made by etching away the chip in a special way. The etching leaves mounds or hills that look like mesas.

Metal Film Resistor: A resistor made by depositing a thin layer of metal on a substrate.

Metal Oxide Semiconductor (MOS): A device formed by diffusing a thin layer of metal oxide and separating or insulating the various parts as required.

Meter: An electrical measuring instrument.

mH: Abbreviation for millihenry.

Mho: Previously used as the unit of conductance.

Mica: A transparent insulating material which is used because of its heat resistance.

Micro: A prefix meaning one millionth (1/1,000,000).

Microcomputer: Another name for a personal computer. A computer designed for business, home, or personal use.

Microelectronic: Reducing the size of electronic parts and circuits so that they are extremely small in size.

Microfarad (mF, mfd, or μF): One millionth of a farad.

Microprocessor: The main integrated circuit that controls the operations of a computer. Also called the CPU.

Microvolt: One millionth of a volt.

Microwave: Short wavelength radio frequencies used in certain types of communication systems.

Mil: One thousandth of an inch. Also, a term used for wire measurement.

Milli (m): A prefix meaning one thousandth (1/1000).

Milliammeter: A meter used for measuring small current values.

Milliampere (mA): One thousandth of an amp.

Miniaturization: The process of making something smaller in size.

Dictionary of Terms

Minority Carriers: The normally undesirable current carriers in a doped semiconductor. These are electrons in P material and holes in N material. They flow opposite the direction of majority carriers.

Modem: Electronic device used to connect two computers together with phone lines to exchange information.

Modulation: The process of varying the amplitude frequency or phase of a carrier wave, depending on how you want to transmit the signal.

Molecule: The smallest division of matter that has the characteristics of that substance.

Monochromatic: Something that consists of a single color.

Monostable: A circuit having only one stable state.

Morse Code: System of dots and dashes used in telegraph systems.

MOS: Abbreviation for metal oxide semiconductor.

Mosfet: Abbreviation for metal oxide semiconductor field effect transistor.

Motherboard: Main printed circuit board found on a computer.

Motor: A device used to convert electrical energy into rotating mechanical energy.

Mouse: Device used to position the cursor on a computer screen.

Mu (μ): The Greek letter used as an abbreviation for micro.

Multimeter: A meter that can measure different values such as voltage, current, and resistance.

Multiplex: A method used in radio and telephone communications where several messages are transmitted in one or both directions over a single path.

Multivibrator: A circuit using two transistors that oscillate. The output of one is coupled to the input of the second. The output is a series of pulses.

Mutual Inductance: The condition that exists when the magnetic field of one conductor is linked to the magnetic field of a second conductor. In this way, each field will have some affect on the emf of the other conductor.

Mylar: Trade name of a transparent plastic used as dielectric material in capacitors.

N

N: Symbol used for the north seeking pole of a magnet.

NAND Gate: The combination of an AND and a NOT used in logic circuits.

Nano: A prefix meaning one billionth.

National Electrical Manufacturers Association: Abbreviation NEMA. It is an organization of companies that manufacture electrical products.

National Electrical Code: A set of regulations that deal with electrical wiring of buildings and construction requirements to make sure they are safe and free of hazards.

Natural Magnet: A substance which when found in its natural state has the properties of a magnet.

NC: Abbreviation for normally closed. It is a term that deals with the contacts of a relay.

Negative: The terminal having an excess of electrons which flow toward the positive terminal.

NEMA: Abbreviation for the National Electrical Manufacturers Association.

Neon Bulb: A glass bulb that will not light until the ionization point of the neon gas inside has been reached.

Network: The combination of two or more electrical circuits.

Neutral: Neither positive nor negative.

Neutron: One of the three parts of an atom. It is the one having no electrical charge and is located in the nucleus of the atom.

Nichrome: A high resistance wire used for heating elements.

Nickel Cadmium Cell: An electrical cell which is popular because it has the ability to be recharged.

NO: Abbreviation for normally open. It is a term that deals with the contacts of a relay.

Node: One of the computer stations used to make up a network of computers that are connected together.

Noise: Unwanted electrical disturbances often found in communications and circuits. Many times this disturbance results from a source outside the circuits.

Nomograph: A chart with three values in which a straightedge is placed across two of the known values, and the third is read directly off the chart.

Nonferrous: Not made of iron.

Nonflammable: Material that will not burn very easily when exposed to flame or high temperatures.

Nonmagnetic: Material which will not be attracted to a magnet.

Normal Condition: A relay that is de-energized.

Normally Closed: Contacts that are closed when the relay is in the de-energized state.

Normally Open: Contacts that are open when the relay is in the de-energized state.

NPN Transistor: A transistor that has N type material for both the emitter and collector and P type material for its base.

N Type Material: Semiconductor material that has free electrons for its majority carriers.

Nucleus: The core of the atom.

Numerical Control: A method of controlling the motion of machines by using a coded message, which is read by a computer.

O

Ohm: The unit of measure for resistance. It is symbolized by the Greek letter omega (Ω). There is one ohm of resistance when an EMF or one volt causes a current of one amp.

Ohmmeter: A meter used to measure resistance.

Ohm's Law: A relationship between the values for voltage (E), current (I), and resistance (R). Discovered by a scientist named Ohm, it states $E = I \times R$.

Ohms Per Volt: A term used to describe the sensitivity rating of a meter.

Omnidirectional Microphone: A microphone that picks up sound waves from almost any direction.

On Delay: A circuit that will produce an output signal after a time lapse. Often found in relay circuits and logic circuits.

Op Amp: Abbreviation for operational amplifier.

Open: To break the path for current in a circuit.

Operating Life: The minimum length of time a device is normally expected to operate without failing.

Operational Amplifier (Op Amp): A special circuit device used to do mathematical operations such as add, subtract, average, etc.

Opposition: Two forces which act against one another.

Orbital Electrons: The electrons that orbit around the nucleus of an atom.

Ordinate: The vertical line on a graph.

OR Gate: A logic device that produces a signal when one of the inputs is present.

Orifice: A small opening in the path of flow.

Oscillator: An electronic device that generates ac voltages.

Oscilloscope: An electronic test instrument that uses a cathode ray tube for visually displaying signals.

Outlet: The point where current can be taken from an electrical circuit.

Out of Phase: A term used to describe alternating current or voltage waveforms that do not pass through the minimum and maximum values at the same time.

Output: The energy delivered by a device or circuit.

Overload: To apply excessive load to a device, which results in a distorted output and, in some cases, damage to the equipment.

Oxide: The thin layer of ferric oxide put on magnetic tapes for the purpose of being able to magnetize them to produce a sound.

Ozone: A type of oxygen produced during an electrical discharge.

P

P: Abbreviation for power.

Padder: A small variable capacitor usually placed in series with a tuning capacitor to adjust for the lower operating frequencies of the tuning capacitor.

Panel: A material on which electrical parts or controls are mounted.

Panel Meter: A measuring instrument built so that it is easy to mount on a panel.

Paper Capacitor: A capacitor which uses a special paper for its dielectric.

Parallel: A method of connecting electrical components so that there are two or more paths of flow.

Parallel Circuit: A circuit which contains two or more paths for electrons to flow from a common voltage source.

Parallel Port: Location on a computer that will accept or send data in parallel fashion.

Passband: The frequencies that will pass through a filter network without reducing the amplitude.

Paste: A thick, moist material that acts as the electrolyte in a dry cell.

Patch: To connect a circuit by using a temporary wiring hookup.

Peak: The highest point on a sine wave.

Peak Inverse Voltage (PIV): The value of the voltage applied across a diode in the reverse direction.

Peak to Peak: The value of a sine wave from the positive peak to the negative peak.

Period: The time required to complete one cycle.

Permanent Magnet: Bar of steel or other material that has been magnetized and retains its magnetism for a long time (years).

Permeability: The relative ability of a substance to conduct magnetic lines of force as compared to air. It is symbolized by the Greek letter mu (μ).

pF: Abbreviation for picofarad.

Phase: The relationship between the current and voltage in an ac circuit with respect to their angular displacement.

Phase Shift: The change in the relationship between two alternating current voltages with the same frequency.

Phone Jack: A receptacle designed for use with phone plugs.

Phone Plug: A special plug used with audio equipment such as headphones.

Phono Jack: A receptacle designed for use with phono plugs.

Phono Plug: A special plug smaller in size than a phone plug. It is used on shielded wire for feeding audio signals to speakers and audio preamplifiers. Sometimes called an RCA plug.

Phosphor: The layer of material coating the inside of cathode ray tubes that produces light when hit by an electron beam.

Photocell: A way of saying "photoelectric cell."

Photodiode: A PN junction device that will conduct electrons when exposed to light.

Photoelectric Cell: A cell that will change its resistance when struck by light.

Photovoltaic: A device that will generate a small voltage when struck by light. It is used to convert light energy to an emf.

Pi (π): A value given to a ratio used when working with circles. It is approximately equal to 3.1416.

Pi Network: A three branch network of components hooked up in the shape of the symbol π.

Pico (p): A prefix meaning 10^{-12}.

Picofarad (pF): A way of labeling a capacitor equal to one millionth of a microfarad (one millionth of one millionth farad).

Piezoelectric: The ability of some types of crystals to produce a voltage when put under certain types of stress.

Pile: A nuclear reactor.

Pilot Lamp: A light used to indicate whether a circuit is energized or operating in the proper sequence.

PIV: Abbreviation for peak inverse voltage.

Pixel: Contraction for picture elements. A single dot from the group that makes up the screen on a computer monitor.

Plate: A term used to refer to a single electrode found in a capacitor or battery.

Plug: The male part of a connector.

Plugging: A way of slowing down a motor by hitting the reverse button while the motor is still running in the forward direction.

PN Junction: The line of separation between P type and N type semiconductor materials.

PNP Transistor: A transistor which has P type material for its emitter and collector and N type material for its base.

Polarity: The property of a device or circuit to have positive and negative poles.

Polarization: The property found in an electrolytic cell to increase its resistance during electrolysis, thereby, shortening its life. Also, a way of making plugs and receptacles so they can be mated together only one way.

Pole: One of the ways used to name the ends of magnets. Also, one electrode found on a battery.

Polygraph: A recorder that can measure small changes in blood pressure and body resistance. Often called a lie detector.

Polyphase: Having more than one phase.

Positive: A point that attracts electrons (as opposed to negative, which is the source of electron flow). Also, any number that is numerically greater than zero.

Positive electrode: The positive terminal of a battery or electrolytic capacitor.

Positive Ion: An atom that has lost electrons. Therefore, it is positively charged.

Positive Plate: The plate in a capacitor or battery that has the fewer number of electrons.

Pot: A short way of saying "potentiometer." Also, the process of completely covering and sealing a component or circuit with a hot liquid insulating material that turns solid as it cools.

Potential: The difference in the voltage between two points of a circuit.

Potentiometer: A variable resistor used as a voltage divider. Also, an electrical device used to give an electrical output signal that is proportional to some rotary movement.

Potted Circuit: A circuit that has been completely covered and sealed with an insulating material.

Power (P): The rate of doing work.

Power Amplifier: A special amplifier used for providing a lot of current to a load, such as a motor or speaker.

Power Dissipation: The ability of a device to get rid of the heat it generates.

Power Factor: The ratio of the true power to the apparent power of a circuit.

Power Factor Correction: The addition of capacitors to an inductive circuit to increase the power factor by putting the current more closely in phase with the voltage.

Power Gain: The amount that a device will amplify a signal. It is the ratio of power output to the power absorbed by the input.

Power Line: The conductors used to transport electricity from one point to another.

Power Loss: The loss in a circuit caused by resistance, heat, etc. Sometimes called the I^2R loss.

Power Transformer: A transformer used to supply output voltages from an ac power source.

Power Transistor: A transistor that can deliver high current and power without overheating.

Preamplifier: An amplifier between the signal source (usually a low level output) and the main amplifier.

Precision: The ability to make the same measurements a number of times and have them as close together as possible.

Pressure: The force per unit area.

Pressure Switch: A switch that is activated by a change in the pressure of some liquid. It is also used with gases.

Primary: The input winding on a transformer.

Primary Cell: A cell that is not designed to be recharged.

Primary Current: Current that flows through the input side of a winding of a transformer.

Printed Circuit: A circuit made on a special insulated board on which thin strips of copper are the wires.

Printed Circuit Board: The insulated board on which the printed circuit is formed.

Printed Wiring: A method of making the conductors by printing very thin ribbons of material on an insulated board.

Probe: A test lead with a pointed metal end used to contact the part of a circuit to be measured by a vacuum tube voltmeter or observed on a scope.

Programmable Logic Controller (PLC): Computer installed to control the various motions of a robot through the use of special input code.

Proton: The positively charged particle in the nucleus of an atom.

Prototype: A hand-assembled model of the finished product used for evaluation of design, construction, and operation before mass production begins.

Proximity Switch: A switch designed to open or close when an object, such as a piece of metal, is brought very near.

P Type Material: A semiconductor material which has holes for its majority current carriers.

Pull In Voltage: The minimum voltage which can be used to energize a relay.

Pulsating Current: Current that will rise and fall, but generally not fall below the zero reference point.

Pulse: A momentary voltage or current.

Pulse Generator: A device used for generating a controlled series of electrical pulses.

Punched Card: A card slightly larger than 3 in. × 7 in. used for coding information in the form of punched holes. Normally, each card has 80 columns with 12 locations in each column where a hole can be punched.

Push Pull Circuit: A circuit having two components hooked up 180 deg. out of phase with one another so that each one will operate on one-half cycle.

Pyrometer: A device used to measure high temperatures, such as the temperature of molten iron.

Q

Q: Figure of merit. It is the ratio of the reactance of a capacitor or inductor to its resistance.

Quad: A combination of four items used in a circuit. Also, the short way of saying "quadruple."

Quadrant: One fourth of a circle or 90 deg.

Quality Control: To control the appearance and operation of a finished product by inspecting it during manufacturing.

Quantity: The amount or number of an item.

Quartz: A mineral (silicon dioxide) used in some electrical devices because of its piezoelectric properties.

Quick Disconnect: A device used to quickly lock and/or remove two connecting halves.

Quiescence: The condition in which a circuit has power supplied to it but does not have a signal supplied to it.

R

R: The symbol for resistance.

Raceway: Channel that holds electrical conductors (wires, bars and cables).

Radar: RAdio Detecting And Ranging is a term used for a system of measuring the speed and location of an object by measuring the amount of time required for a signal to bounce off that object and return.

Radial Lead: The lead coming out of the side of a component rather than from its end.

Radian: A system for measuring angles in which π is the unit of measure rather than degrees. A circle contains 2π radians.

Radiate: To give off rays.

Radiation: To give off electromagnetic waves into space.

Radio: Electronic equipment used to transmit or receive electromagnetic waves without the use of sending or receiving wires.

Radioactivity: The emission of alpha particles, gamma rays, etc., from an unstable nucleus as it decays to a more stable state.

Radio Fix: A method used to find the position of a source of radio waves. Also, a method used by ships and planes to determine their own location by using radio signals from stations whose locations are known.

Radio Frequency Choke: An inductor that has a high impedance to RF currents.

Radioisotope: A radioactive particle used as a tracer in the medical and science fields because it emits rays that can be traced with instruments.

RAM: Abbreviation for random access memory.

Random Access Memory (RAM): Temporary storage memory in a computer which is lost when the machine is turned off.

Range: The maximum distance a radio transmitter can effectively send signals.

Raster: The lighted area on a television picture tube produced by the scanning lines moving across the screen when there is no picture on the screen.

Ratio: The value obtained by dividing one number by another.

RC: Symbol for resistance capacitance.

RC Time Constant: The time period needed for the voltage across a capacitor in an RC circuit to increase to

63.2 percent of the source voltage or decrease to 36.7 percent of the voltage across the capacitor. The t (in seconds) equals R (in ohms) × C (in farads).

Reactance: The opposition to the flow of alternating current in a circuit because of its inductance or capacitance. It is expressed by the symbol X.

Reactive Load: A load caused by capacitance or inductance (as opposed to a resistive load).

Reactor: A device used to split the atom under controlled means.

Read/Write Head: The portion of the computer disk drive that senses the magnetic particles on a disk and writes information to the disk for later use.

Receiver: That part of a communications system which accepts radio waves and converts them into audible form.

Receptacle: A contact device installed at an outlet so that a plug can be connected.

Reciprocal: A number found by dividing it into 1. Therefore, it is 1 over the number.

Rectification: The conversion of ac into dc.

Rectifier: The component used to convert ac into pulsating dc.

Reed Relay: A relay that is made with two magnetic strips inside a coil. They are attracted to each other each time the coil is energized, closing the contacts that are mounted on the strips.

Reed Switch: Two overlapping magnetic strips, mounted inside a glass housing, that are closed by a magnetic field.

Reel: A cylindrical device used for holding wire for storage purposes.

Reference Level: The starting point from which other measurements are made, such as 0 deg. on a thermometer or 0 deg. on a sine wave.

Rel: The unit of measurement for reluctance.

Relay: An electrical device that will open or close contacts through which another circuit can be opened or closed. In this way, the relay can be used in conjunction with one circuit to control a second circuit.

Release: To disconnect.

Reluctance: Opposition to the flow of magnetic flux.

Remote Control: A method of controlling another device from some distance away by the use of wires, light or other means.

Renewable Fuse: A fuse that can be repaired by changing its link, then it is reused.

Repel: To force away or apart, as like magnetic poles do.

Repulsion Induction Motor: A squirrel cage type motor having two sets of windings, one for repulsion and one for induction.

Repulsion Start Motor: A motor that develops starting torque by the interaction of rotor currents and a single phase stator field.

Residual Magnetism: The amount of magnetism left after the magnetic force is removed or the source of electromagnetism has its circuit opened.

Resist: The material placed on printed circuit boards to prevent the copper from being etched away by chemicals used in the process.

Resistance: Opposition to the flow of current.

Resistance Substitution Box: An assembly of resistors connected by switches to a pair of test leads. Any one of the resistors may be connected to a circuit for checking purposes. This device is not left in a circuit permanently.

Resistance Wire: A wire such as Nichrome® that has high resistance to the flow of current. Therefore, it is used in heating elements and wirewound resistors.

Resistor: A device that will oppose the flow of current in an electrical circuit.

Resistor Color Code: A means of identifying the various values of resistors by coding them with colored rings around the body. Each color represents a specific number or multiplying value.

Resolution: The degree to which nearly equal values can be distinguished from one another.

Resolution (Computer): The number of individual pixels that can be displayed on a video monitor at one time.

Resonance: The condition that exists when the inductive reactance equals the capacitive reactance in the circuit.

Resonance Curve: A graph that shows how a tuned circuit will react at various frequencies.

Resonant Frequency (f_r): The frequency at which inductive reactance equals capacitive reactance in a tuned circuit.

Retentivity: The ability of a material to retain its magnetism after the magnetizing force is moved.

Reverse Bias: The voltage applied to a PN junction so that it does not conduct or conducts only a very small amount.

Reverse Breakdown Voltage: The point at which a further increase in voltage in the reverse direction on a semiconductor causes a sharp increase in current without much more voltage.

Rewind: The process of repairing a motor by removing and replacing its wound coils with new coils.

RF: Abbreviation for radio frequency.

RF Choke: A coil that has a high inductive reactance at radio frequencies.

RF Signal Generator: A test instrument that will generate many bands of radio frequencies. It is used in the repair and alignment of radio equipment.

Rheostat: A variable resistor placed in series with the load to control current. It has one fixed terminal and a movable contact called a "slider."

Right Hand Rule: A method used with motors to show the direction of the field (first finger), direction of current (second finger) and motion of conductor (thumb).

Ripple: A series of peaks found after ac has been rectified to dc.

RMS: Abbreviation for root mean square.

Root Mean Square: The value of ac that would produce the same heating effect as an equal amount of dc. In ac, the value is 0.707 times the peak value, and it is the same as the effective value.

Rosin Core Solder: A material used to join electrical components. It is a mixture of tin and lead, and it has a fluxing agent in the hollow center.

Rotating Field: The magnetic field found in electrical motors where the poles keep shifting to cause rotation.

Rotor: The rotating part of an electric motor.

rpm: Abbreviation for revolutions per minute.

RTL: Abbreviation for resistor transistor logic.

S

S: Symbol for siemen. (s) Symbol for second.

Safety Factor: A way of rating a component so that its stated limit may be exceeded temporarily without causing failure.

Sal Ammoniac: Ammonium chloride. It is a material found in electric cells as part of its electrolyte.

Sapphire: A gem used for bearings in electrical instruments.

Saturated: A point where a transistor will not give an increase in current if the base current is increased. Also, a permanent magnet or the core of an electromagnet which is conducting as many lines of magnetic flux as it can be made to conduct under normal conditions.

Sawtooth Generator: An oscillator which produces an alternating waveform that has the shape of teeth on a saw.

Scanner: Device that works very similar to a copying machine. Used to capture graphics images for saving to a computer disk.

Schematic: An electrical diagram that shows components as symbols and electrical connections of components to each other.

Scope: Short way of saying "oscilloscope."

SCR: Abbreviation for silicon controlled rectifier.

Screen: The surface of an oscilloscope that shows the visible pattern traced out by the electron beam.

Sec: Abbreviation for the secondary winding of a transformer. Also, abbreviation for second.

Secondary: The output winding of a transformer.

Secondary Cell: A cell which, after it has been discharged is meant to be recharged.

Sectors: Pie shaped subdivisions produced on a computer disk after it is formatted.

Seed: A single crystal from which semiconductor crystal material is grown.

Selenium Rectifier: A rectifier made by depositing selenium on aluminum plates and coating it with a conductive metal.

Self Induction: That property which causes a counter emf to be generated to oppose a change in current.

Semiconductor: An electronic device that has been made from material somewhere between the range of conductors and insulators.

Semiconductor Chip: A small piece of material from which semiconductor devices are made.

Semiconductor Diode: A device made from P and N type material forming a PN junction that passes current easily in one direction but opposes the flow of current in the other direction.

Sequence: The order in which operations occur.

Serial Port: Location on a computer that will accept or send data bit by bit in serial fashion.

Series Circuit: A circuit in which components are connected from end to end, and the current must flow through each one in sequence to complete its path.

Series Parallel Network: A circuit which has only one path for current in some places but more than one path for current in other places.

Series Resistor: A resistor that is connected in series to some device to control voltage or current.

Servo: A device that controls and delivers power to move something. Short for servomotor.

Shelf Life: The length of time a component may be stored and still be useful.

Shell: The various energy levels of electrons around an atom.

Shielded Cable: A cable that has an outer shield or casing which is intended to decrease the interference from sources outside the cable.

Shock: Current flow through a living organism, especially a person.

Short Circuit: A usually undesired path for current which bypasses a desired path.

Short Out: A method used to bypass some component by connecting a wire between its terminals.

Shunt: A low value resistor used in parallel with a meter to increase the amount of current it can measure. Also, a component or circuit connected in parallel with another component or circuit.

Sidebands: Frequencies above and below carrier frequencies as a result of modulation.

Signal: The part of an electrical voltage or current that is used to carry intelligence or information.

Silicon: A material used to make semiconductors.

Silicon Controlled Rectifier (SCR): A semiconductor device having an anode, cathode and gate used for current values that are usually higher than those carried by transistors.

Silicone Grease: A material used to aid in heat dissipation of semiconductors.

Sine Wave: A wave form of a single frequency alternating current whose displacement is the sine of an angle proportional to time or distance.

Single In-line Memory Module (SIMM's) Chips: IC's that are used for computer RAM memory.

Single Pole Double Throw (SPDT): A switch used to connect one terminal to one of two other terminals.

Single Pole Single Throw (SPST): A switch used to open or close one circuit.

Single Shot Multivibrator: A multivibrator designed to provide a single pulse on demand.

Sink: A device used to drain off excess energy, such as a heat sink drawing off excess heat.

Slice: A wafer cut from a silicon ingot and used for making integrated circuits.

Slider: The movable contact in rheostats.

Slip: The difference between the actual speed of a motor and its synchronous speed.

Slug: An adjustable metallic piece found inside a coil used for tuning circuits.

Solar Cell: A cell which converts the energy of light into electrical energy. A photovoltaic cell.

Solder: An alloy of tin and lead used for providing a low resistance electrical connection which is also mechanically strong.

Soldering Iron: One kind of device used to provide the heat to melt solder.

Solderless Connector: A device used to connect wires to terminals or other wires by means of crimping, etc.

Solenoid: An electromagnet that has an air core in which a small magnetic shaft is free to move and operate a valve or other device.

Solid State: Electronic circuits using semiconductor devices such as transistors, diodes and silicon controlled rectifiers.

Source: One of the leads of a field effect transistor. Also, a device or part of a circuit that supplies electrical energy to another device or circuit.

South Pole: The pole of a magnet where the lines of force enter after having left the north pole.

Spaghetti: An insulating tubing used in electrical work.

SPDT: Abbreviation for single pole, double throw.

Speaker: A device used to convert electrical signals into sound.

Speed of Light: The distance light will travel in one second, which is approximately 300,000,000 meters per second or 186,000 miles per second.

Speed of Sound: The distance sound will travel in one second, which is about 1080 feet per second.

Spike: A usually undesirable very narrow pulse of electricity with so great an amplitude that it interferes with or deteriorates normal circuit operation.

Spkr: Abbreviation for speaker.

Splice: Joining two or more conductors.

SPST: Abbreviation for single pole, single throw.

Spurious Pulse: A pulse or spike which was not generated on purpose.

Square Wave: An electrical wave which alternates abruptly between high and low values of approximately equal duration.

Squirrel Cage Induction Motor: An induction motor having a rotor that looks similar to a squirrel cage in construction.

Static Electricity: Electricity at rest. Also, electricity caused by friction.

Stator: The stationary (nonrotating) part which contains the primary windings of a motor.

Stator Plates: The fixed plates of a variable capacitor.

Steady State: The condition of a circuit after all the transients have settled down.

Step Down Transformer: A transformer used to reduce the voltage.

Stereophonic: Sound that is broken into two or more channels to give the effect of depth because different signals can be received by each ear.

Storage Battery: A common name for the lead acid battery used in automobiles. It is made from storage cells connected in series.

Storage Oscilloscope: A scope that has the ability to retain the image on its screen for a period of time so it can be observed or studied.

Stranded Wire: A conductor which is made from fine strands of wire twisted together.

Strip: To remove insulation from wire.

Stroboscope: A bright light that can be adjusted to flash a specific number of times to coincide with some repeating motion.

Subminiaturization: A method of reducing the size of a circuit by using different construction techniques.

Substation: A place where electrical power is transformed for a large number of users.

Substrate: An insulating material on which circuits are formed.

Surge: A sudden change in current or voltage.

Sweep: The crossing rate for the electron beam on the CRT of an oscilloscope. The horizontal line caused by the deflection of an electron beam across the face of the CRT from left to right.

Switch: A device used to make and break the path for current in a circuit.

Symbol: A method used to represent an electrical or electronic component by using letters, numbers or designs on a schematic drawing.

Synchronous: Two or more actions of a similar or related nature occurring at exactly the same rate at the same time.

T

Table: A collection of data displayed in chart form.

Tank Circuit: A parallel resonant circuit.

Tap: A fixed electrical connection on a transformer that is used to provide another voltage level.

Taper, Potentiometer: The way in which the amount of resistance between the wiper and an end terminal of a potentiometer varies. Common tapers are linear and audio or logarithmic.

Tapped Resistor: A wirewound resistor having additional terminals at points along its length. It is often used for voltage divider circuits.

Telemetry: The transmission of analog or digital information recorded on instruments by radio or telephone to another point some distance away.

Television Signal: The audio, video and sync (timing reference) signals that are broadcast by a television station. These signals are used by a television receiver to produce the picture and sound.

Temporary Magnet: A magnet that will hold its magnetism for a short period of time after the source of magnetism has been removed.

Terminal: A point for electrical connections.

Terminal Strip: An insulated base on which a number of terminals are mounted so that wiring connections will be easy to make.

Test Clip: A spring clip used to make temporary connections to circuits, especially when they are being tested.

Test Lead: A flexible insulated wire used to connect testing equipment to circuits to be tested.

Thermal Overload: A device used to protect electrical circuits from overheating. It will open the circuit when the temperature gets too high because of excessive current.

Thermal Radiation: Heat.

Thermal Runaway: A condition where rising temperature causes the current to increase which in turn, causes the temperature to rise, etc.

Thermistor: Thermal resistor. A device that will decrease in resistance with an increase in temperature.

Thermocouple: A device used to measure temperature by the use of two dissimilar metals which are joined at the point where the measurement is being taken. As heat is applied, the voltage generated can be read on a meter calibrated in degrees.

Thermostat: A device used to control the amount of heat in a building by setting it at some desired temperature level.

Thick Film Circuits: Films are deposited on a substrate to act as certain components, then transistors and diodes are soldered in place as the active components.

Thin Walled Conduit: Metallic tubing used to hold and protect insulated wires in various circuits.

Three Phase Motor: An alternating current motor that operates from three phase current.

Three Phase System: Using three wires to carry current and simultaneously act as the return wires for alternating current with a phase difference of 120 deg. or one third of a cycle.

Three Way Switch: A switch that connects one conductor to either of two other conductors. It is used in places where a light can be turned on from either the top or bottom of a stairway.

Threshold: The point where something first happens, such as a transistor beginning to conduct.

Time Delay Relay: A relay that can be set so that it will not activate its contacts until after a measured amount of time delay.

Tinned: A coating on wire used to make soldering easier.

Tip: The end of a probe.

TO Can: One of the shapes used for packaging integrated circuits in which the shape is similar to that normally used with transistors.

Toggle Switch: A two position switch that is opened and closed (operated) by a lever.

Tolerance: The permissible amount from which a value is allowed to vary.

Torque: A force that tends to produce rotation.

Trace: The pattern on the screen of an oscilloscope.

Transducer: A device that will convert a signal from one form to another, such as converting pressure to electricity.

Transformer: A device used to step up or step down voltage by induction. Also, an electrical device used to transport energy from one circuit to another circuit at the same frequency.

Transient: A sudden change or pulse that is not intended in a circuit.

Transistor: A semiconductor made from germanium or silicon with leads known as emitter, collector and base. It is made to conduct by forward biasing an emitter-base junction.

Dictionary of Terms

Transistor Transistor Logic (TTL): Digital circuits used with computers in which transistors control other transistors.

Transmit: To send a signal from one point to another point.

Triac: A three terminal, bi-directional thyristor device that is triggered into conduction by applying a signal to its gate.

Trickle Charge: A very slow rate of charging, usually taking many hours.

Trimmer Capacitor: A small variable capacitor that is connected in series with another capacitor. It is used to fine adjust a circuit.

TRL: Abbreviation for transistor resistor logic.

Troubleshoot: The process of working with equipment to locate and correct any faults.

Truth Table: A table used to show the output with all the possible combinations of inputs for various AND, OR and other logic functions.

TTL: Abbreviation for transistor transistor logic.

Tuned: Adjusted to resonate at a specific frequency.

Tuned Circuit: A circuit which consists of capacitance and inductance that is adjustable for resonance at a desired frequency.

Tungsten Filament: The filament used in incandescent lights because of its ability to glow white hot.

Tunnel Diode: A special PN junction diode in which initial forward biasing causes the electrons to tunnel through rather than over the barrier. These diodes have special properties that make them suited to high frequencies and use in space.

Turns Ratio: In a transformer, it is the ratio of the number of turns in the primary to the number of turns in the secondary.

Tweeter: A speaker that is designed to produce high audio frequencies.

U

UHF: Abbreviation for ultra high frequency.

Ultra High Frequency: The frequency band from 300 to 3000 megahertz.

Ultrasonic: Having a frequency above audible sound (average 20,000 Hz).

Ultrasonic Welding: Bonding two pieces of metal without reaching melting temperatures.

Undercut: The process where the metal foil on a printed circuit board is etched under the edge of the resist material.

Ungrounded System: An electrical system in which no point is connected to ground.

Unidirectional: Current that is flowing in only one direction.

Unijunction Transistor: A three terminal transistor that has one junction with two base leads and one emitter lead.

V

V: Symbol for volt or voltmeter.

VA: Abbreviation for volt amperes.

Vacuum Tube Voltmeter (VTVM): A voltmeter that uses a vacuum tube to perform the functions of amplification and rectification. It is used to make electrical measurements.

Variable Capacitor: A capacitor whose capacitance can be adjusted by turning a shaft to change the distance between its plates or effectively change the area of its plates.

Variable Speed Motor: A motor which, regardless of loading can be adjusted over a range of speeds.

Varistor: A two electrode semiconductor device that drops in resistance as the voltage is increased.

Vector: A quantity having both magnitude and direction.

Vitreous: Having the characteristics of glass.

Volt (V): The unit of measure for emf or potential difference.

Voltage (E): The electromotive force which will cause current to flow.

Voltage Divider: A method of using a series of resistors across a voltage source so that multiple voltages can be obtained.

Voltage Drop: The difference in voltage between two points in a circuit.

Voltaic Cell: Another name for a primary cell.

Voltmeter: An instrument used for measuring the difference in potential between two points.

Volt Ohm Milliammeter (VOM): A meter that can be used to measure a number of different voltage, resistance and current levels.

VOM: Abbreviation for volt ohm milliammeter.

VTVM: Abbreviation for vacuum tube voltmeter.

W

W: Symbol for watt or work.

Wafer: A thin slice of semiconductor material used for making integrated circuits.

Wall Box: A metal or plastic box used in house wiring to enclose a switch or receptacle.

Watt (W): The unit of measure for power (rate of doing work).

Watt Hour: A unit of measure for electrical power that says you have used one watt for one hour.

Watt Hour Meter: A meter connected into a circuit and used to determine the amount of energy used, usually in kilowatt hours.

Waveform: The graphical shape of a wave which will show the amount of variation in amplitude over some period of time.

Wavelength: Distance between a specific point on a wave and same point on next cycle of the wave.

Wet Cell: Cell that has electrolyte in liquid form.

Wheatstone Bridge: A means of measuring an unknown resistance by comparing it to a known value in a special circuit that will be balanced when its value is found.

Whisker: A thin piece of metal (resembling a cat's whisker) used in making semiconductor devices.

Wideband: Able to pass a broad range of frequencies.

Winding: In a transformer, it is the length of conductor that is wound in a coil shape to serve as the primary or secondary.

Wiper: The moving contact of a potentiometer that is adjusted to change the resistance.

Wiping Contacts: Contacts that rub between two other contacts, usually found in switches.

Wire: A solid conductor or stranded group of electrical conductors (copper, aluminum, etc.) that serve as one conductor. It is said to have low resistance to the flow of current.

Wirewound Resistor: A resistor whose resistance element is a piece of resistance wire wound onto some insulating form. Many of them are then coated with an insulating material.

Wiring Diagram: A drawing used to show the circuit and electrical connections needed.

Woofer: A large speaker specifically designed to produce low frequency sounds.

Working Voltage: The maximum voltage at which some device should be operated.

WVDC: Abbreviation for working voltage direct current, which is maximum safe dc operating voltage across a capacitor at normal operating temperature.

Wye Connection: A method of connecting three phase electrical devices so that the end of each winding has a common neutral point. Symbol is Y.

X

X: Symbol for reactance measured in ohms.

X Axis: The horizontal axis on a graph.

X_C: Symbol for capacitive reactance.

X_L: Symbol for inductive reactance.

X Rays: Radiation of very short wavelength generated by bombarding a target with a stream of high speed electrons.

Y

Y Axis: The vertical axis on a graph.

Yoke: A set of coils used on the neck of a cathode ray tube to deflect the electron beam.

Z

Z: Symbol for impedance.

Zener Breakdown: A breakdown in a reverse biased semiconductor device. It is caused when electrons in the depletion layer knock other electrons loose until a large reverse current is flowing across a reverse biased junction.

Zener Diode: A silicon diode that makes use of the breakdown properties of a PN junction. If reverse voltage across the diode is increased, a point will be reached where the current will greatly increase.

Zero Potential: Zero voltage or "earth potential."

Index